C. SLOAN LEWIS

THE
SOUL
CHILD

ISBN: 979-8-89342-264-1

Cover design by: MiblArt

To my husband,
my rock,
my world.

Chapter One

By their very nature, libraries are magical places. This was especially true for the library of the Enlightened in Gibbous Tower, a place of sanctuary for Sybil Dawn. Four years ago, the Enlightened chose her to be his apprentice, and she began her studies in divination, the art of foresight and insight. The first moment Sybil stepped into the Enlightened's library, a vast collection of histories, magic, and practical knowledge, she fell in love with it.

And what was not to love? The bookshelves stood from floor to ceiling, holding books with elegant covers, most of which the Enlightened had restored himself, all of them inviting her to read. The bibliosmia in the library, that comforting smell of old books, was a better scent to her than even the most expensive fragrances. It was a wonderful place to spend your time because between some of the bookshelves were sitting areas with comfortable wingback chairs and wide tables, providing plenty of space to stretch out all your books, papers, and notebooks as you studied. In the center of the granite floors, white with black flecks, was a long, red carpet with intricate designs and patterns made by the elves in an ancient time. In a line, nearly stretching as long as the carpet, were globes, some surely even older than the carpet, placed in order of their date, which showed the evolution of cartographers' understanding of the world. By this time, the true geography of the world was known; nearly everything had been discovered. But even so, that didn't mean everyone knew everything about these places, some barely knew the history of the kingdom they grew up in.

Sybil, with all her knowledge of the arcane, was one of these people. She had grown up in a village which had kept its distance from the rest of the Kingdom of Irminshu, and when she arrived at the tower, she shut out the world to focus on her studies. But there was only so much studying to be had cooped up in the tower, and Sybil's progress, despite all her effort, was slowing down.

While she could have asked for help or gone to find a stool, Sybil was the type of person to manage things on her own and tried her best to shimmy out the thick tome on clairvoyance which she had been searching for all morning. Getting it off the shelf was easy, if not a bit awkward, but the challenge came with managing the weight of it with her outstretched arms. This she could not do.

The realization of this came too late as the burden of the tome overcame her and dropped to the granite floor. A low, resonant boom echoed through the library, causing her to wince. It was quiet in the library, and she had only seen the old, hard-of-hearing librarian in there for the last few hours, so she thought her mishap would go unnoticed. However, a throat clearing behind her caused the blood to rush to her face. When Sybil turned, pivoting on her feet, she found the Enlightened, known to her simply as Leon, standing just inside the doorway with a hooded stranger, dressed all in black.

"My dear girl," Leon said, his white, bushy eyebrows raised and golden eyes sharp. "I was showing my newest recruit around the tower and thought I would introduce the two of you." The way Leon spoke was always slow, purposeful, and it often took him a long time to say what he wanted to say. On the outside he appeared frail and sunken, but on the inside, he wielded a tremendous amount of power Sybil could only dream of wielding. "Mordecai, this is Sybil, my apprentice."

The hooded figure watched Sybil with a slight smirk on his face. He was a younger man with gray eyes that gleamed like silver, jet black hair that swooped to one side at the top and cut short along the sides, and pale skin that looked smooth and delicate, handsome but in an unorthodox sort of way. Sybil did not like the way this stranger was looking at her, and it made her self-conscious about her own appearance. While she had grown into a beautiful young woman with icy-blue eyes, glossy raven hair, and smattering of freckles along her face, she still imagined herself as the strange-looking child she had been. Her big eyes and ears and small nose made her look quite a bit like a mouse. The ridicule she had received from other children was enough to keep her from realizing she had long grown into her looks.

"I can already tell she has a lot to learn from you, Leon," Mordecai remarked, his voice deep and harsh. "She's a bit careless."

Sybil's self-consciousness melted away as anger bubbled in her belly at this stranger's condescension, but she remembered her place and said, "Welcome to Gibbous Tower, Mordecai. I hope you're not one who lets first impressions dictate your judgment. It will be a difficult time for you here, if you're one to take everything at face value."

Leon frowned and flattened his lips, picking up on Sybil's tone, but instead of being insulted, Mordecai looked amused.

"Yes, well, nothing is truly as it seems, is it?" he asked, raising an eyebrow.

Using her legs, Sybil hoisted the tome into her arms, struggling a bit with its weight but managing to get it supported by her forearms, and said, "Which is why it is important to gather as many facts as you can before coming to a conclusion. Now, if you gentlemen will excuse me, I have some studying to do."

She gave a staggered bow to Leon and the rude stranger and headed toward an isolated corner of the library to carry on with her studying. Her anger toward the man's arrogance made it hard to concentrate, though, so she ended up having to read passages and even whole pages over again, getting little done.

Just after lunchtime, Rani joined her in the library with some books of her own. Rani, a fiery haired halfling from the Northern Realms, was the tower's potion master. A brilliant potion maker and inventor, and a bit of a spellcaster herself, Leon had taken her under his employ only a few months after she had arrived in the Kingdom of Irminshu to follow her dreams which could not have been met in her small village. At times, Sybil found herself envying the value Rani brought to Gibbous Tower because most of Sybil's days were filled with studying and training, trying to perfect her spells. Rarely did she ever contribute anything of tangible valuable to Leon or the others in the tower.

"There's a new fella joinin' the tower," Rani said, her accent thick on each word she spoke. "I hear he's rather mysterious."

"I was introduced to him just a little while ago, actually," Sybil said, flipping to the next page in her book.

"Well? What'd ya think of him?"

"Let's just say that I hope his second impression is better than his first," she replied with a sigh. "I might have embarrassed myself in front of him and Leon. No matter how much I learn or how much my magic grows, I still come off as an oaf sometimes."

"Oh, come off it. I'm sure it wasn't that bad," Rani said with a wave of her hand. "Though, I'm sure ya probably let him have it if he made any indication that he thought ya were an oaf."

"In front of Leon?" Sybil asked, putting a hand to her chest, and Rani grinned knowingly. "Only slightly."

Rani laughed and shook her head before saying, "That pride of yar's gonna get you into a world of trouble one day."

The messaging stone in Sybil's pouch began vibrating. She pulled out the smooth, blue stone, and heard Leon's voice summoning her to his office.

"And perhaps that's today," Rani whispered.

Sybil made her way up the winding staircase of the tower toward Leon's office. Ever since Sybil arrived at the tower, she had worn robes, the traditional garb of wizards and mages. Not all robes looked the same, though, unless you were a student in one of the mage colleges of the Four Kingdoms. Sybil's robes were white with black trim and around her waist was a belt with a silver clasp that held her pouch, spellbook, and various other trinkets she needed on a regular basis. Across her chest was an embroidered raven, its wings outstretched in flight, in black thread. It was her symbol, something she came up with shortly after receiving her robes, though she could not explain how the idea came to her. Her robes were special to her because the day she first put on her robes was the day she officially became a wizard.

Leon's office was on the seventh floor, the exact middle of the tower, and on the same floor as the kitchen and dining hall. When Sybil reached the plain, wooden door, she wished Leon hadn't placed protective wards on it so she could use her magic to see inside the room. She hated being caught off guard by people, and people were usually in Leon's office for one reason or another. Even on the best of days, Sybil did not much enjoy speaking with people, especially not strangers, which is partly why she spent so much time in the library and avoided gatherings whenever she could. Silence, more than any person, was her friend.

Taking in a deep breath, Sybil knocked on the door, and it immediately opened. As soon as she stepped inside, it closed with a soft click. The heat of the room warmed her skin, which was usually chilled by the cold, open spaces of the tower. Leon was at his desk, scribbling away on some parchment with a quill, the feather dancing about as he wrote. She wandered over to the armchair across from his desk and waited. Like the rest of the rooms in the tower, his office floor and walls were made of a smooth, dark-gray stone and wooden beams crisscrossed along the ceiling. In the middle of the far wall was a large fireplace, which was always filled with a roaring fire, despite the season, and banners, trophies, and various other trinkets covered his walls which his people had brought back as gifts for him after their travels. Whenever Sybil waited in Leon's office, she always found herself staring at them and wondering where they came from and how her colleagues in the tower had come to acquire them.

Leon finally returned the quill back to its rest and looked up at her, his hands folding over the surface of the desk.

"Do you know why I have asked you here today?"

With all her skills in divination, Sybil never knew what Leon was thinking or what his grand scheme was in any situation. With a sigh, she said, "My magic must be weak today. But perhaps it's not a coincidence that you've summoned me on the same day someone new has arrived at the tower."

"Yes, indeed. This has to do with the young man I introduced you to this morning," Leon said. "Mordecai has a tremendous amount of skill and talent; I thought it would do well for the two of you to spend time together. There is much you must learn about the world outside this tower, and there are things you can teach him, as well."

"Such as?"

"There have not been many magic users who have happened upon his life with as strong of a will as you. It would do him some good to work with someone who he is not able to easily influence."

"Well, what *can* you tell me about him?"

"Not much beyond what I would prefer you to learn on your own. He is strong in the arcane and his expertise lies with his charisma and ability to manipulate those around him. When I first met him, he was disguised as the king's advisor, who, in reality, had actually been two years deceased." Leon raised his hand before Sybil could make a snipe comment. "And, no. He did not kill this man, though his hands are by no means clean."

"You know what's best," she replied, clenching her fists against the top of her thighs. "If you want me to work with him, then that's what I must do. What exactly do you have in mind?"

"Nothing quite at the moment, but I wanted you to be aware of my plans. I shall give him some time to settle in the tower, and we can reconvene at a later date. Continue with your studies, but please…," he said with a smirk. "Do take care with my books."

A feast was held in the dining hall that evening to welcome Mordecai to the tower. Even though there was a regular stream of visitors coming and going from the tower, it was rare for someone new to join as a permanent member. At any given time, there were nearly thirty people living in the tower, students and workers alike. They were a collection of people from all over the world who had either sought out the Enlightened or had been recruited by him. It was Leon's mission to establish and maintain peace across the continent, and more specifically the Kingdom of Irminshu, and he used his people to do this, despite how impossible it seemed at times.

The only one who Sybil paid much attention to, other than her mentor, was Rani. She understood Sybil's introversion and they had a deep, shared love of all things magic. While Rani sat to Sybil's right, Tanele always sat to Sybil's left. Tanele, a half-giant with snow-white skin and starkly contrasting black hair, was one of the warriors Leon brought under his service. In a past life, she had been a chevalier in the Four Kingdoms, at first a guardian and then a bounty hunter of aberrant mages, before Leon found her. She was quiet, perhaps even a bit shy, and having her there created a buffer between Sybil and the others that Rani, who stood only past Tanele's knees, could not provide.

At the other end of the table, in the guest of honor seat to Leon's right, was Mordecai, who was wearing fashionable garbs that matched the cloak he was wearing earlier in color. To Leon's left was Giselle, a descendant of an ancient, nether race from the Northern Realms, known to southerners as infernals, who was skilled in the art of stealth, thievery, and sabotage. Giselle was beautiful with satiny hair such a dark red it looked almost black, the true color only revealed in strong light, and deep purple skin without a single scar or blemish, the same hue as her amethyst eyes. Despite such a striking person sitting right across from him, Mordecai's eyes continued drifting across the table to Sybil, who was growing more and more frazzled by his gaze. Each time their eyes met, he would smirk or raise an eyebrow. Not wanting to be part of his amusement this evening, Sybil did her best to keep from looking over at him, though his silver eyes seemed to have some strange pull over her.

"What do ya suppose Leon wants with someone like that?" Rani asked Tanele and Sybil in a hushed voice. "Do ya think Leon's wanting to infiltrate a royal court or spy on someone powerful?"

"I stopped trying to determine Leon's motives a long time ago," Sybil told her with a shrug before taking a sip of wine.

Tanele nodded in agreement, but Rani looked unsatisfied as she stared across the table at the newcomer, who was now listening to one of Giselle's many thrilling tales. Though his attention stayed on her during the tale, he appeared bored, resting his chin in his palm and staring at her without expression. To Sybil, all of Giselle's tales were exciting and thrilling –and Giselle was quite the storyteller– so she couldn't help but wonder what sorts of things did keep his interest. Sensing her gaze, Mordecai once again locked eyes with Sybil, and a surge of embarrassment ran up her spine as she quickly looked away. She scolded herself. A newcomer had never piqued her curiosity so strongly before.

The feast started winding down, and Sybil returned to the library, still having two-thirds of the book she pulled that morning left to read. Not particularly fond of change, Sybil always sat in the same spot whenever she studied in the library. It was a perfect place to study in peace as no one could see her until they passed the bookcase it was next to and was the furthest distance from both the front door and the librarian's desk. On the large table, Sybil had her journal on top of her spellbook next to the clairvoyance tome and was scribbling notes and ideas into it as she read.

Being in the library at night, with candles and lanterns flickering all around her, their warm light illuminated her pages, brought her a great sense of calm. It felt impossible for her to fall asleep without an hour or two in the calming library before bed. If she had it her way, she would have spent every hour in the library both sleeping and awake. There was a back storage room, and she had asked Leon to let that be her bedroom, but he didn't like the idea of her completely isolating herself. At least with a room on the tenth floor, she had to pass a good number of people and exchange pleasantries before reaching the library on the ground floor.

Sleep started to weigh down her eyelids, so Sybil decided to wrap up for the night. Just as she was writing the last note in her journal, a shadowy figure appeared in her peripheral. With a jerk, she dropped her quill and splashed ink across the open page. When she turned to face what it was, though, the figure had disappeared. The first thought she had was that it might have been Mordecai in his dark cloak, but there was no trace of anyone in the library. It had been over an hour since the librarian had retired for the evening, and she never saw another soul in there at night.

The candles closest to her began to dance wildly, sending jagged shadows this way and that on the walls. Then, there was a hiss in her ear, like someone was trying to speak to her, and she leapt from her seat. The table jostled, sloshing ink as she moved around the table and turned to face where she was sitting. Pulling out her wand, something she only used when her staff wasn't around, she muttered an incantation which would reveal any creature in the room by forming a bright light above them.

But there was nothing. The library was silent, empty.

Taking a steadying breath, she decided that it really was time to retire for the evening. After casting a light spell, creating a small glowing orb that floated next to her, Sybil blew out the candles and cleaned up her workspace. The book would be fine to stay there until morning, but she took her journal and spellbook so no one wandered off with them. With hurried steps, she made her way out of the library, closing the door firmly behind her.

Moving through the tower at night usually didn't bother Sybil, but now she was nervous with every corner she turned and flinched at every sound. She made her way to the tenth floor where most of the dormitories were and, as she rounded into the hallway, came face to face with Mordecai. Nearly dropping her books, Sybil staggered back and let out a gasp.

"Do you really scare that easily?" he asked, his voice even more hoarse from the day's exhaustion. "What are you doing lurking in the halls?"

"I was going to ask you the same."

He thought for a moment before answering, "I was enjoying the night air up on the roof. You should try it sometime as opposed to the stale air of the library."

"How did you know I was in the library?" she asked him in a firm but hushed voice. "Were you in there just now?"

"I just said I was on the roof," he said, furrowing his eyebrows. "I just assumed, what with you holding books and your general reputation around the tower." She relaxed a little, and he eyed her suspiciously. "Did something happen in the library?"

"I... no," Sybil replied, deciding to forget the experience. "It's late. Good night, Mordecai."

He paused, watching her for a moment as she headed down the hall, and said, "Sleep tight."

The first of Sybil's thoughts the next morning were about Keijin, Leon's most dutiful and heroic warrior. Still lying in bed, the idea of him popped into her mind, though she rarely thought of him. This always meant he would be returning to the tower soon, a strange bit of foresight that only seemed to work on him. She sat up in bed, stretched, and then moved to her wardrobe to change. Her room wasn't much, but she loved that it was hers. There was a twin-size bed against one wall and a desk and two bookcases against another where she had started collecting books of her own, and just above her desk was a square window she could open and let in the autumn breeze. It was not yet time for breakfast, so she decided to head down to the front of the tower and greet Keijin upon his arrival. No one else would bother to, and she needed something to keep her mind off the fright she had the night before.

The Asbriand Forest surrounded Gibbous Tower, providing protection for the tower and a beautiful view from each window. As part of a symbiotic relationship, Gibbous Tower did its best to protect the forest as well. The forest was enchanted, long ago ruled by elves and druids, and all manner of magical creatures and fauna called it home. While there were some in the tower who studied these creatures and fauna, the Asbriand Forest was more or less left alone. Far to the east of the tower, there lived a unicorn, a powerful creature which as rumored to be the very source of the forest's magic. Sybil had never seen it. In fact, she hadn't traveled more than a mile away from the tower since Keijin first brought her here.

As a small child, Sybil decided that she wanted to grow up to be a powerful wizard, possibly the most powerful the world had ever seen. Soon after starting her studies, she learned about the Enlightened, who knew far more about magic and the world than a hundred thousand books could hold. Wanting to learn all he knew, Sybil set out for the Gibbous Tower, leaving the village of Morningbreak for the first time at sixteen.

While Irminshu had been an established kingdom for centuries, there was still a lot of untamed land between one village or city and the next, and traveling alone was dangerous. With Sybil knowing so little about the world, she believed the hardest part of her journey was going to be the many miles she would have to walk.

Just as a group of goblins had her surrounded on the road, not yet across the river east of her village, Keijin found her and saved her from a terrible fate. Keijin was a knight of an organization known only as the Ancient Order and was one of the last surviving members. He had sworn an oath centuries ago as a young man, not much older than Sybil's nineteen years, to protect the lives of the innocent across the lands. While most of his skills he learned over the years, the oath gave him extraordinary powers and a long life. Magic had that effect on powerful wielders, such as Keijin and Leon, and Sybil hoped the same would be true for herself one day.

Despite her deep respect for him and the fact he saved her life, she was not close with Keijin. She wouldn't have even said they were friends. But every time he was due to return to the tower, she felt him approaching within the hour of his arrival. It might have been some sort of bond that was formed when he rescued her from the goblins, but no matter how ridiculous she thought it was, Sybil always found herself sitting on the bottom step of the tower, waiting for him. Maybe it was some strange, unconscious way of thanking him.

This ritual, at the very least, gave Sybil an excuse to leave the tower, something she did on rare occasions because she much preferred to be behind the protective barrier of the tower's wards. She enjoyed listening to the birds chirping, the wind rustling the trees, and the muffled sounds coming from all the life going on inside the tower. Within the hour, Keijin came riding up the road on a beautiful white horse named the Captain with a smile gleaming on his face when he saw Sybil sitting there. It delighted Keijin that she did this every time he returned, and he had even admitted once that sometimes he left earlier or later than intended to test her strange, specific ability.

"My fair lady," he called out as he pulled his horse to a stop. "What joy it brings my heart to see such beauty so early in the day. Tell me that you are well and happy."

"As well and happy as I was when you left," Sybil said with a shrug before standing to her feet. "Only five days, a short trip this time."

"Oh, yes," Keijin said, dismounting his horse, his plate armor clinking. "There was a dragon problem to the southwest, a small town with little defenses, and I offered them my aid. It was only a young dragon, though, nothing a trained knight couldn't handle."

"I'm sure the maidens were thrilled," Sybil responded in her usual monotonous tone.

This made him laugh.

"Oh, Sybil, I always miss your odd sense of humor when I'm away. Tell me, any news in the tower?"

"Just another lost soul Leon recruited. Don't know much about him at this point, and I feel like he's not one to share."

"Well, I look forward to meeting him," Keijin responded, exuding his usual air of positivity that always made Sybil feel a little more pessimistic. "Sounds like an interesting fellow."

A stable hand came to greet Keijin and lead his horse away to the stables behind the tower. Sybil accompanied Keijin up to Leon's office as he told her his valiant tale of dragon slaying. "Unfortunately, red dragons simply cannot be reasoned with once they've set their mind on something," he said, ending his story.

Sybil had never met a dragon, or even seen one from a distance, but she would have never thought to reason with it. Keijin was a special sort of person, kind and pure, but still willing to slay those who threatened the lives of others. It was hard for her to understand him sometimes. They said goodbye at Leon's door so Keijin could debrief him on his latest quest, and Sybil headed toward Rani's workshop to see what she was up to.

There was always a thick, bittersweet humidity in Rani's workshop from all the fumes the potions created which immediately greeted Sybil when she entered. There were various sizes of cauldrons stacked along the right wall as she walked in, and Rani's workspace, where the current cauldron she was using steamed and bubbled, had a large round window above it. On shelves were piles of books, all of them about potions and their ingredients, and vials and scrolls were tucked anywhere they had seemed to fit. The room was colorful with all these things, and Sybil always found it fascinating to be in there, especially while Rani was working. She was in the middle of mixing a potion when Sybil arrived, so Sybil sat in the corner and flipped through one of Rani's potion books. Sybil had dabbled in potion making from time to time, but she knew it would limit her time for spellcasting if she studied it too heavily. Rani was there to make all the potions she needed, though the actual need for them was rare.

A cloud of smoke puffed out of the caldron into Rani's face, causing her to choke and cough. After she was able to breathe, she started cursing and threw a vial across the room, shattering it against the wall. Sybil sat there patiently, watching her friend go from furious to embarrassed.

"Took me nearly a month to gather all the resources for that potion, and I botched it," she said with her head down and arms hanging limply at her side. "I don't think I'll have enough for another go."

"Well, Keijin's just returned, so maybe he'd be willing to gather what you need next time he leaves," Sybil suggested, gathering up the broken pieces with her wand and mending the vial back together. "Until then, you can work on figuring out what you did wrong."

"I suppose ya're right," she mumbled before turning back to her workstation. "Suppose I'll just make some health potions today. We always

11

need those around here. But I think I'm due for a break. Want to help me raid the kitchen? I'm starved."

The two of them walked together in silence down to the kitchen which was full of any food anyone might crave. Sybil didn't have much of an appetite, she saw food as merely a necessity to fuel her throughout the day. On the other hand, she was convinced that Rani had stayed at the tower in large part due to the various types of cheeses, too many for Sybil to remember, an assortment of cured meats, breads from every region in the world, and desserts left over from previous meals Rani could access any time she wanted.

Sybil sat on the butcher-block countertop as Rani rummaged around the pantry for ingredients to make herself a sandwich, the construction of which she had put nearly as much planning into as some of her inventions. After taking a couple bites of this culinary wonder she had created, Rani looked up at Sybil with a curious expression and said, "Ya're awfully social today. What's goin' on?"

"Does something have to be going on for me to spend time with you?"

"For ya, yes. Unless it's my idea, of course. This is out of the ordinary, so what happened?"

Chewing the inside of her cheek, Sybil thought for a moment before answering.

"Something frightened me in the library last night. I haven't really thought about it, but I guess I'm just a little weary of being alone after that."

With a mouthful of food, Rani asked, "What was it?"

"A specter? I have no idea. I saw a figure for only an instance then heard some sort of dark voice in my ear." Sybil wrapped her arms around herself as if she were cold. "It sounded hateful."

Rani was silent for a moment, thinking while she chewed.

"Didn't think ghosts could get into the tower with all the wards Leon's casted," Rani said as she tried to make sense of it. "Do ya think it might've just been someone trying to play a trick on ya?"

"Who would do that?" Sybil asked, and Rani gave a shrug. "The only other person I saw last night after it happened was Mordecai, but he told me he was on the roof. Unless he was lying, it was impossible for him to be in the library one moment and then the roof the next. Leon doesn't allow conjuration magic within the tower unless someone has distinct permission to use it."

"Mordecai's a suspicious character, probably dangerous, but a trickster, I think not. Leon doesn't care for tricks."

"It could've just very well been my own imagination," Sybil offered, though she didn't believe it herself. "In any case, I suppose I shouldn't avoid the library all day. Leon wants me to increase my clairvoyance to see and hear through walls, and there's still a lot I have to learn about such a spell."

Rani had a limited understanding of how wizards learned and used spells, but she understood the process of mastering skills. With a nod, she said, "There's always lots to do."

Despite there being five other perfectly adequate sitting areas, when Sybil entered the library, she found Mordecai reading in her usual spot where she had left her book the night before. She approached the table and saw that the book was open, but he had another book in his hands, one she had never seen before. Its pages looked like they would turn to a pile of dust if you blew too hard on them, the writing on it was jagged and reminded her of ancient texts that witches and other unsavory magic wielders used to create curses, and the cover appeared to have survived a fire. This book must have been from Mordecai's own collection Sybil would have remembered a book like this in the library. She knew the collection nearly as well as the librarian.

Mordecai didn't look up as she walked toward the sitting area, but when she started to slide her book off the table, he said, "Divination magic, probably the most underutilized school of magic, but a very powerful asset to have."

"You're in my spot."

He glanced up from his reading, his silver eyes reminding her of something nocturnal, something feral, and raised an eyebrow.

"Sorry, didn't know it belonged to you. You're more than welcome to join me if you wish."

Hesitating for a moment, Sybil thought about rudely rejecting him, but she did prefer to sit in this corner of the library when she studied. She neither wanted to sit next to him nor sit somewhere else, so with a huff, she sat in her usual chair only a couple feet away from him. Mordecai watched her slide the large tome over to her side before returning to his book, completely at ease with the company. The constant twinge of discomfort from sitting next to a complete stranger, the silent air thickening between them and threatening to choke her, kept her from staying focused on her studies.

Eventually, Sybil grew more and more curious about the foreign book Mordecai seemed to be reading with ease, so she silently cast a spell, allowing her to view from a different perspective. From this new view, she was now able to see the text clearly, though it did little good as she could not read the letters. The best guess she had of its origin was some dialect of ancient elvish, but she knew little of that language, too.

"You know," he breathed, not looking up from the page. "You could just ask."

"Sorry," Sybil said, flushing with embarrassment and releasing the spell. "What... what are you reading?"

Mordecai laid the book on the table, and Sybil could feel something dark and mysterious seeping from it as her true eyes gazed over the text. There was a draw to this book; she could feel some sort of strange power in it. Her fingers found the pages and traced along the letters, but Mordecai reached out and grabbed her wrist, pulling her hand away.

"You'll smudge the ink," he explained, letting go. "This is a very old book with very complicated magic. You seem skilled, but I don't think you're quite ready for this level of the arcane. This magic could break the mind of a mage who isn't ready for it yet, and I don't think Leon would be too pleased if I let that happen to his apprentice."

"You believe my mind is that frail?"

"I believe this magic is that powerful, and you seem rather young to be at a level that's ready to handle this."

"Oh, and is your true, aging face hidden behind some illusion magic?"

A small smile twinged at the corner of his lips.

"I picked the wrong spot in the library to study my books," he noted. "You make it impossible to get any reading done."

"Well, if you must be so dramatic, I'll be quiet and let you study. I must focus on strengthening this frail mind of mine, after all."

Mordecai said nothing, but amusement was clear on his face as he stared at Sybil from the corner of his eyes. Saying nothing more, he pulled the book back toward him and continued reading. They both stayed silent, reading and scribbling notes into their journals well into the afternoon. The dinner chime, a soft but distinguishable ting, rang throughout the tower, but when Sybil started gathering up her things, Mordecai told her he wouldn't be attending dinner that evening.

As he said this, he looked preoccupied, as if his mind were in another time and space. There was darkness, and perhaps even pain, in his eyes. Everything in Sybil wanted to inquire, for even though she didn't enjoy talking to strangers, she could not ignore a mystery. But there was something instinctive in her that knew he was not one to share his thoughts with strangers. Instead, she bid him good night and headed up to the dining hall.

"Ya're broodier than usual," Rani noted halfway through the meal.

"No, I'm not," Sybil replied, staring down at her plate, poking a piece of chicken with her fork. "I'm the normal amount of broody. Just been struggling with spells lately… I just can't seem to make any progress on them." She lowered her voice a bit. "What if Leon made a mistake in picking me as his apprentice?"

"Leon doesn't make mistakes. Ya know this as well as I do," Rani said, pointing her butterknife at Sybil. "I think this newcomer has thrown ya off a bit."

"I haven't even seen him use his magic, but I still know he's powerful… and far more knowledgeable. He's probably seen every corner of the continent and met all sorts of magic users, and me? Perhaps he's my replacement."

"Oh, come off it," Rani hissed. "If anything, Leon brought him on board to be your tutor or something, get ya learning about whatever dark magic I can feel dripping off him. He's a steppingstone to ya one day taking over all this." Sybil nodded but stayed silent. "It's been a while since ya've used your magic in the training rooms. Maybe showing yarself how powerful ya are would be good practice for ya. I don't mind being the target… as long as there's no lasting damage that is."

"You're just trying to get me to test one of your new potions, aren't you? Tit for tat, and all that?"

"No, but since ya're offering…" Rani said with a mischievous smile. "Skip the library tomorrow if ya want to know where ya stand."

As Rani and Sybil discussed heading to the training rooms at breakfast the next morning, Giselle and Tanele overheard their discussion and invited themselves to the practice. With Tanele leading the way, Sybil headed up to the training rooms after breakfast with these smart, capable women. It was a little intimidating to be around them, actually, despite her status in the tower. They had decades of worldly experience between them, and she felt child-like beside them. When they entered the training room, she hoped there was something she could do to impress them.

The training rooms were on the top floor of the tower and even extended to the roof for more dangerous or distance-based training. In the middle of the floor was the largest of the training rooms, which was filled with various training instruments and weapons along the walls, and there were several dummies fighters used for practice that were all piled up together along the far end of the room. Sybil had only used these areas a handful of times, as most of the spells she had learned over the years had little to do with fighting.

Keijin was already in there training when they entered the room. He was dressed in lightweight garbs and had his greatsword drawn, practicing movements with beads of sweat forming along his hairline. Rani called out that they needed the room, and he happily stepped aside for them, returning his greatsword to its sheath. With four other people in the room, Sybil grew nervous, especially when Rani had her stand uncomfortably in the middle of the room, clutching her magic staff in both hands. Rani, Tanele, and Giselle all stood across from her, several feet from each other, and Keijin and moved off to the side to watch. They were all waiting, but Sybil wasn't sure what to do.

"Well, go ahead," Tanele boomed. "Show us a spell!"

Sybil took a deep, steadying breath and moved her staff out in front of her and tapped the end of it on the ground. Conjured from nowhere, water started bubbling up in the middle of the room. The puddle grew and grew, gathering until it stretched from the floor to ceiling, blocking everyone but Keijin from view like a wall. She had never used this spell, having only learned it after Leon suggested she branch out to other schools of magic, but she knew it would shield her from Tanele, Rani, and Giselle. She glanced over at Keijin, who was the only other person in the training room. Even though he must have seen much grander spells in his travels, he seemed impressed by the water barrier she had created.

To Sybil's great surprise, Giselle used the moment she was distracted to burst through the wall, flying toward Sybil with one of her daggers.

Due to Leon's abilities and the magic imbued within the tower, training could turn deadly. If someone was mortally wounded in training, Leon would be able to revive them, allowing the students and warriors in the tower to train the same as they would engage in combat outside the tower. But Sybil certainly didn't expect to have a deadly assassin fly toward her while practicing her spells. Giselle, now drenched in water, caught her completely by surprise.

Without thinking, Sybil lifted her staff and attempted to temporarily paralyze Giselle. She was nearly successful, causing Giselle to falter for a moment, and this gave Sybil enough time to lunge out of the way and cast a protection spell on herself. The dagger caught her in the side, and she let out a yelp. It would have gone much deeper without her spell, but she still felt blood starting to trickle down her side. Distracted by the pain, the water barrier came crashing to the ground, spilling water all across the floor. The water started vanishing as Sybil stood to her feet, and the other two came to join them, Tanele partnering with Sybil and Rani partnering with Giselle.

Tanele drew her longsword and lunged toward Giselle as Rani ran around the room with magically enhanced speed and threw a spell at Sybil, conjuring acid that formed into a ball as it flew in the air. Bringing her staff above her head, Sybil countered Rani's spell, deflecting the acid away from everyone on the training floor, and conjured a giant web that managed to get tangled on one of Rani's feet. While her friend struggled to get loose from the web, Sybil turned her attention to Giselle who was going toe to toe with Tanele. Giselle was the fastest fighter in the tower, and despite all her skill, the half-giant was struggling to keep up with her. Pointing her staff at Giselle, Sybil caused her motions to slow enough to give Tanele the upper hand, and the halfling, now free, used the opportunity to throw another spell.

A great force hit Sybil in her side, sending her flying across the room. She rolled into Keijin's feet, who was watching this fight with what could only be described as glee. As she stood up, Sybil noticed that another spectator had entered the room. Mordecai was standing in the doorway with his arms crossed, looking displeased at the scene he had stumbled upon.

Feeling frustrated by his judgmental glare, Sybil reached out to the three women fighting in the middle of the room and unleashed a ball of fire between them. It exploded in a flurry of sparks and flames, throwing all three of them nearly a dozen feet from where they stood. Exhausted and fairly burnt, all of them lay on the floor as smoke rose from their charred clothes. Sybil had won the fight, but by the look on Mordecai's face, she felt that she had also lost something.

"That was reckless; a wizard should know better," he said, standing over her, his low voice dripping with spite. "Act with your head, not your heart, or you'll never be what you aspire to be."

Before Sybil could say anything, he headed up to the rooftop, slamming the door behind him. Her face and chest burned, and her stomach felt like lead. She couldn't explain why she cared what he thought of her, but she did. Even though everyone else in the room remarked how incredible her spellcasting abilities were, she felt embarrassed and more insecure about her position under Leon than ever. What if she wasn't cut out to be a great wizard like she thought?

Chapter Two

After the way Mordecai had spoken to her in the training room and the embarrassment she felt, Sybil had been sure to keep a safe and comfortable distance between the two of them. Despite Leon's instructions that they should work together, she had managed this quite well for nearly four days until Leon invited her to his office for a meeting. When she arrived a few minutes later, the office door was already open, and Mordecai and Keijin were sitting on the couch in the corner near the fireplace. Mordecai had the hood of his cloak down, his oddly beautiful face warmly illuminated from the fireplace, and the fabric of his cloak was spread out along the cushion and arm of the couch on either side of him, revealing the dark tunic, loosely tied and made of fine fabric, he wore underneath. Keijin was also looking rather casual on the opposite end of the couch with his brown hair down around his neck and shoulders and was wearing a long-sleeved shirt made of cotton, trimmed in an intricate design of silver, which he usually wore under his armor.

When Sybil walked in, she first looked at Keijin and then over at Mordecai. As their eyes met, a humorous grin spread across Mordecai's face, as if he were teasing her. She did her best not to let it bother her. Standing from his desk, Leon asked Sybil to sit with them, and Mordecai moved his cloak out of her way, watching her as she moved to the couch between him and Keijin.

"I have carefully selected the three of you, soon to be the four of you, for an important set of missions. The time has come for you to grow stronger together, to learn from the strengths and weaknesses of each other and become better people because of it," Leon explained to them, slowly pacing back and forth in the middle of the room with slow, deliberate shuffles of his feet. "The first task I have for you as a party is to travel to the nearby village of Spindlewood. There are children going missing there with no clear trace of what or who is taking them. I thought this would be a good opportunity for you to start small and come together as a group."

After the initial shock of what Leon explained to them, Sybil asked, "So… who's the fourth one?"

There was a tingle of nervousness and excitement running through her, and she had to cover her hands with her robes so no one saw them shaking.

"You will pick him up along the way. He is one of my men who has never been to the tower before. In fact, he does not even know who I am… technically speaking. But he has been working for me, out in the field, for several years now," Leon explained. "He is known as Redbeard, though that is not his given name, and he was last seen near the Crossroads hunting orcs and goblins who had been attacking travelers on the road in recent months. You will know him when you see him."

"Because of the beard, right?" Mordecai asked dryly, gesturing to his chin.

Keijin quietly laughed, but Sybil let out a long, quiet sigh before asking, "And when shall we leave?"

"With children at risk? As soon as possible," Keijin answered as he stood and turned toward his new companions. "We shall get a good night's rest tonight and set off on the road by sunrise."

Leon nodded along to Keijin's words but said nothing, and Sybil looked over at Mordecai, who glanced down at her, the flames near him dancing in his eyes. It was impossible for her to tell what he was thinking, but he didn't appear pleased. Sybil couldn't help but wonder what traveling on the road with him and Keijin, and whoever this Redbeard person was, would be like. Keijin was someone she got along well enough with in short spurts, and he and Mordecai didn't seem to have much of an issue with each other, but she knew the three of them stuck traveling together would be a recipe for disaster. Quite frankly, she felt exhausted just thinking about it and could only hope the fourth member of their party would smooth things over once he joined them.

Later that evening, Sybil found Rani, Giselle, and Tanele at the foot of the dining table, waiting for her to join them. Since the fight in the training room, they had all formed some strange sort of bond Sybil didn't quite understand. She went from silently passing them in the hall and occasionally sitting with them at meals, to saying hello and asking them how they were – only after they asked her because she knew it was the polite thing to do– and sitting with them at each meal. They had even convinced her to join them that day at lunch, a meal she usually skipped, and Sybil was a little socially whiplashed from the sudden change in their relationships.

"You don't look at all well," Giselle said to Sybil in her sultry voice as she looked her up and down. Comparatively to her, no one looked well, so Sybil was able to shrug off her comment. "I think all that spellwork is bad for your health."

Rani stared at her wizard friend, clearly concerned, and said, "Did something happen in the meeting with Leon?"

"He's sending me away… with Keijin and Mordecai," Sybil answered weakly, glancing over at where her future travel companions were sitting at the other end of the table. "Not sure how long we'll be gone for, either."

"Keijin and Mordecai…" Giselle breathed, looking up as she thought about them. "Well, at least you won't be bored. I'd love to spend some time in the wilds with that Mordecai fellow. So dark and mysterious. Though, Keijin is a fine specimen as well."

Tanele made a face and said, "You've spent too much time seducing old men for profit in the field. Please, raise your bar a little higher. You're better than them."

The two of them had been bickering back and forth since the four of them started spending more time together. It didn't make sense to Sybil, but they both seemed to enjoy the bickering, and even times she would have been mad at what they said, they seemed to light up from it.

"I could raise it to your level, if that's what you're asking," Giselle said with a gleam, resting her elbows on the table and raising an eyebrow.

"That's…not what I'm asking," the half-giant whispered, her massive frame seeming to shrink, as her pale face turned a light pink, and her eyes remained glued to the table for the rest of the meal.

Rani steered the conversation back on course by asking, "So, where's he sending ya?"

"The Crossroads first, I believe, though I'm not even sure where that is, and then onto a nearby village," Sybil replied. "We're going to be picking up this guy named Redbeard. Have any of you heard of him?"

Both Rani and Giselle shook their heads, but Tanele didn't move, still in shock from what Giselle said. They assured her that Leon wouldn't have picked this Redbeard character to join the party without good reason, though. Each of them had been on an expedition for Leon at least a handful of times, and over the past decade Giselle had become as prolific in her adventuring as Keijin.

Once dinner was over, the four of them headed out of the dining hall toward the stairs, and Tanele, who seemed to have recovered, put a hand on Sybil's shoulder and said, "The best advice I can give you is to trust in the companions Leon has picked for you." Her rich brown eyes landed on Mordecai who was nearing the top of the stairs. "Even if their very nature shouts untrustworthy. As long as you don't get personally attached, it'll all work out just fine."

Sybil said goodnight to her new group of friends and headed to bed. In the far corner of her room sat her travel bag, mostly packed, with her staff leaning against the wall beside it. She stared at her bag for a while, sitting on the edge of her bed. Even though she was tired, she knew she wouldn't be able to sleep muchthat night. The tingling jitters she had felt earlier in Leon's office had never left her. Once she did finally manage to get herself into bed, she tossed and turned for several hours. The restlessness finally overwhelmed her, and she decided to head up to the rooftop for a few minutes to get some fresh air and clear her head.

When Sybil made it to the rooftop, it didn't surprise her to see that another person was already there. Had Mordecai spent every night since arriving on the roof? He was sitting on the edge of the tower, his feet dangling a good hundred and fifty feet from the ground, and staring up at the night sky. The chill of the night air hit Sybil unexpectedly, and she wrapped her robes tighter around her body as she approached him.

"Searching for your fate in the stars?" she asked softly, knowing he had already sensed her presence.

"Not searching, but keeping watch," Mordecai said before looking over at her, his silver eyes glimmering in the moonlight.

He gestured for her to join him on the edge. Looking over and seeing how far the drop was, her stomach lurched, but she trusted in her magic enough to know, if she fell, she would be able to reach the bottom unharmed.

Once she was sitting next to him, his gaze returned to the sky, and he said, "Tell me, how did you come to wield magic?"

Sybil didn't like this question because it was complicated and hard to explain, but it was one she received often. People liked to test her, to see if she was really meant to be Leon's apprentice.

"Due to some...complicated circumstances, I was born with it, to a certain extent. But when I was a child, I decided I wanted to wield it differently than what was expected of me," she tried her best to explain. Mordecai was listening intently, his eyes locked onto her face as she spoke. "In the forest near the village where I was raised, there lived a hermit, Roland. He understood how to wield magic without having been born with such abilities, and after seeing his power, I asked him to make me his student.

"As often as I could, I would sneak away, and Roland would teach me what he knew. I would borrow books from him and practice when I was alone, which was a rare occurrence in those days. Overtime, I learned enough to allow me to escape my village and set out for whom the hermit called 'the greatest of all wizards,' wanting to become powerful enough in my own magic that the other magic tied to me no longer mattered."

"Well, that explains it," he breathed, smiling a little. "The moment I met you, I could feel there was a power radiating from you a mere student wouldn't be able to wield. Something more powerful attaches itself to you, just as it does to me." His gaze once again returned to the sky. "And from what it sounds like, you are a prisoner to it, too."

Sybil waited for him to say more, but when he didn't she asked, "What exactly are you a prisoner to?"

Mordecai was silent for a time, and Sybil could see the stars above shimmering in his eyes. The moonlight made his face unnaturally white, and it reminded her of the stories she used to hear of beautiful, dark creatures that lured mortals into the woods, never to be heard from again.

"Absolute darkness, a hungry void that's never satisfied," he finally said, his gravelly voice causing a shiver to run up Sybil's spine. The way he said this, staring up at the sky, made her follow his gaze. To her own eyes, she couldn't see more than a gaseous star cluster of which she was unfamiliar, but she knew there was more he was seeing. "He's always watching and waiting, so I make sure to watch him right back."

"Mordecai, why are you working for Leon?" she asked, and he twitched at the sound of his name. "What do you get out of serving him?"

"Symbiosis," he answered with a simple shrug. "I give to others to get something else in return."

"And what is it that you want?"

"The same thing you want," he breathed, his eyes moving to her face in her peripheral. "Power."

Sybil lowered her gaze down toward the ground. It was so dark below her only looked like emptiness. Was that truly what she wanted? To be godlike, in order to not fear the power of the gods, yes. But what was it she wanted with that power? More than anything, it came down to freedom and showing the gods, who believed they could control the lives of mortals, did not hold all the power. But from the rate she was going, she had centuries ahead of her before she could wield that sort of power.

"Can this hunger hear us? Does it know your plans?"

"Haborym," he said, giving the hunger a name. "I give him just enough to make him believe he understands me. He's powerful, but I understand how he uses his power. And no, he cannot just hear us. There are too many other things he's listening for to catch enough of what I say."

She thought for a moment, back to the first night she met Mordecai, and asked, "Can he come down here, existing as a shadow?"

His eyes met hers, and she knew he could see the fear she was feeling. Anger flashed across his face, and he turned away.

"When did this happen?" he asked.

"That night I ran into you in the corridor... you asked if I really startled that easily."

"I was afraid of that," he sighed. "Haborym must have sensed your power the first time we met. He's targeted you."

Sybil thought, for the first time in years, of Shuheyr's protection, of the powers he gifted her with at birth. But she pushed the thought away; it was too dangerous to think of him here, outside of the tower.

"What does that mean?" she asked with a shaky voice, pushing her thoughts of Shuheyr aside.

"It could mean a lot of different things. What else do you remember happening?"

She thought back and said, "There was a voice... it was in a language I had never heard, and it sounded angry, spiteful, as if I had wronged it in some way."

To Sybil's surprise, Mordecai let out a short laugh.

"He must be fearful of you, though I don't see how. The only time he tries to intimidate someone is if he feels threatened." A sly smile spread across his face. "You must be more interesting than I gave you credit for."

"Thanks," Sybil said, frowning. "Should I be worried about this? We're going to be leaving the protection of the tower tomorrow, and I don't want something attacking me in the shadows because I'm traveling with you."

"Trust me, you're safer with me than without me," he replied. "Speaking of our travels, you should really go and get some rest."

"And what about you?"

"Don't worry about me."

After a moment of hesitation, Sybil carefully stood up from the edge of the tower and headed toward the door. Just before going inside, she turned around to see Mordecai casting a spell toward the sky, a black flurry of sparks spinning from his open palm, and wondered how much of what he told her was true and how lies might have served him. Even though she trusted Leon's reasons, she didn't trust Mordecai in the slightest.

Dawn was only a few hours away, so she had to push all those thoughts aside if she had any hope of getting rest before they set off on their adventure. Thankfully, sleep took her soon after she crawled into bed, and it felt like only minutes when she woke to a banging at her door as the sunlight poured into her room.

Realizing she was late, Sybil sprung out of bed. As soon as she was dressed, though still a little unkempt, she opened the door and found Keijin impatiently standing there, fully geared up in his plate mail armor and ready for his next mission. He told her to quickly grab her things because they were wasting daylight. She grabbed her bag, heavy with all the stuff she packed into it, and placed it on the bed to buckle it up. Keijin made a face and shook his head.

"Sybil, you can't pack so many books," he told her, knowing what she had prioritized for her bag. "Pick two, and save the rest of the space for the supplies we'll need on our travels."

Keijin watched as she pulled five books out of her bag, consulting which two were most important to her, and she could feel the irritation growing in him, though he would never have expressed it outwardly. Just as she had narrowed down the books she wanted to bring, he approached her and gazed into her bag.

"And only one journal," he said, pulling two others from the bag and tossing them onto her bed. "I highly doubt you will have the time to fill a single one on our journey."

"You know of many things, sir, but of that you do not," she replied but still relented, leaving the other journals behind.

With her bag properly packed, Sybil followed Keijin down to the bottom of the tower and out through the front doors where Mordecai was waiting for them. It was early morning, so no one was there to see them off, but Sybil didn't mind. It was easier to just leave knowing you would be back than saying a bunch of goodbyes and putting on a whole show. The stable hand brought out two horses, the Captain, Keijin's white steed, and a gray mare that Mordecai had not bothered to name. Sybil wanted for him to return with another while Keijin and Mordecai attached their packs to the saddles, but he never returned.

"As soon as we're able, we'll find you a horse," Keijin explained. "But until then, you must ride with one of us. There are no horses the stable can spare for the long journey we have ahead of us."

It was just as well; Sybil never learned to ride a horse. But, by watching what they did and getting used to being in a saddle, she hoped that she would learn by the time she had her own.

Without saying a word, it was clear who Sybil would choose to ride with, and Mordecai was already mounted on his horse and waiting while Keijin to help her into the Captain's saddle. Keijin then took her bag and tied it to his own, along with her staff that sat on top of it all, and slid into the saddle behind her. With his feet in the stirrups, the fronts of his legs were pressed against the back of hers. It was the closest she had ever been to Keijin, or any man for that matter, and she felt herself flush as he nonchalantly pushed her forward by hips to give him more room in the saddle to sit comfortably.

With the black hood over his head and his dark cloak draped over the horse, Mordecai looked like the villains from the storybooks Sybil used to read as a child. The villain was always clothed in black with their faces hidden, and they always had some sort of secret they kept from those around them. Keijin, on the other hand, was the white knight, wearing shining armor and a green cape with golden trim, who saved the fair maidens and village children. Sybil wondered if they saw these things in themselves and each other, as she did. But whether they did or not, she just hoped they didn't see her as a damsel in distress and rather for the powerful wizard she was becoming.

Keijin wrapped his arm around Sybil's waist and kicked his horse into a canter, starting them off down the road. Mordecai rode a bit ahead of them, the tails of his cloak fluttering in the wind, and Keijin explained more of the plan to Sybil she had missed sleeping in that morning. They would be spending the night in an inn at the Crossroads, a place established for every sort of traveler in the kingdom, where they would make contact with Redbeard. The following day, they would make their way to the village of Spindlewood and immediately start their investigation of the missing children. As he explained this, Sybil couldn't help but notice how matter-of-fact he was about something so strange and unsettling to her. He had done missions like this hundreds of times, had fought countless monsters, and knew the roads they would be traveling on like the grooves in his hands. On the other hand, Sybil was scared and nervous for so many reasons, but she was glad to have an experienced adventurer like Keijin to guide her.

Sybil had rarely ventured outside since she joined the tower, and there was a good reason for that. The life she had been trying to escape by seeking out the Enlightened tended to come crashing in on her all at once as Shuheyr, the god of light, sought her out. With all the excitement and nervousness she felt about going on this new adventure, she had forgotten what she was trying to avoid outside of the tower. That is, until she started feeling the weight of Shuheyr pressing down upon her once more.

It was subtle at first, just a slight tingle at the base of her skull she always felt when going outside, but as time went on, her whole body started to tremble and feel like it was being crushed under the weight of a giant's foot. Her hope was he had forgotten her, or the village she grew up in had birthed a new Soul Child, but it was clear that he had just been waiting for her to leave the protective border of Leon's tower. Fearful, her thoughts became consumed by Shuheyr and the destiny which had been given to her the day she was born.

Only an hour down the road, Sybil's hands started to shimmer with radiant light, and she asked Keijin to stop so she could get off his horse. Without question, he did as she requested, and trying to get off the horse without assistance, she nearly collapsed to the ground. Keijin followed close behind her to see if she needed help, but she told him to leave her be, that she just needed a moment. She headed into the tree line, just out of sight, wanting to avoid being seen by the other two as her entire body began to glow.

"Leave me alone," she begged the ethereal being, falling to her knees. "I don't serve you."

Sybil's vision turned white, and a piercing noise rang in her ears, blocking out all other sounds of the forest around her. She wanted to scream, but she couldn't find her voice. Without a doubt she knew: Shuheyr was coming for her.

Unexpectedly, she felt cool hands clasped around hers, and Mordecai's voice was in her ear saying, "Breathe deeply and empty your mind. You're letting him in."

Sybil tried her best to do as he instructed, taking slow, deep breaths and clearing her mind of everything. The panic started to fade, and her vision returned to normal. Mordecai's face was close to hers, and he was staring hard into her eyes. Then, Sybil's thoughts turned to Haborym, to darkness and hunger, and the light and power of Shuheyr which was fading all at once vanished.

Keijin was standing beside them, his face filled with deep concern, but Sybil's attention was still on Mordecai, who asked, "Better?"

"I-I think so," she breathed, realizing he was still clasping her hands.

"I never knew," Keijin spoke up. "This whole time you've been hiding from Shuheyr. Why?"

"It wasn't my choice to serve him," Sybil said weakly. "My connection to him was forced upon me the day I was born."

"The village where you grew up, they were worshipers of Shuheyr?" Mordecai asked, and she slowly nodded. "That would explain why you left. Shuheyr worshippers are the most fanatic of them all."

Sybil glanced down at their hands, and Mordecai quickly pulled his away. Keijin pulled out a flask of water and handed it to her. Sitting back against the tree behind her, Sybil brought the flask to her mouth and drank deeply. There was silence for a few minutes before Keijin spoke up again.

"If you're feeling better, we should be on our way. These woods are home to all sorts of dangerous creatures that would love to catch us off our guard," he suggested and then turned to Mordecai. "Perhaps she should ride with you while she works through this... issue."

"Fine by me," Mordecai replied as he stood, his black cloak flowing back into place.

Keijin helped Sybil back on her feet, and they returned to the horses. Just as Mordecai was helping Sybil into his saddle, they heard an "Oi!" coming from the tree line in the opposite direction. They all turned to see three hobgoblins, hairy creatures about the size of dwarves with primitive weapons and clothing, coming out of the woods with spears and javelins in hand. Sybil heard Mordecai let out a little groan behind her.

"You ain't going nowhere with them horses. We seen 'em first!" the leader and tallest of the short creatures yelled to them as they continued moving toward the horses.

"They were already our horses, you oaf," Sybil said without thinking, causing Mordecai to elbow her.

"Right, if you wanna play it that way," the leader said and snapped his fingers.

One of the hobgoblins behind him reared back and threw his javelin toward them. In one quick motion, Keijin pulled the shield from his back and held it up to deflect the attack. The tip of the javelin made a sharp chime as it met with the metal of the shield, and Sybil watched as the javelin spun wildly in the air and landed in the dirt with the point sticking up.

Seething with irritation, Mordecai stepped out in front of Sybil and raised his arms. Black smoke started bellowing out of his sleeves and drifted swiftly over to the hobgoblins. None of them noticed the smoke until it was upon them, and then they all started clutching their heads and letting out terrible yowls. In a moment, the smoke faded, and the hobgoblins seemed to return to normal, the look of shock on their faces. This spell, though it lasted for only a moment, had terrified them, and they took off back the way they came, yelling that they could keep their stupid horses.

Mordecai looked back at Sybil just quickly enough for her to see his eyes change from a terrible black to his usual gray. She couldn't help but look away from him. His power and this connection he had to such a dark entity terrified her. Without saying a word, he moved closer, practically pinning her between him and the side of his horse, and offered her his hand. Her heart was racing, and she wanted to ride with Keijin instead but said nothing as she took his hand.

Once Sybil was in the saddle, Mordecai settled in behind her. Keijin, silently fuming from the hobgoblin attack, rode on ahead. Grasping his arm which was now around her waist, Sybil winced as Mordecai kicked his horse, sending it into a gallop.

"It wouldn't benefit me to hurt you," he whispered in her ear as they rode. "You don't have to be afraid of me."

"Who said I'm afraid?"

He laughed humorlessly.

"I can feel you... you're terrible at masking your feelings. That's something we'll need to work on."

"Among other things," she breathed, trying her best to calm down and just focus on the mission at hand.

Just as the sun was beginning to set, they came upon the Crossroads. At first glance, it almost looked like a town, but there were only six buildings, all taverns and inns. It was a place only few actually lived; everyone else was just passing through. Some were traveling north to the City of the King or beyond that to the port town of Bream. Others were heading south to the city of Taragpass or beyond the mountains to the realm of the Four Kingdoms, and some parties would head east to the more prosperous towns of the kingdom or west to the rural villages in the Untamed Lands. Around the inns and taverns there were camps and caravans, lighting up the night with a smattering of campfires, for those who had a particular method for travel or who couldn't afford one of the establishments. As the party rode closer to the Crossroads, they could hear the noise of all the people gathered in this one unique spot.

The place where they would find Redbeard was called the Filthy Lantern, and it lived up to its name. Out of all the inns and taverns there, it was the bottom of the barrel. Sybil hoped and prayed this wouldn't be where they would stay for the night; she would have preferred to join one of the campsites.

The smell of alcohol, sweat, and blood hit Sybil in the face as soon as they stepped through the rickety door, and it took everything in her not to clog her nose. The room was dimly lit with only a few lanterns, filthy ones of course, scattered around, and the furniture was all in disrepair and appeared to have been hastily built in the first place. There couldn't have been more than a dozen people, a stark difference from the bustling establishments they passed to get to this one. Each of the patrons sat on their own or in a pair, no one making eye contact with one another, and they were all grungy and beat up with dried blood caked to their face and clothes.

When Keijin, Mordecai, and Sybil stepped in, they immediately drew the room's attention. All three of them looked significantly younger and better kempt. Of their small party, Mordecai would have been the only one to pass unnoticed in this place because he was practically a shadow already. What bothered Sybil most about this place, besides the smell, was that despite her robes fitting as modestly to her form and figure as a woman could get, many of the men were eyeing her lustfully. Feeling uneasy by this, Sybil shrank closer to Keijin and Mordecai.

"Three ales, my good man," Keijin called to the bartender, a half-orc with a hook for a hand, as he headed to the bar with Mordecai and Sybil following behind him.

The half-orc grunted and pulled out three tankards from under the bar and started filling them. They sat in a row along the bar, and Sybil strategically chose the middle seat. The bartender placed the filled tankards in front of them and barked for three copper pieces. Keijin reached into his purse and provided the coin, and the bartender left them alone with their drinks.

"Do you know what he looks like?" Sybil asked them in a whisper as she pulled her large ale toward her.

"Well, I would assume he'd have a red beard..." Mordecai said and smiled when Sybil glared at him. "But no. Leon didn't give us a description."

Trying her best to be subtle, Sybil glanced over her shoulder at some of the other patrons in the room. There were a lot of beards, but none of them were red, save for a few trails of blood from mouths and noses. When she accidently met eyes with a particularly brutish looking man, she quickly turned back around to the bar and kept her head low. Keijin had finished his tankard within the first few minutes and had been slowly spinning it between his hands, but Mordecai had not even touched his. Just as Keijin was leaning over Sybil to ask Mordecai for his now flat ale, the front door to the tavern burst open.

A dwarf, a bit tall for his kind but still a foot shorter than Sybil, came bursting into the room with his greataxe in hand. He was covered in dirt, leaves, and various types of blood, some of which covered his bright red beard. Along his bare arms were intricate tattoos of runes and wolves, and he wore a studded leather tunic which would barely protect his chest. He meandered over to the bar, placing his greataxe on top of it and yelled at the bartender for a pint.

Mordecai was closest to the dwarf, and he was leaning away from him and into Sybil with a disgusted look on his face. The bartender set down an ale, and Redbeard downed it in one breath, some of it spilling over the edges of his mouth. Then, he turned to the three at the bar, noticed the difference in their appearances from the other patrons, and let out a snort.

"I suppose you're the group I've been paid to accompany," he said through a burp, a bit of a twang to his accent. "Not quite what I expected, but gold is gold."

"Pleasure," Keijin said, extending a hand. "My name is Keijin Ravara and these are my traveling companions, Sybil Dawn and Mordecai."

"Redbeard," the dwarf burped. "That's what they call me. You get us lodging for the night, yet?"

"Couldn't we perhaps go to one of the other establishments?" Sybil asked, her voice strained.

Redbeard stared at Sybil, sizing her up, and she could tell he did not approve of her as one of his new colleagues.

"Suppose," he said finally. "Just other places around here are more expensive, so it'd be up to you to pay for the increase in expense."

The need for money outside of the tower was something Sybil had never considered, and it had only just struck her in that moment she didn't have a single copper piece to her name. Keijin, of course, came to her rescue and offered to pay for a nicer room at a cleaner establishment for the night, having plenty of coin from all his adventures. After paying for the last room at the inn two doors over from the Filthy Lantern, the group headed upstairs, and Sybil sighed when she saw there were only two beds and a small lounge chair.

"Much prefer the floor anyway," Redbeard spoke up before Sybil could say anything. "The girl gets that bed to herself, and you two pretty boys get to keep each other warm tonight."

Mordecai and Keijin both looked over at each other and made a face. Sybil offered them one of her spare pillows to use as a barrier, but Mordecai tossed it back and said, "I'm good with the chair."

After Redbeard had settled himself on the floor, Sybil turned to him and asked, "So, what's your story?"

"Story? No story," Redbeard grunted, staring up at the ceiling. "Just an axe for hire. Your boss, whoever he is, has been using my services for several years now. But he's never asked me to work alongside anyone before. Not even sure what we've been assigned to do, quite frankly."

"Saving children... you know, hero stuff," Mordecai said monotonously from his chair in the corner.

"Don't usually get myself wrapped up in so-called hero stuff, but it sounds like an easy enough job," he said, stretching his arms underneath his head.

Keijin was standing in the corner of the room and started removing his armor, draping it over their packs. Underneath was just a simple tunic and knee-high pants. Sybil decided that she would be comfortable enough in the clothes she had on under the outer layer of her robes. When she started pulling them off, though, she caught the attention of everyone in the room. Realizing what she was doing, Keijin quickly looked away. The other two eventually diverted their eyes, but far more slowly. With a huff, Sybil crawled under the covers, still completely clothed, and rolled away from them so they could only see her back.

Chapter Three

It was deeply upsetting to Sybil to wake up the next morning in a strange bed with a shirtless dwarf stretching beside her. His entire body was rippled with muscles and fine, red hairs covered his chest, blending in with his long beard. The wolf tattoos on his arms stretched up and over his shoulder, and across his chest and belly there were four jagged scars that looked as if they had taken weeks to heal. Seeing this first thing in the morning and realizing she was still on the road in an inn at the Crossroads, Sybil let out a groan and covered her head with the blanket. Eventually, it was Keijin who got her up, pulling the covers completely off her and telling her they needed to be off. There was no time for breakfast, but they managed to snag some stale bread and jam from the kitchen on their way out, free of charge.

Back on the road, Sybil still sat in Mordecai's saddle, preferring to sit with him now she was comfortable instead of against Keijin's hard armor. They rode behind Keijin on the Captain and Redbeard on his small quarter horse he named Frenzy. Since passing the Crossroads, heading south toward Spindlewood, the road had turned into more of a trail than a road, and the ride had become far more uncomfortable, especially to an inexperienced rider like Sybil.

"Could you stop bouncing so much? You're going to bruise my horse, and you're driving me insane," Mordecai growled, trying to keep Sybil down in the saddle with his one arm. "Stop letting the motion fling you around. Go with it; anticipate the movements."

"Sorry, I've only been on a horse a handful of times," she said quietly enough so the other two couldn't hear.

"Clearly," he huffed. "Take the reins and focus."

Mordecai handed Sybil the reins, which she had no idea what to do with. She just held them up a little so the horse would stay straight. Then, he placed his hands on her outer thighs causing her to flush and jump.

"Hey, what are you doing?" she hissed.

"Just shut up and listened," he replied, grumbling in her ear. "Imagine you and the horse as a single entity, that you are moving as one rather than the horse doing all the movement for you. You need to engage your thighs, hips, and abdomen."

Mordecai placed one of his hands on her stomach, pressing her to him, to show her the rhythm of his body on the horse. It was almost too much for her to bear. She was feeling both fearful and excited at once and couldn't determine whether she wanted him to never touch her again or never let go.

"You're not concentrating," he said in a low growl. "Stop being a prude and ignore my hands. Feel the motion of the horse."

Truly wanting to learn, despite the unfamiliar touch, she steadied her breath and looked straight ahead as she tried to think of nothing else but the horse. All at once, she became aware of the horse's steady, heavy breaths, the strength of its legs, and the smoothness of its motions despite the rocky terrain it traveled across. The way it moved, its body rocking forward and back as well as up and down as its legs made swift motions below it, all became increasingly clear to her. Then, connecting this understanding to the movement of Mordecai's body, she understood how to move with the horse.

"Better," he told her, returning his hands to the reins. "Trust me, I wouldn't come onto you in such a crude way. It does you well to get out of that damn head of yours and have an experience for what it is. Not everything is like what you read in books."

Sybil was annoyed and a little insulted, but learning how to properly ride a horse helped her to push those feelings aside. The ride became far smoother for her, but the muscles she was engaging to match the horse would surely be sore the next day. She didn't care. Somehow, despite his aggressive methods and unkind words, Sybil was able to learn things quickly with Mordecai to guide her. At that moment, she understood why Leon decided to put them together. Now, for the other two, she thought, staring back at Keijin and Redbeard, as Redbeard dug his pinky around in his ear, she still had to figure out their part in all this.

The village of Spindlewood was not a usual destination spot for travelers on the road. It was a bit out of the way of everything else and nothing particularly exciting ever happened there, up until recently, that is. It was a small village with only a few hundred people and had the white-washed mortar and thatched roofs of older architecture. The roads had not been paved with stone, nor did they need to be as they were lightly traveled on. It was a simple village, they had everything they needed and nothing more.

Following the signposts, the party rode up to the lord's manor. It was a building out of place from the rest of the village with sturdy stone walls and clay shingles on the roof, and starting at the front of the property, there was a lavish garden that stretched out of sight behind the manor. They rode along the short, stone wall marking the perimeter of the estate and turned down the lane toward the front of the manor. A plump, balding man in fine garbs came rushing out of the front door and trotted down the path to meet them. He reached the adventurers, out of breath, just as they were dismounting and clapped his hands together with a smile.

"You must be the heroes we requested," he said and then got a better look at them. "Quite an eclectic group."

"Lord Osric," Keijin said with a deep bow. "I am Keijin Ravara, at your service, and these are my companions, Sybil Dawn, Redbeard, and Mordecai." Unsure how to respond, Sybil gave a shaky curtsy, which caused Mordecai to glare at her. "We are here about the missing children and intend to get started on our investigation right away, if you would only point us in the right direction."

"Gods be praised," Lord Osric breathed. "You'll find the captain of the guard, who has been responsible for the investigation thus far, in the village meeting hall just down the road. But, fair warning, he's a proud man and isn't pleased that we've sought outside assistance."

"Most people aren't pleased to see me, so nothin' new there," Redbeard said with a hearty laugh.

The party walked their horses to the meeting and found a sizable group of people gathered there as they entered. Most of them were villagers with makeshift weapons strapped to their person or town guards with ill-fitted armor. This place was so far off the beaten path their only worry had been the occasional wild animal or village troublemaker finding their way into the village. Whatever was going on there was far outside their realm of capabilities, whether they wanted to believe it or not.

"Ah, our lord's lack of faith in us is walking through the door," the captain of the guard said, causing everyone in the room to turn toward the strangers.

"Good evening, ladies and gentlemen," Keijin announced, ignoring their glares, as he walked to the front of the room. Sybil hung back at the front door with Redbeard and Mordecai while he spoke. "We are here to assist you in finding and protecting your children from whatever monster has been plaguing your lovely village."

The manner in which he spoke caused everyone but the captain to relax a little. As he walked through the crowd to stand by the captain, everyone watched him intently, some of them with awe. With his long, glossy brown hair pulled back in a ponytail, his handsome face shining brightly, and his armor gleaming in the afternoon light pouring in through the windows, he looked like a prince. The strong but soothing tone of his voice brought a calmness to the room. At the tower, these traits had irritated Sybil at times, but now she understood the value in his looks and behavior. It caused the common people to listen to him, helping him get the job done.

"If it pleases you, we would like to begin our investigation right away, so if any of you have specific details to share that would help us find this creature, please see my associates in the back," Keijin clarified, gesturing to his companions.

He turned to speak with the captain of the guard, but Sybil couldn't hear what he was saying as the townspeople started to approach her, all of them talking at once.

Digging into her pack, she pulled out the one journal Keijin had allowed and a quill Rani had fashioned for Sybil to hold ink for quick writing. As the townspeople poured out details of what they knew, she made sure to write down everything. Much of the information was useless, having mostly to do with where they were when someone reported a missing child or what sort of animals they had seen around the village lately. Out of the nonsense, she did learn of three houses and an orphanage which had been hit as well as a mother who reported getting attacked only to wake up and find her child missing. In her notes, Sybil circled "the orphanage," a perfect feasting ground for anything that enjoyed the taste of children. After the townspeople dispersed to return to their homes for dinner, Keijin returned to them and consulted Sybil's notes. They decided to first seek out the woman who was attacked to get what information they could from her.

On the edge of town was a line of small cottages, each one looking practically identical to the other, and the party had to knock on a couple doors before finding the right one. A woman with deep bags under her eyes and knotted hair opened the door and asked them what their business was. For some reason, Sybil found herself being the one to speak up this time, despite her aversion to talking with strangers.

"We're here about the missing children," Sybil stated, noticing the state of the woman's cluttered and grimy home behind her. "May we come in and ask you a few questions?"

The woman eyed the others standing behind Sybil before giving a little nod and opening the door wider. Without a word, they entered her den and saw toys and clothes scattered around the furniture. She apologized for the mess and slid everything off the couch onto the floor so they could sit down. Only Redbeard and Keijin sat while Mordecai roamed about the room, and Sybil stood close to the woman.

"Can you tell me what happened?" Sybil asked in a low voice. She couldn't quite understand the loss this woman suffered, but she could feel it.

The woman sniffed and said, "It was my wee one, little Bally. He'd been up most of the night with an earache, and I'd just put him to bed when something struck me from behind. When I came to, Bally was gone... without a trace." A sob kept her from saying more.

"Was there anyone else in the house?"

"My two oldest, Gingy and Dom. Gingy shared a room with Bally at the time, but she has spoken nary a word since the attack."

Sybil glanced over at Keijin, who gave her a nod.

"May I speak with Gingy?" she asked, turning back to the woman.

"I don't know if that's a good idea... not sure what you could learn from her, anyway," the woman said apprehensively.

"It may help," Sybil told her. "Any information could bring us closer to finding Bally."

Relenting, she led them up to the bedroom. In the room, sitting on the edge of the bed, was a small girl, about five, with a doll in her lap. She was staring out the window and didn't make any motion when the strangers entered. Sybil turned to the woman and asked her if she could make them some tea while they introduced themselves to Gingy. Redbeard helped by offering his assistance in the kitchen and asking if she might have any meat or cheese she could spare. Overwhelmed by their presence, the woman headed toward the kitchen to do as they asked. The wink Redbeard gave Sybil said he would keep her distracted down there as long as needed. Sybil turned to Gingy and kneeled beside her. Mordecai closed the door and stood by it while Keijin hovered near the empty crib.

"Hey, Gingy," she said in a soothing voice. "My name's Sybil, and I'm here because I'm going to find your little brother. The thing is, I need your help in order to find him." Sybil paused to see if the little girl would respond, but she just continued to stare out the window. "When I was about your age, I saw something pretty scary, too. But I want you to know people like me and my friends here, we make sure those scary things never come back." The girl's eyes drifted over to Sybil's. "Sometimes people like us protect with shields and swords, but we also sometimes protect with magic. I can use magic, Gingy." She lifted her hand up and created colorful lights that danced between her fingers. "Part of my magic allows me to see what others have seen, and that's how I'm going to find your little brother. But the thing is, I need your permission. Can I see what you saw the night your brother was taken?"

With her palm up, Sybil moved her hand toward Gingy. Slowly, Gingy nodded and placed her hand on top of Sybil's. She sandwiched the little girl's tiny hand in both of hers and closed her eyes, saying an incantation under her breath. In an instant, she found herself in the dark consciousness of Gingy's mind. Swirling all around her, she could feel the girl's fear, confusion, and sadness. Just by her emotions, Sybil knew she had seen whatever it was they were looking for, so Sybil probed deeper into her mind to access her memories.

There was nothing but darkness until the sound of the door creaking brought the room back into her view. This time, the room was lit only by the moonlight showing through the four-pane window. The open curtains flapped from the gentle breeze blowing through the few inches the window was cracked open. Gingy's mother walked through the door, holding a small boy, not yet two, in her arms. She moved over to the crib and placed the little boy down, tucking him in. The perspective returned to the window and a billow of smoke started trickling through. A form appeared behind the mother, its features distorted and terrible. It was nearly as tall as the ceiling with sharp claws, long hair in a dark shade of blue, and gray, muddled skin. Just as she was about to turn around to stand face to face with this hideous creature, it hit the back of the mother's head so forcefully it knocked her out, and she collapsed to the ground. Gingy hid under the covers, terrified, and all Sybil could hear was the whimpers of the little boy as the monster picked it up and, then, its footsteps as it headed back toward the window.

The spell became too much for Sybil, and out of exhaustion she lost hold of Gingy's mind. She found what she needed, though. When she could see the girl's face again, she saw there were tears streaming from her eyes. Sybil placed her hand on Gingy's cheek and thanked her for the memories. Gingy was too young to understand what had just transpired, and she only looked at Sybil with hopeful eyes. But, after seeing what she did, Sybil had little hope Bally, or any of the missing children, was still alive.

With a frown, Sybil turned to Mordecai and Keijin and said, "We need to talk."

"Y'all ever heard of a creature that can do something like this?" Redbeard asked, chewing on a piece of dry meat from the mother's pantry. The party had gathered together outside of the cottage, and Sybil had shared Gingy's memories. "I'm not much experienced with things that don't adhere to the laws of nature, but y'all seem like you know more about unnatural magic."

Mordecai was thinking, deeply searching his mind, and Keijin started to pace back and forth. This was something beyond the scope of Sybil's understanding. She had studied elementals and demons and fey creatures and so on and so forth, but never anything that fit this description. This creature, just as Redbeard suspected, must have been created through unnatural means.

"Is there a library nearby?" Sybil asked, wishing she had access to Leon's collection. "Maybe we can do some research on these traits."

Mid-step, Keijin laughed and then realized she wasn't joking.

"Libraries don't exist in places like this," he informed her, continuing to pace. "We have to rely on the knowledge we carry with us, unless one of the books you chose to bring would help us."

"We don't necessarily need to know what it is to stop it," Mordecai suggested, returning his focus to his companions. "Knowing would certainly benefit us, but with the abilities we have between us, we should be able to take it out."

"If we can even figure out where it'll strike next," Redbeard said, scratching his head. "Which will probably happen again tonight, by the way."

Sybil glanced up at the sky, which was full of pinks and purples as the sun was setting past the trees. Remembering her notes, she pulled out her journal and flipped to where she had circled the orphanage.

"This is our best option," she told them, pointing to it. "We set ourselves up in the sleeping quarters and wait for it to slip in during the night. Then, we ambush it."

"We're off to a good start, but there are several problems with this," Keijin said, stepping toward her. "Namely, the monster is surely attracted to the scent of its victims and if we left said victims to attract it, they would be in the middle of the fighting once we ambushed it."

"We don't have much choice," Mordecai said with a shrug. "If we want to keep it from taking any more children, we have to risk putting a few in harm's way. But we're careful." He paused and eyed Redbeard. "Most of us, at least. We should be able to keep the children from any harm."

"Especially if we make an exit plan with them," Sybil added.

Keijin still seemed uncomfortable with the idea but said nothing for a while as he thought it through.

"I suppose we are running out of time. And if it's between a child being in harm's way in a fight or one getting taken and befalling whatever terrible fate this creature has in store, the former is the better option, even if it's not a good one."

In the center of the village, a two-story building had been converted into an orphanage decades ago. Its outer walls were made of splintering wood panels, and it appeared to have structural issues because it was leaning slightly to the left and looked ready to topple over with the right amount of force. Being a home for up to ten children, it was smaller than Sybil had expected, though it was now down to seven since the recent kidnappings. The home only had an average sized kitchen and living area, and the upstairs had been converted to one large bedroom with small beds a couple of the older children were starting to outgrow. There were three caretakers who worked in shifts, never having enough time to care for the children and clean up after all of them, so there was an odd sour smell lingering in the air and nearly every surface was covered in grime. When the adventurers entered this place, seeing the state of this poorly cared for orphanage, Mordecai's face grew grave.

The seven children, between the ages of about two and eleven, were still downstairs eating dinner. Only four of them were able to fit around the table, so the rest were sitting on the floor. A portly woman in gray clothes, who had been trying to feed a toddler some sort of orange mush, came up to them. Sybil asked her if they could see where the missing children were taken, and just as they had suspected, she led them up to the dormitory and explained how the children were taken from their beds in the middle of the night, choking up a little as she explained this. With a sigh, Sybil looked around at all the windows in the room, a bed by each of them. Then, an idea struck her, and she turned to Keijin.

"We need to warn the villagers to lock their windows tonight," she said, thinking back to the billowing smoke in Gingy's memories. "I need you to ride around the village and warn everyone you can."

"Aye, and I can help to cover more ground," Redbeard offered, jabbing his chest with his thumb.

Keijin nodded and said, "We'll be back post-haste."

The two of them headed down stairs, and from the window Sybil and Mordecai could see them mounting up their horses and riding off in opposite directions. Mordecai then looked to Sybil, waiting to hear what the rest of her plan was.

"The caretaker said this place was hit only a few days ago," she told him. "If we both work together, we might be able to get a better sense of what this thing is with any traces of magic it might have left behind."

"Very well," Mordecai said, and it was only then when she noticed how uncomfortable he looked.

His brow was set in a constant frown and his shoulders were rolled forward as if he were bracing himself to be struck. She wanted to ask him what was wrong, but they didn't have time now that the night's sky was in full view.

"Give me your hand."

Sybil did as he asked, and he wrapped his hands around hers. Then, he told her to cast the spell. As she started saying the incantation, a surge of energy started pulsing through her. Sybil had never felt power like this before, but something told her it was only a taste of what was possible. With his assistance, her spell was able to stretch out across the entire room, showing traces of the creature's magic. These traces showed up in various colors as the non-magical elements in the room turned grayscale. Along the window at the front of the orphanage were splotches of green light that led onto the floor and ended at one of the beds. On the pillow of the bed was a splash of pink light. Whatever this creature was, it was a skilled spell caster. Using transmutation, it entered through the window as smoke and reformed itself once inside. Then, when it found its victim, it put the child to sleep with an enchantment, most likely to keep it from waking the others in the room.

Sybil turned to explain this to Mordecai and saw that he was alight in a purple aura. From head to toe, he was covered in illusion magic. Surprised, she let go of his hands, and her spell started to fade. The color started to return to the world, and the purple surrounding Mordecai faded to black as his cloak and perfectly formed face came back into view.

"We do what we have to to survive in this world," he said with coldness in his tone. "You'll learn that soon enough."

Sybil wanted to say something, but the children started entering the room to ready themselves for bed, causing her to lose her train of thought. They headed back downstairs and discussed their plan with the evening caretaker. She wasn't pleased with the idea but, after some convincing, agreed that it was what needed to be done in order to stop whatever this thing was. Just as Sybil was about to head back upstairs, Mordecai grabbed her arm and pulled her close to him so no one else could hear him speak.

"You've done well up until this point, but when it comes time for us to fight this thing, you need to keep your distance and not draw its attention."

"You still don't see me as capable, do you?" she asked, growing angry at him with how tight his grip was.

"Not in a fight, no," he replied. "You're intelligent and have mastered spells that get you the answers you seek, but I've seen you fight."

"I beat Rani and Giselle," she reminded him, wanting to scream but keeping her voice hushed. "I can handle whatever this thing is."

"You had been stabbed and knocked flat on your back. And then, you hit your own teammate in order to win the fight. Just admit you had no idea what you were doing in that training room, just admit you're not a fighter."

Keijin and Redbeard walked through the front door, causing Mordecai to release Sybil's arm. She thanked them for riding around to warn the villagers, trying to pretend like nothing was wrong, but Keijin looked at her with a knowing face before glaring over at Mordecai. He knew Mordecai had done something to make her uncomfortable, and for the first time, she saw anger in Keijin's eyes. But Mordecai either didn't seem to notice or didn't care because he continued with the plan.

"From its track record, the creature is drawn to the youngest child in the room, so I think we should get the youngest to sleep the furthest from the windows to allow us to trap it in the middle. Once it makes it to the middle of the room, I can close the window and lock it so it doesn't have a clear escape."

"We should leave the rest locked, then," Sybil said, shaking off her anger and discomfort from a moment ago. "And crack the window open to provide more of an incentive for it. For all we know, that might be the only way it knows to get in and out."

"Where'll we be while we wait?" Redbeard asked, running his beard through his calloused hands. "I don't feel too comfortable hiding under some kid's bed or in their closest or nothing."

"I'll make sure we're unseen until the creature arrives," Mordecai answered. "Once I use another spell, we'll be visible again, but it will have served its purpose by then."

With their plan in place, Sybil headed up to the second floor to arrange the youngest in the right spot and situate the windows. She told all the kids that as soon as they heard her voice to slide off their beds and hide underneath them. Most of the children didn't understand what was going on and were just excited with the change in their routine. Once everything was ready, Sybil headed back downstairs where Mordecai used his magic to turn all four of them invisible. As the spell took hold, a strange coldness to wash over Sybil's body.

Whether or not they were ready to face this monster, there was no turning back now.

For over three hours, they stood in the four corners of the room. It was dark, and Sybil hated not being able to see her companions, so she waited with little bouts of fear trickling up her spine. All the children were sleeping soundly in their beds by the time she saw movement through a window. A shadow lingered by one window and then another, until it found the one that was cracked opened. Just like in Gingy's memories, the shadow turned to a bluish-gray smoke and seeped in through the gap in the open window. The smoke floated through the air, going from one bed to the next until it reached the bed of the youngest child in the center of the room.

The smoke started to take shape, forming into a massive creature whose form nearly reached the ceiling. Gingy's memory of the creature had been off, but not by much. It was a massive, horrifying creature with giant, curved claws that shimmered in the moonlight. It reached those claws out toward the youngest child, a chubby-faced two-year-old, but snapped back when the window slammed shut behind it and the four adventurers appeared. Sybil shouted to the children, and they all ducked under their beds, some more quickly than others. The creature let out a horrible shriek and took a couple of steps back. It started to revert to its gaseous form, but Sybil reached out with all the magical strength she could muster and held it in place.

Whatever this creature was, it was strong, and she could feel her power draining as she held it there long enough for Keijin and Redbeard to draw their longsword and greataxe. Coming from either side, they slashed into this creature's flesh, causing it to let out another horrible cry. Despite their strength and blades, their attacks seemed to do little more than piss it off. Some of the children underneath their beds screamed in fright. Sybil's magic waned for a moment, giving the creature enough time to pick up one of the beds and throw it at Redbeard, hitting him dead on and throwing him back against the wall. Sybil was the closest one to the stairs, so she called the children, who were now exposed to the monster, over to her. Little bodies darted through the room as Mordecai gathered up a ball of dark energy and hurled it at the creature, sending static bursts shooting throughout the room as it made contact. The children made it to Sybil by the time Mordecai had gathered enough dark energy for another attack, and the force of it hitting the creature finally broke her hold on it.

Furious, the creature moved toward Mordecai. Sybil was gathering up her strength to send another spell toward it, but Mordecai raised up his arms and waved them slowly through the air. More kids screamed and made a mad dash to Sybil as an inky black material started seeping up through the floorboards and formed into large tendrils. The magical limbs wrapped around the creature, bringing it to the ground, giving Keijin and Redbeard another chance to get a few more strikes in, this time leaving a deep gash in the creature's flesh. Being mindful of the small space, Sybil sent a bolt of lightning crackling across the room, hitting the creature square in the chest.

Rearing his longsword back, his shield at his side, Keijin called on the divine powers of his oath, filling the room with a bright light that radiated off his sword, and brought it down on the creature's back. It let out a final shout, speaking in an unfamiliar language, before the radiant light overcame it, causing it to explode into dust that blanketed the room. Sybil quickly covered her eyes with the sleeve of her robe and when she lowered it again, the only ones left in the room were Keijin, Redbeard, Mordecai, and her.

They had done it; they had stopped the monster.

Overcome with exhaustion, Sybil fell onto the nearest bed and heaved a sigh. When she glanced out the window to her right, she could see the faintest hint of the sunrise as the sky was turning from black to gray.

Keijin came to sit next to her, exhausted as well, and patted her knee as his way to show she did well.

"Well, that went better than expected," Mordecai said, staring at the spot where the creature had vanished, and brushed off the dust that had gathered on his cloak.

"Speak for yourself," Redbeard said, poking at the giant gash above his eye where the bedframe hit him. "Never had to fight in such close quarters before, and never expected a bed to come flying at me."

Sybil couldn't help but let out a little laugh. Redbeard glared at her for a brief moment before bursting out into laughter himself, only causing her to laugh harder. Watching the two of them laugh, Keijin cracked a little smile, but Mordecai turned away from his companions, as if their laughter was more upsetting than the creature's shrieks. Then, something occurred to him, and he breathed, "Dammit."

"What?" Keijin asked.

"We were so preoccupied in stopping the thing, we didn't even bother to figure out what it was doing with the children," he growled, causing the other three to grow deathly quiet. "If some of them are still alive, we have no idea where it was keeping them."

"It might've left a trail on its way over here we can follow," Redbeard suggested, wiping some of the blood off his face with a dirty handkerchief. "It might not be too late."

Between Redbeard's tracking skills and Sybil's ability to trace magic, it didn't take them long to find the creature's trail as they searched around the outside of the orphanage. The sun was rising above the trees, and Sybil was starting to feel the overbearing weight of staying up all night, but the group trudged along, following the trail, so they could finish what they started. Just outside of the village's border, they found a cave with a foul-smelling odor wafting out of it. Heading inside with Keijin leading the charge, they were immediately discouraged with what they saw.

The cave was the size of a small room, and with the morning sunlight pouring in, they could clearly see everything in it. A large, flat boulder was resting against the wall to their left, and Sybil determined the creature must have used it to close the entrance when it hibernate. There was nothing else in the cave other than what could only be described as a nest and what Sybil thought at first were small, white rocks. With a grave face, Mordecai bent down and picked up one of the rocks to show it to her. Even though she had anticipated the creature's intentions with the children from Gingy's memory,

Sybil let out a gasp when she realized the rock was in fact a small bone. It was something they had all suspected, but it became crushingly clear, seeing the small bone, that the creature had been eating the children it took.

The other three started to leave the cave, but when Keijin saw Sybil hanging back and staring down at the piles of bones, he turned to her and placed his hand on her shoulder.

"This is why we do what we do," he said softly, giving her shoulder a gentle squeeze. "We can't keep everyone safe all the time -the world just doesn't work that way- but we can do what we can to keep anyone else from coming to harm. We did a good thing here today, even though, standing in this cave, it doesn't feel that way."

She gave a nod and said in barely a whisper, "I guess I still have to get used to all this."

"Believe me," he said with a nod and humorless laugh. "It takes time."

Tired and feeling a little ill by how the mission ended, the party returned to the meeting hall to inform the captain of the guard the monster was dead. Many of the villagers were there, and the good news quickly turned into a celebration as more and more villagers filled the space, laughing and cheering and some even drinking. All in all, Sybil felt good about her part in saving the village, but she was so exhausted from the fight and lack of sleep that all she cared about was rest. Eventually, Lord Osric joined the festivities and, after seeing how tired they all were, offered his manor's guest rooms for the village's heroes. Mordecai, however, declined the offer and left the meeting hall without a word as to where he was going. Sybil was too tired to care, and still a little mad at him from his behavior before the fight, so she didn't ask where he was heading.

Lord Osric led Sybil, Keijin, and Redbeard to three guest rooms on the top floor of his manor and told them to take as much time as they needed to recover from the fight. Being able to close herself in a room alone was such a luxury to Sybil from the past couple of days. She disrobed down to her undergarments and joyously got into bed, feeling the quality of the fabric soothe her skin as they rubbed against each other. Within minutes, she was asleep, but to her misfortune, she fell into a deep, horrible dream.

The darkness swirling around her was palpable, and she could hear faint cries of anguish and fear coming from all around her. Then, a voice like daggers and ice reached her ears. Even though it spoke in a language she did not understand, she knew what it wanted:

her death. This entity was drawing closer and closer to Sybil, and she didn't know how to escape it. There was nowhere to run where it wouldn't find her.

Just as she was beginning to feel the darkness wrapping around her limbs, a light appeared above her. It grew brighter, reaching for her. These two powerful elements began to tug at her, and she felt as though she was about to split in two. She let out a scream as the pain became unbearable.

Something was shaking her, and Sybil opened her eyes to find Keijin sitting on the edge of her bed, his long hair down around his shoulders. Realizing who it was, she reached out for him and buried her face into his chest, letting out a whimper of fear. Keijin held her in his arms, placing his chin on the top of her head, and ran his warm hand up and down her upper back to soothe her. Sybil had never been embraced like this before, even as a small child, and she held onto him until he pulled away to look at her face.

"Thank you," Sybil breathed as they moved away from each other.

Keijin nodded, his eyes full of concern.

"I'm here for you, Sybil. As long as I am able, I'll do all in my power to keep you safe. Even if all I can do is stir you from a nightmare."

"Something's happening to me… I can't quite explain it," she told him, wiping the sudden moisture from her cheeks. "In my dream, something was coming for me. But Shuheyr, he was trying to get me first."

"Perhaps Shuheyr was trying to protect you," he suggested, but she shook her head. "The power of the gods can feel dangerous, even when they are trying to aid us."

"If I give into Shuheyr," she breathed, continuing to shake her head. "I would lose myself. It's not like the connection most have with him or the other gods… you wouldn't understand."

"How can I help you if you don't let me in?" he asked, his voice going low.

Anger rose in her belly.

"Who says I want your help, Keijin? I'm not one of those helpless maidens you save from bandits."

He leaned away from her and frowned.

"No, you're not. You're Sybil Dawn, a wizard so skilled and powerful that the strongest and wisest magic wielder in the world has taken you in to be his apprentice. I don't see you as some helpless maiden, but I do see you as a friend." He paused to take a steadying breath. "Your youth is a disadvantage to you because you believe you can push through whatever it is that you're dealing with on your own. But I learned long ago that we need our friends to help us through hard times. So let me help you."

Keijin's words hit Sybil's heart, and she placed her hands to her face before whispering, "I don't know how."

"It might take some time," he said, placing a steady hand on her forearm. "But as long as you don't stop trying, you'll get there."

A knock sounded on the door, and Keijin got up to open it just wide enough to allow him to look out but not to reveal Sybil, still in bed and in her undergarments, to whoever was outside. Keijin took an envelope before thanking whoever was there. He closed the door and returned to where he was sitting on the bed. She watched as he opened the letter and read it to himself. Then, a small chuckle escaped him.

"Leon knows we were successful in our mission and has already sent us another one," he explained and handed her the letter.

Dear adventurers,

The monster you fought in the orphanage was known as an oni: an ancient creature that comes forth every few hundred years to feed on the young before returning to its long slumber. You have saved countless lives by putting the oni to rest, but now it is time for you to venture forth from the Village of Spindlewood and travel toward the mountains, to a town called Taragpass. There are many threats to the people of Taragpass, but it is for each of you to decide what those threats are and how to defeat them. For centuries, this town has been the stronghold of the Kingdom of Irminshu, and if it falls to the dangers surrounding it, Irminshu would be made vulnerable to the Four Kingdoms of Thedaras.

Best of luck to you all.

Leon

"An oni?" Mordecai asked when Sybil read the letter to him and Redbeard at dinner that evening. He had returned just an hour before, his eyes still fading from black to gray, which she now understood as a sign of him using some sort of dark magic. "I think I remember that name from an old wives' tale I heard as a child."

Lord Osric, who left that afternoon for what he felt was a well-earned vacation, instructed his kitchen staff to prepare a three-course meal for his guests, which they were now enjoying. They all sat at the end of his long, extravagant dining table, eating as they traced out the next leg of their journey on the map of the kingdom Keijin carried with him. It would be a four-day ride to Taragpass, and Sybil was still without a horse. To make the journey even more uncomfortable, there were no settlements between here and Taragpass. Staring down at the map, Sybil heaved a sigh and longed for the comfort of the tower and the familiarity of the library. Redbeard, on the other hand, had a twinkle in his eyes, thrilled for this next stage in their travels and longing to be in the wilderness again.

"How long do you suppose he'll keep us away from the tower?" Sybil asked as the servants cleaned up their plates from the final course. "Do you think it'll be mission after mission, or we will be able to return once we settle whatever business there is to settle in Taragpass?"

"It depends on what Leon is truly wanting us to accomplish," Keijin said, removing the map from his lap and setting it on the cleared table.

"If it's to get you trained up, we'll be out here a while," Mordecai added, causing both Sybil and Keijin to frown at him. "What? Is it not obvious to anyone else that Sybil is our real mission? He wants his reclusive assistant to become knowledgeable about the world. Which could also explain why he stuck us with this one." He pointed his fork toward Redbeard, who was still gnawing absentmindedly on a chicken bone before looking back to Sybil. "Let's just all be honest: she has a lot to learn."

Unable to stand his words any longer, Sybil stood up from the table, causing the chair to scrape loudly across the floor, and stormed out of the room. He was right of course, but she hated him saying it in front of Keijin and Redbeard, making it sound like she was a child. Unsure where to go, she headed outside to the back garden. There were rows of flower beds and fruit trees with cobblestone paths weaving between them, which was idyllic compared to the simplicity of the village.

She found a bench near the back of the garden and sat down, deciding to stay away from the others until sundown, when she would reasonably retire for the night. The spot she chose was peaceful, but she wished to have one of her books. Instead, she spent some time practicing a few minor spells, being mindful not to damage any of the nearby foliage. As she was manipulating the wind to spin some of the fallen leaves up into the air, she caught Mordecai's dark features in her peripheral. When he sat down on the bench next to her, she stopped her spell but didn't turn to him.

"They made me come talk to you," he said, adjusting his robes. "Apparently, I was out of line."

Sybil thought for a moment and sighed.

"No, you were right," she said in a soft, defeated tone. "There's a lot for me to learn, and I'm struggling." Staring down at her hands, she fought back tears, not wanting him of all people to see her cry. "Leon could've picked anyone to be his apprentice, but he chose me. And I have no idea why."

Mordecai was silent for a while. The breeze picked up, cutting through the thin fabric of Sybil's robes and causing her to shiver. The sky was turning dark, and the moon had appeared from behind the clouds. When she looked over at him, Mordecai's gray eyes shimmered like mercury in the moonlight.

"I can teach you," he said, leaning closer to her as if he were telling her a secret. "But you would need to trust me... completely. What we were able to do in the orphanage by enhancing your magic, you would need to trust me just as you did then."

"You would need to give me a reason to trust you, then."

He raised an eyebrow and asked, "How?"

"Tell me something about yourself, something that doesn't have to do with magic or a dark entity watching over you."

"Like what?"

"Tell me why you were uncomfortable in the orphanage," she said, remembering his behavior before they fought the oni. "I could see it in your face and hear it in your voice. It didn't have to do with the oni –you were fine facing that– so it must have had something to do with the orphanage."

"Fine," he said gruffly, shifting on the bench. "If you must know, I was an orphan. Not a particularly cheery tale in my life. Though, I suppose none are." He gave a shrug, though his face appeared pained. "After several years of living in the orphanage, eating watery stews made of table scraps and sleeping on old rags on the floor, the so-called caretakers started selling us off as slaves to make a bit of extra gold for themselves. From there, it doesn't get any better for me... But you only asked about the orphanage, so perhaps let's leave that story to another day."

"What happened to your parents?"

"None to speak of," Mordecai replied, not looking particularly bothered by it. "A common tale, I was abandoned on the street in the City of the King as a baby, and some merchant found me and brought me to the orphanage in the Outer Ring." He realized Sybil did not understand what he meant and clarified. "The slums of the City. The further into the City you get, the better the conditions. I didn't see the Inner Ring until I was an adult. Though, it was not as myself."

"Leon said that you had been acting as the king's advisor when he found you," she told him, thinking back to the first day she met Mordecai.

A smile spread across his face, and he said, "Yes, that was fun. The king was a fool, but when he died and the new king took over, my services were no longer wanted."

"Why did you pretend to be the king's advisor?"

"Why not?" he asked with a laugh. "And I didn't pretend. I *was* the king's advisor. Decisions were made in that city and in this kingdom through my counsel. And soon, you'll find that with our abilities, the only limit is our imaginations."

Sybil chewed on the inside of her cheek as she thought about what he said. Having limitless power sounded nice, in theory, but she didn't want to lose herself in gaining it. She had read many stories about magic wielders who allowed their hubris to lead to their destruction and knew she had to be careful.

"If you let me, if you trust me, I can open up an entire world of possibilities for you," he whispered, leaning just a bit closer.

"I trust what you're saying is true," she began, tucking her hair behind her ear. "But I'm not sure I trust the motives behind them. If you want me to trust you, then treat me with respect, especially in front of other people. I'll eventually master my skills in magic and will someday be worthy to take up Leon's place as the Enlightened, but however long it takes me to get there depends on the choices I make along the way."

Sybil rose from the bench, feeling stronger and more confident than she had in a while, and Mordecai looked up at her with an expression mangled between confusion and frustration.

"Thank you for sharing with me a bit of your past, and believe me when I say, I want to trust you. But trust is not something I give freely."

"I... can respect that," he said, struggling with his words for the first time since she met him.

Glancing up at the night sky, she felt the fear from her nightmare trickling up inside her.

"I think I'll turn in for the evening. Good night, Mordecai."

As if he knew what happened earlier that day, he said, "Sweet dreams."

She turned back to look at him, and his face was entirely covered in shadow. Wrapping her robes tighter around her, she headed inside, her pace quicker than usual. Something about Mordecai truly terrified her, but she did not believe it was him, rather this Haborym, the dark entity he was connected to. It wanted something to do with her, but she didn't know what, and there was a suspicion, a fear, that it was using Mordecai to get to her. Passing by Keijin's room, she was glad to be sleeping so close to him. He would keep her safe.

Chapter Four

The sun peeked through a slit in the gossamer curtains and hit Sybil's eyes, causing her to stir. Wanting to be timelier with their departure than she had been at the tower, Sybil didn't roll over and go back to sleep, despite how much she wanted to. Instead, she rolled out of bed and started getting dressed and packing up her gear. Still, Redbeard and Keijin had made it down before her, both waiting on the manor's porch, but Mordecai was nowhere to be seen.

"Haven't seen him all morning," Redbeard said when Sybil asked about him. "In fact, the last time I saw him was when we had him apologize to you last night. Which I'm sure he did well with," he added with an eye roll.

As Lord Osric's stable hand arrived with their three horses, Mordecai came riding down the road with a forth horse, this one white with black spots. When he reached his companions, he dismounted the horse, turned to Sybil, and said, "So? What do you think?"

"Is this for me?" she asked.

"Well, I certainly can't ride two horses, can I?" he replied gruffly. "I was tired of having to share a saddle with you, so I bought this one off the captain of the guard."

Sybil approached the horse and patted its neck, unsure of how to respond. The horse gave a little whinny, which made her smile. Even though his excuse for buying it was purely a selfish one, she felt touched by his gift. He could have just found any old horse, but he picked one that was strong, beautiful, and well-mannered.

"Thank you," she said, turning back to him.

This seemed to throw Mordecai, and he made a face that was difficult for her to read.

"Yes, well, you're welcome. Let's just get on the road. I'm ready to leave this dingy little town."

The stable hand frowned at Mordecai's insult before taking his leave. They mounted their horses, and Keijin and Redbeard started off down the road. Mordecai waited for Sybil, but she had no idea how to make the horse move.

He rolled his eyes and said, "To get the horse moving, press your heel into the horse's side, giving it a light kick will tell it to move faster. Move the reins to whichever side you want to turn and pull back on the reins to get the horse to stop. It's really not that hard."

"Can you ever just give directions without being insulting?" she asked before pressing her heel into her horse, causing it to lurch forward and start trotting down the road.

Mordecai moved his horse to keep in step with Sybil.

"Once you stop needing simple directions, then yes," he replied. "Now, pick up the pace. The others are a mile off by now, and Keijin's the one with the map."

"I thought an all knowing being such as yourself wouldn't need a map," she told him before giving her horse a kick to move into a canter.

The annoyed look on his face as she moved ahead of him made her smile.

It was nearing midday when the party stopped for lunch, pulling out some cured meat, cheese, and bread Lord Osric had his servants pack for their journey. As they ate, Redbeard entertained his companions with a story about the first time he fought a troll by himself. Sybil had been interrupting him so much with questions he had to request her to wait until the end so he could think properly. Once his story was over and all Sybil's questions were answered, they mounted up once more and set back out on the road.

The sun was beginning to set, so they pulled off the road and made a campsite under the shelter of the trees. Keijin built a fire as Sybil laid out the bedrolls and other supplies and Redbeard hunted for dinner further into the woods. Pacing along the border of their campsite, Mordecai created wards to protect them from monsters and other creatures in the night. With a roaring fire and a soft spot to sit, Sybil let herself relax a little. Nearly eight hours of riding had left her legs and abdomen aching and the reins had rubbed the beginning of sores into her hands, which had seen nothing more than paper and quill all her life. Keijin noticed her rubbing her hands and offered to heal them with the magic his oath bestowed him.

"If you keep healing her, how will she ever grow stronger?" Mordecai asked, joining them by the fire and pulling off his cloak to reveal the dark tunic and trousers he wore underneath. "Let the pain in. It's good for you."

Sybil tucked her hands away under the skirt of her robes and stared into the fire, wanting to ignore both of them.

"You know, it isn't showing weakness to help soothe another or accept help," Keijin offered to Mordecai. "In fact, there's a tremendous amount of strength in it. Have you ever tried to show anyone compassion?"

"Compassion can get you killed," Mordecai remarked. He picked a stray stick off the ground, broke a piece off, and tossed the piece into the fire. "I wouldn't have survived this long if I let people distract me from what needed to be done. You have the luxury of time, Ravara. I do not."

Redbeard interrupted the intensity of the conversation by throwing down two hares and a squirrel next to the fire. When Sybil looked up at him, there was a spark of triumph in his eyes. Without a word, he kneeled down and started slicing into the dead animals' skin. When he started pulling the skin away from the flesh, creating a strange, muffled ripping sound, Sybil gagged. She excused herself from the circle, but as she was wandering off, Mordecai reminded her of the wards, which she would break if she walked through them. Instead, she leaned against a tree, facing out into the starless woods, as she waited for Redbeard to finish mangling his prey.

"Ya'll are in for a treat," Redbeard said, putting the skinned and decapitated animals on the fire spit, as Sybil rejoined the party. "My roasted hare is the best in the kingdom." He pulled out a jar from his pack that contained a brown liquid, the consistency of jam. "All thanks to my secret sauce."

The hare was indeed delicious with the sweet and savory flavor of the sauce. When Sybil asked him what it was, he told her it was an old family recipe and only those in his bloodline could know the secret.

"Are you close with your family?" she asked him after licking her fingers clean, both to savor the sauce and to prevent her white robes from getting stained.

Redbeard was surprised by her question and laughed.

"Not even sure how to start with answering that," he said. "Dwarves, especially ones in the clan I come from, aren't particularly affectionate with one another. Didn't have any siblings, and my mom ran off to do gods know what when I was a lad. Dad trained me like any other dwarf boy is trained, and since he was the clan leader, I was pushed extra hard, which I'm grateful for now. He died about, oh, five years ago, but it's not like I went through a grieving period or nothin'."

"What happened to your clan?" she asked. "If your dad died, you're here, and you didn't have any siblings..."

Redbeard tensed at this question and didn't say anything for a minute or two. Just as she was about to change the subject, growing uneasy with the awkward silence, he spoke up.

"I had left the clan over a decade ago. When my dad died and I returned to fulfill my duty, they treated me like an outsider, which was understandable. After a vote, they decided to banish me from the clan, officially ending my line." His face had been grave as he explained this, but after a moment, he perked up and laughed. "So that's why I ain't telling any of you about my secret sauce. It's all I got left."

Even though he said this as a joke, it made Sybil a little sad. Thinking back to her past, she wondered what she had left of it. Shuheyr and his ever-looming presence over her was the only thing that came to mind, and as soon as it did, she remembered what Mordecai told her that first day on the road. Taking a deep breath, she let the idea go… she wasn't going to let him in.

"What about your family?" Redbeard asked, and shock spread across her face. "What? You asked me about mine, so it's only fair."

Sybil gave a humorless laugh, realizing he was right.

"My family… hmmm…" she said slowly, thinking about what she was comfortable sharing. "Well, like you, I don't have any siblings. At least, none that I'm aware of. The place I grew up was dedicated to worshiping Shuheyr, a small village called Morningbreak." She cracked her neck as she continued to think. "My parents were just responsible for my birth, but the elders of the village raised me. They all sought to my needs, but none of them were loving to me. Apparently, I was designed for a greater purpose, so I was barely even considered a person. To them, I was a Soul Child, just a vessel for Shuheyr, the God of Light, to one day inhabit." Sighing, she shrugged. "I have no idea if any of them are still alive or if I even care."

"What finally made you leave?"

Sybil tilted her head and stared at Redbeard for a moment, feeling like the answer was obvious.

"Probably similar reasons to why you left: escaping a destiny that was chosen for me."

The group fell quiet, and the silence of the evening creeped in around them. There was only the sound of the crackling fire and the gentle rustling of the trees in the cool night breeze. Eventually, they all started to drift off to sleep one by one, except Mordecai who stared thoughtfully into the fire. When Sybil awoke several hours later, he had a book in his lap, one that looked similar to the book he was reading in the library, its pages and cover ancient.

Sybil sat up and turned to him, and he said, "Go back to sleep. It's still a while until sunrise."

"What's keeping you up? I thought the wards were to keep us safe so no one had to keep watch," she said in a low, sleepy voice.

"I try not to sleep if I can help it, which I usually can," he replied, his eyes moving from the page to her. "And who says I'm keeping watch?"

"Do you never tire?"

"Not anymore."

She sat up more but still tried to keep her voice quiet to avoid waking Keijin or Redbeard, both of whom were snoring softly.

"How far away from human are you willing to go in order to reach the power you seek? In the end, will it even be worth it?"

"In the end, will it even matter? My humanity means little to me. In fact, it's been nothing but a hindrance thus far." For the first time, Sybil felt sad for him and all the terrible experiences he must have had to feel this way. "Don't give me that look. I don't need your pity."

"Sorry," she breathed, surprising herself. "I just suddenly realized I don't want you to feel pain; I want you to experience... good things."

Mordecai's face flashed from anger to confusion to sadness.

"Caring about me will only cause you problems. Just... go back to sleep."

Not wanting to push him too far, Sybil did as he asked and laid back down, closing her eyes. The sounds of camp breaking down caused her to rouse a few hours later, and soon after she sat up, Keijin offered her what was left of last night's dinner for breakfast. He then started to pack up their supplies to ready for the next day of their journey. Sybil was slow moving, eating her small breakfast leisurely. By the tree next to her, Redbeard moved over and started relieving himself, causing her to jump and grab her bedroll to keep it clean. He hadn't noticed her until she moved and chuckled as he carried on with his business. As Sybil backed away, she rammed her back into Mordecai who let out a little grunt. He nudged her away and grumbled something under his breath as he headed over to the saddles. Sybil really hated this whole camping situation.

Keijin brought over Sybil's saddle to her new horse and slung it over the horse's back. Sybil watched carefully as he cinched up the straps, and he explained how it needed to be loose enough so it wouldn't pinch the horse but tight enough so the saddle wouldn't slide off mid-ride. Then, he removed the bridle that was slung over his shoulder and slid it onto the horse's head, showing her where all the leather pieces needed to rest.

"You still haven't named her, yet," he told her, petting the horse's neck. "Bad luck to ride a horse with no name."

"I've never named anything before," she said, unsure. "What do you suggest?"

"I'm afraid that one's up to you," he said with a shrug before heading over to the Captain.

Thinking, Sybil looked over at Mordecai who had just mounted his horse. He had not bothered to name his horse, probably because he didn't want to appear sentimental or superstitious. Looking back to hers, noticing the black speckled pattern in its coat, she thought of the name Dusk, and when she looked at her horse and thought about her own name, she felt like it was a pretty good fit.

Sybil rode Dusk alongside Redbeard and his horse, Frenzy, for most of the day. She continued finding herself asking him all sorts of questions about his time out in the wilds, though she made sure not to interrupt in the middle of his stories. Redbeard, a natural storyteller, was happy to entertain her for most of the day, and she wished she could take notes in her journal as she rode because the details he provided of creatures like goblins and ghouls were things she wanted to keep track of. For a short stint in his early adventuring days, he had traveled with two gnomes and a halfling and, together, had saved a village from a blue dragon and her followers, which they just barely survived. Sybil listened intently as if she were a child again, listening to the children's stories the nursemaids would read to her before bed.

Near the end of their day's journey, the party came across a barricade in the road made of carts and wide logs. Three men, heavily armed, stepped out from the tree line and greeted the adventurers. They said they were under the king's orders to inspect travelers on the road, but by the state of their clothes and unkempt features, they were not fooling anyone into believing they were soldiers.

Speaking only so his companions could hear, Mordecai said, "Bandits. There's bound to be more in the trees."

Keijin turned to the bandits and tried to be diplomatic.

"Good sirs, we are but simple adventurers who are on a mission to aid a town in much need of assistance. If you could make an exception and let us on our way, we would be quite appreciative."

Just as Mordecai predicted, four more men came out of the tree line behind the party, boxing them in. Redbeard's eyes flashed with a combination of fury and glee as both Mordecai and Keijin heaved a sigh. Knowing there was about to be a fight, Sybil whispered an incantation and placed a protection spell on herself as she eyed the bows slung over the bandits' shoulders.

Then, everything seemed to happen all at once.

Keijin and Redbeard leapt from their horses in opposite directions, heading for the two groups, and the bandits pulled their weapons as they approached them. Still on his horse, Mordecai pulled energy from the air around him and created a fog that engulfed the surrounding area. As Keijin and Redbeard engaged in combat, Mordecai slid out of his saddle, moved to Sybil, and yanked her down to the ground. Their horses ran off the road into the trees, fleeing from the danger. Thanks to the fog, the bandits couldn't see Mordecai or Sybil, but they shot a few arrows wildly in hopes of hitting one of them. Mordecai pulled Sybil back by her robes, and an arrow landed in the ground by her feet, missing her by only an inch.

"Use your magic, tell me where they are," he growled as he gathered up a ball of dark energy, creating a small, black sun between his palms.

Pulling out her wand –her staff still attached to her saddle– Sybil waved it through the air and bright lights appeared over everyone in the battlefield. Because she knew them, Keijin's and Redbeard's auras shone brighter than the others, so she could tell them apart. She pointed to where one of the bandits was, and Mordecai shot the ball of energy toward him. It landed, and they could hear the man cry out in terrible pain. Turning to the other side, she pointed to another bandit, and Mordecai unleashed his second blast.

Just after his attack hit, an arrow appeared through the fog and landed in Mordecai's shoulder. He let out a moan as the pain caused him to buckle over. The fog he created suddenly vanished because he was no longer able to hold it. Distracted for a moment by the sudden change in the battlefield, Redbeard was knocked back and fell hard to the ground. He jumped back up, and Sybil watched as his muscles bulged and his eyes filled with fury and madness. Sprinting straight at the one who knocked him over, Redbeard drew back his greataxe and swiped through the man's neck, cutting his head clean off.

In horror, Sybil looked away, back toward Mordecai. But as Mordecai was getting up, the archer launched another arrow, and Mordecai had to quickly deflect it with his magic to keep it from hitting Sybil. She turned to the archer, and unable to think of another spell, reached into his mind, and brought his greatest nightmares to the forefront of his consciousness.

It was a spell Sybil didn't have a name for, nor did she need to mutter any words for. Her desperation and fear caused this power to surge through her like an instinct, and she had no idea where it came from. The man buckled to his knees and collapsed to the ground, clutching his head and screaming at the top of his lungs, until he laid still.

Sybil pulled her shaking hand away, only realizing too late what she had done. Killing someone in that way… she felt like a monster.

With blood spilling out between his fingers from the wound he was grasping, Mordecai stared at Sybil. Shame bubbled up inside her, but she didn't have time to think because a bandit was running toward her with his sword raised above his head. Just as she thought to shoot a lightning bolt at him, Mordecai put his hand up and a tremendous amount of magical force caused the man to go flying back. When he landed, the bandit cracked his head on a rock and fell still. Just as Sybil turned to see if Keijin was okay, he was finishing up the last of his bandits by driving his longsword through his belly.

Everything went silent, and seven men lay dead around them. Sybil felt like she was going to be sick. But Mordecai put his hand up to her face, a bit of his blood getting on her skin, and said, "Whatever you're thinking, stop it. They would've killed us if we didn't fight. You did the right thing."

Keijin came over to him to tend to his wounds, and Sybil looked away as Keijin placed one hand firmly on Mordecai's collar bone and pulled the arrow from his flesh. Blood splashed onto the ground, and Mordecai's breath hitched, but he didn't make a sound. Keijin's hands filled with radiant light, and he brought them to the wound, causing Mordecai to squirm in pain, gripping Keijin's forearms tightly. As the magic healed him, Sybil wiped the blood off her face and searched around for Redbeard. He was looting the bodies, pulling coin and other valuables from their person as if none of this phased him anymore. When he saw her watching him, he held up a gold necklace and waved it around for her to see. She tried to return his smile but couldn't manage it.

After removing the dead bodies and barricade from the road, it was nearly nightfall, so they decided to make camp for the night. As Keijin and Redbeard were preparing dinner, Mordecai found Sybil sitting on a boulder near the edge of camp where he had laid out his wards.

"Mind if I join you?" he asked, and she slid over enough for him to sit. They sat in silence for a while before he spoke again. "That spell you used today... I get it now. You're powerful."

"I wish I hadn't used that spell," she breathed, feeling a lump forming in her throat. "It's a horrible way to die. It's just... it's so easy for me to reach into others' minds, and when I panicked, that was the only thing I could think to do."

"Back in the village, you said you needed permission, though," he recalled.

Sybil nodded and sighed.

"Without permission, going into someone's mind is extremely painful and dangerous for them. When they let me in, they barely feel it, depending on how long I'm in there. The first time I killed someone, I was trying to steal information from their mind. I... I didn't know it would happen."

"Who?"

A sob tried to bubble out of her, but she suppressed it. She turned away from him and put a hand up to her face.

"My first mentor," Sybil finally said. "The very person who taught me how to use spells in the first place. He had information I thought was too important for me not to know, and I killed him for it. He was a good man; he didn't do anything wrong."

"So, in theory," Mordecai began, shifting uncomfortably on the boulder. "You could kill anyone with this power, anyone who resisted, that is?"

"In theory, but I've only done it twice," she answered, turning back to him. It was hard to tell what he was thinking because his face had become impossible to read. "What?"

"Just finding this all very fascinating."

Redbeard called out to let them know dinner was ready. When Sybil stood up to head back to the campfire, Mordecai grabbed her wrist, pulled her close to him, and warned her to keep this information just between the two of them.

"This kind of power would only make people fearful of you or want to use you," he told her with a strange gleam in his eyes.

Sybil stared down at him, her expression hard, and asked, "And which one are you?"

The question took him by surprise, causing him to let go of her wrist, and she headed back to the campfire where Keijin and Redbeard were waiting for them. Several minutes passed before Mordecai joined them, but he stayed silent for the rest of the night. As Keijin sharpened his sword and Redbeard sang a song in dwarvish, Sybil read one of the books she packed and tried her best to ignore Mordecai. Eventually, the fire died down a little, and they went to sleep, ending another tiring day of their adventure.

Chapter Five

By the end of their third day of travel, with still a full day ahead of them before they reached Taragpass, Sybil was exhausted and sore from head to toe. The others, though, seemed no worse off than when they started, and she could only hope that her outward appearance did not match how badly she felt. Relief hit her when Keijin announced they would make camp where they were for the night, and she dismounted Dusk as quickly as she could. Standing next to her horse as she removed her saddle, Sybil could feel the muscles in her thighs shaking, and her fingers were so tender it was hard to undo the harnesses. Just as she had slung the saddle over the limb of a tree and felt ready to lounge by a fire for the rest of the night, they all heard a long, high-pitched shriek coming from the trees.

Running through the woods toward the party was a young woman, her blue skirt and blonde hair flowing wildly behind her. Just a half dozen yards from her, a hill giant was bumbling through the trees heading toward them, knocking branches out of its way with its club. Redbeard, with a light in his eyes, held out his arms for the woman, who seemed to be heading straight toward him. But he was mistaken, and the woman fell into Keijin's arms instead, begging for him to save her from the monster that was rapidly approaching. Redbeard despite the sprinting giant fast approaching, dropped his arms to his side, looking dejected.

Keijin instructed her to hide behind a tree and then drew his longsword and shield. Sybil pulled her staff from the saddle as her heart began to race. With his greataxe out now in front of him, Redbeard's attention moved to the fight, laughing with excitement, and Mordecai raised his arms up, channeling energy for an attack. Seeing the adventurers, the hill giant came to a stop and yelled in a foreign language. Then, pulling a rock from his loincloth, he hurled it at Keijin.

As the rock clanged loudly off Keijin's shield, Sybil attempted to hold this monster in place, just as she had the oni, but it managed to resist her hold and started moving toward them. Redbeard ran up to the giant and slashed its belly. The giant let out a cry of pain and swung his club in an arch, hitting Redbeard in the side and sending him flying against a tree. Keijin moved around the giant and lunged toward it with his sword, catching it in the arm. The blade stabbed through the flesh of its forearm, and the giant pulled his arm away before Keijin could pull out his sword, causing it to spin in the opposite direction, blood twirling off it as it flew. To keep the giant distracted while Keijin grabbed his sword, Sybil took a few steps forward and shot a couple blasts of fire toward it.

Not realizing until it was too late, Sybil had moved way too close to the giant. Out of fear of the flames, it let out a horrible yell and started waving its club around to keep the fire away. The club landed squarely in Sybil's chest, knocking her prone. Realizing the flames came from Sybil, the giant moved forward and lifted its club to crush her with it. Mordecai stepped out between Sybil and the giant, and the world turned dark around them. Black smoke billowed around Mordecai's arms, and when he thrust them forward, a sharp snap cracked through the air as black spikes of energy shot toward the giant. The spikes pierced into the giant's flesh and exploded out through its back, sending blood and entrails splattering over the trees behind it. With a short, labored exhale, the creature collapsed to the ground, its eyes still open.

The horrible capabilities of Mordecai's powers were only starting to show, and as he turned around to look at Sybil, her heart raced just as it had when staring down the giant. She was terrified of him, but at the same time, she felt something more. She admired him. And when he bent down to check if she was alright, she realized she also liked the way he looked at her and the way his cool hands felt when they touched her skin.

When Mordecai saw that Sybil was mostly unharmed, he heaved a sigh, and said, "I told you you're not a fighter."

Something about this tickled Sybil, and she started laughing, despite the pain in her chest. At first, he raised eyebrow, but then a small smirk formed on his face as he looked down at her.

"Okay, you've obviously received some head trauma. Let's get you up."

The woman who had been running from the giant was practically in hysterics. Keijin had his hands firmly on her shoulder and was trying to calm her down when Mordecai and Sybil approached them. Redbeard, having taken quite a blow, both physically and emotionally, was sitting under the tree he was thrown into looking a little shaken, but like Sybil, mostly unharmed.

"Everything's alright now," Keijin was saying. "The danger has passed. Please, can you tell me your name?"

"I'm… Mary," she said between deep breaths as she tried to calm down.

"Mary, that's a beautiful name," Keijin replied with a charming, reassuring smile. "Where do you live, Mary?"

She pointed in the direction from which she ran and said, "Back that way. It's just a small cottage in a wide clearing of the woods. My husband, George, he was chopping wood when the monster attacked… said for me to run, and I did. I don't know if the monster got him or just went straight after me."

Keijin turned to Sybil and Mordecai, and Sybil winced when she knew what he was going to say.

"We need to return Mary to the cottage and find George," he told them, and it took everything in Sybil not to groan. She just wanted to rest.

The cottage was nearly two miles from where they fought the giant, a long way for a commoner to run, and Sybil's already tired legs and feet were screaming. By the time they made it to the cottage, it was already dark, so Sybil created an orb of light and placed it on the top of her staff to illuminate their path. They searched the entire property, inside and out, but they didn't find Mary's husband. Starting to panic, Mary tried yelling out into the forest for him, but Redbeard stopped her and explained why that might be a bad idea. Everyone headed inside and lit several lanterns to brighten up the cottage.

"I don't understand," she whimpered as they all sat around her living room. "We've lived here nearly three years now without any trouble at all. Why is this happening now?"

"Has anything changed in the past couple days or weeks? Anything that might have attracted unwanted visitors?" Sybil asked, squished between Redbeard and Keijin on the couch.

"Not that I can…" Mary started to say, but then her face turned white. "But that can't be."

"What?" Mordecai asked, turning from the window to her.

Mary's face turned from white to a deep pink, as she said, "Well, I…
I just found out I'm pregnant."

Taken aback, Sybil stared at the woman for a moment before looking
at the other three, who all seemed equally surprised.

"And what exactly might be after a pregnant woman and her
husband?" she asked softly, not sure if she wanted the answer.

"There are countless dark creatures with countless reasons that
would target a pregnant woman," Mordecai said with a groan. "Not three
days ago, we fought one that ate babies."

Mary clutched her stomach with a gasp, and Keijin put a steadying
hand on her shoulder.

"Don't worry," he told her. "We won't let any harm come to you or
your child."

"What about my husband, won't you go looking for him? What if
he's dying out there somewhere?"

"It's the middle of the night, and past experiences have taught me
that's the worst time to look for a missing person," Redbeard said, shaking his
head.

Mary brought her hands to her face and wept.

"But we can't just leave him out there. What if he dies and we
could've done something to save him?"

"The problem is," Keijin said. "If we were to go out there and look
for him, we'd have to leave you here, and that would leave you all alone. I
think it would be best if we all tried to get some rest and leave together at first
light. Sybil and Redbeard here can find whatever clues we might be able to
use to figure out where he's gone. Another possibility is that he ran off
looking for you and will return when he sees that the hill giant has been
slain."

Unable to refute Keijin's logic, Mary excused herself and headed up
to her room for the night, her soft cries coming through the closed door.
Redbeard and Sybil did just as Keijin had suggested and headed outside to the
wood chopping block where Mary had reportedly last seen her husband.
Redbeard, skilled in tracking, searched around for a trail. Sybil increased the
orb of light still flickering on her staff to see better, though Redbeard had the
night vision of dwarves, developed after generations of living under hills and
mountains. When Redbeard only found the tracks of the hill giant and strange
lines leading away from the house toward the forest, Sybil cast the spell
allowing her to see traces of magic, just as she had done in the orphanage.

The spell was far weaker without Mordecai's help to amplify it, but when she approached the giant's footprints, she could see the faintest splotches of pink in them.

"The hill giant was being controlled by someone else," she told him, recognizing the sign of an enchantment.

Redbeard gave a grunt and then pointed out toward the forest.

"And it dragged the husband out into the woods in that direction. I bet it left a pretty easy trail to follow, too."

"Have you ever encountered something like this?" Sybil asked, looking over at the cottage. Through the window, she could see Keijin and Mordecai talking.

"I've been at this whole adventuring business for a while," Redbeard said. "But I've seen more crazy shit happen this week than I have in all the years before. I'm in brand new territory; I just hope my skills are useful."

"They are," she told him with a smile. "You kind of want to be a hero, huh?"

Redbeard sniffed and said, "Now, what on earth would give you that idea?"

"I've just been thinking about your reason for leaving your clan to become an adventurer," Sybil replied with a shrug. "It wasn't for lack of excitement; I've heard about the lifestyle of barbarian clans. But then, I saw you reach out for that scared woman running toward us. You wanted to be there for her, to make her feel safe."

"Or maybe it's just 'cause I like tall women," Redbeard retorted with a smirk.

"Sure," Sybil laughed. "That might be a part of it, but you're well on your way to becoming a hero, whether you realize it or not."

"Careful now, little lady. You just might make me blush."

"No, really," she said with another laugh. "You're a good person. Scary on the battlefield, but I know you have my back."

"Well, same goes for you," Redbeard replied, looking both pleased and uncomfortable. "Come on, let's get back inside before we feel obliged to hug or something."

There was only one guest bedroom, so after some deliberation, Redbeard was given several blankets and pillows to sleep on the floor, and Keijin and Sybil decided to share the bed with a pillow between them, at Keijin's suggestion. After the boys had fallen asleep, Sybil snuck out and headed downstairs, unable to quiet her mind. Mordecai was lounging on the couch, one of his legs out straight on the cushions and the other one on the floor to keep him propped upright as he read his book. It was the same one he had been reading for a few days, so she asked, "Slow reader?"

Mordecai's eyes slid up from the page and glared at her for a moment before returning to his book.

"It takes time to master the concepts here," he replied, his low voice rumbling. "If you ever develop your maturity, I might teach some to you one day."

He moved his leg as she approached the couch, giving her room to sit. After she had been watching him read for a moment, he looked at her from the corner of his eye.

"Yes?"

"I wanted to thank you for saving my life today," she told him, a flush of embarrassment burning her cheeks. "All I was thinking about was keeping it distracted so Keijin could grab his sword. I didn't realize how close I was to it."

He closed his book and sighed.

"Yeah, well, I guess stepping out in front of it when it was just about to strike wasn't the brightest move on my part, either."

"Why *did* you do that?" she asked. "It's just… a bit outside your character."

Mordecai frowned as he thought about it.

"I'm not sure. I just didn't like the thought of that thing killing you. If you're going to get yourself killed, it needs to be by something better than a hill giant." Sybil gave a little laugh and shook her head. "What?"

"I bet it will be quite a show if something ever threatens someone you actually care about."

"Not sure that will ever happen," he said, his tone turning dark again.

"Have you ever? Cared for someone, I mean."

"That's precisely why I know how dangerous caring for someone is." Pain spread across his face, and then he turned to her, angry. "Have you? In fact, have you ever loved someone before? You and the others look at me as if I am heartless, but it's only because I know what it's like to have your heart ripped from you."

Mordecai's words stung Sybil as he hurled his pain toward her.

"I've never loved because no one has ever let me love them," she replied, her voice catching in her throat.

Mordecai frowned, not knowing what to say, and looked away from her. Feeling her face grow hot and her eyes start to water, she excused herself and headed back up to the guest bedroom.

Sybil had to be quiet as she crawled back into bed and silently cried for a moment or two. Once she had settled, Keijin rolled over in his sleep, and she stared at him, taking in his purity and goodness. His hand had fallen near hers, and she slowly moved to where they were touching. She wondered if she could love someone like him, someone good who could bring only good things into her life. Or would she grow old and alone like Leon, living in a cold tower for the rest of her days? Her thoughts as she drifted off to sleep were of Mordecai and this tragic person, probably long dead, who he once loved. But the last thing she remembered before sleep took her is Keijin's hand slowly wrapping itself around hers.

The party, along with the calmer, more exhausted Mary, was out the door of the cottage before dawn, following the trail Redbeard was tracking. The horses were left hidden in the stable with plenty of straw and water in case something kept them in the woods overnight. Sybil stayed close to Redbeard at the front while Keijin kept a close watch over Mary. Mordecai, who did not look pleased to be traipsing through the woods, brought up the back. Every now and then, Sybil could hear him grumbling something about how nature was messy and chaotic and should only be observed from afar.

The trail took them deep into the woods where the canopies, untouched by hands, grew thick and blocked out much of the sun. It struck Sybil as odd how quiet the woods were. With the Asbriand Forest being just below her bedroom window, she had grown accustomed to the sounds of birds chirping and fluttering about, the calls of predators and whines of prey, and the creaks and rustling of the trees as the wind blew across and through them. The air here, though, was still and humid, and the only sounds to be heard were of the four humans and dwarf making their way through.

After a couple hours of hiking, sweat starting to appear despite it being the tail end of autumn, Redbeard put his arm up to stop Sybil from walking forward and said, "It's the darndest thing, but I've lost the trail here.

This giant seemed to just vanished… or very cleverly retraced his steps, which I doubt."

"We're not lost yet," Sybil said, pulling out a bronze medal.

Before they had left the cottage, Sybil had asked Mary to give her something important to George. With this medal, which had a symbol on it she was unfamiliar with, she cast a spell. The spell was one of the first divination spells Leon had taught her, and it allowed her to see a shiny, golden line that would lead her to the item's owner. It only worked within a certain distance of the target, but thanks to Redbeard's tracking, they were close enough. The golden line stretched out further into the woods, though no one but Sybil could see it.

"I'll take the lead from here," she told Redbeard with a pleased grin.

Every now and then, the line fluttered, but Sybil said nothing about it. Her magic was fine, nothing was weakening it, but it seemed that George's lifeforce was dimming, wherever he was. Still, it was strong enough to give her a solid direction, and they hiked another mile or two until they reached a decrepit cottage in the darkest part of the woods.

It looked ancient, and the wood panels were only still standing because most of them had been painted in a thick tar. Sybil could feel negative energy radiating from this place and started to regret every decision she made that led her there. Turning to the others, she could tell they were thinking similar thoughts.

"Let's get this over with," Keijin said, not sounding like himself.

The door was unlocked, and Sybil pushed it open with the butt of her staff before casting a spell that lit up the room.

Mary hesitated at the bottom of the porch and asked, "Might it be possible for me to stay outside?"

Seeing the genuine fear in her eyes, Keijin heaved a sigh and said, "Very well. But if you see or hear anything coming toward you, come find us immediately."

As Mary nodded, Sybil stepped inside the cottage. The smell hit her instantly: a combination of rotting flesh, bitter herbs, and fermenting liquids. Sybil covered her mouth as she gagged at the smell. Mordecai followed in behind her and covered his mouth and nose with a black shawl he kept tucked in his cloak, only leaving his eyes visible, and Keijin cursed under his breath, putting his hand to his mouth, as well. Redbeard, looking displeased but mostly unfazed, moved further into the room, and his companions followed after him.

Whoever lived here clearly dabbled in multiple forms of the arcane. Vials and jars of various liquids, creatures or their parts, and potions lined the walls in a disorganized manner, and there were countless spellbooks and potion books as well as scrolls, some looking centuries old, scattered about the room. Everyone looked to Sybil, and she returned to the glowing trail, which led her to the center of the room where an old rug lay. Redbeard moved the rug out of the way, revealing a hatch.

"I don't like this," Mordecai warned.

"Noted," Keijin said in an usually gruff voice before grabbing the handle of the hatch and lifting it up.

The smell intensified, and they all choked. There were stairs leading down, and because she had been following the trail, Sybil was about to head down first. But Mordecai grabbed her wrist and held her back. The other two didn't notice this and headed down the stairs. She looked up at him, confused, and with his own confused expression on his face, he let her go. Without a word, they both followed after their companions.

Immediately, Sybil recognized they were in a dungeon. The light from her staff and the spell she cast in the room above only illuminated the space so much, and it was hard to see the walls from the base of the stairs. She stepped forward, and a figure came into view. Flinching, she held her staff up and realized it was a man chained to the wall. He had a giant gash across his head that had trickled blood down to the collar of his shirt. Reaching out her hand, Sybil could feel his lifeforce. He was just barely hanging on.

"Oh no," she heard Redbeard breathe, his dwarven eyes trained on something, and she turned to him, shining the light toward what he was looking at.

It was Mary, lifeless, with her belly cut open. Just as the realization hit the party, they heard a cackling laughter as the trap door above shut and its lock snapped.

"The witch fucking tricked us!" Redbeard boomed.

A rattling of metal filled the room, replacing the cackling, and chains started moving toward them. They all stood close together and tried to fight them off with magic, staff, and blades, but it was no use. Within a minute, they were all shackled and pulled against the wall. Sybil had been pulled to the far wall next to George and the others had been pulled to the wall directly across from her. Panicking, Sybil started screaming and tugged against the chains with all her might. But the more she tugged, the tighter the chains became, and her hands started tingling from the lack of circulation.

"Sybil, look at me," Keijin called out to her. She forced herself to look at him, her breathing heavy. "I need you to calm down, or you're going to hurt yourself. Can you do that for me? Take some deep breaths, that's it. We are going to get out of this."

Sybil's heart rate slowed, and she nodded along to Keijin's words. Tears were streaming down her face, but she couldn't wipe them away because her hands were high above her head. Using her magic was impossible in this position as she needed her hands to perform all but the weakest of spells. All the noise she had made stirred George awake, and he was looking over at her, barely able to lift his head from his shoulder.

"Who are you people?" he asked in a weak voice.

"Just a bunch of idiots, that's who," Redbeard answered, his face nearly as red as his hair and beard. "We were attempting a search and rescue for you, but got tricked by the witch."

"The witch," he said, closing his eyes. "She took everything…" He took a big, labored breath. "I broke our deal, and she took everything."

"What deal?" Mordecai asked, but the man passed out again before he could answer.

When the hatch opened again sometime later, Sybil's heart nearly leapt out of her chest, and it took everything in her to not pull against the chains. What they knew as Mary started heading down the stairs, but with each step, she changed into something different, something horrible. Sybil had never seen a hag before, but it was worse than she could have ever imagined. Her skin was scaly and gray, stretching taut across her bony frame, her hair was black and matted around two jagged horns that rose out from her temples, and she had sharp, yellow teeth and long, black claws.

"What a real treat this is," the hag hissed as she made her way to the center of the room, eyeing her new victims. "Such supple specimens for me to continue on with my fun."

"What do you want from us?" Sybil asked in barely a whisper.

The hag turned to her, smiling with her razor teeth.

"I want your *pain*, of course. And with a whole group of you, I can really savor it. You see, I came up with a rather ingenious system long ago: I cause one physical pain and then feast on that pain *and* the pain of the others watching someone they care for hurt and bleed." Sybil glanced over at the real Mary and realized she was used to suck the pain out of her husband, until she died. "Getting to observe you all last night, it became extremely clear to me just who that person would be."

The hag started moving toward Sybil, her claws extended out in front of her, and the panic started rising in her again. Laughter burst from Mordecai, and the hag turned to see what he was laughing about.

He shook his head and said, "Do you seriously think we care at all about her? She's just some child we're escorting, and quite frankly, you'd be doing us a favor by taking her off our hands."

His words hurt for a moment until Sybil realized what he was doing. If he convinced the hag they didn't care about her, then she might leave her alone. At the very least, it might buy them some time to think of something. But the hag knew better. She had observed too much the night before for them to fool her now. Even though she was wracked with fear and panic, Sybil couldn't help but notice the irony of finally having people care for her only to be punished for it.

When the hag continued to move her claws toward Sybil, Mordecai saw his attempt had failed and yelled, "Don't touch her," as he pulled against his chains.

As the wicked smile spread on her face, the hag gestured to Mordecai.

"See? Even the shadowed one is affected," she said with a horrible giggle. "This is going to be *delicious*."

Without any further hesitation, she slowly drove her five extended claws into Sybil's belly. The pain was immediate and intense. As much as she wanted to fight it, to keep the others from hearing it, Sybil let out a bloodcurdling scream as tears streamed down her face. The others were yelling at the hag to stop and thrashing against their chains, but she just continued, slowly running the claws up toward Sybil's chest. Blood spilled out, and Sybil could feel the warm liquid soaking through her robes. Her entire body was radiating pain, and she felt like she could die from it alone.

"Please," she heard Keijin beg. "Please."

The hag's face was inches from Sybil, and she leaned in to lick the tears from Sybil's chin with her blistered tongue. Trying to leave this place in her mind, Sybil closed her eyes and prayed.

Lord Shuheyr, hear my call. Save me from this anguish.

Though she could still feel the pain and the blood trickling down her body, Sybil felt herself leave the dungeon. Like in her dream at Lord Osric's estate, she was surrounded by a swirling darkness. A form began to solidify in front of her, as tall as Leon's tower, and it could barely be described as humanoid, with four gangly limbs and a long torso. Through the darkness, she couldn't see its face, even as it spoke.

"Bind yourself to me," it spoke in language she had never heard before but could somehow comprehend. "And I shall save you from this torture."

The knowledge struck her of what this creature was all at once, and she breathed, "Haborym."

"I will make all the pain go away; I will give you my power," it continued in a foul hiss. "All you have to do is submit."

The pain was unbearable, and even though she could hear herself screaming and feel the hot tears streaming down her face, all she could see was Haborym. But she didn't want his darkness. She didn't want to be his slave.

"No," Sybil breathed, accepting her fate with her ethereal hands pressed against her chest. "I would rather die."

Haborym's body convulsed in pain, and he let out a horrible, high-pitched shriek like nothing she had ever heard before. Within an instance, he was gone, and all she could see was the hag and the darkness of the dungeon surrounding her. But then, she felt a trembling coming from all around her, and she remembered the power granted to her as a child.

Shuheyr, she begged. *Help me.*

Sybil's pain started to diminish as the light inside her grew, and she could feel him reaching out for her. The God of Light engulfed her, holding her safe in his arms. She opened her eyes, lighting up the hag's face, which turned from gleeful to fearful, as Sybil's entire body began to glow. The power radiating off her was so intense it caused Sybil to scream as it passed through her body and shot out into the room. The others closed their eyes just in time as the bright light of Shuheyr filled every inch of the dungeon and caused the hag and her chains to disintegrate. All five of the prisoners fell to the floor, and Sybil passed out before she could see if anyone was okay.

Chapter Six

Sybil was back in Mary's guest bedroom, though she had no idea how or when she got there. When she lifted her head and looked around, becoming aware of the intense pain radiating through her body, she found Keijin reading in a chair across the room. It was one of the books she had packed for their adventure, *the Wilds of the West*. When he saw her rouse, the book fell to the ground, and he moved to her side.

"Stay still," Keijin breathed, pressing down on her shoulder. "You aren't completely healed yet."

"What happened?" she asked, her voice barely usable after the intensity of her screams.

"It seems like Shuheyr has his uses in your life after all," he told her with a smile, brushing some hair out of her face. "You saved us all down there by calling him forth."

"Are Mordecai and Redbeard, okay?"

"They're a little shaken by what happened, but they're alright. Just waiting for you downstairs," he said and then shook his head with a small smile. "Those two... I never thought I would say it, but you really mean something to them." He looked away, and his smile turned to a frown. "You mean a lot to all of us... and seeing what that thing did to you was hard."

Sybil placed her hand on his, causing him to look back over at her.

"Thank you," she told him. "Your voice in the dark... I might have lost myself, if it wasn't for you."

Keijin touched her cheek and leaned forward, like he wanted to tell her all his secrets. But then, something changed in his expression, and he pulled back.

"I'll always be here for you, just know that," he told her, and then looked down at his hands as they began to glow. "Just one more round of healing, and you should be good to go."

After Keijin excused himself to check on George, who was resting and recovering in the master bedroom, Sybil slowly made her way out of bed. Instead of her robes, she was wearing a nightgown that must have once belonged to Mary. It was low cut and didn't cover her arms, so she felt a little exposed compared to her usual attire. Then, a trickle of embarrassment shot through her when she realized one of them, or perhaps even all of them, had to see her naked to get her into the nightgown. With a shake of her head, she tried to ignore that thought and just be thankful for clothes that fit. However, when she passed the master bedroom and saw George staring at her through the door frame, her embarrassment was replaced with shame. He was propped up in bed as Keijin treated his wounds, and at the sight of her in his wife's nightgown, his eyes started welling up with tears. He turned his head away, and Sybil hurried passed.

The memories of the hag's dungeon flashed in Sybil's mind: the chains, Mary's limp and mutilated body, and the indescribable pain. She stopped in the middle of the staircase and clutched her chest as the memories overwhelmed her, but she inhaled deeply and let it out slowly, pushing down the memories along with the others she kept at bay, and continued on her way.

When she walked into the living room, Mordecai rose from the couch, his cloak falling around his legs. His silver eyes were locked onto Sybil, and she could see something new in them. She felt strangely immodest standing in front of him wearing nothing but a nightgown and crossed her arms behind her back.

"I just needed to stretch my legs," she said in a hoarse, weak voice.

"It's good to see you up and about," he said, looking uncomfortable. "I was… hoping to talk to you. If you'd like, we could take a short walk outside."

It unsettled Sybil a little how cordially he was behaving, but she agreed. They made their way outside and walked around the property for a while, slowly because of how sore Sybil was from her still healing wounds and the days of traveling before that. It was several minutes before Mordecai spoke up again.

"I wanted to apologize for what I said in the witch's hut. I was only trying to-"

"It's okay," she interrupted. "I understand what you were trying to do. If she had been heading toward you with those claws, I probably would've tried the same thing."

"Good, I'm glad you understand," he said with a nod. "Do you feel okay? I mean, does Shuheyr have some hold over you now?"

Sybil thought for a moment and felt the sensations in her body and listened in her mind to see if anything was different, but whatever Shuheyr had done in the hag's dungeon was temporary, possibly just a gift for rejecting Haborym. For a moment, she was sure she was going to tell Mordecai about Haborym's call, but she didn't know how he would react to it. Besides, she just wanted to forget about the whole incident.

"No hold on me yet," Sybil replied, trying to smile but failing.

Just then, Redbeard came trudging out of the woods with a small deer draped over his shoulders. He dropped it and ran over to Sybil. After a moment of hesitation, Redbeard pulled her into a hug, his head coming just above her chest. She winced a little from the pain of Redbeard squeezing her, and he quickly pulled away.

"Sorry, sorry. It's just so good to see you up and about again," Redbeard said. "It was touch and go with you for a while. That Keijin fella was mighty tense, and this guy looked like death."

Mordecai made a face as Sybil asked how long she had been out.

"Going on three days, just about. You were in awful shape. That witch nearly bled you dry, and that light show you did that burned her up sapped all that was left of you. But I don't think we would've made it out of there without it."

Redbeard then excused himself to dress and butcher the deer for dinner, and Mordecai and Sybil headed back inside. She hadn't noticed before, but on the couch were her old robes, and Mordecai picked them up and handed them to her.

"While Keijin was patching up your wounds, I thought I would try to be useful and mend your clothes," he explained. "There wasn't much I could do about the bloodstains, but I managed to mend the holes well enough."

Sybil turned the robes over in her hands and stared at where the hag stabbed and tore into her with her claws. Pushing away the memories again, she thanked him for the repairs. Her blood stained the white fabric from her chest down to where the robes ended at the knee, and she didn't see any use for them looking like this.

"You don't have to wear them," he said as if he could read her thoughts. "I just thought you might like the option. I'm sure Mary has some spare dresses you can wear that she no longer has use for. You'll just be a distraction if you continue wearing what you have on."

Mordecai glanced down and placed his cool fingers on her upper arm, causing her heart to flutter.

"You're blushing," Mordecai noted with a grin. "Never thought I would be thankful to see those silly, girlish things you do."

Sybil gave a small laugh and said, "Even when you're being nice, you're still such an asshole."

Sybil dressed herself in one of Mary's light blue dresses the following morning and moved to the mirror to assess how it fit. It had been nearly a decade since Sybil had worn a dress, but it was nothing as nice as this one, and it looked foreign on her. At the same time, though, she liked the way it showed her features. The neckline fell below her distinct collarbone, the sleeves came up just before her shoulders —the only thing covering them was her dark brown hair that fell past her shoulder blades— and the skirt started at her waist, forming nicely to her womanly figure that had fully developed under her robes over the past few years. The blue of the dress brought out the blue in her eyes, and for the first time in her life, staring in that mirror, she felt like an actual woman.

If things had been different, if she had grown up in a village with normal people and normal parents, she might have been somebody who men tried to woo, a fair maiden like the ones Keijin always found himself assisting or a lady of a great house. But that reality would never be.

With a small, sad smile, Sybil turned away from the mirror, knowing what she was seeing wasn't the true her. This dress was only temporary, and they would get new robes for her as soon as possible. Perhaps Leon had already sent some to wherever they would stay in Taragpass. However, when she headed down for breakfast that morning wearing the dress, she did enjoy the look on everyone's faces. Redbeard was in the middle of eating oatmeal and dropped his spoon, sending it clattering and flinging oatmeal across the table.

"Good, it fits," was all Keijin was able to say.

Mordecai just stared at Sybil, his eyebrows raised, watching her as she took her seat at the table next to him. When she glanced up at him, he looked away, returning his attention to the food in front of him. Putting a hand up to her face, she tried to hide the grin she couldn't get rid of. Who knew there was magic in simply being a woman?

Once Sybil started eating, Keijin updated the others on the state of their host. He would be well enough to ride in another day and had decided to accompany the party to Taragpass where he had a cousin he could live with. If he had any hopes of moving on from the tragedy of his wife and unborn child, George would need to leave this place and start a new life over.

Thinking back to the dungeon, Sybil frowned and asked, "Has George explained anything more about the deal he had made with the hag?"

"Only that when he learned of his wife being pregnant, he broke whatever deal it was," Keijin replied. "He said that the child would have been at risk if the hag still had hold over his life."

"The fool," Mordecai muttered. "You can't just break a deal with a dark creature like that. Something has to be given."

Sybil nodded slowly and said, "Perhaps he didn't fully understand what it was. Things like this are hard for the common people to comprehend. She could have disguised herself as something else to make him feel like she wasn't as big of a threat."

"Well, whatever the case, I want to learn what this fella had been doing for the hag," Redbeard said, having recovered his spoon. "I know the man's suffered, but he might be responsible for a lot of pain himself doing the witch's bidding."

"Give him another day," Keijin suggested. "Before we set out for Taragpass, we'll set the matter straight. If need be, we can always deliver him to the authorities when we arrive in town."

"Still no word on what it is we'll be doing there?" Mordecai asked, clearly annoyed at the ambiguity of Leon's instructions.

Keijin shook his head and said, "Not a clue. Perhaps he wants us to determine what needs our assistance, to see how well we can assess problems and situations."

A cold thought passed through Sybil's mind, causing her to grip the skirt of her dress. The thought was so terrible that she couldn't hold on to it.

"What if this was the reason Leon wanted us to head to Taragpass? What if he knew we'd face this hag?"

Heavy silence fell over the table as the idea hit the others. Keijin mulled over the idea and shook his head but said nothing.

"So what if he did? It doesn't change the fact that it happened," Mordecai replied, sounding indifferent to the whole situation.

"Well, it would for me," Redbeard said, bending the spoon a little in his hand. "Don't want to be working for some all-knowing wizard that sends me off into situations like that again."

Mordecai ignored Redbeard and turned to Sybil.

"If this whole journey is to train you, to get you ready for the legacy he's leaving you, and if you trust that anything he's actively pushing us toward is to make you stronger, then you have to accept that this is something you needed to go through."

"If this is what it costs to be Leon's heir, I'm not sure I want it," Sybil muttered, staring down at the table.

"Power isn't just handed to you," he told her, his voice growing harsher with every word. "You have to sweat for it, to bleed for it. Anyone who acquires power without pain squanders it and suffers in other ways for it. If you just want Leon to hand over his power to you because you've read every book in his library or can explode a ball of fire in the middle of a group of people, then I suggest you just keep that dress and give up the life of a wizard."

When she looked back up at him, Mordecai's eyes were intense, waiting for her to argue back. The other two just stared at them, not sure what to say. Eventually, she relented and heaved a sigh.

"You're right," Sybil said, her voice tired and defeated. "Whatever we come across in our journey, whether it was designed by Leon or not, will help me strengthen my powers… and it will help me to understand the misery of others."

Everything was silent for a moment before Redbeard turned to Mordecai and said, "You can be a real dick sometimes, you know that?"

"Yes, Redbeard," Keijin said. "I believe he does,"

Mordecai rolled his eyes at the two of them.

Sybil spent most of the next day practicing her spells in the field near the cottage. The helplessness she felt when the hag chained her to the wall made Sybil determined to practice her spells with limited hand gestures, but she was only successful with minor ones. As she practiced, her frustration and anger grew. The sky above her turned from blue to gray, and large clouds started to form, the weather reflecting the intensity of her soul. Lightning snapped across the sky, sending a boom of thunder that shook the earth. The clouds grew darker and more threatening, but Sybil stayed in the center of the field, not frightened by the storm she created. Thrusting her staff upwards, she sent the coldness of her heart into the sky, and the clouds started shooting down shards of ice all around her. She had never been able to cast a spell like this before, and as the field filled with jagged ice spears, it became clear what Mordecai had said was true.

The pain and anger and coldness Sybil was feeling had made her stronger and allowed her to harness her power in a new way. Her emotions overcame her all at once, and she released the spell, falling to her knees. The sky cleared up, returning to the blue, sunny day it had been before, and the ice melted away.

When she looked up, breathing heavily and wiping the tears from her cheeks, she saw Redbeard watching her from the tree line. His face was hard, and when their eyes met, he turned away and started heading back toward the cottage. She didn't know what to make of his reaction, but her stomach felt like lead thinking of the expression on his face, like he was disappointed. They were all starting to realize she was someone who could wield a great deal of power, but in what ways would she end up wielding it?

In the evening, Mordecai and Sybil were reading on the couch when George finally made his way down the stairs with Keijin following close behind him. They both looked up and watched as he slowly made his way over to the table, glancing up nervously at them a couple times. Redbeard offered him a cup of water as Keijin helped him into the chair. Sybil got up from the couch and moved to the table with Mordecai following suit. There were only four chairs at the table, so Redbeard stood behind Sybil, making her a little wary since they hadn't spoken to each other since she saw him earlier.

"Listen, we need to know what that deal you made with the hag was about," Redbeard began, crossing his arms.

There was a long moment of silence from George as he stared around at his saviors from the hag's cellar. He rubbed his hands together and his eyebrows were high on his face. It was clear he was nervous, but there was also a heavy weight of shame blanketed over him. Eventually, knowing they wouldn't let it go, George shared his story.

"My wife and I came here several years ago to escape a life that put us both in danger because of the people we knew and the things I had done in my youth. There was no one really around, but it wasn't too far off the path where we had to totally fend for ourselves. For nearly a year after settling here, we lived here peacefully and talked about starting a family.

"But then, a dark shadow fell over our land. It was like something cursed this place. Nothing would grow and all sorts of dangerous creatures started coming right up to our doorstep." He paused, pinching the bridge of his nose. "That's when I met her. An old, kind-looking woman who told me she had the power to make everything prosperous and good again. Of course, I didn't believe her at first. But then she cast a spell over my crops, giving me the most beautiful harvest I had ever seen. We were nearly starved by this point, so I saw it as a miracle."

"What did she want in return for this prosperity?" Mordecai asked, his voice rough.

George looked over at Mordecai with fearful eyes. To a common man, Mordecai looked like a dark creature himself, and Sybil wondered if he had disguised himself for that very purpose.

"Sacrifices," the man breathed. "She wanted lives… it didn't matter whose. Not wanting innocent people to suffer -I didn't even let myself think what she was going to do with them- I decided to find people who deserved some sort of punishment: criminals. There were people after me, mobsters from my life before, and I started with their lackeys and worked my way up. Once I was facing people who matched my fighting abilities, I turned to bandits and other ne'er-do-wells on the road nearby."

"So why break the deal? It seemed to be working out for you," Redbeard said in an icy tone.

"Because… after my wife told me she was pregnant, I realized I didn't want to be that man anymore. I didn't want to give into a witch's demands." He put his hands to his face, grieving for what he lost. "I was planning to leave the very next day… but the hag feared this would be the last time she would get to feed for a while, so she sent her creatures after Mary and me. And the rest… well, you know the rest from there."

The table was silent for a while, everyone processing this man's story. Helping the hag gather victims was a terrible crime, no matter who they were, and Sybil didn't know if Keijin would just let him go. Or if Redbeard would even let him live.

"How many people did you bring to the hag?" Mordecai asked, clearly not satisfied with the man's story. "How many lives did you sacrifice for your own gain?"

"Uh, I... I don't know. Nearly twenty, I suppose. One per month was what she demanded."

"You helped her torture twenty souls to death?" Mordecai asked, his voice growing more spiteful with every word. "Or I should say, twenty-two since you chose to stay here and do the witch's bidding, getting your wife and unborn child killed. You could've left, but you decided to put yourself above the lives of so many others."

George was staring down at the table, trembling, and Sybil could see the life, the will to live, leave his eyes as Mordecai spoke. She placed her hand on Mordecai's forearm to make him stop. He glanced over at her, and the fury and hatred in his eyes dwindled into a gentle rage. Turning away from Sybil, he huffed but stayed silent.

"Unfortunately, there's some truth in my companion's words," Keijin said slowly. "This isn't something we can just let you get away with, despite the suffering you experienced at the hands of the witch. We would need to deliver you to the proper authorities and tell them of your crimes, and my greatest hope is that you would cooperate to help set things right. As much as they can be, that is."

George let out a deep, shaky breath and slowly nodded his head.

"That's more than fair."

"You're damn right it is," Redbeard muttered under his breath to where only Mordecai and Sybil could hear.

Keijin locked George in his bedroom after dinner, now he was technically their prisoner. When Keijin came back downstairs, he sat down on the couch between Redbeard and Sybil and heaved a sigh. Redbeard clasped Keijin's shoulder roughly, showing his support in the least vulnerable way possible. All of them sat there in silence for a while. Mordecai was in a chair in the far corner, staring out into the darkness through the window to his right. They were all tired and weary from the events of the past few days, but Sybil found herself feeling hopeful for the next leg in their adventure. She wanted to see this town of Taragpass and discover what it had to offer. Besides, nothing could get much worse than a hag nearly bleeding you to death in a dark, smelly dungeon, and she survived that.

For breakfast, before the next leg of their journey, Sybil helped Redbeard prepare some of the deer he had caught a couple days before along with some eggs she found in the chicken coop around back. Due to their neglect, there had only been a few, but it was enough to get the party fed for the morning ride to Taragpass. As she was setting the table, and Mordecai was unhelpfully reading in the corner, Keijin came downstairs, his face white. She asked him what was wrong, but he didn't respond for a moment. They all watched as he moved to the couch and slowly sat down.

"George is dead," Keijin breathed, taking the other three completely by surprise. "He... he killed himself."

Sybil's stomach dropped, and she put her hand up to her mouth.

Keijin rubbed his face before continuing. "He strung himself up by the rafters in the middle of the night," he said, his voice breaking a little. "I suppose it had all just become too much for him. He knew he wouldn't be able to escape his past."

"It's probably for the best," Mordecai said. When Sybil frowned at him, he added, "The man was just going to suffer for the rest of his days, anyway. For common folk, it's sometimes better to die than suffer."

"Killing yourself because of pain ain't a good way to die," Redbeard said, staring down at the floor.

"I know what he did was awful but no one deserves to suffer like that," Sybil agreed, and then she turned to Keijin. "We should bury him before we leave, right?"

Keijin shook his head, looked up at her, and said, "No... no, I think I have a better idea."

After packing up their bags and readying their horses, Sybil aimed her staff toward the cottage and, as requested by Keijin, unleashed a stream of fire toward its facade. There was no one left to occupy this home other than the ghosts and memories of its former owners. It was better destroyed and the land freed up for someone to start anew, if they so wished. The party watched, standing by their horses, as the flames engulfed the house. It was purifying in a way, cleansing a house full of dark memories from the world, and Sybil found a weight lifted off her chest as the structure went tumbling in on itself.

With the remains of the house still burning, they mounted their horses and set off down the road, leaving that forsaken place forever.

Chapter Seven

     The forest they had been riding through seemed to all at once turn into desolate land, nearly void of life. Craters of dirt sat where great trees once stood, and a smog was hovering in the air, creating a haze in the sky that turned the whole world gray. They were nearing the town of Taragpass, which sat near the base of the Wintry Tops, the mountain range which ran through the continent and separated Irminshu from the southern kingdoms. Taragpass sat at the mouth of a trail leading through the mountains and into the south, which was the easiest way for their kingdom to establish a trade route with the others. Because of this, it had become a booming hub of industry, bustling with traveling traders, merchants, and all sorts of other colorful characters. While the town grew in prosperity, though, the land underneath it seemed to suffer.

     Riding into the city, their horses' hooves clomping along the cobblestoned roads, it became nearly impossible to navigate. There was not a lot of space in between the tall and narrow half-timbered buildings of the villagers' homes and shops. And since it was the early afternoon, the busy people of Taragpass were coming and going from all directions.

     Pushing their horses through the crowd, various people cursing and spitting at them as they did, they arrived at an inn near the center of town. After paying for a stable hand to care for their horses, they headed inside. The first floor of the inn was completely dedicated to the tavern with a dozen or so tables sprawled across the room, a wide stage directly across from the front door where a band was playing lively music, and a large crowd trickling in as the day was coming to a close.

Keijin found one of the maids and rented the last room available. Thankfully, it had two full size beds and a couch that was big enough for Redbeard to sleep on so he didn't have to take the floor again, though he claimed to prefer it. Sybil chose the bed furthest from the door because it had a vanity screen next to it, and even though she knew that at least one of them had seen her naked to change her into that nightgown, she liked finding privacy wherever she could. Sitting on the soft bed and watching the others settle in, she noticed this room was far nicer than the one they had stayed in at the Crossroads but paled in comparison to the guest rooms of Lord Osric's manor.

Curious about the view, Sybil went to the window and stared down at all the busy people on the street, darting in and out of buildings and selling or buying various wares from booths. She had never seen so many people in one place before, and she found it fascinating to see them going about their lives all as one but independent from each other.

"This is nothing compared to the City of the King," Mordecai told her, leaning up against the window frame and watching the people below with her. "All those busy people with their seemingly busy lives. They believe the world revolves around them and any inconvenience to them is life-threatening."

"I can't quite tell if you pity them or if you're disgusted by them," she said, glancing up at him and seeing his chillingly gray eyes staring down at her.

"Can it not be both?" he asked before gesturing back to the window with his chin. "Look at them. What do you feel when you watch them scurry about?"

"I suppose, mostly curious," she responded with a shrug, looking back. "I have no idea what their lives are like. I've never experienced common people before all this." One woman on the street was carrying a basket full of food in one hand and dragging her stubborn, screaming child behind her with another. "Like, what is it that keeps them moving forward? What are they living for?"

"You're going to be disappointed by their answers," he said with a sigh, turning his back to the window. "Their motivations are only a little above the motivations of animals."

Keijin threw his bag down on the bed and nearly yelled, "Says someone who only spends time around the commonfolk when using them for your own gain. Thinking of them that way only helps you to manipulate them."

Mordecai's eyes flashed over to Keijin, furious.

"And believing there's something more to them helps you play the hero. You think you're doing such grand and noble gestures for these people, but it wouldn't be as rewarding if you let yourself realize just how simply they view you. That connection you feel with them is in your head."

"And you thought nothing of the children we saved from the oni? Or the man and his wife who suffered at the hands of that hag?" Keijin asked, raising his voice.

Sybil started backing away to where Redbeard was standing, surprised to see the two of them suddenly fighting. It was especially shocking that Keijin had been the one to start the fight. Redbeard stared at them, equally confused.

"Of course, I thought something," Mordecai retorted as his irritation caused the lanterns in the room to dim. "As much as you all would like to believe it, I'm not heartless. I'm realistic."

Keijin was opening his mouth to say more when Sybil shouted, "Stop it, both of you."

The room grew uncomfortably silent, as Mordecai and Keijin turned to look at her, their anger slowly fading as she glared at them. Then, in unison, they realized what had just happened and turned away from each other. With everything they had been through so far in their journey, stress and tension had been rising in each of them, and it was just starting to bleed through the cracks. If something didn't change, she knew their group was going to fall apart. Then what would they do?

"How about we all just take a little break?" she asked with a huff. "We've been on the road for a long time, and we're all tired and stressed. Let's just take it easy."

"Not a bad idea," Mordecai grumbled. "I think I'm going to take a walk to get some… well, not fresh air, but air."

"Well, I haven't had a decent drink in days, so I'm heading down to the tavern," Redbeard said, slapping his stomach. "Ya'll can join me, or not. I don't rightly care."

Redbeard left without another word, and Mordecai followed shortly after him, going his own way. Not sure what to do, Sybil stared out the window again. Most of the town was visible from here, but all the buildings seemed to just run together, so she couldn't tell what was what. She could have gone down to the tavern with Redbeard, but the way he was talking, it sounded like it would be better to just give him his space, and there was no way she was following Mordecai to wherever he was heading. Seeing Sybil standing by the window, unsure what to do, Keijin hesitated at the door and turned to her.

"There's a library," he said, his tone back to his normal, charming self. She looked over at him and a smile spread across her face. "Come on, I'll show you where it is."

Out of habit, Keijin extended his arm to escort her, and being a little overwhelmed by all the people and not wanting to offend him, Sybil wrapped her arm around his. He told her about the last time he had been in Taragpass when rock trolls had come down from the mountains because of all the blasting they were doing in the mines below. They had been woken up from their hibernation five years early, so they were reasonably upset. Instead of fighting them, he helped them find a new home in the mountains, one far enough away from Taragpass that the mining and other ruckus from their industries no longer bothered them. In order to lull them back to sleep, he sang them a song, which promptly did the trick.

"I'm no bard," Keijin said with a laugh. "But rock trolls are so bad at music, they didn't even notice my tone-deafness."

"With your skills in fighting, I'm sure you could have easily defeated them. Why go to all that extra trouble?"

"The oath I swore to my order long ago compels me to protect all the people of this land, not just the humans," he answered. "Killing those rock trolls would have only brought further pain to this land, especially since they act as the guardians of the mountains. They had their reasons for attacking the town, reasons I couldn't argue with, and didn't deserve to be slain for them. Sometimes there are creatures of complete evil, like the oni or the hag, which we must deal those fatal blows, but for everything else, it is better to preserve life than take it."

Just as Sybil was about to ask another question, they turned a corner, and Keijin announced that they had arrived at the library. Untouched by any of the surrounding buildings and looking rather out of place from the rest of Taragpass, a white building the size of a small chapel stood before them. On the top half of the building, just over the front door, was the symbol of Minerva, the Goddess of Wisdom and Knowledge, Sybil had seen the librarian at the tower wear around her neck. It was a tree made of knots with branches that stretched upwards and long roots that swerved this way and that underneath the trunk. Of the gods' symbols, it was Sybil's favorite.

"There are some old contacts I need to speak with to settle up on a few things," Keijin informed Sybil as he led her to the front door. "I'll come find you in an hour or two so we can walk back to the inn together."

With that, he turned to leave, and Sybil excitedly headed into the library. The inside was bigger than the outside facade appeared as it was narrow in width but stretched a ways from the front door. There were several rows of bookshelves, but this collection was barely a forth of the tower's collection. Still, it was the first library Sybil had seen in a couple of weeks, so she was just happy to be there. There were two people working in the library, one scribbling on paperwork at the front desk and the other reshelving books, both wearing the same pendant of Minerva around their necks. With how busy the tavern and the town were, it was surprising to see so few people in the library. None of them paid Sybil any mind, though, as she wandered around and eventually pulled a couple books, *The History of Taragpass* and *Varric's Book of Fairy Tales*, off the shelf and headed over to a secluded corner to read them.

Flipping through the book on fairy tales, she came across a tale about the oni and read through it. It talked about how disobedient children would be taken by the oni and made into his stew. The tale sent a shiver up her spine, so she closed the book and turned to *the History of Taragpass*. She learned the town had once been an elven settlement, the last one in the north before the Kingdom of Irminshu made their final push against the elves, sending those who survived to the east and south. Since then, Taragpass had been ruled by the noble class, starting with Lord Eryl, who had been the youngest son of the king three generations ago.

In the corner Sybil was sitting, she could hear a door open to her right, and three hooded people stepped into view, unable to see her from their perspective. They stopped to discuss something in low voices, eyeing the others in the room to make sure they weren't listening. Just in case they looked her way, Sybil disappeared under a spell because she wanted to hear these strangers' secrets.

"Pandyr said more recruits are trickling in by the day," one of the females whispered. "Soon, we'll be strong enough to start our attack."

"Do we really need to start a revolution, Saffra?" the male asked. "Surely, if there are enough people behind us, Lord Maerel will give into our demands. Can't we just sit down and talk with him?"

"We've talked enough with him and his people," the other female said with a hiss. "For too long, our people have suffered and starved while the nobles have lived soft, cushioned lives. It's not just about meeting our demands anymore, it's about removing them from power, whether they decide to go willingly or not."

The male sighed before nodding his head. "You're right. I'm just so nervous about the whole thing."

"Well, get it together," the first female said, clapping him on the arm. "Come on, we've lingered here too long."

As soon as they left the library, Sybil pulled out her notebook and jotted down everything they said. If Leon had truly sent them here to find their own missions to help Taragpass, she might have just stumbled across hers. A jolt of excitement surged through her as Keijin walked through the door, looking for her. She had forgotten about the spell, so she suddenly appeared into view when she removed it. Confused, he came to sit down next to her.

"Do you really hate interacting with people that much?" he asked, being mindful to keep his voice down.

"Only slightly, but that's not why," she told him and handed the notebook over to him.

He read over what she wrote and said, "A revolution? That's a bit extreme."

"If we let it get to that point. Maybe we could find a way to appease both sides or something. The people I overheard seemed pretty adamant about removing the leaders of Taragpass. Maybe we could even remove them ourselves, so no one has to fight."

"This is some pretty serious stuff you've stumbled upon," he remarked, sliding the notebook back over to her. "Lord Maerel is part of the royal family, nearly all the lords of this kingdom are. If we make enemies with him, we could make enemies with every noble in the kingdom, putting targets on our backs. But... if we side with him, it might lead to worse outcomes for the peasants. There's a lot to consider here; we may not want to get wrapped up in all of this."

"But what if this is what Leon wanted me to accomplish here? What if this is the mission I needed to find?" she asked, her voice straining a little.

The idea Sybil had at the cottage of Leon tricking them into getting captured by the hag had hurt her so much that she needed what he said in the letter to be true. She believed Keijin sensed this because of the way he was looking at her, concern and apprehension spread across his face.

When he didn't say anything, she asked, "Should we talk to Redbeard and Mordecai about it?"

Keijin's face contorted into a scowl.

"I have a feeling I know what they would want to do. Redbeard is a man of the people and clearly loves rebel-rousing, and Mordecai would love the opportunity to sink his claws into a noble."

"You make it sound like he's a monster," she noted, her tone softening.

"Am I far off?" he asked. When she frowned at him, he heaved a sigh. "Honestly, I have been trying to figure out what possible reason Leon could have had for bringing Mordecai into the fold of his entire operation. He clearly just sees everyone as tools to manipulate or objects to own."

She didn't say anything for a moment, so he continued.

"And I see the way he looks at you, like you're a prize to be won. He sees you as a way to get more power, through the magic you wield or the position you hold with Leon or both. No matter how much he grows to care about you, those feelings will only come second to his ambitions and greed."

"Why are you saying all of this?"

"Because I've seen the way you look at him, too. You admire him and care for him, and I know he is going to use that against you one day." He sighed and reached over to take her hand. "Mordecai is one of those people who makes you feel like you're getting through to him, like he's becoming a better person. But it's just an act. Just... please be careful around him, okay?"

Sybil wanted to say something, to defend herself, or even Mordecai, in some way, but nothing came to mind. He was right; she did need to be careful. Even though it was clear Mordecai wanted to use her in some way, she couldn't help but feel a growing connection to him.

A librarian pulled her from her thoughts as she approached and informed them that the library would be closing soon. Sybil returned her books and headed outside after Keijin. Their walk back to the inn was silent, a strange heaviness had fallen between them, but as soon as they stepped into the tavern, it faded away.

The band was playing a lively song, and the place had become even more crowded since they left with people sitting around tables, playing games with dice and cards, and drinking copious amounts of ale. Everyone in the room seemed to be having a grand time, especially Redbeard, who was standing on top of the bar, raising a sloshing tankard high in the air and singing along with the lead singer of the band, another dwarf who was dressed in fancy garbs and far cleaner than Redbeard had ever been. Sybil and Keijin both lit up at the sight of their dwarf friend making such a fool of himself in a crowd full of people, his round cheeks rosy with delight. It was heartwarming for Sybil to see him so carefree and happy after the intensity of the past few days.

With smiles on their faces, they joined Redbeard at the bar, sitting near his feet that were thumping along to the music, and Keijin ordered them drinks. The bitter, but slightly sweet, liquid went down smooth and warmed Sybil's belly. Within minutes, the ale started to soothe her in a way she couldn't explain, and liking the sensation, she continued to drink. Other than the drink she sipped on the night they first met Redbeard, she had never consumed ale before and found herself loving it more and more as she continued to drink. Three tankards in, the music began to feel as though it was a part of her, like a heartbeat, and the nervousness she usually felt around a room full of strangers melted away.

Redbeard had moved from the bar to a card table in the middle of the room while Sybil was making her way through the large amount of liquid now sitting in her stomach, and she wanted to join in on his fun. She wandered over to where he was playing with five rather brutish-looking men and women, swaying a little as she did, and watched them play a game she had never seen before as she rested her elbow on Redbeard's shoulder. Each of them had two cards face down in front of them and there were three cards in the middle of the table surrounded by small piles of bronze, silver, and gold coins. After watching them play a couple of rounds, Redbeard winning one of them, Sybil realized she hadn't played, or even knew of, many games, which made her incredibly sad.

"I don't have coin, and I don't know games," was all she was able to mumble when Redbeard asked if she wanted to join them.

Everyone at the table looked up at Sybil like she was crazy, and even Redbeard raised a scruffy, red eyebrow at her. All their faces blurred together for an instant, and she couldn't remember where the bar was until she turned around and wandered over to it. A woman in a red dress was sitting at the end of the bar with one of her girlfriends, and Sybil approached them, her feet struggling to keep up with her. She had black hair with wide curls that fell in every direction over her shoulders and red lips that matched her dress.

"You're pretty," Sybil announced, pointing at her, and gave a giggle before moving on.

The women both watched her with confused frowns as she left. Keijin was still at the bar, several ales in him as well, and was watching the band with his arms spread out along the bar's surface, taking up a couple seats of room. She gave him a wave, and he waved back with a smile. He was an attractive person, probably the most handsome man Sybil had ever seen, and she was going to head back over to him to tell him this when Mordecai suddenly appeared at her side, looking rather miffed.

"You're drunk," he observed glaring down at her. Somehow, she had made it all the way over to the front door, which must have been how he was able to sneak up on her like that.

"And you're bossy and mean," she said, poking him in the shoulder, and was surprised, even in her drunken state, he just let her do that. "But that's okay. We've all got our flaws, right?"

"Come on," he huffed, grabbing her arm. "Let's get you to bed before you pass out in the middle of the tavern and make even more of a fool of yourself than you already have."

"There you go again, telling me what to do," she slurred as they started heading up the stairs, her feet struggling to find some of the steps. Mordecai caught her a couple times, making sure she didn't tumble down the stairs. "You're always telling me what to do, like I don't know what to do. You just looooove telling me what to do."

"Figuring you've never been drunk before, you don't know what to do," he told her, turning her around the corner. "Other times, it's hit or miss."

"So mean," she whispered loudly as he opened the door to their room. "I want to like you, but you make it so hard."

"Thanks for that," he grumbled and moved Sybil next to her bed. "Lie down."

She put her hand on her hip and made what was meant to be a seductive face, but it didn't land well.

"Oh, you'd like that wouldn't you."

"Stop being an ass and just lie down. You're in serious need of rest."

When he said this, Sybil could suddenly feel how true that was. She sat down on the bed and slowly kicked off her boots. He pulled the sheets back and helped her get inside. Once her head was on the pillow, she let out a soft whimper and said, "I don't know how to play games."

"I'll teach you," he said as he sat on the bed next to her.

"Really?" she asked, propping herself up a little.

He rolled his eyes.

"Yes." Pushing her back down, he said, "Now, just go to sleep."

She closed her eyes and laid there silently, suddenly feeling the weight of the ale she drank. The last thing she remembered was his fingers running through her hair, soothing her to sleep.

Redbeard was the first face Sybil saw the next day.

"Here, kiddo, drink this," he said as she struggled to sit up. "You need to rehydrate." The water he gave her was cool and crisp, soothing her aching throat and nauseous belly. "Slow down or all that's gonna come back up."

"I feel awful," she said, clutching her throbbing head.

Redbeard laughed a deep belly laugh and said, "That means you had a grand ol' time last night." He took the cup of water from her. "Come on, let's get some food in you."

Sybil followed him down to the tavern, which, with its mostly empty tables and the lack of music, felt like a completely different place. They found a table away from the other patrons, and when the barmaid came over, Redbeard ordered a ridiculous amount of food.

"Where are Mordecai and Keijin?" she asked after the barmaid left them alone.

"Keijin told us about the discovery you made at the library last night, so they went to see what they could learn about it around town," he answered. "I figured one of us should stay behind and help you through your first hangover, though."

She laughed and said, "I appreciate it." Looking over at him for a moment, she saw the brightness in his eyes and the gentle smile he seemed to always wear when nothing bad was happening. "I meant what I said the other day. You're a really good person, you know that?"

"Good?" he asked with a chuckle. "I'm not so sure about that, at least not in the traditional sense. But I try to do right by people."

"No, you are. You think about others and their needs, making sure everyone's protected and has their fair share. If that's not being a good person, I don't know what is." Sybil thought for a moment before adding, "There's always been this lingering question in my mind, especially now, which has me asking whether what I'm doing is good or bad. I just want to do the right thing, but I don't know how."

"Listen," Redbeard said to her, shaking his head. "People are going to tell you where to go, this path or that, good decisions or bad. But as long as you listen to your heart and follow what it says, you'll be alright."

"Yeah, I suppose that's true," she said, not entirely convinced.

The barmaid, along with two other waiters, returned to their table and laid out the food, the number of plates taking up the whole of the table's surface. Nausea gurgled up Sybil's esophagus as she stared down at all the food, most of it heavy and greasy, but Redbeard assured her she would feel better after putting something on her stomach. Trusting his experience in the matter, she did as he instructed. By the end of the meal, she was stuffed but, just as he advised, felt loads better than she did before.

Despite the dent Redbeard and Sybil made, there was still plenty of food for Keijin and Mordecai when they entered the tavern a bit later. Besides petty complaints and the usual dissatisfaction of commoners, they weren't able to learn anything about a rebellion or a plot against Lord Maerel. The town was struggling with overcrowding and pollution, but that was more to do with the industries there than decisions made by the nobility.

"What do we know about Lord Maerel? What kind of leader is he?" Sybil asked, pulling out her notebook.

"Well, we know he is in his position based on birthright rather than any merit he earned to win over people," Keijin began. "That alone could cause some people to fight against him, especially with more and more settlements in the south electing their own leaders since the War of the Five Queens. People no longer revere those of royal birth as they once did."

"Probably 'cause people've come to realize they're just as fallible as the rest of us. More so, oftentimes, with how spoiled they are with all their gold and servants," Redbeard rambled on. "In my clan, and many clans like it, we pass along titles in the bloodlines insofar as you could prove yourself worthy, prove yourself to be a good leader. That's why they didn't want me as leader in my own clan. I went off on my own path in my youth and left them behind."

"Leaders should also be capable and wise," Mordecai added. "They should know how to give the people just enough to not want to rise up against them and ruthless enough to never even let that thought cross any of their minds."

Their ideas of leadership were all so varied, which helped Sybil better understand just how difficult leading an entire community of people would be. Thinking about this, she decided she wouldn't make a very good leader. She liked doing things her own way and found compromises annoying and a waste of everyone's time. The others sitting at the table, though, would all make great leaders in their own way. It would depend on who they were leading, sure, and whether or not their decisions were morally correct, especially when it came to Mordecai, but they would keep things running as smoothly as possible. Sybil wondered if she would be ready to lead by the time Leon passed the tower down to her.

"I don't know," she said, returning to the conversation. "There must have been something Lord Maerel or his people did to hurt the peasants in some way. The people I overheard last night sounded hateful toward the man, like they wanted him dead."

More and more people started trickling into the tavern as the time approached when most villagers took a break for their midday meal. With the number of people sitting close to the party now, Mordecai suggested they return to their room to discuss this matter in private. Sybil sat in the center of her unmade bed as Keijin and Mordecai, back working together after their fight the night before, sat on the couch with a map of the town on the coffee table in front of them. Redbeard was leaning against Sybil's bed with his arms crossed, staring thoughtfully out the window.

"What if we went back to the library?" Sybil asked. "Those three came out of a back door. Maybe that's where the rebels regularly meet."

"That's an option," Mordecai breathed, eyeing the map closely. "But I think we need to learn more about this Lord Maerel directly."

"And how do you suppose we do that?" Redbeard asked, his head snapping back toward the room.

"Before joining Leon, I had created several persona, many of which have a good deal of renown associated with them," Mordecai explained. "I can infiltrate the estate with one of those personas, getting us all in so we can learn more about Lord Maerel and the way he runs things here."

There was still so much Sybil didn't know about Mordecai's life before Leon found him, and she realized in moment that she wanted to hear all his stories. It was an unexpected realization. Only a week ago, she bubbled with annoyance every time he spoke, but now, she couldn't get enough of what he had to say. Still, knowing his already inflamed ego, she would never dare to tell him that.

Mordecai went on to tell them about a lumber merchant named Render Valkalyn, a wealthy man who had made powerful friends over the years. This Render was not someone who had ever existed, but Mordecai had played him well enough that most nobles accepted his position and fortune without question. For them to enter Lord Maerel's estate, he would pose as Render and the rest of them would have their own personas to accompany him. Sybil would be disguised as Lizlisa Valkalyn, his wife, and Keijin and Redbeard would be their accompanying guards, Samson and Rex, respectively. Mordecai and Sybil would be able to speak privately with Lord Maerel and his wife while Keijin and Redbeard would try to get some information from the other guards or servants.

When Sybil asked about buying disguises from a clothes merchant, Mordecai gave a little laugh, took off his cloak, and said, "No. We're using magic for the disguises."

With a wave of an arm over his body, Mordecai completely changed in front of them. His dark clothes turned into a green tunic with gold trim and brown pants with fine leather boots, his black hair changed to a sandy brown, his light skin turned sun kissed and warm, and his gray eyes became a vibrant green. To Sybil's surprise, he could even change his voice. What once sounded rough and gravely was now smooth and sultry when he talked.

"Now, it's your turn," he said, turning to Sybil as Render.

With a flick of his wrist, the plain blue dress she had on turned to a shimmering silk, the color of the sky. Her hair turned long and blond, and half of it was styled in a braided bun, and her skin became unblemished and matched Mordecai's new persona in color. When she had a chance to look in the mirror while he was casting the spell on the other two, Sybil noticed he had kept her eyes the same. When she turned back around, Keijin and Redbeard looked similar in features, but they were now wearing new sets of armor, better than the minimal armor Redbeard wore and far worse than Keijin's shining armor. The four of them looked the part, but Sybil still had no idea what Mordecai's plan was.

"When a merchant is wealthy enough, they are immediately welcomed into a lord's court in hopes they'll be able to strike a lucrative deal with the merchant," Mordecai explained. "I've never met this Lord Maerel, but in theory, we should be welcomed as soon as we arrive."

"In theory?" she asked.

"Nothing's ever a sure thing," he said with a shrug. "Some lords see themselves above the assistance of merchants. But, at the very least, he won't want to appear rude to someone of my class status in fear of turning other merchants against him."

Redbeard stared down at his disguise and gruffly said, "Okay, let's just get this over with. I feel ridiculous."

By the time they made it to Lord Maerel's estate, it was late afternoon. The estate was on the easternmost side of Taragpass and had a large, stone wall with iron pikes at the top to prevent people from climbing over the wall. They had been made to look more aesthetically pleasing, but all the same, their use was clear. Despite the lack of space within the town for the peasants to live in, Lord Maerel had a lavish, two story home with plenty of lawn that stretched between the outer walls and the walls of the estate. If Sybil was a commoner living there, she would have been at least a little annoyed every time she walked passed this place.

As they made their way over to the estate, Mordecai had instructed Keijin and Redbeard not to speak, as guards were to be seen, not heard, and told Sybil to keep her comments to a minimum unless someone tried to engage in conversation. If that was the case, she had to maintain small talk and not let them venture into topics she knew nothing about. He was probably worried she would be the one to mess all of this up.

The gate was open, the only way in or out of the estate being watched by silent, armed guards, and when Mordecai knocked on the front door, another guard opened it and glared at the strangers before asking what their business was. As he spoke with the guard, explaining how they were passing through and thought to pop in for a visit, Sybil repeated his pseudonym in her head to make sure she didn't slip up. Eventually, the guard stepped aside and let them enter.

The disguised party walked into the large foyer that, with its marble floors and golden trim along the walls and ceilings, was so elegant it was a little hard for Sybil to take in. A butler moved to greet them and asked them to wait there while he fetched Lord Maerel. Several minutes went by before the butler returned with Lord Maerel following slowly behind him, looking bored. He was an older man, nearing his winter years, and had the round face and stocky frame of someone well-fed and inactive.

"Valkalyn, I recognize that name," Lord Maerel said, extending his hand to shake Mordecai's. "You're the lumber merchant? My cousin, Lord Geryl, has spoken highly of you, though he hasn't heard from you in many months."

"Thought I would spend a bit of time on the road before my age caught up with me," Render replied with a laugh. His acting made it easy for Sybil to forget it was really Mordecai under the disguise. "This is my wife, Lizlisa. Fortunately, she has the same wandering heart I do."

"And a great deal of beauty," Lord Maerel said, turning his attention to Sybil. She gave a small curtsy, not sure how else to respond. "Tell me, how does a lumber merchant get his hands on one so fair?"

She forced a laugh and said the first thing that came to her mind. "The heart wants what the heart wants."

"Too true," he said with a smirk before turning his attention back to Render. Once he wasn't looking, Sybil took a deep, steadying breath, nervous about her lack of acting skills. "Well, I was just about to sit down for supper, and my cooks always prepare more than enough, so why don't the two of you join me this evening? Your guards can join the servants for their meal downstairs."

"That sounds like an excellent idea," Render replied, and they followed Lord Maerel into the dining room, leaving Keijin and Redbeard to their side of the plan.

Just as the food was being served in Lord Maerel's dining room, a tired looking woman joined them at the table, a glass of wine already in hand as she entered the room. Back in the inn, Mordecai had mentioned Lord Maerel had a wife, Lady Joylane, who he wanted Sybil to speak with if she could get a moment alone with her. This older woman took her seat to Sybil's left and let out a sigh. Then, Lady Joylane leaned in and asked her, "And who are the two of you?"

"Oh, um, we're the Valkalyn's," Sybil answered shakily. "My husband's a lumber merchant."

"Lumber," Lady Joylane shouted with a laugh, causing the wine to slosh out of her glass. "Well, I suppose we're in for a fascinating evening. Tell me, how is the lumber industry doing?" Every word she spoke was dripping with sarcasm.

"As lucrative as ever," Render responded before quickly changing the subject. "Taragpass appears to be doing well. It's been nearly a decade since I've passed through this way."

"Yes, we've had our ups and downs over the years, but we've managed to keep everything running smoothly," Lord Maerel replied with pride in his voice.

"Despite these ungrateful peasants causing unrest," Lady Joylane muttered as she brought the wine glass to her lips.

Lord Maerel shot a warning glance at his wife before saying, "Yes, well, every lord must navigate the free will of the peasants. These settlements to the south of us have started to convince them it's in their best interest to elect their own leaders. If they only knew the challenges of ruling, they wouldn't be giving us so many problems."

"And how do you plan to deal with this ideology?" Render asked. "As a business owner, I can simply fire those who oppose my ruling and find someone else, but that's not the case for citizens."

"We have our own ways of dealing with them, but never you mind about that," he said and changed the subject to more mundane topics for the rest of the meal.

After dinner, Lord Maerel invited Mordecai to smoke with him in the parlor, leaving Lady Joylane and Sybil to have drinks together in the library. Sybil glanced over at all the books next to her as Lady Joylane poured them both some sort of brown liquid and moved to sit next to her. The liquid burned going down, and Sybil let out a little cough after the first sip.

"You're young," Lady Joylane said, eyeing her up and down. "You'll get used to the taste soon enough. Wives of powerful men must learn to push away our thoughts and inhibitions, and this is one of the best ways to do it."

"Are you unhappy as the lord's wife?" Sybil asked, the question escaping her before she could review it.

Lady Joylane looked at Sybil as if she had called her a whore, and just when she thought Lady Joylane was going to slap her across the face, she let out a laugh.

"Well, aren't we all, my dear? Don't tell me you married your husband, with a purse like his, out of love and the pleasure of his company."

"No… I mean, aren't there a lot of reasons to get married?" she asked, genuinely confused.

"Not for women like us," Lady Joylane said before taking another swig. "I might not look it now, but I used to be a beauty, just like you. Maybe even more so, if you don't mind me saying. And have you ever wondered if you said no to your husband's proposal? I came from a well-respected but financially unstable family, and I knew that rejecting Maerel would have led to my family's ruin. Now, they are prosperous and happy thanks to my sacrifice."

"That's not fair," Sybil breathed with a frown.

The older woman eyed her, and Sybil realized she was not playing the part Mordecai had instructed her to play. It was possible Lady Joylane was starting to see through her, though she hoped she just saw her as naive.

"We were born with an advantage over other women, and it would have been unfair to them if we did not take the opportunities we've been given," she corrected. "That is why these peasants frustrate me so. They are threatening all I have sacrificed for. If they were to overthrow my husband, where would that leave me? If they didn't kill me, too, I would become just like them but rejected due to the life I live now."

"Is there anything you can do to keep that from happening?"

"All I've been able to accomplish is providing reminders of where their place is in all this, showing them that as lord and lady over this land we hold all the power. As your husband expressed, your situation is different. People can choose whether or not to work for your family, but for us, we must establish our authority wherever possible."

"How so?"

"We deal with the rebel rousers, of course," Lady Joylane said with a humorless laugh. "Usually, it's just settled through a warning, but oftentimes it must be so permanently." Unable to control herself, Sybil made a face, and Lady Joylane rolled her eyes. "Oh, don't you dare judge me. I'm sure there are many within your circle who have done the same, perhaps even your husband if the situation called for it."

Their conversation dwindled after that, shifting to complaints Lady Joylane had about her husband, the house staff, and various other people in her life. Sybil's thoughts remained, though, on the reasons she married Lord Maerel and how miserable she seemed. It didn't seem to bother her that Sybil had little to contribute to her conversation. She probably just enjoyed having someone she believed to be close to her equal listen to her complaining. Sybil's heart was overjoyed when the men found them in the library, ready to call it a night.

Mordecai wrapped his arm around Sybil's waist, causing her to blush under her disguise, and bid goodbye to Lord Maerel and Lady Joylane, who had both escorted them to the door, keeping several feet apart from each other. They found Keijin and Redbeard waiting for them in the hallway, and they quickly moved to follow step with each other as they headed outside. Keijin's face was blank, and he stayed silent based on Mordecai's instructions, but Sybil could tell by the way he was clenching his jaw something was wrong.

It wasn't until they were a good distance away from the estate that Keijin finally spoke up and said, "We have a lot to discuss."

Chapter Eight

As soon as the door to their room in the inn was closed, Keijin turned to his companions and said, "The nobles are definitely up to something."

A consistent supporter of the nobles, Keijin appeared genuinely upset by this. Though Sybil didn't know the extent of it, she knew he had close ties with the royal family, and the nobles who extended from them, for several generations.

"When we were dining with the staff, I saw a glimpse of someone being dragged into the back," he continued, rubbing the inside of his palm with his thumb. "They had a hood over their head, but their clothes were clearly of a female commoner. When I asked the maid I was standing near about it, she told me not to ask questions I wouldn't like the answer to."

"Do you think they're killing peasants?" Sybil asked as she put her hand to her chest.

"More likely torturing for information, bringing them back to their estate like that," Mordecai corrected. "If they wanted them dead, they could just hire someone to take them out."

"If that's the case, though, I doubt they're getting out of there alive," Redbeard added, shaking his head.

"But why?" she asked, turning to Mordecai with a frown. "Did you learn anything more from Maerel?"

"He knows there are those who would have him step down from his rule," Mordecai answered. "It annoyed him, but he wasn't particularly upset by it. In fact, he seemed in denial that the people could ever overpower him."

Redbeard plopped down on the couch with a huff and asked, "Well, what'd you guys learn from Joylane? The staff I talked to seemed terrified of her and didn't even want to speak about her, especially around strangers. They acted as though we might be her spies trying to catch them speaking ill against her."

"Joylane definitely has a strong dislike of the peasants," Sybil told them, moving past Mordecai to sit next to Redbeard. "She believes that her marriage to Lord Maerel was a sacrifice, and by wanting to depose her husband, they're a threat to her."

"Provides us with a solid motive," Mordecai pointed out. "And if the peasants are being rounded up, tortured, and killed by the nobles, that would provide them with enough motivation to go to war."

Sybil frowned, taking in all this information.

"But nothing is concrete. We're just working on theories and piecing together the ideas of people we've never met before. It just feels all too… convenient."

"What do you suggest then?" Mordecai asked.

"I think we need to infiltrate the rebels, figure out their side of things and learn their plans, if we can."

"Are you sure we want to get in the middle of this?" Keijin asked, looking at his companions with confliction and concern burning in his eyes. "It's possible we could make this worse for everyone involved."

Sybil knew why he didn't want to get involved. The nobles and the common folk. They had always been two sides of the same coin for him, and choosing a side would be painfully difficult.

"If this rebellion is going to lead to innocent people dying, we need to do something to stop it," she told him. "But this doesn't have to be something we all get involved with, if you want to sit this one out and find another way to help Taragpass, none of us would think less of you for it."

"Speak for yourself," Mordecai grumbled, and she flashed him a seething look.

Keijin took in a deep breath, his pride not easily tarnished by someone like Mordecai, and said, "The contacts I spoke with yesterday informed me of some troubles my skills would be better suited for. Perhaps, for the time being, I can see to those. Of course, if you need any help, I will come straight to your aid."

There was something deeper, something intimate, in the way he said this, looking only at Sybil, but she tried her best to brush off the feeling.

"Thank you," she said. "And we'll make sure we do this right, get all the facts, and not just jump into the middle of something dangerous, like we did before."

Everyone made a face, thinking back to the hag.

"Fine then," Mordecai said, joining Sybil and Redbeard on the couch. "We'll seek out the rebels tomorrow and see what we can learn from them."

Before heading to the library, Mordecai decided it would be useful to teach Sybil how to use her magic to create her own disguises. Wanting to get to the library by nightfall, they were only able to manage her physical features in that time. Sybil was still unable to change her clothes and, wearing the same dress she took from Mary's wardrobe, had used her magic to temporarily become a redhead with bright green eyes and remove the splattering of freckles across her face. Even though it wasn't quite where it needed to be, Sybil felt a great sense of pride looking over the handiwork of her new spell in the mirror. She couldn't help but think of all the possibilities it would allow her to explore in the future.

Keijin had been gone all day, attending to a goblin problem to the west of Taragpass, but Redbeard was still with Sybil and Mordecai, boredly watching their magic lesson for hours in between trips down to the tavern for food. Mordecai provided Redbeard with a new disguise, and because his beard had changed from red to brown, Sybil joked that they would have to change his name.

"Are you ever going to tell us your real name?" she asked him as they were preparing to leave.

"Nope," Redbeard, temporarily known as Brownbeard, said with a huff. "I left that name when I left my clan, and I don't like hearing it. Not gonna to tell you just for you to use it when you want to annoy me most."

"But I would never," Sybil said with a fake gasp. Redbeard glared at her, and she laughed. "Alright then, keep your secrets."

"Stop messing around, and let's go," Mordecai grumbled, acting like an older child who was asked to watch over the little ones.

Without another word, though Sybil had several for him, they headed out the door. Remembering the way was a bit of a struggle for Sybil because all the houses looked the same, but she managed it and was surprised to see there were several people waiting around right outside the library. The lingering group eyed the three adventurers as they entered, both parties probably wondering in the same instant if the other was part of the rebellion.

The library itself was free of patrons, and the librarians had their heads tilted toward books laid out on their desks, paying no mind to anyone. Sybil led Redbeard and Mordecai to the door she had seen the hooded people come out of two days before, and Redbeard gave it a tug. When it didn't budge, he knocked quietly. The door opened only a few inches, and there was a chain between the door and the frame pulled taut to keep the door from getting ripped open.

"Password?" a gruff voice behind the door asked.

Redbeard turned to Sybil, and she shrugged. After a moment, she said, "We're friends with Pandyr."

"Nobody's friends with Pandyr," the voice said.

Coolly, she replied, "He just says that to people he doesn't like. If people knew he was friends with just a few, others would get their feelings hurt."

There was silence for a moment before the door closed. Sybil looked over at Mordecai, who was glaring impatiently at her and made an expression to say, *at least I tried*. But then, the door opened, and a burly man pulled them inside, quickly closing the door behind them.

"You better know, Pandyr," the man grumbled, returning the chain. "He's there in the back with a few of his lieutenants. Meeting'll be starting soon."

The size of the room the man pulled them into surprised Sybil as the library must have stretched twice its size with this addition in the back. The walls were all painted white like the outside, and with no books to muffle sounds, all the voices speaking echoed off the walls, creating a constant sound of muttering and whispering. There were more than a dozen people gathered around here, and it was hard to distinguish one from another. Other than the door they came through, there was only one other door, which must have led to what the guard referred to as "the back" where Pandyr was.

From this point, Sybil felt completely lost. She didn't know what to say or how to act to not get found out by the rebels. Perhaps they would think her and her companions were new recruits, but without another rebel with them, it would be hard to explain what they were doing there. Thankfully, more and more people started trickling in, and it was clear not everyone knew each other because nearly everyone was looking around with part curiosity and part suspicion. As the crowd grew denser, the three adventurers stood closer together until Sybil's back was pressed into Mordecai's chest and Redbeard's shoulder was digging into her upper arm. The more people who arrived, the quieter the room became, everyone slowly starting to anticipate something with bated breath.

The back door opened, turning everyone's heads, and an elven man stepped out with a few people following behind him. Sybil had never met a full-blooded elf before but immediately knew he was one by his sharp features and slightly upturned eyebrows. His skin was like porcelain, clear and beautiful, and his eyes were of a dark green which reminded her of the forest. He was wearing gray leather armor with a green cloak and silver trim with a matching sash around his waist, and his golden blonde hair was pulled back to reveal the pointed tips of his ears. Sybil's eyes followed him across the room as he stood on a small platform against the far wall, unable to recall if she had seen any man more beautiful than him.

"For anyone new here today, I am Pandyr Faywind, and have been a citizen of Taragpass for more than fifty years," he began, his voice deep and inviting. "In that time, I have seen the leadership of our beloved city pass from father to son for generations, despite the understanding of the people or the knowledge of how to lead. When I was a young boy, it was Lord Maerel's grandfather, Lord Eryl, who was lord over this land. He was a good and responsible leader, but his heirs, who we must follow without say, have not cared for this land as Lord Eryl did. In fact, they have actively exploited it for their own gain." The crowd started to perk up with his words, some of the groaning or shouting in agreement. "When we stood up to Lord Maerel years ago, asking for what is fair, what is due to us as those who tend to his land, care for his home, and provide services for his people and guests, he spat in our face, saying we should be grateful for the scraps we have. This is unacceptable."

His eyes landed on Sybil as he said this, and a bolt of nervousness shot through her. She took a deep, steadying breath as he moved his attention elsewhere and continued.

"The more we stood against him, the more he lashed out at our people. We have suffered and lost those we love at his hand, and it is time for this age of tyranny to end. Together we will rise up against the nobles and remove them from their post."

The crowd exploded into a roar of applause and cheers, nearly deafening Sybil in both ears, and she tried to clap and yell to not seem too out of place, but it just wasn't in her nature to do so. Pandyr left the stage, heading toward his office, and a group of people swarmed him, wanting more. Mordecai moved around her as an idea came to him.

"You need to get information from Pandyr directly," he whispered loudly to Sybil through the yelling and other ruckus going on in the room now that the crowd was invigorated by his speech. "We'll split up and work the rest of the crowd while you do."

"And how do you suppose I get close to him?" she asked with a frown, a little annoyed that he was telling her what to do again.

"Think of something. Use your womanly charms," he suggested, vaguely gesturing over her body. "He noticed you during his speech. I'm sure he'll at least give you a moment of his time to get something out of him."

"Well, I'll just do that, then," she said snarkily, returning the gesture over his body.

Sybil's heart pounded as she moved through the crowd of people, heading to where Pandyr was standing near his office. The crowd was swarming Pandyr, so she had to hover around him for a moment, standing right in front of his office door and trying to think of how to get closer and what she was going to say. Sybil was bad at talking to people in the best of circumstances, but she realized Mordecai was onto something when Pandyr's eyes flashed over to her again. A few people were clearly trying their all to get his attention, and their faces fell when he breezed past them and came to stand next to her.

"I've not seen you here before. Welcome," Pandyr said with a warm, charming smile. "How are you finding everything?"

"A little overwhelming," she answered honestly. "There's so much to take in with all the people and your speech."

"I'm sure it is for first time visitors. Tell me, what brings you here today?" he asked, moving closer to her.

"Oh, well, my family's new to town, but the friends I have made so far told me about what was going on. I thought I would at least hear you out."

"Well, I appreciate that," he said, smirking. "What brings your family to Taragpass?"

"Lumber," she answered too quickly, immediately regretting that decision.

As she learned through the mindless chit chat the night before, lumber had not been an industry here for over a decade. He raised his eyebrow when she said this.

"I mean… My father used to be in the lumber business, but we moved here so he could find a job when the foreman fired him. No luck so far."

"I see," he breathed slowly and then straightened. "Say, it's awfully loud in here. Let's step into my office so we can hear each other better."

He didn't give her time to answer before he opened the door and moved her inside. When the door shut, it was as if they had entered an entirely new world because of the sudden silence. The office was small with nothing but a desk, two chairs, and a small bed tucked in the corner. Immediately, his face went from warm and chipper to stern, and just as Sybil had the thought to leave, he pressed his arm up against the door, pinning her to it with his body.

"So who are you really? And don't lie because you're terrible at it," he growled, his warm breath flowing over her face.

Just as Sybil was about to continue with her feeble attempt of espionage, he brought his hand up to her face and little sparkles, like tiny fireflies, fluttered out of his fingers. It was magic, but none she had ever seen before. She could feel her magical disguise fade with this motion, and he seemed surprised to still see a young woman behind the false face. His expression and body loosened, but he kept her between him and the door.

"I'll only ask once more: who are you?"

"Just someone who wants to help," Sybil replied, trying to be as honest as possible without giving too much away. "I overheard something about a revolution when I was reading in the secluded nook the other night, and the idea sounded awful, so I wanted to try to stop it."

Pandyr thought for a moment before saying, "So your plan was to seduce me into giving up the secrets of our rebellion?"

"Seduce?" Sybil couldn't help but laugh, causing his face to twist in frustration. "I wouldn't know the first thing about how to seduce someone. And how sexist of you to assume that I'm some sort of seductress." She took a deep breath to stay her anger. "No, all I wanted to do was see what this whole rebellion was even about. I just wanted to learn more."

"I see," he said, removing his hand from the door. "And what did you plan to use this information for?"

"To decide whether or not to help you. I was sent to Taragpass to help the people in some way, and I've been trying to figure out how."

"And what help could you be to us?"

Sybil smiled sweetly at his ignorance and said, "Loads."

This intrigued him, and he stepped away from her, asking her to take a seat in the chair closest to his desk. Eyeing him as she moved, Sybil did as he asked and flipped her skirt out in front of her as she sat. He moved to his chair and rested his elbows on the desk, ready to conduct business.

"Well, then, have you decided?" he asked, his mossy eyes gleaming. "Or is there more information you seek?"

Sybil leaned forward in her chair and said, "I'm just wondering: why lead the charge in all this?"

Pandyr considered her question, taking a deep breath.

"By no doubt you've noticed I'm an elf. The rarity of my kind in these parts makes it hard to miss," he began, tucking a strand of loose, golden hair behind his pointy ear. "As humans traveled east across our lands, my people were pushed south or forced to leave this continent entirely. When they came here, the last place we called home in the north, we made a deal with them: they could have these lands if they carried on our stewardship of them."

He continued with a humorlessly laugh, "Unfortunately, my people were too trusting and believed the humans when they agreed to their terms. A few of my people stayed behind, my mother and father being among that group to ensure they kept to their end of the bargain. As more of the trees were cut away and the pollution spread throughout the lands, the light in my parents both started to fade, the long lives of elves dwindling in them. Since I was raised in this place, it did not affect me as it did them, and shortly after their deaths ten years ago, I started building my rebellion here."

"I'm really sorry to hear that," Sybil muttered, truly feeling what she said.

"But in addition to my own family being wronged at the hands of the nobles," Pandyr went on with a sigh. "My anger towards them also comes from decades of exploitation and cruelty to countless other families."

Sybil thought for a moment before asking, "Why not leave if it's so terrible here?"

"You've clearly never lived a commoner's life, if you think that the solution to this problem is as simple as leaving," he told her, frowning. "Some have left, sure, those who have the means to, but most of us have to stay. For me, perhaps it's a bit of stubbornness on my part. This was my family's home long before it was settled by the kingdom, and I don't feel like I should have to leave. The nobles should be taking care of the people in their charge."

"Besides poor leadership and pollution, have the nobles ever committed crimes against the people of Taragpass?"

Pandyr eyed Sybil, and she could tell he knew she knew something.

"Over the past year, members of our rebellion have been going missing, never to be heard from again. When city guards investigated, they found nothing. And then when we started our own investigations, there was still nothing." Heaving a sigh, he shook his head and continued. "There's no doubt in my mind the nobles had my people kidnapped to silence them, and I have no hope I will see any of them alive again."

Sybil thought back to Keijin's story of the commoner being dragged into a back room in the lord's estate and asked, "Has anyone gone missing recently?"

"Yes," he replied, that spark of knowing returning to his eyes. "My left-hand lieutenant, Saffra, just yesterday. She was supposed to meet me here last night, and when she didn't show, we went looking for her, again finding nothing."

"What if I could help you find out what happened to her? Would you trust me then?"

Leaning back in his chair, Pandyr thought for a moment. Sybil waited patiently, maintaining eye contact with him to show she was being truthful, and she wasn't intimidated by him.

"Possibly," he breathed.

Tearing a piece of paper out of one of the notebooks in front of him, he scribbled down some information. Sliding it over to her, he said, "Meet me at this address at midnight. And, please, don't bring any friends. A group of people entering her home would draw attention from the neighbors and anyone else who might be watching it."

Sybil took the piece of paper and rose from her chair, his eyes watching every movement she made. Without another word, she read the address, gave a nod, and headed out of his office to find Mordecai and Redbeard. They must have seen her enter the office because they were standing right outside the door, and Mordecai was fuming.

"Have you lost your damn mind?" he asked with a growl, grabbing her by the arm and leading her outside. "I told you to get his attention, not lock yourself up in a room with him."

"Yeah, what if he was some sort of sex criminal?" Redbeard asked, struggling to keep up with the gait Mordecai was setting.

Once they were outside, Mordecai swung Sybil around and looked her over.

"Did he hurt you? Touch you?"

"No," Sybil snarled, feeding off his anger, as she yanked her arm away. "I was getting answers while the two of you were just meandering about. However much you like to believe I'm just a weak little girl, I'm a powerful wizard, and I'll kick your ass if you grab me like that again."

"Uh, we probably shouldn't be having this conversation here," Redbeard said, pointing to her magically inflamed hands. It was still mostly daylight out, so thankfully no one had seen the flames.

Sybil thought the way she had responded to Mordecai would have angered him further, but he had seemed to calm down from it. He was still frowning, but a twinge of a smile was starting to pull at the corner of his lips. For whatever reason, he liked it when she shot back at him, and it made her want to light him on fire all the more. The three companions made it back to the inn unscathed, though, which was more than they could say for Keijin. He was sitting on his bed, continuing his reading of one of the books Sybil brought, with a deep gash across his forehead.

"What happened?" Sybil asked as she moved to his bedside, forgetting her anger toward Mordecai for a moment.

"There were way more goblins than my contacts had anticipated," Keijin replied with a laugh. "Good thing I was there or they wouldn't have made it."

"Why didn't you heal it?" she asked, moving to look at it.

The wound seemed to have been made with a fairly dull blade, more of a bludgeon wound, like running into the corner of a table.

"Used up all my powers in combat," Keijin replied, nonchalantly turning the page. "I'll be able to heal it after some rest." Then, as if he could sense the tension in the room, he looked up at his companions. "What happened at the library?"

"I had a meeting with the rebel leader," Sybil replied before Mordecai or Redbeard could find a way to twist the truth around. "He told me he would let me in on his plans if I met him, alone, at his lieutenant's house tonight. I suspect she's the one you saw being dragged away in the estate."

"Please, tell me you're not planning on going to a secondary location with this creep," Mordecai grumbled. "He might have just let you go at the library because there were so many people, including us, who saw you go in there with him."

"Mordecai's jealous that I made a new friend," she told Keijin with a shrug.

"Why do I bother with her?" Mordecai asked, looking at Redbeard, who shook his head in reply. "Fine, whatever, where's this location?"

Sybil gave them the address, and Keijin pulled out one of the maps to show her where it was in the city. Since none of them thought it was a good idea for her to go alone, they decided they would follow close behind her, staying in the shadows, while she headed there on her own out in the open. Keijin and Redbeard headed down to the tavern for a bite to eat, leaving Sybil alone with Mordecai. After a moment or two of awkward silence, he pulled out a large box from under Keijin's bed and handed it to her.

"What's this?" she asked him, not at all expecting a gift from him.

"Just open it."

Sybil did as he instructed and found brand new robes inside. Instead of white robes with black trim, they were black robes with white trim. The raven sigil she had created for herself when first becoming Leon's apprentice was emblazoned across the chest with silver thread.

"Black doesn't get ruined by bloodstains."

"You bought this for me?" Sybil asked, all the anger and frustration she had felt toward him earlier melting away.

"I was just getting tired of that dress. It doesn't suit you," he explained, his voice going lower as it quieted. "Now, hurry up and change. It's almost midnight."

When Sybil found Pandyr outside of the address he had given her, he gave her a look over, taking in the new robes and staff, and flashed a humorous smile.

"So, you're a wizard, then? Fascinating," he said in a quiet voice, his pale face gleaming in the moonlight. "Come on. Let's head inside before anyone sees."

The house they entered was small, not much bigger than the room at the inn, but it was homey. There was a fireplace in the corner with various kinds of folk art decorating the mantle, and even though her furniture was old, it gave a pleasant and cozy aesthetic to the room. It was clear this place was well-loved by its owner as soon as you entered. The thought that whoever lived here might have been tortured and killed by the nobles caused Sybil stomach to turn.

Pandyr watched as Sybil glanced around the room, waiting to see what she could find. She waved her staff out in front of her, trying to reveal any magic that might have been used there. But there was nothing. Whoever took Saffra must have used natural skills if they even took her from this house at all.

"Is it possible they could have snagged her from the road?" she asked, turning back to Pandyr.

He thought for a moment, his arms crossed over his chest.

"Possibly, but the others who've been taken were taken from their homes. We knew as much because of how things were out of place, but a couple of them had even been taken when their family or friends knew them to be home. It could have been different for Saffra, but I don't see why they would suddenly change their methods."

"Is there anything here that you know of being particularly important to Saffra?"

Pandyr glanced around the room and grabbed one of the pieces of art from the fireplace and handed it over to Sybil.

"Her partner had died in the mines awhile back; this was the last piece of artwork he made her."

Holding it in both hands, Sybil muttered an incantation, but her clairvoyance line only sputtered for a moment, heading out the door, before it vanished.

Gravely, she handed back the artwork and said, "I'm sorry, but... I think she may be dead."

"How do you know?" he asked, his voice dark.

"I can only track people who are still living. But she must have died recently, within a few hours, because my spell worked for an instant."

"Can you just keep casting it so we can track where she died?"

She shook her head and said, "I would wear out after a hundred feet. Besides, I think I might know where her last whereabouts were."

"How? Where?"

Sybil bit her lip, thinking about whether or not to tell him. But she could see the loss for Saffra and his concern for his people on his face, causing her to give in. She told him about her group entering into the lord's estate in disguises and what Keijin saw when he was dining with the servants.

She paused, taking a deep breath and hoping she wasn't shooting herself in the foot.

"It's only a hunch," she told him with a shrug. "A simple guess, but if you were to ask me where I thought your friend ended up, it would be there."

Pandyr went silent, thinking deeply, as he moved to Saffra's table and sat down. He was clearly devastated to learn that one of his lieutenants was dead, but she could also see rage filling up inside of him. Slowly, she joined him at the table, sitting across from him.

"What are your plans?" she asked in a soft voice. "I want to help you, I want to keep innocent people from getting caught in the crossfire, but you need to tell me what you plan to do."

His eyes, which reminded her of the trees outside her window in the tower, stared deep into hers.

Then, he looked away, heaving a sigh, and said, "I suppose you've given me no reason not to trust you, thus far." He looked back at her, his eyes hard. "But if you double cross me in any way, I will not hesitate to kill you or your friends. My mission is too important."

Despite him seeing a glimpse of her power, Pandyr seemed to truly believe that he would be able to kill her if he tried. Perhaps he was far stronger than the common citizen of Taragpass. He had been able to dispel her magical disguise earlier that day, after all. Nervousness shot through her, but she maintained her calm composure.

"Consider myself warned."

Pandyr explained to her they were slowly building an army of rebels to overthrow the guards and military under Lord Maerel's control. They had good numbers at this point, but it was still not enough, especially with his top people getting taken every month or so. Once they were strong enough, he would call upon the people of Taragpass to stand with them and lead them to the lord's estate. Then, Pandyr would demand the lord be punished for his crimes. People would die in this battle, but he believed it would be worth the sacrifice to remove a tyrant from his position.

It was getting late, so he suggested they go their separate ways for the evening. Sybil knew where to find him once she decided how she wanted to help in all this. Just before they headed out the door, Pandyr gently grabbed her forearm to turn her back toward him.

"Why do you want to help me, anyway? You could stop all this by simply letting the nobles know of our plans."

"Because I like helping people, surprisingly enough," she told him, pushing his hand away but staying close to him. "There are too many people in this world who have no one to fight for them. And don't mistake me, I'm not helping you but the people of Taragpass. Your side just happens to be the better side."

"Fair enough," he replied with a grin. "You know, I hope that whatever your overall business here in Taragpass is, it will keep you here for a while. I would truly like to get to know you more."

Sybil felt herself blush a little and said, "Perhaps we'll be able to make that happen."

Just before she made it back to the inn, Mordecai, Keijin, and Redbeard converged with her in the street, all coming from different directions. They had been watching the house the whole time, and Sybil felt good to know they had her back. In their room, she told the others about what Pandyr shared with her and felt conflicted about the whole thing. Keijin might have been right to not get wrapped up in this, but it was too late for her now. Too much had already been done, and she knew too much.

"I don't like the idea of you running around the city with that rebel," Keijin said shortly after Redbeard had fallen asleep, snoring on the couch in the corner of the room. "From what you told me, he might have powers that could prove dangerous to you, despite how far you've come in our journey together."

"What makes you think his motives are entirely altruistic, anyway? It sounds like he's using this rebellion as an opportunity to seize control of the city," Mordecai explained, his voice cold. "It's what I would do in his shoes."

"Not everyone's as hungry for power as you are," Sybil retorted.

"I happen to agree with Mordecai," Keijin said, surprising her. "Most men, most people, are ambitious and greedy. If they see a chance to move up in the world, they often take it."

Sybil thought about this for a moment and said, "Fine. I'll be sure to be mindful of that. But I want to help the rebels and to make sure they succeed in a way that limits the number of casualties. I know I can do both."

Both of them looked at her skeptically, and she glared back at them. They didn't think she could do it. What did they see when they looked at her, Sybil wondered, an overly ambitious child or an incompetent woman? She didn't care anymore. She was going to prove to them that she could do this, but most importantly, she was going to prove it to herself.

Chapter Nine

At his request, sent by one of his rebels, Sybil met Pandyr in his office around midday. Three of his lieutenants were already there when she arrived. Two of them she recognized as the hooded, whispering people from the library that first night in Taragpass. Saffra, it turned out, had been the third who was no longer with them. The other lieutenant in the room was the burly man who had allowed Sybil's party into the meeting the night before, and he eyed her suspiciously when she walked in. Pandyr stood behind his desk, looking at a list of names. His eyes were gleaming, and there was a small smile on his face. It was hard not to regard him as handsome, but it was more than that. His presence inspired confidence, and his eyes showed wisdom.

"Our army grows ever stronger with each passing day," Pandyr said to his lieutenants before putting down the paper. "I foresee us being ready to launch our plan by the end of the week."

"So soon?" the nervous male asked. "Shouldn't we do more to ready the people?"

Pandyr stared at his lieutenant with stern eyes.

"The longer we wait, the more likely the nobles will learn what we're planning. Saffra was strong and would never have revealed any of our secrets, despite whatever horrors they threw at her, but some of our people, some of you, are not that strong." The male next to Sybil shrank with Pandyr's words. "No, in three days' time, we will present our demonstration to the people and begin our assault on the lord's estate. Ready your men. Dismissed."

The three lieutenants left without another word, leaving Pandyr and Sybil alone. She was in the middle of the room, standing awkwardly and thinking about what he just told his people. He studied her for a moment and said, "Do you have something you wish to share? You can speak candidly with me."

"I just don't think we should lead a charge on the lord's estate, at least not a full frontal one. The military guards inside the gate will have the advantage, and it could cost unnecessary bloodshed," she explained, moving toward his desk. "Instead, we should use the rebels and crowds to draw the attention away from the lord's estate, reducing their manpower to a minimum. They will still have a guard there to protect the lord and lady, as they will likely hold themselves up until the fighting stops, but that's why we'll take a small team that will sneak into the building to get to them."

"I don't see how this prevents lost lives," he replied, shaking his head. "There will still be fighting."

"The rebels follow your command. If the numbers are as good as you say they are, they will overwhelm the lord's forces, and you can order them not to kill, only to incapacitate the guards."

He thought for a moment, rounding the desk to stand in front of her, and smiled. "You're brilliant, you know that?"

"I've had an inclination," Sybil said with a shrug.

Something changed in Pandyr's eyes as he stared down at her, and his entire body seemed to relax. He reached out and grabbed a lock of her hair and ran it through his fingers. Her scalp tingled at this, and Sybil felt herself drifting toward him. Pandyr leaned closer to her, and she could feel his breath on her cheek like a summer breeze.

"There's something about you; I haven't been able to get you out of my head since we met," he said in barely a whisper. "It's like I was meant to find you."

"I think," Sybil replied, trying to keep her breathing steady. "That I technically found you."

"Hmm...that you did," he noted with a grin.

Pandyr pressed his soft, warm lips to hers. He smelled of oak trees and warm spices, and the scent of campfire smoke lingered on his clothes. Overcome with desire, Sybil moved into him, her lips following his rhythm. As her heart rate increased, his passion for her grew like a stoked fire. Despite the smoothness of his lips, Sybil could feel the rough calluses of his hands as one moved around the nap of her neck and another down her arm. She hesitated to touch him, not knowing what the right thing to do was, until deciding to rest them on his firm chest where she could feel the thumping of his equally racing heart.

Sybil's entire body was shaking, and she could feel her knees grow weak, threatening to topple out from under her. Pandyr moved his hands around her so he could press their bodies closer. When his fingers started to tug at the laces that ran down her back, keeping the outer part of her robe in place, panic shot through her. She leaned away from him and pressed her hands more firmly into his chest to keep a space between them. The thought of what might come next terrified her, but she didn't understand why.

"I'm sorry," she breathed. "I'm just not ready for that. Not yet, at least."

Thinking this would upset him, it surprised Sybil to see him smile.

"I understand," he replied, smoothing out his tunic. "We only just met, and these things take time. As an elf, with all the time in the world, waiting doesn't bother me."

"Thank you for understanding," she said, lowering her hands.

Pandyr nodded and gently ran his hand up and down her arm, thinking.

"How about I take you somewhere for a meal, and we can get to know each other better?" he suggested. "It would be a nice change of pace to spend time with someone who I converse with about matters beyond this rebellion."

Sybil smiled and said, "I would like that very much."

When Sybil entered the room she shared with her companions later that day, she found Mordecai sitting on Keijin's bed reading a book. He looked up at her with a frown and asked, "Where have you been?"

"Never you mind," she told him, sitting down on her bed and kicking off her boots.

Mordecai made a noise of discontent before closing his book and saying, "You're letting your emotions get the better of you again. We're here for a short time. What do you think is going to come from you running around with that rebel leader?"

"I'm not in the mood for one of your lectures. This is none of your business."

"I'm not lecturing you; I'm warning you," he growled. "And it is my business. However much we dislike it, Leon assigned us to work together. If you get yourself into a mess you can't get yourself out of, I'm going to have to come in after you."

"Just admit that you're jealous of him," she said, crossing her arms.

Mordecai's face contorted until there was nothing but spite left in it.

"Jealous? Of him?" he growled. "How could I be? You're nothing but a child, a little girl who does not understand the weight of responsibilities which have inconceivably been put on your shoulders. Your emotions consume you, and it will be your undoing. And when that happens, I'll be there to pick up the pieces and reap the rewards of my loyalty."

"So this has been your plan the whole time?" she asked, raising her voice. "Then why help me? Why teach me?"

"Because for a time, you were proving to be useful, and I wanted to see what your capabilities were," he said and then laughed. "But now I know you'll only be as powerful as your heart allows you to be. It's sad, really."

"If I'm so much weaker, how was I able to resist Haborym and you weren't?"

His anger quickly transitioned into shock.

"What?"

"When the hag was torturing me, before Shuheyr came to my aid, Haborym found me and offered to save me from the hag if I submitted to him," she said, feeling the weight of her words build. "When I rejected him, that's when Shuheyr found me."

"I was a child, a slave, when Haborym found me," he said in barely a whisper as the room around them began to darken. "It wasn't the same."

"And yet you just called me a child, and practically called me a slave to my emotions," she shot back, glaring up at him. "So what other excuses do you wish to throw at me?"

The room grew ever darker as Mordecai's rage started seeping out of him, and Sybil thought he was going to strike her. Instead, all the lanterns in the room exploded, sending shards of glass across the floor. She stared at him, or at least what she could see through the shroud, scared and surprised at his outburst. Letting out what was a mix of a growl and a yell, he stormed out of the room, just as Redbeard was entering. Redbeard stumbled a little, trying to get out of Mordecai's way, and looked at Sybil with confusion.

"What crawled up his butt?" Redbeard asked, looking around at all the broken glass.

Sybil laid back on the bed with a huff and said, "Emotions."

A couple of days went by, and in addition to rarely seeing Keijin, Mordecai was nowhere to be found. When Sybil wasn't at the library with Pandyr, she and Redbeard spent a good deal of time together, eating their meals together and talking in the evenings before heading to bed. There was a knock on their door around midday, just before luncheon, and Sybil opened it to find Pandyr standing there.

Redbeard jumped up from the couch when he saw Pandyr and asked, "What the hell are you doing here?" Sybil turned to Redbeard, surprised to see him so furious at Pandyr. "Did you follow Sybil here?"

"One of my men saw you in the tavern yesterday," Pandyr explained coolly, standing in the doorway. "When I inquired about a young woman traveling with a dwarf, they pointed me in the direction of your room. I wasn't stalking you."

Redbeard deflated a little but stayed standing with his shoulders squared, so Sybil turned to him and said, "It's alright."

"Fine, whatever," Redbeard huffed before returning to the couch.

"Would you like to go for a walk?" Pandyr said, unbothered by Redbeard's outburst.

Sybil glanced over at Redbeard, who was doing his best to silently show how much he disapproved of Pandyr, and said, "I would love to."

Pandyr walked with Sybil for some time, heading away from the bustling center of the town, and they eventually reached a small patch of land with a thick bunching of trees. He led her to the middle of it where there was a small clearing just large enough for them to sit comfortably together. Even though from this spot it felt like they were in the middle of the woods, she could still hear the constant hum of noise coming from Taragpass.

"I often come here to clear my mind," Pandyr said, looking up at the tree branches above that covered the sky. "I've never brought someone here before, though. I've never met someone who could understand my connection to nature and the magic running between me and it, but I thought you might."

"Your magic stems from nature?" Sybil asked, curious. "I've heard of spellcasters like you, but I've never had the opportunity to meet one. There must be so much pleasure that comes from communicating with the natural world and knowing your magic is your own."

"You don't feel connected with your magic?"

"In a way, I do. But it's something I had to develop, something I had to grasp from countless hours of studying," she explained. "Even after decades of practice, I don't think I'll ever know what it feels like to have magic in my blood, to be directly connected to the Mirrored."

She had only read about it in books, but she knew a great deal about the Mirror and how it was the source of magic for all who wielded it. It was a place of pure magic, and many theorized it was the remnant of one of the Old Gods who wanted gifted magic to mortals.

"The Mirrored can be a dangerous place," he said with a frown. "It might be better to wield magic without that connection."

Sybil remembered the stories the nightmarish creatures that roamed in the Mirrored. Decades ago now, one of the mage colleges in the Southern Kingdoms was overrun with these creatures when a student broke the veil between the mortal world and the Mirrored. It didn't end well.

"What does your magic feel like?" she asked, wanting to change the subject.

Pandyr smiled as he reached up his hand, his fingers sparkling with magic, and the trees around them grew thicker and their leaves more vibrant. The number of trees he was able to control with this seemingly simple spell gave her a better understanding of how powerful a magic wielder he actually was.

"It feels... like home." Seeing the confusion on Sybil's face from the corner of his eye, he laughed. "I received my magic from my ancestors. They lived in these lands for centuries, caring for it as much as it did for them." Lowering his hands, he looked at her with sad eyes. "When I was a child, my mother would explain in sorrow how this land was settled upon and used up for lumber and materials. This grove is the only thing left of the forest that once prospered here. Even though I feel at home here and with my magic, it also pains me to know this is all that's left."

"I'm so sorry about what happened to your people, your parents," she told him, knowing but not understanding the pain of the elves. "To have suffered a loss like that and still have to live under the people responsible."

"Yes," his voice went grave as his eyes moved to the ground. "I lived with my own grief and rage for a long time until I found comrades who I could relate my sorrows to. Eventually, we used our hurt to fuel our efforts, to channel it productively."

Thinking back to her conversation with Keijin and Mordecai the other day, Sybil asked, "Do you intend to lead in Lord Maerel's absence? Is your plan to restore Taragpass to what it was to your ancestors?"

"If the people want me to lead them, then that is what I shall do," he replied. "With no better prospects before them, though, it seems fairly likely they will select me. And while I'll ensure this land is taken care of, I don't believe I could restore Taragpass to what it once was without removing a lot of people from their homes. But there are greater things this place could become. It's better to look to the future than the past, anyway."

Pandyr placed his hand on Sybil's, making her smile. But the thought of the rebellion returned to her along with the concern she had for his plan and the people involved in it, making her face fall.

"What's the matter?" he asked, noticing the sudden change in her expression.

"There's something that's been bugging me about the nobles since the night we had infiltrated their estate," she said, still lost in her thoughts.

"And what's that?"

"It's just... we don't know who's directly responsible for all this. We can make educated guesses based on what we saw and learned, but the only way to be sure is to kill all of them. I'm not sure I'm okay with that."

"It can be hard," Pandyr said. "But sometimes sacrifices must be made to make change for the better."

"But if there's a way around it, shouldn't we take it?"

"What are you asking of me, my dear?" he asked sweetly, brushing a strand of hair behind her ear.

"I want to go in as part of your strike team," she replied, trying to ignore the goosebumps that followed his touch. "In fact, I want to get ahead of the strike team and learn what I can from the nobles and their servants. Then, once I know for sure who is behind the kidnappings and attacks, we can take the necessary steps to bring justice to them. For the rest, we can just send them on their way, banishing them from Taragpass."

Pandyr considered this for a moment before agreeing.

"If you believe you are able to do all these things, then I'll allow it. But with fighting going on, I'll only give you a small window of time to do what you need to do before I head in after you to end things."

"Hopefully, a small window is all I'll need."

"Good," Pandyr breathed. "Well, we best be getting back so I can inform my lieutenants of this new plan."

With the rebellion being only a day away and Mordecai still nowhere to be found, Sybil's nerves were starting to get the better of her. As much as she could in their room, she practiced her spells and retraced her steps through the lord's estate. Without Mordecai, she would have to recreate her disguise on her own and pray to the gods she got it right. Keijin entered their room as she was practicing the spell and watched her struggle to change her old dress to finer fabric.

"You're really going through with this, huh?" he asked after a while.

"It's the right thing to do," she said, growing frustrated. "I've already ensured as few people will die in the fighting tomorrow as possible… I just need to make sure the same happens in the estate."

"Sorry if this is overstepping, but this doesn't have anything to do with the beautiful rebel leader you've been spending so much time with, is it?" he asked, sitting on the bed next to her.

Sybil turned to him, ready to verbally jump him for making such a rash insinuation, but then she realized she wasn't entirely sure. Frowning, she looked away from him and said, "It isn't like that. I wanted to help before I met Pandyr. If he has anything to do with my motivations now, it only enhances what I already felt."

Keijin took her hand, his face apologetic, and pulled something out of his pocket and said, "Here, take this. If things get out of hand, if you need help, please use it." The small blue gem he put into her hand was a messenger stone, a magical object connected to another identical one, allowing the users to communicate over several miles. "Sometimes we enter situations, and we think we have it all figured out. When something changes that we don't expect, it's good to have options."

She thanked him, staring down at the stone, and then glanced back up at him.

"Do you know where Mordecai is?"

"Not a clue," he said. "But I have a feeling he hasn't wandered off too far. Redbeard told me about the fight you had with him, and I saw the aftermath of it with the lanterns. Maybe he just needed some time to cool off."

"Yeah, maybe," she breathed, rubbing the messenger stone in her hand as she thought.

"He'll rejoin us when he's ready," Keijin assured her. "And it's probably better for all of us he stays away until then."

The morning of the revolution, Sybil made her way over to the town square, wearing her dress with her wand tucked secretly into a slit she made in the skirt. A crowd started gathering, being directed by some familiar faces of the rebels she had encountered over the past few days. She stood on the edge of the square, by the road leading the lord's house, and watched as more and more people filled the area. Then, Pandyr stepped up onto the fountain in the middle of the square, looking out among the people, and his eyes landed on Sybil for a moment. She nodded, smiling at him, and even though he didn't smile back, she could see the joy in his eyes when he looked at her. That joy turned to triumph and determination as his eyes moved back to the crowd.

"People of Taragpass," he began, his voice steady and booming and his porcelain skin and golden hair gleaming in the morning sun. "Today is the day we take back our fine city from the hands of the nobles. For too long, have we lived under their feet, eating their scraps, and cleaning up their messes. Well, I say, no longer!"

To Sybil's surprise, the crowd was already behind him, most of them shouting out in agreement to Pandyr's call to action. The guards near her were starting to approach, and she knew she would have to be on her way. Still hearing the speech echoing off the buildings, she started to run toward the estate with the skirt of her dress hiked up to keep from tripping.

"We will show the nobles that as a people we are strong," Pandyr continued, his voice growing fainter as Sybil ran. "And their reign will end today."

Once she was out of earshot and away from any bystanders, Sybil pulled out her wand and performed the spell to change her appearance. Concentrating with all her might, she was able to do it perfectly, turning everything the right texture and shade, leaving her eyes just as Mordecai did. By the time she made it to the lord's estate, she was out of breath but looked the part. In fact, she realized she could use her exhaustion to enhance her acting, which needed all the help it could get. As the guard opened the door, she fell into his arms with a dramatic gasp for air, causing the guard to stare down at her with wide eyes and an open mouth as he held her there.

"Oh, thank the gods I made it," she said in a panicked, breathy voice. "The peasants… they're revolting."

The guard nearly dropped her out of fear but managed to help her upright just in time for a butler and maid to rush to their side. He repeated to them what Sybil said, causing the maid to gasp and the butler's face to turn white. The butler told the maid to inform the lord and lady as well as the rest of the staff, and the maid hurried off to do as instructed. Knowing Sybil as one of the lord's guests, the butler escorted her to safety, leading her down through the servant quarters and into the basement. They walked through a cellar with barrels of wine and other stored goods, and he stopped at a back door.

"The lord and lady's safe room," he said, as if he was presenting the grand ballroom. "They will join you down here shortly to wait out this terrible mess."

The butler closed the door behind him, leaving Sybil alone in this dark, underground room. It was small and empty except for a bench on the far end of the room and lanterns spread out every few feet on the walls. Using her wand, she quickly lit the lanterns, putting it back into the slit in her skirt right as Lord Maerel and Lady Joylane came into the room. Joylane immediately moved to hug her.

"Oh, my dear Lizlisa," she said with a cry. "I'm so glad to see you unharmed. But where is your husband?"

"I was on my way to find him when the peasants started gathering in the square," Sybil answered, pretending to still be frightened. "When I heard their terrible words, I came running here right away, knowing you would keep me safe."

Lord Maerel looked confused, almost stunned, and stayed silent as he paced back and forth in the room.

"These damn, ungrateful peasants," Joylane hissed. "If we survive this, we will cleanse this city of them."

"Joy, please," Lord Maerel said, bringing his multi-ringed hand up to his chest. "If we can manage a conversation with their leader, we could meet their demands and end this whole mess peacefully."

"No, they get nothing from us. What we have is ours and no one else's," Joylane nearly screamed at her husband. "They should know their place."

An explosion rang out, shaking the wall around them and causing dust and dirt to fall on their heads. Lord Maerel cried out, "Dear gods, they've breached the walls."

Sybil turned to the nobles, running out of time, and said, "You need to listen to me. They're planning to kill both of you because they believe you've been kidnapping, torturing, and killing their people. If I can prove that not to be true, I can convince them to let you live, but I need your help."

"Lizlisa, what are you saying?" Joylane asked, clutching the wall next to her.

"My name isn't Lizlisa but Sybil," she replied. "I'm a wizard sent to help aid Taragpass in its time of need, and I need you to cooperate with me, so I have enough information to give them a reason to spare your life."

"You know these rebels?" Lord Maerel asked.

"Yes, I infiltrated their ranks to learn of their plans so I could keep things from turning into a bloodbath."

Lord Maerel's face was empty as he asked, "What do you need of us?"

"I need you to let me read your mind," Sybil said, pulling out her wand.

"What?" Lady Joylane asked in both shock and fury.

Sybil used her wand to reveal what she truly looked like and tore her dress off to reveal her black robes underneath.

"With my divination magic, I can enter the minds of those who let me in. Well, actually, I can enter the minds of whoever I'm near, but those who resist don't usually survive."

"Is that a threat?" Lord Maerel asked, backing away.

"No," she said, looking over at him, annoyed. "If you don't let me in and fail to provide me with proof of your innocence, then you will simply die at the hands of the rebels. I wouldn't kill you myself."

"The audacity, how dare you ask such a thing," Joylane spat.

"I'll do it," Lord Maerel said to both of their surprise. "Search my mind, you'll see I've done nothing to the peasants. I've not been the best leader, but I certainly would never try to hurt my own people."

With no time to lose, Sybil placed her hand on Lord Maerel's head and searched deep into his mind. There was nothing about the peasants, other than the small interactions he had with them over the years. Most of his days were spent at the estate or hunting in the nearby forest. He was not a malicious and dangerous leader, just a clueless and careless one. The speed at which Sybil searched his mind had been so much of a strain on them both their noses had started bleeding.

When Sybil turned to Joylane, wiping her nose, Joylane frowned, contorting her face into an ugly expression, and shrieked, "You will not use your magic on me, witch. I have committed no crimes; I have only performed my duties as lady over these lands. It's not my fault my fat oaf of a husband never had the gall to stand up to these peasants."

Just then, there came a banging on the door. Pandyr and his strike team had already made it through the estate. Sybil wiped her nose, looked over at Joylane with spite, knowing full well these crimes were committed by her alone, and said, "Your time as lady over this land is over."

The door came flying toward them, and Sybil deflected it with a spell, sending it crashing against the wall to her left. Pandyr stood there, holding a bloodied shortsword, with four of his people standing around him.

"You really can make your way into anywhere, can't you?" he asked Sybil, impressed. "Now, step aside so I can deal with these nobles."

"Wait, let's take a moment to talk about this," she said with her hands held out and her voice straining.

From the corner of her eye, Sybil watched as Joylane pulled a dagger from her belt, the blade flashing in the lantern light. Sybil only had time to turn her head as Joylane lunged toward Pandyr, and yelled, "Die, you filthy peasants."

Pandyr was quicker to react. He waved his hand, magic sparkling from his arm, and blew Joylane back with a gust of wind just before she was able to stab him. Stepping forward, he jabbed his sword toward her, catching Joylane in the stomach. Sybil jumped at this, horrified to see his blade cut into the woman. Letting out a cry of pain, Joylane crumbled to the floor and went still.

Pandyr started moving toward Lord Maerel, the blade dripping with his wife's blood, but Sybil stepped in front of him.

"Stand aside," he said in a sort of growl, his eyes empty of the kindness and joy they once had. This was a totally different person from the Pandyr she had come to know over the past week.

"Not him. I've searched every inch of his mind, and he's never committed any of the crimes you accuse him of. Joylane must have been the one behind it all. Just let Maerel leave, and you can claim the city for the people."

"Don't you get it?" Pandyr asked, his voice going cold. "With Maerel alive, he still has a claim to this land. There are people here who still support him, and he has brothers and cousins who will provide men for his armies to take back the land from us. The revolution would have been for nothing, if Maerel lives."

"Please, Pandyr," she begged, hoping that the time they had shared together counted for something. "There has to be another way. An innocent man, who is only in this position because he was obligated by blood to fill it, doesn't have to die today."

"Sybil, you're kind and smart and beautiful, but you're also naive," he breathed, a darkness looming on his face. "I'll only tell you once more: stand aside."

How did she not see this malice dripping from Pandyr's heart before? He wanted Lord Maerel dead, no matter what, because he wanted power over this land, the land of his ancestors, whether or not his intentions were good. What Mordecai had said was true. Sybil had let her emotions get the better of her, and now she had to choose between siding with the innocent and siding with one she might have come to love.

Pulling out her wand, Sybil picked a side.

For a moment, Pandyr just stared at her wand, which was pointed at him, his expression void of surprise. Then, he lunged at her with his short sword, and she moved out of the way, hitting him in the side with a blast of fire, the flames singeing his skin and clothes. The other rebels kept a safe distance, their eyes wide as they watched the fight. Like most common folk, none of them seemed familiar with magical combat. He spun around and threw his sword in her direction. Just above her right shoulder, it stabbed into the wall behind her, and she let out a gasp. While he was unarmed, she used the window of opportunity to recite an incantation, creating a protective barrier around Maerel, making him lightly glow. As she did this, Pandyr drew a dagger from his boot and threw it at her, this time hitting his mark. She let out a yelp as the blade pierced into her belly, but then, she reached up and brought down the ceiling in the spot above him. Even though he was able to move out of the way of most of it, some cobblestone smashed into him, leaving him dazed for a moment. While she removed the dagger and put a ward over the wound to stall the bleeding, he extended his hands out, causing the earth below her to shake.

Vines started appearing through the floors and walls, rapidly enveloping Sybil, their rough surfaces rubbing painfully against her skin.

Within seconds, she was trapped by the vines, unable to move any of her limbs. Her breath quickened as panic started to rise in her chest. She tried reaching for the messenger stone Keijin had given her, but she couldn't reach where she stashed it in her boot.

"It's a pity," Pandyr said, brushing some dust off his shoulder. "I thought we really had something. You could have helped me turn Taragpass into something beautiful."

With Sybil secure, Pandyr turned his attention to Maerel and pulled his shortsword from the wall. Twisting her palm away from her, Sybil was able to burn through the vines just enough to allow her to extend her hand a couple inches and reach into Pandyr's mind. Fighting against her, Pandyr dropped his sword and fell to his knees, letting out groans with his struggle. She could see flashes of memories, but because of his resistance, she couldn't place them in time. There was a beautiful elven woman, with hair and eyes which matched Pandyr's, who appeared in various places, and Sybil figured it must have been his mother.

"Get out," she heard him groan, but she just pushed deeper.

This felt different than the times she used this spell before, as if she understood this part of her magic better now, and she could control it and navigate it more easily. Pandyr's nose was starting to bleed, and the vines he had wrapped around her started to recede back into the earth. Once Sybil was free, she let him go, causing him to topple to the floor. He was unconscious but still alive.

The other rebels had run off in the middle of the fight, but one remained, and he was slowly clapping. Sybil's eyes landed on him, finding his display of sarcasm familiar, and as he started walking toward her, he waved an arm over his body, revealing the hood of a black cloak, at first, and then Mordecai's amused smile.

Picking up Pandyr's sword, she pointed it at Mordecai, and said, "You're an ass."

"I knew you could handle it," he replied, in his usual gravely tone. "I was just here in case you did something stupid."

The wound in Sybil's side twinged, causing her to wince. It wasn't in a vital spot, she had plenty of time to find Keijin so he could heal her, but it still hurt terribly. The ward had worn off, and blood was getting everywhere, but at least it wasn't going to stain her new, black robes.

"Yes, well, I'm not feeling particularly smart right now."

Mordecai pulled Lord Maerel to his feet, and they helped her hobble out of the basement. Both Joylane's body and the unconscious Pandyr were lying on the floor, and Lord Maerel locked it just to be sure the rebel leader couldn't escape before the guards could arrive. Once they were in the main foyer, a few soldiers standing close by, Lord Maerel asked Sybil what he should do with Pandyr.

Sybil thought of his beautiful face and the passion he had shown her as sadness washed over her. If he had been true of heart like he had led her to believe, would they have been anything more than a fleeting romance? After a moment, she decided that no, there had never been a future between them, and for some reason, that's what hurt the most.

"If you kill him, you'll make him a martyr to the people," she explained. "But he must pay for his crimes, even if what he did was out of his own idea of justice."

Lord Maerel shook his head.

"I never knew Joylane would've been capable of committing such terrible atrocities… or that she hated her life with me as much as she did."

"This just goes to show how important it is for you to care for all those in and around your life. As lord, you're responsible for the people's happiness, so you must constantly be working toward that," Sybil told him.

"Are you sure you don't want to lead Taragpass, instead?" Maerel asked with a laugh.

"By the gods, no," she said with a twisted smile, ignoring the twinges of pain in her side. Then, her eyes met Mordecai's. "Besides, I have responsibilities waiting for me elsewhere."

After bidding what Sybil hoped was a long farewell to Lord Maerel, Mordecai helped her back to the inn where Keijin and Redbeard found them. They took her up to their room, and she was healed within the hour. It was hard to tell if she had helped the people of Taragpass at all, or if she might have doomed them for an even worse future, but she felt good about the decisions she made, even if they didn't turn out how she wanted them.

That evening, Sybil laid in bed, fully healed by Keijin, listening to the usual merriment of the tavern downstairs and thinking about her short time with Pandyr. She wondered what would become of him now he was a prisoner and an enemy of the royal family and if their paths would ever cross again. She decided to do her best to forget about him, at least the last day of knowing him, and not dwell on his poor decisions. It was something she did well, pushing away painful thoughts and memories.

Despite the noise below her, Sybil was starting to drift off to sleep when she heard footsteps approach the door and the sound of paper sliding under it. Looking over, she saw another envelope made of the same stationary Leon had sent to them previously. Both relieved and nervous, she picked it up and opened its contents.

Dear adventurers,

The town of Taragpass is far better off for you being there, and I foresee a prosperous future for it and its people. Now it is time for you to venture off to a new settlement in need of your help. Blackridge is a small town, newly established, but brimming with promise. A dark shadow has fallen over their land and people have been brutally attacked by what can only be assumed is some sort of creature. I want the four of you to go there, find out what has been attacking its people, and put a stop to it, if you can.

-Leon

Just as she finished reading it, the door swung open, nearly hitting her in the face. She jumped back and frowned at Mordecai as he walked in.

"What?" he asked, and she handed him the letter. He read it over and sighed. "Thank the gods, I hate this place."

Chapter Ten

The party was glad to put Taragpass behind them. It had been a long seven days and an even longer journey thus far. Sybil hoped they would return to Gibbous Tower after they defeated whatever this monster was in Blackridge. Even if it was for a short time, she could use a bit of rest. But until then, it was a two-days ride to Blackridge from Taragpass, and they would have to spend however much time needed to solve this monster issue. She had to steel herself for whatever lay ahead.

The road was easy to travel on, though, and feeling much more confident in her riding abilities, Sybil cantered up to Mordecai with a smirk to show off how well she was doing. He rolled his eyes and said, "Congratulations, you can do what people have been able to do for centuries."

"Thanks," she said, deciding to deflect his sarcasm. "So, had you been stalking me the whole time or just that morning?"

"Just that morning," he answered, looking annoyed. "If you must know, I had taken up a mission of my own while you were galivanting around with that rebel."

"Oh?"

"The children in the orphanage looked malnourished so I might have… convinced some of the gentry to donate money to make sure the children were better cared for," he explained and then noticed that Sybil was smiling at him. "Stop that."

"Very well," she breathed, looking away. After a moment, she said, "By the way, I wanted to apologize for what I said the other night. It wasn't fair to compare your situation to mine."

"There's nothing to apologize for," he said flatly.

"It's just… I wanted to make sure things are okay between us."

Mordecai's eyes flashed over to her, and she could see a coldness in them.

"Somehow along our journey, you have come to believe we're friends, but we're not. We're associates, colleagues, our relationship only goes as far as Leon requests it. Stop being such a child about everything."

Mordecai kicked his horse and moved up to be in front of Keijin and Redbeard, leaving Sybil stunned at the back of the party. So that's how he wanted it to be then? Even though it seemed like they had been growing close, all of that meant nothing to him. But then, she wondered if what she said to him before affected him more than he let on. Instead of trying to press the issue, she decided it would be best to leave him alone for the time being. He was much like a cat and would return to her when he was ready, not a moment before.

Instead of camping out, Keijin had another place in mind for where they would spend the night. A road to a small hamlet appeared just as the sun was beginning to set, and Keijin led his companions to one of the four houses. The house was small, but big enough for a family. It looked practically identical to the other houses in the hamlet, except this one was covered in flowers and beautiful artwork, adding an array of colors over its bare wood facade.

Keijin knocked on the door in a specific rhythm, and a few moments later, an elderly lady, perhaps in her late eighties or early nineties, opened the door. She smiled brightly up at Keijin when she recognized him and said, "Oh Keijin, it's so good to see you. And you've brought friends this time. Please, do come in." They all entered her home, and she directed them to the living room. "Quite an interesting bunch of characters you all are."

"We're on a mission for Leon," Keijin said as he embraced the old woman. "We're heading to Blackridge."

"Well, I'm glad to have kept my children's bedrooms much the same since they left home. It looks like we'll be needing all the rooms tonight," she said. "But Keijin, you have yet to introduce me to your friends."

"Oh, forgive me. Alina Sarazana, this is Sybil Dawn, Redbeard, and Mordecai," Keijin said, gesturing to each as he said their names.

"It's a pleasure to meet you, Alina," Sybil said with a gentle smile. "And thank you for letting us stay here tonight."

Alina's eyes gleamed when she looked at Sybil, and then she turned to Keijin and said, "Well, this one's certainly pretty."

Keijin gave an uncomfortable laugh as he rubbed the back of his neck. Was he blushing? It was a little hard for Sybil to tell because, after hours of riding, his face was always a little flush.

After clearing his throat, Keijin asked, "So how are the kids? The grandkids?"

"They're all well and healthy, which is everything an old lady like me could hope for. We celebrated little Joseph's tenth birthday here not a fortnight ago," she answered sweetly. "And Conner has recently joined the College of Scholars in the City."

"So, uh, how do the two of you know each other?" Redbeard asked from where he had plopped down on the couch.

"You know, it's been such a long time that I can't quite remember how we came to meet. It has been decades since then," Alina said, thinking. "In my youth, I was an adventurer, seeking fame and glory wherever I could find it. And Keijin often traveled alongside me."

"I believe it was technically on the road, but you were so stubborn back then, that you rode off, not wanting to admit I had saved you from that rock troll," he said, looking down at this old woman with what Sybil could only describe as love, though she was still fairly unfamiliar with the idea.

Alina waved her hand as the memory returned to her and said, "I still stand by it. I was only seconds from slaying it when you arrived, and you riding up so gallantly on that horse distracted me just long enough for the troll to get that hit in."

Mordecai, Redbeard, and Sybil sat on the couch awkwardly as the two of them continued sharing story after story of their travels together, laughing and believing they were entertaining the others. Seeing the way Keijin interacted with Alina and knowing they knew each other when she was young, Sybil couldn't help but get the sense there had been feelings between them far deeper than friendship.

Later that night, after Alina had gone to bed, Sybil was sitting on a swinging bench on the front porch, feeling the cool night breeze brush against her skin. It would be winter soon, and she hoped they would be back at the tower by that point. Keijin stepped outside and, when he noticed her, joined her on the bench. He breathed in a deep breath and let it out slowly.

"Do you often stop by here on your travels?" Sybil asked.

"As much as I'm able," he replied. "With how little time she has left, I want to be sure to spend as much time as I can here. Though, it's far less frequent than I would like."

"Forgive me if this is too personal of a question, but were the two of you together? Did you love her?"

Keijin turned to her and smiled.

"With all we've been through, I suppose you're allowed a personal question or two," he said. "Yes, we were together. We were in love, though I still love her in a way." His voice grew sad as he spoke. "After nearly a decade of traveling together, Alina decided she wanted to settle down, to get married and have kids, but I would've had to step away from my oath, give up my immortality and duties. I wasn't ready to do that, not yet. It was always the question of: without me to help them, how many people would suffer and die because I was selfish enough to abandon them?

"Honestly, it was my fault for getting involved with her in the first place because I knew we could never be more than lovers on the road. When she asked me to move here with her, I had to reject her. I had to break her heart, and my own. Within a year, she had met another man, a former adventurer himself, and they married shortly after. The next time I saw her, she had a ring on her finger and a baby on her hip. This man, who was good and kind, lived the life with her I always wanted but could never have, not without sacrificing who I am."

Keijin's eyes started welling with tears, and Sybil reached over to put her hand on top of his. Looking over at her, he gave a gentle smile as a tear rolled down his cheek.

"But I'm just so thankful she's been able to live such a long and happy life," he continued. "Her husband died several years ago, but she has four kids and nine grandchildren who bring her such joy."

"Even though it's a different kind of love now, I can tell she still loves you with all her heart," Sybil told him. "The way she looks at you, I can see how deeply she cares for you. And I know she would want you to find the same amount of joy for your own life."

"Perhaps I will, someday," he said, gently squeezing her hand.

It looked like he was about to say more when Mordecai appeared from out of the dark, returning from his evening walk. Sybil felt Keijin's hand flit away from hers, and Mordecai stared at them with narrowed eyes.

"It's late," he grumbled. "Shouldn't the two of you be asleep by now?"

"Dear Sybil, could it be Mordecai cares for our wellbeing?" Keijin asked in a dramatic tone, all the sadness in his voice replaced with jest.

"Why, yes," she said, feeding off Keijin's playful nature. "It would appear Mordecai wants us to take proper care of ourselves."

Mordecai rolled his eyes and said, "Do what you want then," before heading inside.

Looking back at each other, Keijin and Sybil laughed at their little joke.

"I suppose he's right, though," she said after a moment with a small smile still on her face. "I will be in no shape to ride tomorrow if I don't get some rest."

"Sybil," Keijin breathed as she stood from the bench. When she looked back at him, he said, "I just wanted you to know that you bring me joy."

His words surprised her, and she felt herself blush. Not knowing what to say, she gave a smile and a nod before heading inside. As soon as she was in her room, Sybil wished she had said something, but what? Even as she had time to think, she couldn't come up with a good response. With a groan, she covered her face and fell asleep.

Alina had prepared a lavish breakfast for the adventurers the next morning with all the breakfast staples: eggs, bacon, biscuits and gravy, hash browns, and toast. She told them when she had been an adventurer, she always dreamed of waking up to a breakfast like this before setting off on the road. They all ate with gusto, especially Redbeard, who was acting like he hadn't eaten in days, and as they ate, they shared with Alina some of the stories they had accumulated so far on their journey, while avoiding some of the grittier details. From the smile on her face and contentment in her eyes, Sybil could tell how much Alina was enjoying having all of them, including the brooding Mordecai and boorish Redbeard, around the table with her.

As the others were packing the bags and preparing the horses, Sybil offered to help Alina with the dishes. The old lady handed her a rag and said she could dry. For a few minutes, Sybil stood next to her, silently drying the dishes and setting them on the counter, until she thought of a question to ask.

"So, what made you want to become an adventurer?"

Alina, who had been lost in thought, glanced over at her and then smiled at the question.

"Oh, who can remember these days?" she replied with a laugh. "I was young and couldn't sit still, and besides, between you and me, I didn't know how hard it would be when I set off on the road."

Sybil smiled at this and said, "Yeah, I know what you mean. I expected challenges and hardship, but nothing like what we've faced so far."

"Being on the road isn't an easy life," she said, nodding. "But even when you eventually settle down, you find yourself missing it from time to time. All those crazy adventures and interesting people you meet along the way."

"Is it worth it, though, settling down?"

Alina stopped washing her dish to look more closely at the young woman standing next to her and said, "When you do it at the right time and with the right person."

Sybil opened her mouth to say something but just as she did, Keijin called into the house, saying that it was time for them to leave.

"Best not keep the road waiting," Alina told her, taking the dish from Sybil's hand, with a twinkle in her eyes.

Standing on the porch, Alina watched as the party mounted their horses and headed off down the road. Keijin and Sybil looked back at her, and she gave them a wave. Sybil hoped that she would be able to meet Alina again. There were so many questions she had, and she knew Alina had a lot of stories to tell. But for now, they made their way to Blackridge and rode late into the evening.

Just after nightfall, it had started to rain, so when they entered the town, it was muddy and bleak. Most of the buildings were shoddily made, probably within a matter of weeks, and the road was just a long patch of dirt, turned to a sticky sludge by the weather. Despite her best efforts to stay dry, Sybil's clothes were soaked through by the time they made it to the sad excuse for an inn which lay in the center of the settlement. When the party walked in, the young woman behind the counter shouted at them to remove their boots by the door so they didn't track in mud. Begrudgingly, they did as she asked before Keijin approached her and asked for four rooms.

"All we've got is the common room upstairs," she replied, jabbing her thumb back toward the staircase. "Should be plenty of space for you, though. We only have three other guests tonight."

With this being their only option for accommodation, Keijin paid the fee for the room and led his companions upstairs. Despite their best efforts, the four of them entering the common room and shuffling around to find empty beds made enough noise to wake up everyone else in the room. One of them even shouted in a groggy voice, "Oi, shut the hell up, you lot!"

There was a hearth in the center of the room, and after removing the heavy top layers of their clothes, they warmed themselves by the fire. It was moments like this in their journey when Sybil felt closest to her travel companions. Even though she and Mordecai were in the middle of a spat, she and Keijin were working through some strange tension between them, and she and Redbeard had practically nothing in common, she felt like the four of them were one solid unit. Whatever was going on between them, they were in this together. As the fire pushed the cold away from their bodies, she and Mordecai used a simple spell to dry out their clothes. Once they were dry and warm, they all miserably crawled into their beds, which were little more than cots, and fell asleep.

But the next morning didn't prove to be any less miserable as the rain was still falling, filling the roads with slick mud, and every inch of the town was cast in gloomy shades of gray. What was worse was no one looked pleased to see newcomers in their settlement. Everyone was dressed in dirty, wet clothing, and it looked like the men hadn't shaved and the women hadn't combed their hair in weeks. It made Sybil uncomfortable just to look at them.

The party managed to find their way through the muck and unfriendly faces to the building with the sheriff's office and small jail and, being mindful to take their muddy boots off by the door this time, entered. With hard eyes, the scrawny, bald man at the desk stared at them as they approached and asked what their business was.

"Good morning, good sir," Keijin said, returning to his gallant knight persona. "We are here to help you and your settlement with the recent attacks you've been experiencing in town. As we've come to understand it, it's still unknown what or who is committing them."

"Don't know who sent for you, but we've got everything under control here," the officer said, crossing his arms. "You lot can just be on your merry way."

"So you've stopped the attacker?" Mordecai asked, his eyebrow raised but his tone bored.

The man thought for a moment, his determined demeanor shaken by the question.

"Well, I mean, no. But we'll get it soon enough. The sheriff's gonna save us from it."

"At the rate he's going, I wonder how many more people are going to die," Redbeard said with a shake of his head. "Seems like we ought to talk with this sheriff and set him straight."

"He's busy working on the clues and asked not to be disturbed," the officer explained, looking up at the ceiling as if he were reciting word for word what the sheriff told him to say.

Keijin leaned in, putting on the charm, and said, "You seem to be a very capable chap, and a hard worker at that. Would you mind making this one small exception for us? Then, we'll be able to leave you alone so you can get back to all the important work you're doing."

These simple compliment really buttered the man up, and he was beaming.

"Well, I suppose this once. He's been at it for hours, anyway."

The officer showed the party to the sheriff's office door, knocked, and announced them to him. In the back of the room, the sheriff stood in front of three large boards, each of them covered in notes, maps, and drawings, and thread was stuck in the board with small nails, zigzagging from one note to the next. The thread had been intended to connect the clues together, but they all ended up connecting in some way, making it just as useful as if there were no string at all. The sheriff, a broad, middle-aged man with salt and pepper hair and beard, had been looking at these boards when they walked in but was now glaring at the four of them, trying to figure out who they were. When the officer explained they were requested, the sheriff frowned deeply.

"We've got everything under control here," he grumbled with a wave of his hand.

"Clearly," Mordecai remarked, glancing over the boards.

"Don't know who sent you, and don't rightly care," the sheriff said. "But as sheriff, I'm telling you all to leave. If I see you roaming my streets, messing with my investigation, I will have you arrested."

Mordecai and Redbeard both chuckled at this. The sheriff looked at the two of them with fury blazing in his eyes.

"Well, boys," Sybil said to distract the sheriff from his rage. "It's clear that the sheriff has everything under control here, and we best be on our way."

The other three looked at her, and she gestured for them to leave. Trusting in whatever she had planned, they followed her out. She led them out of the building and around the back to a thin alley before she spoke again.

"We don't need the sheriff's help, but we might need those clues," Sybil told them, pulling out her wand. "I'll use my magic to take a look around from out here and let you guys know what I see."

Using the same spell she cast on Mordecai the first day they met, Sybil created an invisible lens allowing her to see from any perspective she wanted within a certain distance. In the sheriff's office, looking over his shoulder, she could see names of the victims, drawings of various humanoid shapes, places marked on maps where she assumed victims had been attacked, dates and times when the attacks took place, and descriptions of the wounds. As she scanned over the boards, she described everything to the other three. Once her spell ran out of energy, she turned to them to see if they had any ideas.

"With the vague descriptions in the drawing, the slash marks on the victims, and organs missing, that could still be a number of things," Mordecai said, thinking through all the monsters he knew of. "But at least we can cross out the idea of it being one of the settlers, unless one of them has become seriously deranged."

"We'll need to talk to someone who's witnessed an attack," Keijin suggested.

"Memory's a tricky thing, though," Sybil said with a frown. "If there's some psycho with a bunch of blades attacking people, someone who witnessed this could have created something entirely different in their head. The oni in the girl's memories, for instance: its features were all distorted because she only had so long to process them."

"There's no harm in checking it out, though." Redbeard said with a shrug. "There might be something the sheriff missed."

"I'm sure there is," Mordecai said, glancing over at Sybil. "Especially without a divination wizard in his employ."

The board had given her three names of witnesses who saw at least some glimpse of different attacks. After asking a couple people, they were able to find the home of one of them, the others having left town the first chance they had. The remaining witness was Nill Shastra, the settlement's cobbler. The party found him in his small shop just under the apartment he lived, doing some leather work in the back. When they entered, he slowly rose, noticing their weapons and armor, and asked, "You here about the monster?"

"Yes," Keijin replied, stepping forward. "We were sent here to investigate and deal with the problem, but the sheriff has asked us to stand down."

"That prideful bastard," the cobbler muttered, tossing the brush he had been holding onto the table. "The sheriff doesn't care about people's lives around here. He only sees this issue as something he can solve to get a promotion. All he's thinking of is getting out of this place." Nill stood and walked toward the adventurers. "I had my daughter send your master a note. She's the writer of the family. I knew without the help of the Enlightened, we'd surely all fall prey to whatever this fiend is."

"How did you know to seek his help?" Sybil asked, surprised someone like him would know about Leon.

"My mother told me about him before she died, said that his people helped her once before, but she wouldn't say with what," Nill explained. "I didn't believe he was real until I saw that monstrosity, whatever it was, kill my friend Carl right in front of me."

"Do you remember much from that night?" Mordecai asked.

"Far more than I would like to, at the very least," the cobbler said, scratching his head. "I could describe it to you, if you'd like."

"Actually, there's a more effective method we've got to get firsthand accounts of incidents," Redbeard said, looking over at Sybil. "Brought to you by the Enlightened's apprentice herself."

The cobbler's eyes widened, and he said, "You must be a powerful wizard if you're his apprentice, then."

"Well, I know my way around a spell or two," Sybil responded uncomfortably, and her modesty caused Mordecai to glare at her. "If you let me, I can go into your mind and watch the memory of what happened to your friend."

"But… only that right?" the cobbler asked, his eyes shifting around at the adventurers.

"If that memory is all you are focusing on and you let me in to see it, yes," she said, raising an eyebrow. "Trust me, I won't pry around in there."

Nill relaxed a little and said, "Okay, well, that sounds just fine then."

Sybil instructed him to think clearly on the night of the attack and nothing else, hoping she wouldn't come across anything unseemly in his mind, and placed her hand on his head. Immediately, her vision shifted to the town's main road at night. Seeing things through Nill's perspective, she could see his friend, Carl, a dwarf far smaller in both size and stature than Redbeard. They were talking with each other about a girl they noticed at the tavern when something large and hairy flashed in front of them. It was impossible to tell what it was with how fast it moved. Carl and Nill both stood frozen in the middle of the street, their breathing heavy and their eyes darting this way and that. Then, large claws appeared in Nill's left periphery and sunk deep into Carl's shoulders. Nill turned around to see a hideous creature dragging his friend away and screamed in horror but stayed stock-still. Carl gave one last cry, calling for Nill, before the creature bit him in the throat and pulled away at the flesh. Disgusted and horrified, Sybil released Nill's mind, returning to the present.

Tears were streaming down Nill's face, and he said, "I was too much of a coward to do anything to save him. But please, tell me what I can do to prevent this horrible fate befalling anyone else."

"You've already been such a huge help," Keijin said, placing his hand on the cobbler's shoulder. "How about you take a little break from work and rest up?"

Nill headed up to his apartment for a nap, and once the party was outside of Nill's shop, Sybil described his memory to the others.

"Sounds like a werewolf to me," Redbeard said, running his fingers down his beard.

"A werewolf?" Sybil asked, having only ever heard of them in scary stories. "I had no idea they actually existed."

"Oh, believe me. They're real," Redbeard said before lifting up his shirt to reveal the four jagged scars running from his right shoulder to his left hip Sybil had seen glimpses of before. "This one nearly did me in."

Now understanding the source of the scars, Sybil stared them with wide eyes. When he lowered his shirt, she looked at him and realized there was still so much about him she didn't know. He had over a decade of adventuring experience when they joined up with him at the Crossroads, and that was only after his decades living in his clan, doing gods know what on the regular.

"How did you defeat it?" she asked.

"Weakened it with wolfsbane and then chopped its disgusting head off," Redbeard said proudly. "It's how I earned my totem in the clan." He pulled out a black stone carved into the shape of a wolf. "Earned the wolf totem just like my father before me."

"That explains those hideous tattoos all over your arms," Mordecai said, gesturing with his chin.

Redbeard stretched his arms in front of him before flexing them and saying, "These? Yeah, they're pretty gnarly, aren't they? Strikes fear into my enemies' hearts and really wins over the ladies."

Mordecai rolled his eyes, and Sybil giggled.

"Tell me, are there any ladies in your life, Redbeard?" Keijin asked as they continued down the road, smiling but not rude enough to laugh.

"Well, now that you mention it, there's one special lady in a village not too far from here," he explained, his eyes going a bit dreamy as he spoke. "Her name's June. She's a widow with two kids, but she is quite the catch, and I don't mind kids. I helped save her village from a dragon a couple years back, but her husband's death was too recent for her to be able to think of me in that way just yet. But I'm betting when I return, she'll be ready."

Sybil patted Redbeard on his shoulder, looking at Keijin and then Mordecai, before saying, "I'm sure she will, Redbeard. I'm sure she will."

Redbeard smiled up at her, nothing but hope in his eyes. He was such a strange man. So brutal and fierce on the battlefield, but so sweet and gentle with those he felt close with. Even though they were both so different, he was one of the most important people to her. When they returned to the tower, Sybil decided she would ask Leon to make him an official member under his employ. The idea of them just parting ways after all this was too sad not to fight.

With her hand still firmly on Redbeard's shoulder, the adventurers started heading back to the inn from the cobbler's shop when five armed officers approached them followed by the sheriff. The officers all carried shortswords and wore black studded leather, ready for a fight.

"I thought I told you that if you messed with my investigation that I'd arrest you," the sheriff announced from behind his men. "It seems like the four of you have a bit of a listening problem."

Redbeard, Mordecai, and Sybil all looked at each other, ready to spring into action, and Keijin sighed before whispering, "Just don't kill them."

Taking the lead on this, Mordecai stepped out in front of the men and raised his arms. The officers grew uneasy as the world around them darkened, and then fear flashed across their faces when black ichor started rising out of the earth. They all screamed as black tendrils trapped them where they stood, wrapping around them up to their necks. With Mordecai concentrating on holding them there, Sybil stepped forward with electricity sparkling from her hands as a warning to them. Redbeard stood right behind her, brandishing his greataxe, just waiting for an excuse to use it.

"My associates and I have been sent by the Enlightened himself to deal with the recent slaughtering of your people," Sybil announced, her voice louder than she had ever made it before. "If you interfere with *our* investigation again, we will have no choice but to use force against you, as you will have made it clear by your actions that you are on the side of the murderer's and must be stopped."

"Do ya understand, you ungrateful bastards?" Redbeard asked in a crazed voice, squeezing his meaty hands around the wood of his axe.

The officers all let out some form of acknowledgement as they sniffled in fear. But the sheriff, on the other hand, just stared at the party with wrath in his eyes. Without his officers to fight for him, the sheriff was no match for the four of them, but there were other ways he could cause problems. Still, there was nothing more the adventurers could do to him at this point without the entire settlement being after them with torches and pitchforks, so they had to let him and the rest of his officers go.

Thankfully, it was clear that the officers were not going to put up a fight, despite any orders, because as soon as Mordecai released them, they scrambled away. The sheriff eyed the party for a moment before heading back down the road to his office.

To Sybil's surprise, Mordecai turned to her and said, "You're starting to sound more like you know what you're doing."

A double-sided compliment, but a compliment nonetheless.

"We should get a move on," Keijin told his companions, stepping forward. "I have a feeling that wasn't the last of the sheriff's attempts to stop us."

To continue their investigation, now that they had a good idea of what the creature was and how to kill it, they tried searching for a trail from the places where it attacked one of the victims. The rain over the past two days, however, had ruined any chance of finding one. With nothing to go on, the rest of the party decided to accompany Redbeard in his search for wolfsbane in the nearby woods. It was a scarce resource, but with his keen senses and knowledge of nature, Redbeard was able to find a tiny patch of the bright purple flowers hidden between a tree and a boulder.

As Redbeard retrieved the wolfsbane with his knife, Sybil glanced around the forest, feeling something odd about it.

"There's a strange magic here," she said as she realized what it was. "Something's poisoning these lands."

The other three turned to her, looking for more of an explanation, but when she gave Mordecai a moment to think about it, he said, "I can feel it, too. It's like some sort of curse."

"Could that be what caused the werewolf?" Keijin asked in a whisper as if they were suddenly hiding from something.

"There's plenty of legends pointing to the idea that werewolves are just cursed men," Redbeard said, tucking the wolfsbane into his pocket. "But in my experience, it's always seemed like more of a disease, spreading from one to the next through bites."

"Maybe that's just how it's spread after the initial curse," Sybil suggested. "I'm starting to think just taking care of the werewolf, if there is only one, won't solve the overall problem."

Mordecai was staring down at her, thinking deeply, and just when she was about to ask what he was thinking, he said, "You seem to have a strong sense of this magic. Using your skills in divination, we might be able to track the source of it."

Sybil wrapped her arms around her and turned in the direction of where the magic felt strongest.

"Not sure I want to track it," she breathed, starting to feel a little dizzy. "It feels... like a sickness."

"Well, we ain't going traipsing into the forest just yet," Redbeard said, starting to hike back to town. "Not when this wolfsbane's not properly prepared."

While Redbeard led them back to town, Sybil continued looking over her shoulder, fearful something might be stalking them from a distance. When they made it back to the inn, she felt a little better, but the smell of the wolfsbane as Redbeard extracted it brought the dizziness back. Once the oil from the flower had been removed, Redbeard placed it into a vial for them to use when they were ready.

"So what's the plan, then?" Mordecai asked, watching her as she paced back and forth in the middle of the room.

"If we follow this magic into the forest, we might not be prepared for what we find there or what it could possibly do to us," Keijin said. "I say, we figure out a plan for this werewolf and then go from there."

"With all this rain, I doubt the beast will strike tonight," Redbeard told his companions. "Not many people will be out, and it's hard to track prey when it's raining."

"So we just have to hang out here until the rain let's up?" Sybil asked, and both Keijin and Redbeard shrugged. "Brilliant."

Mordecai moved to a table in the corner of the room which had a deck of cards sitting in the middle. Slowly, he pulled out a chair, sat down, and looked over at Sybil.

"Sit," he said, gesturing to the chair across the table from him.

"Why?" she asked, walking toward him.

"Because when you were drunk and babbling back in Taragpass, you asked me if I could teach you how to play games," he explained, grabbing the deck of cards. "Since we have time, I'm going to teach you now."

Surprised, Sybil sat down and stared at him. He seemed annoyed, so she didn't understand why he was doing this. He started shuffling the cards, and as he divided up the deck between the two of them, she couldn't help but smile a little. Even though he said they weren't friends, that they'd never be friends, she couldn't help but wonder if somewhere along the way she had, in fact, become his friend, and he didn't even realize it. When he glanced back up at her, Sybil stopped smiling and looked at the cards seriously.

Mordecai taught her a number of games that night, and Redbeard and Keijin eventually joined them around the table. All the rules were far more simplistic than she had anticipated, so she caught on quickly to these games they had known for years. When the other guests in the common room started shuffling in to go to sleep, they had to stop playing, mainly because Redbeard was being far too loud. At one point, he had stood up on his chair to yell down at Mordecai for taking his entire hand, though Mordecai was unfazed by this.

That night, Sybil went to bed happy about everything feeling back on track with her group. However, when she opened her eyes in the middle of the night to find a man pointing his crossbow in her face, a feeling of dread quickly filled her stomach.

Chapter Eleven

"Sit up, slowly," the arbalist instructed.

When Sybil looked over at her companions, there were men pointing crossbows at them as well. She did as the man commanded, and then he tossed her a pair of shackles.

"Put them on."

"I would really rather not," she breathed, staring down at them.

The man moved the crossbow closer and growled, "Put them on or you get a bolt in your head."

Sybil wondered if Keijin was powerful enough to heal a head wound and if he was fast enough to keep her from dying. Deciding it was better not to test it, she slid the shackles over her hands and closed them around her wrists. The man leaned forward and tightened them to the point where they were pinching her, and she could feel her stomach start to cramp. Keijin's eyes met hers as he put his own shackles on and gave her a nod. *It will be okay,* he was telling her.

The men pulled the party out of the common room, the other patrons sleepily watching them being taken away, and out of the inn. Even though the rain had let up, the road was still slick, and Sybil almost slipped as the man dragged her behind him. Both Redbeard and Mordecai's faces were filled with fury, and Keijin was just watching Sybil with concern. It was not a surprise to any of them when the arbalists pulled the party into the sheriff's office, led them to the jail, and locked them up in individual cells, leaving the shackles on. Once they were secure, the men left the jail, locking the door behind them.

"So, we kill the sheriff now, right?" Mordecai growled, attempting to pull his hand out of one of the shackles. "That's my plan, anyway."

"Not if I get to him first," Redbeard muttered as he started pulling his wrists apart over and over again, trying to break the chain.

"Why take us prisoner?" Sybil asked with a shake of her head. "He could've just taken credit once we killed the werewolf."

"He could've just ordered them to kill us," Keijin added. "So I guess we have something to be thankful for, at least."

The door unlocked, and the Sheriff stepped through, wearing a smug grin on his face. He walked between their cells, clearly enjoying the sight of those who bested him earlier trapped in his jail. Sybil wanted to slap him, or perhaps set him ablaze.

"Great, noble adventurers," he said with a laugh. "Bested by four mercenaries? Not so fearsome, after all."

"Put a crossbow in my face when I'm awake and you've got another thing coming to you," Redbeard snarled, grabbing the bars of the cell and pulling against them. "In fact, let's go right fucking now."

"Oh, please," the sheriff scoffed. "Like I would ever sink down to your level. No, I am a man of wit, and I use my brain, not my brawn to do my fighting." Sybil laughed at the idea of him using his brain, causing him to turn toward her. "And what's so funny, little girl? You were dumb enough to fall asleep in my city after making a mockery of me and my men."

"I suppose you're right," she said, taking a dramatic tone. "How could we ever be so foolish? Your power is clearly so much greater than ours." Raising her hands, she continued. "There's simply nothing our magic can do against your shackles and bars. Oh, wait... there is."

In an instant, Sybil had hold of the sheriff's mind, causing him to relive some of his darkest memories, though they were nothing compared to trauma she had seen in other minds. She didn't dig as deeply or viciously as she had with the bandit she killed, trying her best to keep the sheriff alive and conscious. Clutching his head and crying out, he fell to his knees. And after only a few seconds, she released him. There were beads of sweat forming on his forehead and his face had gone completely red.

Through labored breaths, he said, "You're all creatures of evil."

"Evil is such a strong word," Mordecai remarked with a smile on his face. "Evil would be you suffering in that state far longer than it took to get the message across, which is what I would've done. What she's shown you is mercy, so you better make the most of it and release us."

"How do I know you won't kill me?" the sheriff said, tears starting to stream down his face.

"Quite frankly, whether you let us go willingly or not, we're killing you either way," Redbeard said. "No one puts me in shackles in the middle of the night without me getting something good out of it. And if your death's all I get, I'll take it."

"We're not killing anybody," Keijin announced. "But quite clearly, you're not well suited for your post, sir. Release us, and we'll spare you, but your punishment will be stepping down as sheriff."

The sheriff thought on Keijin's proposal and then looked at Sybil.

"Fine, I'll do it."

Strategically, he unlocked Keijin's cell first and then gave him the key so he could keep a safe distance away from the other three. Redbeard tried to charge him, but Keijin, who matched Redbeard in strength, stepped in front of him, holding him back. The sheriff shied away from Sybil as she approached him and flinched when she held out her hand.

"What are you doing?" he asked after a moment.

"Your badge, give it to me," she said, and he just looked at her with confusion. "The deal was that you would step down if we spared your life, so I'm taking your badge."

Slowly, he pulled the badge of his coat and placed it in her hand. She stuck it in her pocket and nodded.

"Good. Now that that's settled, get in the cell."

"What?"

"You think we're just going to let you go after you've repeatedly hindered our investigation?" Sybil asked him, raising an eyebrow. "No, you're going to stay nice and cozy in a cell until we figure out what is going on around here."

Once the sheriff was secure, the party moved into his office to regroup. The sun was just beginning to bring color back to the sky, so there was really no point in going back to the inn to get a little more sleep. They made a plan for the day, and just as they were about to head back to the woods, they heard a crying woman coming into the front. The sight of four strangers heading toward her at once caused the woman to gasp.

"Don't worry," Keijin said. "You're safe here. Please, take a seat and tell us what's the matter."

"My husband," the woman whimpered as she sat on the bench against the wall. "Something attacked him in the night. There's blood everywhere."

"Did you see what it was?" Redbeard asked, though it was easy to guess.

"No, but I heard it," she said, wiping away tears. "My husband and I don't share the same room at night on account of his snoring. There was this horrible snarl, and Patrick was yelling at the top of his lungs. At first, I thought I was just having a nightmare, but by the time I mustered up the courage to see what I was hearing for myself, Patrick was gone and his bed was covered in blood."

There was a cot in one of the back offices, so Keijin had the woman rest and wait for the party there while they went to investigate her house. She had given them directions, and it annoyed everyone in the party to see that her house was right next to the inn. If it hadn't been for the sheriff's stupidity, they probably would have heard the attack and could've stopped the creature right then and there. Patrick would probably have still been killed, but at least the party would have arrived in time to keep the creature from returning to its lair and dragging his body away with it.

Just as the woman described, her husband's bedroom was covered in blood. It was mostly on the bed where the man was sleeping, but it had also reached the floors and walls in various splatter patterns as the man struggled against the monster. The window right above the bed had been shattered, sending glass everywhere, and the man drug through it, a piece of his nightgown stuck on one of the shards still in the frame.

"The poor bastard," Redbeard said with a shake of his head. "But at least we'll be able to track it to its lair from here."

Heading outside around the back of the house, the drying mud had allowed for distinct prints, something between a paw and a foot, both heading toward the house and away from it. Even though the tracks were easy to follow, the other three let the resident werewolf expert take the lead on this, and Redbeard started heading back into the forest.

"Looks like it had been checking out different houses before deciding on Patrick's," Redbeard explained, pointing out how the tracks heading to the house came from the direction of the settlement. "This thing's smart. It made specific decisions rather than acting on impulse or instinct."

The tracks led the adventurers to a cave a mile or so into the forest, and Sybil was thankful the sickening magic was not stemming from this place but further into the woods instead. Redbeard and Keijin both readied their weapons, dosing them in wolfsbane, and Mordecai pulled Sybil aside.

"Remember, you're not a fighter. Don't get up close to this thing," he instructed. "If it has an opportunity to strike you with its claws, it will shred you to bits."

"And suddenly you care about my wellbeing again?" Sybil asked him softly enough so the other two didn't hear. "Careful Mordecai, only friends do that sort of thing."

"Of course, I care about your wellbeing," Mordecai growled, his grip tightening. "You're important to me, okay? But I wouldn't call us friends."

"Then what would you call us?"

"It doesn't matter. We need to focus on the task at hand. Stop getting distracted by petty matters."

Just then, Keijin and Redbeard turned to their companions, ready for the fight. They decided it would be best to go into the cave rather than draw it out so it didn't have anywhere to run. The two fighters would rush the creature, and the magic wielders would offer support from behind. As Keijin and Redbeard headed inside, Sybil cast a spell creating a glowing orb, like a tiny sun, at the top of the cave to provide them with plenty of light. The creature, who was slumbering in the back of the cave, gave out a shriek as it was awoken by Redbeard's greataxe slashing through its shoulder. The wolfsbane must have felt like acid to the creature because as the wound started to bubble the werewolf let out a painful moan.

It rose to its feet, standing nearly a foot taller than Keijin, and brandished its long, dagger-like claws. It tried slashing at the two of them, but they had anticipated its movement and lunged out of the way. Sybil sent a dart of fire at it, catching it in its stomach and singeing some of the hairs. The creature's attention turned to her for an instant, but Keijin came at it with his longsword, slicing it across the chest, and Mordecai sent a sphere of dark energy toward it, hitting directly on the wound. The werewolf let out a howl of rage and pain, staggering back as it clutched its chest. The wolfsbane Redbeard found was hurting it far more than their weapons on their own would have, but it was also pissing it off.

It swung its arm around, and sparks flew off Keijin's armor as its strong claws scratched across his chest plate. The force of the creature's attack caused Keijin to go flying back, hitting the wall of the cave.

Sybil started moving forward to help, but Mordecai grabbed her by the arm and hissed, "No." He was right. The way that thing had knocked Keijin prone and damaged his armor, it would have killed Sybil in an instant.

After pulling her back, Mordecai sent a bolt of lightning crackling through the air at it, causing it to turn toward him. As Keijin struggled back up to his feet, Redbeard had just enough time to catch it unaware. With all of his might, Redbeard drove his greataxe into the werewolf's back, right between the shoulder blades. The sound it made was horrible as it crumpled to the ground, but Redbeard cut it short by pulling his axe out of its back and bringing it down on its neck.

Despite all they had seen on their journey together, watching the werewolf's head roll across the ground a few feet made Sybil sick. As Redbeard went to extract a tooth from the creature, muttering something about adding it to his collection, she left the cave and tried to breathe in some fresh air. But the air here had grown sour, and it caused her to buckle over and gag. Keijin placed his hand on her back and rubbed it to help soothe her, not feeling the same sickness she was. On the other hand, Mordecai's face was scrunched up in disgust.

"What is it?" Keijin asked the magic wielders. "The same thing from before?"

"But stronger this time," Mordecai answered. "Whatever it is, its strength is growing. It's quite likely it's connected to the werewolf's victims in some way. There were no bodies or remains in the cave."

"Necromancy… it must be, if they're using the bodies to enhance their magic," Sybil suggested, straightening back up.

"Or something far fouler," Mordecai said, staring off in the direction the magic seemed to be radiating from. "It takes a lot of power to make an entire forest feel sick."

"If that's true, then the entire settlement is at risk," Keijin said, sheathing his sword. "We must do something."

Redbeard walked out of the cave, his axe still dripping with black blood. When he saw his companions' expressions, he asked, "We're not done yet, are we?"

"Not yet," Sybil breathed.

"Let's approach it cautiously," Mordecai suggested. "We can scout it out, and if we know it's not something we can handle, then we turn back."

They all agreed to this plan, so Mordecai used his magic to turn his companions invisible, making it easier for them to retreat if they needed to.

The closer they moved toward the magic, the sicker Sybil started to feel. But, other than the initial shock of it, Mordecai seemed fine. The adventurers all held onto a part of another to make sure they stayed together: Redbeard holding the edge of Keijin's shield, Keijin grasping Sybil's sleeve, and Sybil's arm wrapped securely around Mordecai's because it was growing hard to stand on her own from the nausea. After another mile or so of walking, they came across a clearing and stopped when they saw what was in the center of it.

Four necromancers, mages who could control dangerous magic which mostly involved the dead, stood chanting an unknown language in a circle. Sybil could point out their kind anywhere. Not only did she know of a former one who now worked in Gibbous Tower, but she also did a great deal of research into their kind of magic in morbid fascination. The ones before them wore robes made of black, rough spun fabric and had their faces covered with hoods. Around their waist, instead of a belt or rope, there were metal chains with a sharp spike at the end, dangling near their feet.

None of them noticed the presence of the party, only in part because they were still invisible, but the necromancers' attention was elsewhere, and it immediately drew the attention of the adventurers. In the center of the clearing, what the necromancers were chanting to, was an enormous, black tumor growing from the earth. It was twice as tall as the tallest among them and equally wide, pulsating and oozing a strange, black liquid from its wart-like pustules. Sybil knew as soon as she saw it that this was causing the sickness. Every time it pulsed, she felt a wave of nausea hit her.

After the necromancers finished whatever spell they were casting, the tumor surged, sending the liquid it was oozing splattering against the nearby trees. This change in the mass caused Mordecai to collapse to the ground in pain, and suddenly the party was visible again. Sybil stared down at him in horror as he clutched his head. Not thinking it through, she placed her hand on his ice-cold forehead and tried to push whatever it was out of his mind.

The horrors she saw in his consciousness were indescribable, and she knew she was seeing things no mortal being should be able to see. Dark arcane horrors from ancient planes of existence swirled around in her head, and she knelt there, frozen in fear, until Mordecai knocked her hand away with his forearm. Just as she was about to collapse to the ground, he caught her and held her in his arms. He placed his hand over the side of her face and spoke in the same dark language the necromancers were chanting, the one she often found him studying in the books. The dread and anguish began leaving her body as Mordecai's eyes turned black, pulling whatever darkness had entered her back into him.

"I won't let him take you," he said in barely a whisper, wincing at the pain he was drawing from her.

Keijin stepped out in front of his two companions on the ground, deflecting a spell that one of the necromancers threw at them with his shield.

"I'm going to need you guys back on your feet as soon as possible," he said in a strained voice. "We've drawn their attention."

Mordecai looked from Keijin to Sybil with worry in his eyes, and she said, "It's okay. I can do this."

Once they were both on their feet, the party immediately sprang into action. Redbeard charged toward one of the necromancers who deflected him with their magic, a shield wall of static electricity, nearly sending him flying into the tumor. He bounced off and hit the ground hard, his back covered in the dark ooze. Using her negative emotions like before, Sybil raised her staff toward the sky and created an ice storm. Shards of ice came shooting down from the sky, and it took a great deal of effort to keep them from hitting her team. Three necromancers were hit by ice shards, two in the shoulder and one in the foot, but it didn't seem to even faze them. Not even when Mordecai set one ablaze with a stream of fire.

One of the necromancers lunged toward Sybil, his eyes black and filled with hate, and she put her staff up to deflect him. He grabbed the middle of the staff, and after muttering something, shattered it into a million pieces. Sybil let out a cry, shielding her eyes from the wood shards, before throwing the necromancer backward with a force spell from her wand. Drawing energy into his sword, Keijin approached the one closest to him and brought his radiant sword down on him. The necromancer shrieked in pain as he crumbled to the ground, dead. Then, the other three held their palms above the ground and started chanting the same incantation.

The ground rumbled, causing the party to freeze, and all the trees surrounding them lost the remainder of their autumn leaves. Underneath the necromancers, the soil shifted and bubbled as though it were water. Then, to everyone's horror, decaying limbs reached out of the earth, their rotting flesh dangling loosely from their bones.

Necromancy was the tabooest of the schools of magic as it dealt with the aspects of life and death. In her studies, Sybil had learned a great deal about their powers and had even used a few minor spells herself. Necromancers could keep people who were an inch from death alive, open scars into wounds, curse, and steal senses, but Sybil had never known any powerful enough to bring a corpse back to life. These three together had risen over a dozen corpses buried in the ground, and the dead dwarf that looked just like Nill Shastra's friend told Sybil these were the victims of the werewolf.

After staring down the small army of the dead, each of the adventurers needing a moment to process, they returned to the fight. Redbeard easily hacked down two of the animated dead in front of him and ran over to Sybil as five of them started encircling her. Keijin and Mordecai were standing together fending off the others and two of the necromancers on the other side of the tumor. As Sybil set fire to one of the undead, she searched around for the third necromancer. Redbeard struck down the last undead near them and then smiled at Sybil and winked.

"I think you're enjoying yourself too much," she said with a twinge of a smile on her lips.

He laughed and asked, "What's the point if you don't love what you do?"

Sybil looked around the battlefield until she found Keijin and Mordecai, who were still dealing with enemies. Just as she turned back to Redbeard to suggest they help the others, the third necromancer flashed into view.

Standing mere inches in front of Redbeard, catching him completely by surprise, the necromancer raised his hand, dark energy swirling around it, and plunged it into Redbeard's chest. Redbeard's eyes widened to huge circles, and he let out a weak groan as he looked down at the necromancer's wrist. The necromancer hissed a spell in the ancient language, and black veins appeared along Redbeard's neck and arms for a brief moment. Just as Sybil was about to attack the necromancer, he ripped his hand out of Redbeard's chest, pulling whatever he could out with it.

"No!" Sybil screamed as she blasted the necromancer back with a beam of light she didn't know she could wield.

In fury, she set the necromancer on fire and got a sick pleasure from hearing his cries of pain. Then, she collapsed down to Redbeard's side and brought her shaky hands up to his wound. He was still alive, but barely.

"Keijin," she yelled, tears streaming down her face. "Keijin, please help!"

Slicing through one of the necromancers, Keijin made his way back over to them. He rushed to Redbeard's other side and immediately started to heal him. As he did this, Redbeard took Sybil's hand in his, and they locked eyes together.

"I-I don't know why it's not working," Keijin said, panic rising in his voice.

"I think this is the end of the road... for me," Redbeard told her, his eyes peaceful, and Sybil shook her head no. "That freak did something to me... I can feel it."

Mordecai, who had been dealing with the last of the undead, joined his companions and tried to remove whatever curse the necromancer had placed on Redbeard, but it was no use. None of them knew what this was, and he was far too injured to be moved anywhere to seek help from someone who did. There was nothing they could do.

The thought of losing Redbeard was unbearable, and the pain caused Sybil to let out a wail. Mordecai and Keijin just sat by them, staring down at the earth, defeated.

With the last bit of strength he had left, Redbeard pulled Sybil toward him and whispered to her.

"My name is Emric... Emric Castellian," he said, his beard hairs tickling Sybil's ear. "Just thought ... you should know."

To her horror, Redbeard gave one final breath and his eyelids closed.

Grief and rage and sadness and hate all swarmed inside Sybil as one of her first true friends laid dead before her. She wanted to burn the whole world down. She wanted to bring pain to everyone who was responsible for this. Sybil stood to her feet and walked over to the giant, oozing, pulsating tumor as the fury raged inside her.

"Shuheyr," she breathed through gritted teeth. "Help me."

Raising her hands up, Sybil pointed her palms toward the mass, as her entire body began to glow. Feeling the weight of her grief, she threw all of the magic inside her at this evil tumor, two beams of bright light shooting out of her hands. The clearing of trees filled with light, but her remaining companions could still see her, staring at this powerful force in awe. Whatever this evil thing was, it trembled and convulsed as the light overpowered it. Then, all at once, it exploded, sending its black ooze like a geyser into the air and the flesh of it dissolved into ash. Using her magic, Sybil shielded herself from the liquid as it rained down around her.

The sickness immediately started to dissipate from the forest, and when everything had settled, Sybil returned to the others and stared down at Redbeard. Mordecai was staring up at her, his silver eyes wide and mouth slightly open, but she didn't meet his gaze. Another sob bubbled to the surface, and she rested her head on Redbeard's shoulder. The other two said nothing for a while before Keijin spoke up and said, "We should leave soon. I'll make a stretcher."

The three companions walked Redbeard's body back to town silently, too exhausted and grief-stricken to think of anything to say. By the time they made it to town, the sun was starting to set, and people were closing up shop for dinner time. The party had saved them, all of them, from a terrible threat, but as they passed the battle- and grief-weary adventurers, the townspeople looked at them with disgust. At that moment, Sybil wished they had let them all die.

Not knowing where else to take his body, they brought Redbeard back to the sheriff's office and laid him down in the back room. They had just started talking about their next moves while standing around the front desk when, to their surprise, Giselle walked through the front door. Dressed all in black, the fabric of her tunic and trousers tailored close to her frame, and her purple skin bright in the evening light, she approached the remaining members of the party, her lightly curled reddish-black hair bouncing with every step.

"Leon saw what happened," Giselle said, glancing at Redbeard's body through the door frame. "He sent me to pull you out of the field."

"We're going back to the tower?" Sybil asked, her voice weak.

"Yes, dear one," Giselle said, looking at her with pitying eyes. "You've all been through enough out here. He wants you to return and rest from your traumas."

"And what about the settlement?" Keijin asked, sounding like he was finally starting to age.

Giselle shrugged and said, "I think you've done enough for them, don't you?"

"Absolutely," Mordecai agreed, not looking up at the others.

"Good, then get your stuff, and we'll be on our way."

They met Giselle in the middle of the road with their bags and horses, and she pulled out a large crystal and threw it on the ground. As it shattered, a portal appeared in a glowing shade of blue, and she stepped through it. Not sure how long the portal lasted, the adventurers all stepped through it quickly after her. It was Sybil's first time using a portal, and it was not a pleasant experience. The world seemed to spin around her a hundred times, and she struggled to find her sense of balance after her feet made contact with the ground in front of Gibbous Tower.

Everything felt like a blur as a few people came up to the party and took Redbeard away. When Sybil tried to follow them, Mordecai took her hand and held her next to him, saying, "Let them clean him up."

So, Sybil just watched as these people she barely knew walked away with the remains of her dear friend.

As was expected of everyone who returned to Gibbous Tower, the three of them headed to Leon's office to debrief with him on their journey. When they arrived, Sybil stared at the door as she had hundreds of times before as she waited for him to let her in, but this time was different. She had become a vastly different person since the last time she stood in this spot.

Leon called them in, and Mordecai and Keijin moved to the couch as Sybil went to stand by the fireplace, feeling incredibly cold.

"I am so sorry to hear of your loss," Leon told them, hanging his head. "What those necromancers did to Redbeard was unspeakable… but I am glad the rest of you came out of it unharmed."

"I wouldn't say we're unharmed," Sybil breathed, staring into the flames.

"Yes, of course. You have suffered greatly, both with Redbeard's death and the other incidents on your journey, there is no mistaking that," Leon corrected. "Tell me, did you get rid of the evil in the forest, the one that was leading the werewolf to kill?"

"Sybil did," Keijin said, his voice void of emotion or melody. "She was the only one who could."

Leon nodded.

"I am glad to hear it. Again, such a tragic loss has befallen you, but you have saved countless lives by ridding the world of that cancer." The party was silent, so he spoke up again. "Perhaps I should let you all get some rest, and we can discuss things on a later date. I will be holding a funeral for Redbeard tomorrow evening, so you will be able to say your final goodbyes then."

Chapter Twelve

Standing in front of Redbeard's funeral pyre, Sybil stared down at his peaceful face. He had been placed on a three-foot-tall bed of wood with his arms crossed over his chest, his skin bare to show off the intricate artwork of his tattoos he had taken so much pride in. Whoever had cleaned him up had braided the front half of his beard, and knowing it would have annoyed him, she undid it.

"There," Sybil sniffed, smoothing out the hairs. "You look like your sloppy, old self again. But you still look nice. June would have gone mad for you if she had a chance to see you again. If I ever meet her, I'll let her know how much of a catch she missed out on." She leaned down and kissed him on the cheek. "I'm so sorry, Redbeard. I miss you."

Before the tears could come, Sybil stepped back from the pyre, joining Keijin and Mordecai where they were standing. Keijin's face was red as he let his tears fall, and Mordecai had his head down and hood up, darkening his face. Even though Sybil thought it was only going to be the three of them, across the pyre were Rani, Giselle, and Tanele, showing their support. After Leon said a few words, thanking Redbeard for his service and acknowledging his importance to his companions and the tower, he set the pyre on fire. It started small at first, but soon it was all ablaze. The fire grew too warm to stand next to, but Sybil didn't want to move away, watching Redbeard disappear through the flames. After nearly an hour had gone by, though, Keijin told her it was time to head back inside. She closed her eyes, the final tears of grief sliding down her cheeks, before she let him guide her back to the tower.

"I think I want to be alone," Sybil said to everyone in barely a whisper. "At least, for a little while."

All of them understood, and she headed up to her room, keeping her head down as she walked. Laying down in bed, she stared at her bookshelves, reading each of the titles on the spines over and over again, until she fell asleep.

Sybil spent several days alone in her room. Leon made sure to send food to her at every meal, but she barely ate any of it. All she did was lay in bed, sleeping off and on, flip through books she had already read, and stare out the window.

It wasn't until the fifth day back in the tower when Keijin decided to try to pull Sybil from her depression. He knocked on the door, and she opened it with magic, not even bothering to get out of bed. His face scrunched up when he saw the state of her room, with books scattered around and a couple of plates of food still lingering from the previous day. Sitting on the bed, he patted her leg and asked how she was doing. She just gave him a shrug, which caused him to sigh.

"How about we go for a ride?" he asked, looking down at the forest through the window. "Dusk has been cooped up for a while."

Somehow, Keijin had managed to convince Sybil to leave the tower, saddle up her horse, and ride off into the Asbriand Forest with him. She had no idea where they were going, but it felt good to be back in the saddle, feeling Dusk's strong but delicate movements, and having the wind in her hair again. He stopped in front of a tree, and she instantly recognized it.

"The tree I made my wand and staff from?" Sybil asked. "Why here?"

Keijin dismounted and started heading to the tree, and she followed suit.

"When you were new to all this, barely a woman with childhood so close behind you," Keijin said, placing his hand on the tree. "Leon asked me to escort you out to the forest to find a tree that spoke to you. Whichever tree this was, I would cut off the thickest branch and help you bring it back to the tower."

"Yes, I remember," she told him, still waiting for his point.

"Why don't you pick another branch?" he asked, a gentle smile on his face.

Sybil looked from him to the tree, gazing around at all its branches. Eventually, she found one that looked the sturdiest and pointed to it.

"Oh, I'm just here to watch. You can cut it down yourself."

Annoyed, Sybil took a step back as she conjured a magical blade, something she had only done a few times, and started slicing it back and forth over the base of the branch. After a few minutes, the branch snapped off and fell to the ground.

"I'm not even sure I want another staff," she told him, staring down at the branch.

"That's up to you," Keijin said with a shrug as he walked up to her. "That wasn't really the point of all this."

"Then, what was the point?"

"Years ago, when we first found this tree, you needed my help to cut down the branch and bring it back to the tower. In fact, it would have been impossible for you to do any of it on your own. But now?" he asked before giving a small laugh. "Sybil, you have grown to be one of the most capable, intelligent, and powerful people I have ever met. You no longer truly need the help of others to get something done. But I don't want you to ever lose sight of what you can do with people at your side.

"I know Redbeard's death was hard, but despair should not have a permanent place in your heart. At worst it should just be a thunderstorm which will eventually yield to the sun, as all storms do," he told her, looking up at the tree with a gentle smile on his face. "Feel your grief and sadness and guilt, but don't let it consume you. Know there's always another friend to reach out to, like there's always another branch to choose. You'll never forget the old one, and you'll cherish the memories of it in your heart, but it's okay to move on."

Thinking back to when she first found the tree four years ago, Sybil was silent for several minutes as she stared up at the tree. She felt so young back then, even though it wasn't that long ago, and Keijin seemed so old and wise. But when she looked over at him now, standing there with the same face, she understood what he was saying about her growth. She didn't need him anymore; he didn't need to protect her anymore. Instead, she had grown to be his companion, his equal, and his friend. When he turned to her, his blue eyes sparkling in the morning sun, she knew he could see all those things in her.

"Thank you," Sybil breathed, moving closer to him. Keijin wrapped his arm around her shoulders and squeezed her to him as they stared up at the tree together.

Later that day, Sybil made her way down to the library, wanting to study some of the spells and monsters they had encountered on their travels. At her usual table, Mordecai had a stack of books he was working through and was scribbling notes in a journal next to him. He didn't look up from his work as she approached, but he moved his stuff out of the way so she could sit next to him. She could tell something was frustrating him, so she didn't say anything for a while, opening up one of the books she found about druids. Eventually, he closed the book he was working on with a loud thud, causing her to jump.

"Sorry," he breathed, pinching the brim of his nose. "It's just…I've been through nearly every book in this damn library, and there's so little information about what happened at Blackridge. Necromancers, sure. But a black mass oozing liquid evil growing out of the ground? It's as if there's been nothing like it before."

"What if there hasn't been anything like it before?" she asked. "It doesn't sound like anything I've ever heard of."

He glared at her for a second and then sighed.

"I'm not ready to believe that's true just yet," he told her. "Haborym has wreaked havoc here before, hundreds of years ago, but there are books in this library that span a millennium with little to no mention of him. He's also shown his face in other planes of existence as well, but there's nothing about him infecting a world with part of himself like he did in the woods near Blackridge. If this is something new he can do, then that must mean his power is growing, which is terrible news for our reality."

Sybil could feel the anxiety and stress radiating off him, so she reached over and held his hand. This took him completely by surprise, and with suspicious eyes, he stared down at their hands.

"What are you doing?"

"Have you had any rest since we've been back?" she asked, keeping her hand there. "I know you said you don't need it, or whatever, but we're safe in this tower, and I think you should try to rest, even for just a day or so."

His grip tightened around her hand, and he said, "I don't have time for rest."

"You know, what happened in the woods… none of that was your fault, right?" she asked, and the look he gave her was twisted between anger and sadness. "I chose to help you, and despite what I saw, I don't regret it. It was killing you, whatever it was. And Redbeard? His death is on the necromancer and Haborym alone. He wouldn't want us blaming ourselves for it."

Mordecai heaved a big sigh.

"I… need to be alone right now, I think," he breathed, his voice sounding younger than it usually did.

Taking the hint, Sybil rose from her seat and picked up her book.

"Well, you're in my spot, but I suppose I could lend it to you for a while," she said, moving around the table. "I know you like doing things on your own, but Keijin and I… we're here for you, okay?"

Mordecai gave a slight nod before returning to his books. Sybil went up to the librarian's counter to check out the book she had, and the old lady gave her a sweet smile as she handed Sybil the book back, her hands shaking. Of all the people in the tower, this woman had been there the longest, and for some reason, Sybil found herself wondering how much longer she would be around, how long any of them would be around, as she headed up to her room to read.

Reading about druids after actually meeting one and seeing their form of magic in real time was strange as Sybil could now visualize what these technical terms in the book were referring to. As she read, her thoughts drifted back to Pandyr and the short-termed but intensely emotional relationship they had. Despite the fact he tried to kill her to get to Lord Maerel, she hoped he wasn't suffering, wherever he was. If it hadn't been for what happened to his people and the neglect of Lord Maerel and the previous lords, he would have been a good person. So, all things considered, she didn't judge him too harshly for his actions.

After Sybil finished the book, she placed it on the small table next to her door so she wouldn't forget to take it back down to the library the next day. Turning around, she stared at the maple branch she had brought in from the forest that morning. Moving toward it, she could feel her connection to the tree, and realized wizards had stolen the focusing of magic in this way from the druids. Putting her fingers to it, she decided she would have it made into a new staff after all.

Rani, Giselle, and Tanele were all surprised to see Sybil at dinner that night, and she felt good to see how happy they were to see she was finally out of her room. After she had some food in her, she told them about the fight with the oni, leaving out the part about the fate of the children, and they all listened as if they were children hearing a ghost story for the first time.

"I've always wanted to see Keijin in action," Tanele said after Sybil described how he slayed the oni. "It must have been quite the sight."

Finished with her meal, Giselle leaned over to put her head on Tanele's shoulder, causing Tanele to beam down at her. Their relationship had blossomed while Sybil was away.

"What was this Redbeard like, if you don't mind me asking?" Rani said.

"No, I don't mind," Sybil said with a sad smile. "He was a lot to take in all at once. When I met him, it wasn't that I was scared of him, more like overwhelmed by him. But over time, he slowly started opening up and showed he had the kindest soul you could ever find. His rough exterior and behavior was due to his upbringing and the expectations put on him by his clan, but at heart he was a gentle soul." She paused for a moment to clear her throat. "He was also a fantastic fighter, to the point of being a little frightening at times."

Sybil's laugh caused the other three to smile.

After dinner, Tanele and Giselle went up to the training floor, and Rani walked with Sybil to the dormitory. As they walked Rani said, "Yer different from the person ya were when ya left." Sybil turned to her, concerned. "Don't get me wrong, it's not a bad thing. In fact, I'm glad to see ya like this now. Ya were so reserved and closed off before ya left, and now? Well, I just haven't seen ya express so many emotions at one time, and I don't think I've ever heard ya laugh before."

"I suppose the journey did just as Leon had planned," Sybil told her with a shrug. "I've changed a lot over the last month. It would've been impossible not to, really."

"Well, I'm glad for it, though I hated hearing all the terrible things ya were struggling through," Rani said softly. "And I'm glad you're back."

"Glad to be back," Sybil said, smiling.

They both said goodnight and headed into their rooms. Sybil spent some time that evening writing in one of her journals, going through all the events she experienced in as much detail as she could remember, not wanting to ever forget, even the bad times. Just as she started writing about

Blackridge, though, the desire to write left her, and she decided to turn in for the night.

A knock on Sybil's door woke her from her dreamless sleep, and the full moon framed in the window told her that it was still the middle of the night. Since she was just in her undergarments, she grabbed her cloak from the wardrobe and draped it around her before opening the door. Mordecai was standing there, a mixture of emotions on his face, and asked if he could come in. She stepped aside, and he walked over to the window, closing the curtains.

"What is it?" Sybil asked in a whisper.

Mordecai turned to her and thought for a moment before saying, "There's something I've wanted to tell you for a while now, but I feared you wouldn't understand."

"I'll do my best to," she told him, sitting down on her bed.

Taking in a deep breath, he leaned against the bookshelf to his right and said, "The night we first met, that first night Haborym spoke to you in the library, he had spoken to me, as well. He commanded me to bring you into his fold, to make you one of his servants. And for a while, I was doing just that." His silver eyes moved from Sybil to the floor in shame. "But after our conversation in Spindlewood in Lord Osric's garden, I realized just how strong your will is, and overtime, I came to care about you, despite what I said and how I've behaved.

"But then, when Haborym reached into my mind in the woods outside of Blackridge and saw you were no closer to being his servant than the first day I met you, he gave me a new command. He told me if I couldn't convert you by the Winter Solstice I had to kill you. And if I failed this, he would send another like me, someone so closely tied to his magic all his humanity has been forsaken, to hunt us both down."

After a moment of taking all of this in, Sybil asked, "Why does he care what happens to me?"

"I wondered that myself for a while," he said, moving over to her bed and sitting next to her. "But after seeing what you were able to do with the power of Shuheyr, like you were working with him, not for him, I realized just how much of a threat you are to Haborym."

"So what's next then?" she asked. "It sounds like you're going to have to kill me. There's no point in both of us dying."

"No," Mordecai breathed, anger rising up in him. "I could never kill you, not without killing the last bit of myself that still lives."

The way he looked over at Sybil, she could tell there was a library full of things he wished to tell her but couldn't bring himself to.

"Then what do we do?" she asked, her voice quiet.

He sighed as he looked away and his hands turned to fists in his lap.

"We defeat the servant, and then... we kill Haborym."

A short, shocked and terrified laugh broke free from Sybil's lips, and he frowned. She covered her mouth and shook her head before saying, "And how do you suggest we do that?"

"I'm... still figuring that part out," he admitted, standing up and moving to the other side of the room. "But if we continue working on honing your power, it could be possible. Perhaps, this is way he fears you."

"I don't know," she breathed. "How do I know you've told me everything?"

Mordecai turned to her, his face showing that she had hurt him, and said, "How do I get you to trust me, Sybil?"

It was the first time he had said her name aloud, and she could feel another meaning behind it as he said it, something that came from deep inside him. Still, it wasn't enough. She stood up and moved toward him, standing only inches from him, and said, "Show me your face, your true face that you keep hidden behind your magic."

Mordecai stared at the wall behind Sybil, a deep frown on his face, and whispered, "No one's seen my real face for fifteen years."

"I want to know the real you, not just what you curate for the world," she said, taking his cool hands in hers.

"Okay," he breathed as his silver eyes met hers, and she watched them slowly turn to a deep brown. Then, his black hair lightened to auburn, and scars started forming on his unblemished face, one running along his left jawline and the other over his right eye and across his nose. Even though the skin around his forehead and eyes showed he was a few years older in age, the structure of his face had remained the same. Still, there were enough differences Sybil wouldn't have been able to pick him out of a crowd.

Sybil reached up to touch the scar on his jaw, wanting to see if it was real, and he flinched when he felt her fingertips. Still, he let her run her a finger across the scar, and she could feel the indentation in his skin as she did. He gently grabbed her hand, closing his beautiful brown eyes, and placed it to his cheek. Then, he leaned forward and pressed his lips to hers, sending a rush through Sybil's body. It only lasted for a brief moment before he pulled away.

"Just… think about what I've asked," he breathed before returning his face to the Mordecai she knew. "Goodnight, Sybil."

He kissed her hand and then left the room without another word or glance toward her. She sat down on the bed, putting her fingers to her lips, and waited for her heart to stop racing and for the blush to leave her cheeks.

Sybil sought out Mordecai the next day, having spent most of the morning getting up the courage to do so. She couldn't find him in any of his usual spots around the tower. Eventually, she ran into Leon as he was making his daily stroll through the tower, and when she asked him where Mordecai was he said, "I sent him to Crescent Tower."

Sybil followed after her mentor as he continued on his stroll.

"Crescent Tower? Why on earth would you send him there?"

Crescent Tower was on the opposite end of the kingdom from Gibbous Tower, passed the City of the King and the Cormyr River, and ruled by Felix, a dark wizard who matched Leon in power and knowledge. Leon only sent people there on the rarest of occasions, and only through portal. Rumor had it that there was no other way to access Cresent Tower than through teleportation. Beyond that, Sybil knew nothing about Crescent Tower or Felix, its master, and could not fathom a single reason why he would send Mordecai there.

"Young Mordecai came to me for resources and answers I could not provide him," Leon explained, turning a corner. Sybil struggled to keep up with the old man. "Felix is well-versed in dark magic and other arcane forces I do not deal with. He should be back soon enough."

"And you won't tell me what this visit to Felix was about?"

"No, my dear," Leon responded. "But I'm sure you can ask Mordecai when he returns."

Sybil stopped following after her mentor and watched until he disappeared down the stairwell. She didn't know who she was more frustrated with: Mordecai, Leon, or herself for feeling like Mordecai had abandoned her here.

To occupy her time, Sybil spent a few hours riding Dusk around the forest, strangely missing being on the road. When she brought Dusk to the stables, she noticed Frenzy, Redbeard's horse, in one of the stalls near the back. The quarter horse looked tired, with its head slumped down low, so she went into his stall and brushed him to keep him company for a little while. Sybil wondered what they planned to do with him, but as she brushed him, she thought that it might be good for him to be set free. When she brought this idea up to Keijin and Rani at lunch, they both thought it was a good idea.

"We could lead him to the Unicorn's Domain," Keijin suggested. "Creatures are safe in the woods there under its blessing."

"Aye, it's probably the safest place in the entire kingdom," Rani agreed with a nod.

"Great, then let's go," Sybil told them.

Rani laughed.

"I can't just go traipsing off into the woods out of nowhere. I've, uh, got potions to make," she said, her eyes darting from Sybil to Keijin as if she was trying to communicate something. "But if ya want to go today, I'm sure Keijin has the time to go with ya. I've seen the unicorn before, anyway."

"I didn't have anything planned for the rest of the day," he said, shrugging. "We can go now if you'd like."

Frenzy seemed relieved to be out of the stable after nearly a week of being cooped up, and he shook his head happily as they led him further into the Asbriand Forest toward where Keijin knew to be the Unicorn's Domain. He warned her they might not get to see the unicorn, as it never stays in the same spot, but that was alright with her. She had no idea how to act around a unicorn anyway.

"What do you know about Felix from Crescent Tower?" she asked after things had been silent for a while.

"Not much is known about him, and Leon certainly doesn't talk about him, but it's rumored they're brothers, Leon being the older of the two. I met him once, a long time ago and only briefly. He keeps to himself, and it's extremely rare that he takes any visitors at his tower," Keijin explained before looking over at her. "Why do you ask?"

"Leon told me he sent Mordecai there this morning," Sybil told him. "He didn't give me any details, and I'm not sure when he'll be back."

"You always knew when I was coming back."

"That's different... I can feel your aura, but I can't feel his through all the darkness surrounding him," she explained with a sigh. "He could be right behind me, and I'd have no idea through my powers alone."

"You sound worried about him," Keijin noted, looking seriously at her. "But he'll be fine. You'll see."

"I hope you're right."

Keijin thought for a moment and said, "It's rather surprising that Felix allowed him to visit with such short notice, though. There must be a mutual benefit for the two of them to converse and work with one another."

"Is this Felix like Leon or is he someone we should be worried about?"

"I can't help but get the feeling he's the opposite of Leon in their very natures, like how water is the opposite of fire," Keijin replied. "But don't let that discourage you. Mordecai is the one person besides Leon who would be safe in the presence of Felix. Like I said, everything will be fine."

The Asbriand Forest was a dense, old forest with trees decades, possibly even centuries, older than the Kingdom of Irminshu. It had once been sacred land to the elves, and as they departed from this continent, they were given assurances by Leon that he would care for it just as they had. As far as Sybil knew, he had stayed true to these assurances.

While the woodland creatures and other beasts kept their distance at the sight and sound of them, the forest was noisy from animal calls, rustling of leaves and branches, and the flapping of wings as birds took flight from their perches. From what Sybil now knew about the druids, this was a place of great magic, and when they had passed into the unicorn's territory, she could feel its own specific sort of magic. Serene and comforting, it was like a cure for the world where the tumor of Haborym had been a sickness to it. Being here felt like nothing bad in the world could happen, even despite their recent memories to tell them otherwise. Sybil and Keijin dismounted their horses and led them for a little way with Frenzy behind them, wanting to ensure he would know to remain here and not venture to some other, more dangerous part of the forest.

Just as they were about to release Frenzy and start heading back, the sight of something truly incredible stopped them dead in their tracks. Sybil's mouth opened as a silvery-white horse stepped from seemingly out of nowhere. Along its neck was a mane shimmering chromatically from white to a spectrum of colors as it moved, and in the center of its forehead was a spiraled horn that exuded radiant magic so powerful she could feel it gently warming her skin from a hundred yards away. The unicorn stared at them for a moment with its dark, beautiful eyes before moving forward, the plant life under its hooves growing more vibrant instead of being crushed by them.

Moving as slowly as he could to not spook the unicorn, Keijin undid the bridle on Frenzy and nudged him forward. Frenzy trotted up to the unicorn, and their muzzles touched for a moment, as if this was the unicorn's way of welcoming him into its home. With a happy whinny, Frenzy moved past the unicorn and headed further into the forest, disappearing into the trees. Sybil's heart swelled and a smile formed on her face as Frenzy joyfully trotted off. Then, the unicorn started to approach them and stopped when it was within arm's reach.

Sybil flinched as magic started pouring out of the unicorn's horn, falling like shimmering snow over both of them. The pain and heaviness of her heart lifted and was replaced by peace and hope. With this new sense of relief, she couldn't help but let out a little sigh. It was as if she could breathe well for the first time in a month. The unicorn then gave a bow and turned to leave. Sybil and Keijin watched it, their eyes wide, until it disappeared behind the trees just as Frenzy had.

"In all my days, I have never seen the unicorn do something like that before," Keijin said, turning to her. "It must have been able to sense how important you are and how much we needed its relief."

"That was remarkable," Sybil said in barely a whisper. "It's hard to believe a creature like it exists, especially with how many dark creatures there are in the world."

"Well, if you think about it, it makes perfect sense for the unicorn to exist," Keijin replied, turning his horse to leave. "I've been in this world a very long time, and I've witnessed how the world always maintains some form of balance. There will always be light and dark. But when you only look at the dark, it can feel like the light doesn't exist. You just have to understand the balance."

Sybil nodded to his words, following his movements, as her thoughts returned to Mordecai. Did Shuheyr claim her to help balance the scales of the darkness Haborym was spreading through his servants? If she and Mordecai defeated Haborym, the greatest source of darkness, what would have to happen to balance the scales? They were frustrating and concerning questions, but not ones that she wanted to burden Keijin with.

They led their horses back out of the Unicorn's Domain and mounted them. There was a companiable silence between Keijin and Sybil, neither of them feeling like anything needed to be said as they made their way back to the tower. When they reached the stable, though, Keijin's face told Sybil his mind had turned to another topic, and as they were heading out of the stalls, he turned to her in the doorway and took her hand in his.

"There's something I've wanted to tell you for some time now, but it never felt like the right time. But now? Now, feels right," Keijin said, moving closer to her. He pulled her hand to his chest, and she could feel the racing of his heart. "Ever since I met you on the road years ago, you have been important to me. But it wasn't until that night on Alina's porch when I realized just how important."

Realizing what he was saying, Sybil sucked in a quick breath. "Keijin…"

He placed his free hand on her cheek, looking down at her with a tenderness she had never seen before.

"Sybil, I love you."

Before she was able to say anything, he leaned forward and kissed her, his fingers running through her hair. His touch felt good, and she felt safe in his arms. But something in the pit of her stomach nagged at her. She kissed him back for a moment before pulling away by lowering her head.

"Keijin, there's something you should know."

When Sybil looked into his eyes, she could see the understanding of what she was going to say on his face. There was a sadness in his eyes, but he smiled sweetly at her and said, "It's Mordecai, isn't it?"

"I don't know," she told him honestly and shrugged. "I don't know who it is. But I didn't want to keep it from you… he kissed me last night."

A look of defeat flashed across his face, but he nodded.

"Thank you for telling me," he said, and then he perked up a little. "But it sounds like you have yet to decide where your heart lies. I have lived for centuries, making me a patient man. You know my intentions, so just know I'll be here if you decide your heart belongs with me."

Keijin leaned forward to kiss Sybil gently on the forehead before heading out of the stables without another word. With a sigh, she leaned up against the wall and looked over at Dusk.

"What I wouldn't give to be a horse right now," Sybil said to her, and Dusk gave a little knicker in reply.

Just as Sybil was leaving the stables, the whole world seemed to fall into shadows. She readied her wand out in front of her as her heart raced wildly. When she heard a harsh whisper to her left, she immediately turned toward it but saw nothing. Her breathing quickened, and she tried to steady it as she waited for something to attack her from the shadows. But just as suddenly as it appeared, the darkness faded, and she was once again back in the daylight. A stable boy, who had been returning from the tower, was watching her curiously.

Trying her best to shake it off, Sybil headed inside, her breath and heartbeat still struggling to slow. She had no idea if that was a message from Haborym or if she was starting to lose it a little. Maybe what Mordecai had said to her last night made her paranoid, or it made Haborym angry. Whatever the case, she hurried back into the tower, returning the protection within its walls.

Chapter Thirteen

Leon found Sybil in the library at the librarian's desk. The librarian hadn't made an appearance that day, something that happened from time to time, so Sybil helped some of the people searching for resources and ended up just sitting at her desk to work. She had three books about gods and their connection to mortals in front of her all turned to various pages, which she was taking notes on. Before Mordecai came back, she wanted to have more information about her connection to Shuheyr so she could make an informed decision about what he asked her the other night. Despite all her studying, though, she felt like she was getting nowhere.

"We have not had a chance to speak in depth about the missions I assigned you," Leon said, placing his frail hands on the desk. "I was hoping we could do that now, unofficially. Think of it as more of a mentor to mentee conversation than how I address debriefings with the others."

Sybil placed her quill down and gave a nod.

"Very well, I suppose I have been caught up in everything going on. It would be good for us to speak."

Leon smiled before taking a seat in the empty chair next to her and said, "Tell me, how are you?"

"Grieving for Redbeard was hard, and the journey the four of us endured together was draining, but after being here for a week, I'm starting to feel refreshed," she answered. "I'm definitely not the same person I was when I left, and I think I'm still getting used to that."

"Yes, you have grown and experienced much in very little time," Leon said while nodding. "It is understandable you would need some time to adjust. But I am proud of what you have accomplished. You were able to figure out how to defeat the oni, you overcame the torment of the hag, you stopped a revolution from tearing Taragpass apart, and you saved Blackridge, and quite possibly the kingdom, from the corruption of Haborym. Though in those moments you might have felt scared, confused, or hurt, you have proven yourself to be a great wizard indeed."

"Leon, what do you know about Haborym?" she asked, letting the mention of his name spur her question.

Her mentor thought for a moment, a frown on his face, and said, "He is the one that young Mordecai and several other unfortunate souls have tied their lives to in order to escape suffering, only to suffer in a new way. He is a parasite, a consumer of all things good and warm and bright. Beyond that, I know little else other than stories that might be tied to him."

"If you don't mind me asking, why did you bring Mordecai to the tower, knowing what he's tied to?"

A gentle smile returned to his face, and he said, "Everyone I bring to this tower is in some way a lost soul in need of direction. Mordecai was consumed with power and corruption when I met him, but I knew if he spent enough time here, especially around you, someone who would hold his intrigue but not be so easily swayed by his charm, he would change. Out of all of the followers of Haborym, he was the only one I have seen who still had a flicker of his humanity. When I saw him, standing there by your side at Redbeard's funeral, I knew his heart was beginning to heal."

"I care for him, but I don't know if I should," Sybil breathed, staring down at the books in front of her. "It's hard to know if what he's showing me is genuine or a ruse."

"If you are hoping I will tell you whether or not you should love Mordecai, or even trust him, I cannot," Leon said with a shake of his head. "You must decide this for yourself; you must learn to read people and trust your instincts. My interference would only hurt you in the end, whether you would realize it or not."

"Is there nothing more you can tell me?"

Leon reached over and patted her hand.

"My dear girl, it would defeat the purpose of all you and I have worked toward if I just start telling you the answers to everything now." The dinner bell rang, and Leon's face lit up. "Ah, good. It is pot roast tonight. Come along, my dear."

After dinner, Sybil headed to the common room with Rani. Much like the training room, it took up an entire floor of the tower, but instead of training dummies and weapon racks, there were lounge chairs and tables for group activities. No one was in there, so she decided she would confide in Rani about what happened between Mordecai and her the night before as well as Keijin's kiss and confession in the stables. Rani's eyes and mouth grew wider and wider as Sybil told her the stories, and by the end, she seemed at a loss for words.

"I'm afraid if I spend too much time thinking about it everything is going to blow up in my face," Sybil added after a moment of silence.

"So, who then?"

Letting out a sigh, Sybil slid down in the chair she was sitting in.

"That's the question isn't it. I mean, let's be honest, Keijin is the obvious choice, right?"

"The obvious one but maybe not the right one," Rani said. "Sure, Mordecai's rough around the edges and isn't the easiest person to get along with, but neither are you to be quite frank." Sybil made a face, and she continued with her hand raised. "All I'm saying is ya need to be with someone who fits ya, not someone ya feel like ya should be with."

Sybil nodded, and said, "I have to figure out who fits, the."

"A task easier said than done," Rani agreed. "But I'm sure it'll all get sorted when the time is right."

Mordecai finally returned to the tower after being gone for three days. Sybil didn't know this, though, until Leon called her into his office the following morning. When she entered, Sybil found Mordecai and Keijin sitting on the couch in the same spots they sat before starting their journey together. Both of them looked over at her, their expressions impossible to read. The idea of sitting between these two men, who had expressed their feelings to her just days before, was too stressful to bear, so instead of sitting on the couch, she moved to the fireplace and stood there like she had done the day they returned. To her surprise, in walked Giselle, looking quite pleased, who took the spot in the middle of them.

"I know your time at the tower has been short since you returned from your journey," Leon said. "But there are urgent matters which must be dealt with in the City of the King. Without delay, I am sending the four of you on your way to deal with threats being made against King Elias' life. We do not know if it is a single person or a group, but they have managed to be successful enough in their infiltration of the palace to kill the king's double. Not wanting to show fear or weakness, the king is continuing on with events and activities in the palace as usual. He is even throwing the annual feast of the Autumn Harvest the day after tomorrow, but I fear he is running out of time."

"Isn't this is going to be fun?" Giselle breathed through a mischievous smile, her purple eyes glimmering with excitement, and Sybil realized she was Redbeard's replacement. She knew it wasn't fair, but she didn't like Giselle's addition to the group because of this.

Mordecai sighed and said, "Yes, loads."

Wanting to have as much of the daylight as possible, Keijin told his companions they had two hours to pack up and ready themselves for the journey. As Giselle and Sybil were heading down the hall to the dormitories, Tanele and Rani found them, and Tanele looked a little crushed when they told her the news.

"But ya've only been back for a couple of weeks," Rani protested as Tanele pulled Giselle in for a hug.

"Urgent matters, I'm afraid," Sybil told her with a sigh and then raised an eyebrow. "We could try convincing Leon to let you come with us."

"No, no. I think my adventuring days, however short lived they were, are behind me now," she said with an uncomfortable laugh.

Rani gave Sybil a hug goodbye before heading back to her workshop, and Tanele and Giselle went off on their own to be alone for the short time they had.

Just below the training room floors was a place for an assortment of other magical studies, such as creatures, plants, and necromancy. Ermid, the man who works in the necromancy lab, kept completely to himself, and Sybil had only seen him a handful of times. The others in the tower often assumed all his time spent with dead things had made him uncomfortable with the living. Next to his lab and across from the kennels and nursery for the magical animals and plants some of Leon's people studied was a workshop, run by a gnome named Luvodert. In this workshop, Luvodert created and enchanted all sorts of magical items. He had been the one to make Sybil's wand and original staff and had been working on the new staff since she brought him the branch a few days ago.

Sybil walked into Luvodert's workshop and found him standing on a stool, leaning over a shortsword with a book in his hand. Enchantment was a form of magic she knew little about but understood that enchantments were somewhat similar to wards, which she had been studying recently since Mordecai had shown her his true face under the protection of Leon's wards.

Luvodert didn't seem to notice when she walked in, so Sybil cleared her throat.

"Yes, yes. Just give me a moment," he grumbled with a wave of his hand. After a few minutes, the sword started to glow blue. With a sigh, he shimmied down the stool and said, "I really wish they would bring me more of a challenge."

"Perhaps you should make people things beyond what they've requested," she suggested. "Not everyone has as creative of a mind as you, Luv."

"Especially not you wizards," he muttered before gesturing to the staff in the corner of the room. "'Exactly like it was,' you said. Well, just as you suggested, I made a few tweaks because I never just repeat. It would go against my code as an artist."

"You're a credit to your culture," Sybil remarked, knowing well enough now, after nearly four years, not to argue with Luvodert. "What did you tweak about it?"

She turned to get a good look at the staff and let out a small gasp when she saw Redbeard's wolf totem, the one he received from his clan for killing a werewolf, embedded into the wood near the top of the staff. Luvodert also made the staff a bit slimmer, which would make it lighter to carry, and the top of it was carved into a design which would do a good deal of damage if something was hit with it. Sybil walked up to the staff and ran her thumb over the black stone of the totem.

"We found that in the ashes of the pyre," he told her, not seeming to understand the value it had. "I thought it would make for an interesting design. Plus, you seemed to really like the guy."

"Yeah, I did," she said softly, thinking back to when Redbeard proudly flexed his muscles to show off his wolf tattoos, and smiled a little. "As always, you've made a masterpiece."

"I know, I know," he replied with another wave of his hand before returning to his work.

With her staff in hand, feeling like she was complete again, Sybil headed up to her room to pack up her stuff. When she entered her room, though, she found herself face to face with a shadow, a smoke-like creature that didn't seem to be bothered by the sunlight pouring into her room. Hate and pain radiated off this creature, making her feel sick to her stomach. It couldn't be real; she was protected by Leon's wards. Surely, this was only in her imagination. It reached out its hand and stepped forward.

Jabbing her new staff forward, the shadow vanished in an instant, and once again, she was alone in her room. Letting out a staggered breath, she was glad to be returning to close quarters with three other people. Something was definitely after her.

It was around midday when Sybil met Keijin outside with the horses, having improved her timeliness during their adventuring together. They hadn't spoken more than a few words since the other day in the barn, but he smiled at her as she approached and helped her strap her bag to Dusk's saddle. She wanted to say something to him but couldn't think of anything. Thankfully, Mordecai and Giselle exited from the tower and headed toward them before the silence grew to be too much.

"I don't know about you all, but I'm certainly excited," Giselle said with a mischievous smile as she attached her bag to her horse, a gray thoroughbred named Nightshade. "Leon's sent me on many missions to the City, but never directly into the palace."

"It's certainly not an easy task," Mordecai said, walking past Sybil to his horse. He moved so close that his cloak brushed against her, causing her heart to flutter. "We'll need to plan every step in order to be successful in this, especially since the guards and staff are already on high alert."

The party mounted up and started off down the road. Sybil kept to the back, feeling the heaviness of what they were about to do and the strange dynamic that now existed in their group. Even though she was sometimes hard to get along with, Sybil was glad Giselle was there to provide a buffer between the three of them. While Giselle and Keijin were at the front, discussing something Sybil couldn't hear from a distance, Mordecai slowed his horse to meet pace with hers.

"Sorry I left so abruptly the other night," he said, still looking ahead. "I needed answers Leon wasn't able to provide."

"And did you learn them from Felix?" Sybil asked, trying to keep her emotions at bay.

"Some," he replied, glancing over at her.

She didn't know if it was her mind playing tricks on she or if she could see through his magic, but for an instant, his silver eyes flashed to brown.

"Most of what he knows about Haborym, I had already learned. And the only insight he had about your tie with Shuheyr was that we would learn more if we sought out his followers. Fortunately, we'll find plenty in the City. The prominent temple in the Inner Ring is dedicated to him."

"I didn't know there were temples for him."

Mordecai nodded and said, "Shuheyr is easily the most important god to the people of this kingdom. With the land being so far north, the days change rapidly in length throughout the year. The ancient people would pray for Shuheyr to save them from the darkness in the winter and rejoice in the summer when he brought long days of sunshine to support their crops." Sybil knew all this, of course, but didn't realize the ideas were so widespread through the kingdom. "It's only a coincidence that we haven't seen one of his temples yet on our travels."

There was silence for a while before Mordecai spoke up again, "So, have you given any more consideration to my question?"

"Of course, I have," Sybil said with a sigh. "If you see no other way, then I am behind you. Just tell me what you need of me, and I will do my best to follow through with it. Just… promise me something?"

"What?"

"If it comes down to dying or becoming his servant," she told him, her voice going cold. "Please, kill me."

Mordecai flinched at this, but after a moment, he gave a nod. "If that's what you wish."

"It is," she breathed, and the conversation died there.

The party was only able to make it a few hours down the road before the sun started to set. The daylight hours were growing shorter as winter approached. After making camp, they all sat around the campfire, eating their provisions and discussing the plan for when they arrived at the City. Mordecai told them even though his old persona, the king's advisor, had been removed from court, he would still be a viable option as a visitor. He didn't think the party would be able to all arrive as a group together, like they had at Lord Maerel's estate, so they would need to enter with their own personas. Keijin, they decided, could go in as himself, having developed his own reputation and renown over the years, and Giselle had close relationships with many of the gentry and would be able to convince one to bring her to the palace. That just left Sybil.

"What if I sought an audience with the king and just told him who I am and why I'm here?" she asked, not being able to think of anything better. "Maybe that would cause whoever's out for the king to focus on me and not notice the three of you."

Mordecai thought for a moment before giving a shrug.

"I don't see why not," he said. "But it could put you in as much danger as the king."

"She'll have us there for her," Giselle said, nudging Mordecai to his extreme dislike. "Besides, from what I've seen and heard, she can handle her own in a fight."

"It would also allow us to communicate with the king more easily," Keijin added. "Honestly, this might be our best play."

"Fine," Mordecai growled before turning to Sybil. "You've done well against our enemies thus far, but anyone who's after the king and yet to be caught will be skilled in fighting beyond your capabilities, so don't go running into a fight on your own. You're too important to die for this king."

"Very well," she said, a little annoyed at him lecturing her in front of Keijin and Giselle. "It's not like I'm looking to get stabbed again or anything."

Giselle let out a laugh. "Well, I guess I will try to keep my blades to myself then."

Something caught Keijin's eye from afar and his face went hard before he said, "Maybe that's not the best idea."

The party turned to look at what he saw. There was a team of orcs heading toward them, holding torches to light their way in the woods. When they noticed the adventurers, the orcs drew their weapons. Unfortunately, there was no reasoning with orcs, who had grown spiteful of humans over the years for settling in lands they once lived, so Keijin said nothing as he rose to his feet with his sword and shield in hand. Sybil reached over and grabbed her staff as Giselle sighed and slunk away into the shadows, using her stealth to sneak around the orcs and catch them by surprise.

There were eight orcs, two for each adventurer, and as the orcs approached the party, Sybil cast an invisible armor around her, something a bit stronger than the ward she used to use on herself. Orcs were strong and their blades sharp. Without magic, they could tear through her with one slice if they managed to get close enough. They were all clumped together, so Sybil pointed her staff in their direction and unleashed a ball of fire, similar to the one she used in the training room but far more powerful. All eight of them

183

flew in different directions as the flames exploded between them, and their leather armor and skin were burned by the heat.

The two who were closest to Sybil charged, and Mordecai sent a thick, black fog toward them, nearly surrounding them in darkness. She could see the orcs' faces as they choked on the fog, and their skin started to shrivel as they aged rapidly before her. One of them fell down dead, and the other, still clutching onto a bit of life, fell to his knees. The other six orcs' attentions were on Mordecai and Sybil completely now, and three of them pulled out their bows and started firing arrows at them. The orcs were skilled archers, and Mordecai was hit in the thigh. Another landed in the center of Sybil's left shoulder, the force of the bow causing it to pierce effortlessly through her protection spell.

Giselle appeared out of the shadows behind the orcs, slitting one of their throats before any of them even saw her, and Keijin moved to one of the archers closest to him and struck him down, slicing through his collar bone. One of the orcs slashed at Keijin, getting him across the chest. Since he wasn't wearing his armor, the blade cut through his shirt and skin, causing blood to trickle down his front. This didn't faze him, though, and he removed the orc's head with one swift motion of his sword. Giselle took out another orc with a blade through his back and out through his chest.

As Sybil was bent over from the pain in her shoulder, another orc rushed her, holding his sword with both hands above his head. Mordecai reached out, black ichor pooling from his skin, and sent spikes of dark energy toward the orc, hitting him with tremendous force on one side and flying out the other. One of the orcs was able to catch Giselle as she swerved around him, and stabbed her in the side, causing her to drop her blades. Keijin was busy with the other one still standing, so Sybil sent a bolt of lightning at the one holding Giselle, which caused him to drop to the ground, spasming. Once Keijin had taken care of the orc in front of him, he pivoted around and stabbed the other through the chest. The only orc left alive was the one whose life had been mostly sapped away, and Mordecai sent a bolt through his head.

"They're sure to have a camp nearby, possibly prisoners," Keijin said, pulling off his bloody shirt. "We should check it out."

"Not without a potion or two, first," Giselle grumbled as she hobbled over to her bag, pulling out a few vials of Rani's potions.

She handed Mordecai and Sybil a potion as Keijin came over to look at Sybil's shoulder. The pain was intense, but she didn't want him to touch it.

"No, wait, please," Sybil cried as he wrapped his fingers around the arrow.

A small shriek escaped her as he pulled the arrow from her flesh. The pain was blinding, and she placed her forehead on his shoulder as she groaned.

"Oh, I hate you."

"I know, I know," he breathed and let out a laugh as he started to heal the wound with his powers. "You're welcome."

Keijin could only do so much in one sitting, so in order to fully heal the wound, Sybil drank the potion Giselle had given her, tasting the bittersweet liquid for the first time.

Mordecai ripped the arrow from his leg, causing it to bleed profusely, and quickly drank a potion. After a moment, the bleeding stopped, but the wound was still partially there. Keijin turned to help him with it, but Mordecai put his hand up.

"I'd rather not, thanks," he said. "Go tend to the girl."

Giselle was leaning against a tree, pouring water over her wound that the potion had had a similar effect on. Keijin placed his hand on her stomach, and it was barely a scar when he removed it.

"Oh, that's a neat trick," Giselle said with a tired laugh. "Shall we venture on toward their camp?"

"It should be in this direction," Keijin said, pointing where the orcs had been heading from. He pulled a new shirt from his pack and slid it on. "I doubt it would be too far from the road."

Keijin had been right, clearly experienced in the methods and behavior of orcs. There was a camp with several tents lined around, made of animal skin, a campfire in the center where two orcs were sitting, eating something they had roasted over the fire, and a cage with a man and woman between two of the tents. To avoid any more bloodshed, Sybil stepped forward as stealthily as she could and reached into the orcs' minds, causing them to fall into a deep sleep they wouldn't wake from for several hours. Once the coast was clear, Keijin moved to the cage and smashed open the lock with the hilt of his sword.

"Don't worry, you're safe now," he said to the two prisoners offering them his hand.

"There was a whole team of 'em," the woman said. "They'll be back soon."

"Don't worry," Giselle said with a smile. "We've taken care of them."

Both the prisoners were frightened when Giselle came into view, but she didn't seem to notice. Common people must have given her looks like that all the time, but while they saw her as terrifying in her differences, Sybil thought she was the most beautiful woman she had ever seen and didn't understand how anyone couldn't see it. When Keijin offered to escort the prisoners back to their homes, they thanked him but said no, eyeing Giselle. Instead, they headed back to the road, heading away from the City of the King.

After watching them go, Sybil shook her head, turned back to the others, and said, "Sometimes it doesn't feel good to help people."

"Oh, you'll get used to it," Giselle said with a shrug. "They mean well. It's just hard for them to understand things different from the world they know."

Chapter Fourteen

Shortly after making it back to camp, Sybil passed out on her bedroll. In her dream that night, she saw a man who had been overtaken by the darkness, by Haborym's influence. While she couldn't see his face, she could feel the anguish in his heart and the familiar pull of the darkness beckoning her forward. Sybil had tried to move closer to this man, to learn more about him, but she was awoken by Mordecai's hand on her shoulder. There was barely any light in the sky, and the other two were still asleep. He gestured for her to follow him, and they left the campsite, going far enough away so they could speak privately. Since he didn't accept Keijin's healing power, he was limping a little from the night before.

"You really should accept his help," Sybil told him.

Mordecai shook his head. "His healing magic is painful, and the way it affects my magic, it might cause Haborym to take notice of me. I do my best to only let him in on my terms."

"Is he the reason why you wear a different face?"

"Yes," he breathed, staring up at the gray sky. "I snuck away from his line of sight and changed my appearance when he wasn't looking, and he's been struggling to find me ever since. The only times he has, he couldn't see my face, only my thoughts, so he can't track me."

"Well, for what it's worth, I like your true face. You're rather handsome," she told him with a smile. He looked at her skeptically. "Truly. I even prefer it to the one you wear now, even if you intentionally made yourself beautiful."

Mordecai turned to Sybil and brought his fingertips to her cheeks.

"I don't deserve to be looked at the way you are doing so now," he breathed, sending a rush through her head. "Despite all I've said and done, you care for me and see the humanity in me. Why?"

"I don't know," she answered honestly. "Perhaps we're simply two sides of the same coin, one shining in the light and the other cast over by darkness. We're the same, and I can feel your heart despite how much you contradict it."

The sound of the other two waking up and breaking down camp kept Mordecai from saying whatever he was about to. Sybil also wanted to say more, to tell him about the dreams and experiences she had been having which she knew were directly tied to Haborym, but she wanted to find a time when they were truly alone to discuss them.

The City of the King was a huge metropolis, bigger than any city Sybil had ever seen. When she was first on her own, free from the cult she grew up in, she had seen the City from a distance, traveling toward Easthaven, a town to its south. In order to reclaim their lands, the elves and orcs created a temporary truce, working together to defeat the humans, and laid siege to the City. But this had been the humans' stronghold, and the elves and orcs were defeated and scattered, their truce broken. Since that battle, the humans governed this land absolutely, just as they did in the Southern Kingdoms.

Being up close to it made Sybil feel overwhelmed before they even entered its gates. On the outer edge of the City was a fortified wall nearly three stories high with guards stationed every dozen feet from each other. It was well lit with lanterns, torches, and magical orbs of light. The giant wrought-iron gate to the City was open, and they were able to enter without much fuss from the guards, though they did eye them and their weapons suspiciously.

Mordecai led his companions through the Outer and Middle Rings into the Inner Ring, and Sybil was able to see the state of the poorest citizens to the wealthiest ones. As they rode through the Outer Ring, some of the street urchins came running up to them begging for coin or a bit of food. Even though they looked sick and hungry, Mordecai told her not to give them anything because it was only going to cause more of them to surround the party, drawing attention to them. It was hard, though, because they were just children. As the party passed them, Sybil couldn't help but imagine a small Mordecai in their faces. What if someone had taken pity on him long ago?

The Middle Ring was much nicer than the slums of the Outer Ring and was bustling with people and was still busy far into the night. This was the market district, made up of various shops and vendors, and according to Mordecai, one could find any good they desired there, for a price. Of the other places they had traveled together, it reminded Sybil most of Taragpass, and she found herself watching the hustle and bustle of the common people with as much interest as she had then.

When the party made it to the wall of the Inner Ring, the guards were suddenly concerned with their presence in the City. The gate to this part of the City was closed, namely to keep out the peasants, and the number of guards bordered on ridiculous for such a small area of the City. Something told Sybil their numbers weren't just because they were on high alert due to the threats against the king's life. Their one and only job was to keep the lower citizens from mingling with the gentry and nobles.

Still, after some convincing from Mordecai and Keijin, they let the party through, and they entered into the Inner Ring of the City. As soon as their horses passed the wall, Sybil felt like they had entered another world. In the center was the king's palace, a gigantic fortress made out of marble and limestone with gold trim that could rival the Gibbous Tower in a feat of architecture. Around the palace were finely built houses three times the size as any seen in the Middle Ring with manicured lawns and gardens similar to the one behind Lord Osric's estate. People dressed in fine garbs and gowns meandered about as if they had all the time in the world, many of them stopping to watch as the party rode up to a building with an ornate sign with "The Queen's Resort" written on its face. It was the inn they would be staying in, but it was nothing like any of the inns Sybil had seen so far in her travels.

Stepping through the doors, Sybil thought they surely must have had the wrong place as this was somewhere fit for royalty to stay. Everything glimmered in the light of the intricately designed lanterns and sconces along the walls. The adventurers, dirty from the journey and bloodied from their encounter with the orcs, were a sight for the workers of the inn, who were used to only the most prestigious of clients. The elven woman at the front desk watched the adventurers approach her with a look of disgust on her sharp face. Mordecai pulled out a small, flattened piece of gold with the inn's symbol, which was etched into the wall above the woman's head, and her expression completely changed.

"Welcome back to the Queen's Resort, my good sir," she said in a pleasant, breathy voice. "Shall it be one room or multiple for you and your companions?"

"Four singles, please," Mordecai answered. "And tell the staff that we wish for our rooms to not be disturbed during our stay."

"Yes, of course, very good sir," she said, pulling out four keys from under the desk and sliding them across to him. "Anything else I can assist you with this evening?"

"That will be all," he said as he passed out the keys to each of his companions.

The room Sybil was given was immaculate and lavished with beautiful furniture made out of mahogany wood and silk. In the center of the room was a four poster bed with shiny blue curtains draped across it that matched the sheets and blankets on the bed. There was a full-sized bathtub in the corner next to a wash basin, and on a table on the other side of the room was a large basket filled with fruits, wine, and chocolate. Sybil pulled a grape off its stem and popped it in her mouth as she walked around the room, dropping her bag next to the bed.

Everything about this place was amazing, until Sybil reached the window and saw the view she had. Just across the road was the temple of Shuheyr Mordecai had mentioned. Right out front, there was a twenty foot tall statue of Shuheyr, which looked strikingly familiar to the drawings she had seen of him growing up. He was covered in gold plating, and his arms were raised high above his head. With a sigh, she flung the curtains closed and readied herself for bed.

In her dream that night, Sybil found herself standing in a lush meadow and glanced around trying to figure out her surroundings. She turned one way, and when she turned back around, a cottage was suddenly there where once there was nothing. Raising an eyebrow, she slowly started moving toward the cabin. Smoke billowed from the chimney, and the scent of home cooked food and the hint of flowers filled the air. She walked up the steps of the porch and turned the door handle. The door creaked as it opened, and in the middle of the room were two high back chairs with a man sitting in one of them.

With his light blonde hair and bright blue eyes, Shuheyr looked just as he did in the iconography Sybil's teachers had her study as a child. But unlike his statue, he was the size of a regular man, perhaps even shorter than Mordecai and Keijin, but it was hard to tell with him sitting down. An affectionate smile grew on his face, and he gestured toward the chair.

"My child, please, sit," he said, his voice airy and melodic. "I have been waiting a long time to speak with you."

After a moment of hesitation, Sybil did as he requested and sat uncomfortably in the chair only a few feet from this powerful and famous god she had been running from her entire life.

"Is this just a dream?" she asked, not sure what else to say.

Shuheyr laughed, shook his head, and said, "No, dear Sybil, this is no dream. Unfortunately, though, the only time I could find my way to you was when you were sleeping, a time when the mind is far more vulnerable to outside influences." Sybil now understood why Mordecai avoided sleep. "I'm sorry to have done this without your consent, but I fear we are running out of time."

"What do you mean?"

"I have been watching you for your entire life, save for the time you have been under the protection of Gibbous Tower, and I overheard the conversation you and Mordecai had on the road the other day," Shuheyr said. "You and he plan to destroy Haborym."

"So, what if we do?" Sybil asked, irritated he had been eavesdropping.

This made Shuheyr smile.

"You will need my help, of course."

"Have you come to make some sort of deal? What else do you want from me?"

"More than anything, right now, I just want you to listen," he told her, putting his hand up. "It has become apparent to me that you do not understand the nature of your tie to me, or what the plan was involving your birth." As much as Sybil wanted to say something, she remained silent. "A Soul Child is a unique being on this earth, so much so there have only been a handful of them since creation. I have come to understand you believe you were promised to me at birth, tied to me like some sort of sacrifice, but this is not the case at all. So, I would like to educate you on the true nature of your birth:

"On the Winter Solstice, the magic in this world is at its strongest and the border between the realities of mortals and the gods becomes razor thin. Twenty years ago, on the Winter Solstice, I was able to use the man you know to be your biological father as a vessel. Using his body, I wed your mother and we consummated our joining. From that ceremony, we were able to conceive you, a Soul Child. Even though I was not in the mortal world physically, a part of my soul was able to transfer over to you at the moment of your conception."

Sybil's body had grown cold, and she was gripping the arms of the chair tightly. She couldn't seem to wrap her mind around what he was saying.

"Sybil, you are *my* child, my daughter," he breathed, leaning forward. "You are the child of a god. You are not owed to me; I do not want to take anything from you. But you are a part of me, and we will always be connected to one another, no matter how hard you fight it."

"Why? Why create me?" she breathed, tears starting to flow down her cheek as the pain from her childhood, a pain she fought so hard to keep buried, bubbled to the surface. "What's the point of all this?"

"There are many reasons," he remarked, watching her with compassionate eyes. "But the one we must concern ourselves with now is that you are to be the one who saves the mortal world from darkness, from Haborym. The power you inherited from me will help you do this, but you need to learn to trust me and work with me for that power to be fully realized.

"Presently, though, there are other concerns for you to take care of. Once those have been resolved, I would like you to come to my temple so that we may speak again of your own free will."

Sybil tried to say something, to ask him more questions, but the cottage was slipping from her vision, and she awoke with a start. The sun was starting to rise, and when she opened her curtains, she could see it framed between the open arms of Shuheyr. Staring at his gilded face for a moment, she felt a storm of emotions swirling instead of her. She didn't know whether or not she wanted to cry or scream or laugh, but she just closed the curtains angrily and fell back in bed until someone came to fetch her.

Mordecai knocked on Sybil's door about an hour later, and she let him in. When he noticed the expression on her face and bags under her eyes, he asked, "Bad night?"

"Something like that," Sybil told him with a sigh. "Shuheyr came to me in my dream. I'm still trying to make sense of what he told me." Mordecai looked at her with great curiosity, but she shook her head. "There will be time for that later. He said to speak with him at the temple once we're done with our mission."

"Pragmatic of him," Mordecai grumbled. "Are you okay?"

"Yeah, I'm fine, just tired," she replied, sitting down on her bed. "Let's talk more about it after we save the king. What's the plan?"

Mordecai nodded and, getting straight to business, said, "You'll go in first, as you are, this morning. Request an audience with the king and be honest with him about why you're here, excluding the part about us. Then, I will return to court as my old persona. Since the king is having his grand feast tomorrow to celebrate the Autumn Harvest, there will be a lot of people arriving at the palace today, so I will not be conspicuous. And the same goes for Keijin, who will be arriving as himself utilizing his fame among the nobles. As for Giselle, she has her own plan of getting into the palace using one of her contacts, which I have no doubt she'll succeed with.

"Also, it's important that none of us behave like we know each other. The assassins should have their eyes on you alone as the king's protection, but we will be keeping close watch over the two of you. If anything happens while we're not around, though, find a way to contact us. Don't just try to handle it on your own."

Sybil's nerves were overloaded as she approached the palace on her own. Even though it was a short distance from the inn, Mordecai suggested she ride in on Dusk to give herself a bit more stature as she arrived. The guards stopped her and asked what her business was, and she told them exactly what her companions planned for her to say.

"I am Sybil Dawn, apprentice to the Enlightened," she said, lifting her chest a little as she spoke. "Here to request an immediate audience with the king on direct business from Gibbous Tower."

The guards were skeptical at first, but after a few moments of thought and murmurs, they called for an escort to take Sybil to the king. A large man with plate armor and a greatsword sheathed against his back found her, introducing himself as Malic, captain of the king's personal guard. He had a scar running from the cleft of his chin down his throat and his black hair was cut so short he was practically bald. With the fairness of skin typical in the north, Sybil knew he was from the Southern Kingdoms, possibly the Southern Isles, by the hickory hue of his skin. His deep brown eyes stared down at her, sizing her up, before he gestured with his chin and led her into the palace.

Without her staff to support her, Sybil might not have been able to walk straight with how overwhelmed she was with everything she saw and the weight of knowing she was now in the royal family's palace. There were nobles and gentry roaming around the palace and servants, most of them of elven descent, darting this way and that to meet the needs and wants of all of them. Sybil kept close behind Malic, not wanting to raise any suspicions, as she glanced around at the majesty of the royal palace. She stared up at portraits of members of the royal family, most of them kings long passed, and famous weapons and armor of warriors both in and working for the royal family. There was so much history in these halls that the nobles who flitted about, talking of superficial things, did not seem to appreciate.

Malic led Sybil to a far room in the back of the palace, opened the large wooden door for her, and announced her to the king as they stepped inside the room. Instead of sitting on a throne, like she had imagined meeting him, the king was sitting at a desk in a leather chair that was certainly grand but nothing compared to a throne. He had been writing letters while two other guards stood watch over him on opposite ends of the room when Malic and Sybil entered, but his dark brown eyes were scanning over her now.

If she had stumbled upon this room, she wouldn't have assumed this man to be the king. While he was dressed in fine garbs, they weren't of the vibrant colors the other nobles wore but darker tones of blue and red. His face and hands, while still youthful, showed experience and hard work. In truth, Keijin looked more like a king than he did. But there was something in his eyes, surety and experience, which told her he was, in fact, the king.

"I wasn't aware the Enlightened had an apprentice," King Elias said, setting down his quill. "What's your business here?"

"It's my understanding that there has been an attempt on your life," Sybil replied, taking a few steps forward, which caused Malic and the other two guards to flinch. "The Enlightened has sent me to help you figure out who they are and put a stop to them. He tells me you are continuing on with your events and meetings as usual, despite your body double having recently been killed."

"It's true nothing escapes the watchful eyes of Gibbous Tower," he remarked with a smirk, making Sybil wonder what all he knew about Leon and the tower. "You seem young, though. Do you truly have the skills to protect me from assassins?"

"Must I prove it to you, your majesty?" she asked, raising an eyebrow.

The king leaned back in his chair, staring at Sybil with an amused smile on his face, and said, "I'm sure that won't be necessary." He rose and moved around the desk to stand in front of her. His presence was intimidating, and it wasn't just because he was king. "Well, wizard, what do you intend to do?"

"I thought I'd accompany you today and then tomorrow at the feast, see if there are any suspicious characters and ask people some questions," she replied, trying to sound like she knew what she was doing. "But I'd also like to investigate where your double was murdered in case there are any clues your men overlooked." Sybil glanced over at Malic, who had a scowl on his face. "No offense, of course."

"Don't mind him. Malic takes his job far too seriously," the king said with a laugh. "Come, let me show you to my bed chambers." Sybil made a face, causing him to grin at her ignorance. "It's where he was murdered."

Embarrassed, she gave a nod and followed him out of the room. As she followed the king through the palace, with Malic close behind them, the nobles and gentry all turned to stare at her, wondering who this stranger to the court was. On the second floor of the palace, in the west wing, was the king's bedchambers, a ridiculously large room with a bed big enough for four people in the center of it. There were tapestries lining the wall, showing various stories of ages past, and she recognized a couple as the story of how the kingdom came to be settled and won against the elves.

"It's been a few days," the king remarked, watching as Sybil roamed about the room. "There might not be anything for you to discover here."

After close inspection, both normally and with magic, the king was proven right as there was nothing here to give her any insight into his double's death. But, at least, she knew it wasn't magic which killed him.

"Why was he sleeping in your chambers that night?" she asked, abandoning her search. "Where were you staying?"

"With my wife, the queen, if you must know," the king said. "I rarely stay in here, I think the design is ghastly, so my double fills the room for me. Only my closest guards and servants know, though."

"Did you have any indication someone was targeting you before this?"

He laughed and shook his head.

"I'm a king, that's why I have a double to begin with. Did I know someone who could sneak their way into my bedchambers was targeting me, though? No, I didn't. Nothing like this has ever happened in the palace before. It's supposed to be impenetrable."

"Then, it must be someone who has access to this part of the palace but who isn't close enough to know you typically spend the night with the queen," Sybil thought aloud. "Have you questioned everyone who fits that description?"

"Yes," the king said, looking slightly annoyed. "Everyone has been accounted for, each of them with solid alibis, and my trust."

Sybil nodded, giving the room one more look over, and headed back out into the corridor. The king followed her and heaved a sigh as Malic shut the door. It didn't make any sense to her. How could someone have made it all the way to the king's chambers without anyone noticing and all the servants and guards being accounted for?

"How was your man killed?" she asked, feeling like she was just grasping at straws by this point.

"Three stab wounds, all in the chest," Malic replied in a grumble. "They stuck him while he slept, probably covering his mouth just in case he screamed."

"And were the guards present outside of the doors?"

Malic shifted and cracked his neck.

"Yeah, but there's usually about a five-minute window when the guards change in the middle of the night. Something we've cracked down on since then."

Sybil frowned and said, "Very well. I suppose all I can do now is accompany you and hope to develop a list of suspects, at the very least."

"I don't mind the company," the king said with a laugh and a wave of his hand. "But we must be off to the throne room. I was due there nearly an hour ago."

The throne room had a crowd of people waiting for the king, each of them more regal than the last. Sybil had never seen so many well-dressed, well-groomed people in one place. A small smile spread on her face as she thought about how much Redbeard would hate it here.

The throne was feet above everyone, needing stairs for the king to reach it. Sybil stood at the base of the stairs, and Malic suggested to her in a low whisper that she might as well sit. They would be there for a while.

Sybil couldn't help but gaze at all the artistry present in the room. This place was the beating heart of the Kingdom of Irminshu. There were six massive columns, three on each side, holding up the vaulted ceiling painted with an assortment of scenes from the kingdom's history, just as the tapestry in the king's chambers had depicted. Between the columns were stained glass windows with statues below them depicting the six human gods standing before them. Shuheyr was closest to the king's right, and then there was Minerva, the goddess of knowledge and wisdom; Faunalynn, the goddess of nature; Lorelai, the goddess of death; Zoltas, the goddess of birth and fertility; and lastly, a shrouded figure to symbolize the god of darkness, whose name had been forgotten by time.

Everyone seemed to quickly grow used to Sybil's presence. As they carried on with their business with the king, discussing economics and other such matters she knew little about, she glanced around at all the people in the room. No one seemed suspicious from what she could tell, but she had little to go on. All of them seemed strange to her, and she could tell they were all forcing themselves to be someone they weren't. What sort of lies did they tell and characters did they play? Seeing all of them in one room, hearing them talk with one another, Sybil started to feel like Mordecai was no more fake in his personas then the rest of them.

Just as Mordecai came into her thoughts, the doors flew open, hitting the walls with a loud bang and causing everyone in the room to turn to look. In walked a short, plump man, wearing a bright green outfit with shiny black shoes and a wide brim hat with a plume that matched his clothes. Mordecai had told her nothing of the king's advisor he once pretended to be, but Sybil knew this was him as soon as her eyes adjusted to the absurdity of his outfit. Thankfully, no one was watching her because she rolled her eyes.

"Your majesty," the advisor announced, making his way toward the throne, his stylish cane clicking as he walked. "It's so wonderful to see you again. My, have I missed the grandeur of the palace and the warm glow of your presence."

The king seemed deeply annoyed to see his former advisor heading toward him, but everyone else in the room was enamored by his presence. Many of the people in the room eyed him with longing, as if their hearts belonged to him. Even though his style was absolutely ridiculous, the face he now wore was handsome, nearly perfect, despite the age it was beginning to show. When his eyes met Sybil's, he winked, causing a couple of women near her to glare.

"Mephidilea," the King murmured. "Didn't expect to see you back at the palace so soon."

"Oh, you should've known I would never stay away for too long, especially for the Autumn Harvest. I just can't help myself," Mephidilea said with a giggle. Could this really be Mordecai? It seemed too opposite to his character. "But, please, carry on with your business. I don't want to be a distraction."

"Yeah, right," the king breathed only loud enough for Malic and Sybil to hear him.

In the far corner of the room was a buffet table with an assortment of foods. After he exchanged pleasantries with the other nobles in the room, Sybil watched as Mephidilea headed over to the table, and as soon as the table was free from other grazers, she joined him. She couldn't help herself; she had to experience this character close up. He looked up at her from across the table, smiled, and said, "Quite the spread we have here, eh?"

"Indeed," she breathed, putting various fruits on a plate. "So, Mephidilea, how long did you work for the king?"

"For this king? Only a couple months," Mephidilea replied before tossing a blueberry in his mouth. "But for his father, I was under his employ for nearly a decade. King Elias decided that he didn't need an advisor, which I'll admit, he's far more capable than his father in matters I typically advised in."

A couple more people came to the table, and Sybil said, "Well, it was a pleasure meeting you Mephidilea."

"The pleasure was all mine," he replied, with a flick of his wrist, flashing his gaudy rings. "Do save a dance for me at the feast tomorrow."

Nodding, Sybil left the table and started to roam around the room, trying to get a better sense of who all these people were. Everyone she met and questioned seemed innocent enough, and the only people who drew her suspicions were the ones who were a bit too curious about her powers as a wizard. Most of them hadn't even arrived before the king's double was murdered, and none of them seemed to know anything bad had happened here when Sybil hinted at it. Eventually, she had spoken to everyone in the room and found herself sitting back down on the bottom step of the throne, trying to figure out what to do next.

The king seemed to be enjoying himself as much as Sybil was, and they both heaved a sigh of relief when Malic concluded the assembly and asked everyone to leave the throne room. Shortly after that, the servants announced that dinner was being served in the grand ballroom, and the king asked Sybil to join his guests. She walked with the king to the grand ballroom, and when they arrived, he sat next to a gorgeous woman with golden hair and blue eyes. She was wearing a crown of silver and diamonds matching the silver embroidery and trim of her red gown. As the king came to her side, he took her hand and kissed it lovingly before sitting beside her. Thinking back to Lady Joylane's words and comparing them to the love and compassion in the king's and queen's eyes, Sybil wondered how a match like that came to be.

While Sybil had been in the throne room with the king, Keijin and Giselle had made their way into the palace. Keijin was wearing his finest garbs, looking like royalty himself, and many of the guests were eyeing him, while giggling and whispering to each other. There was a spot at his table, so Sybil joined him and asked who he was so the other people sitting there didn't assume they knew each other. Giselle sat at the table opposite them with five men who were listening to her stories intently. Sybil couldn't tell which of them had brought her or if she just came with the lot of them.

When Mephidilea entered the grand ballroom sometime after Sybil and the king, he was wearing a different outfit. This one was black with trim that ran a spectrum of shimmering colors around him, as if he had sewed a rainbow into his clothes. He was no longer wearing a hat and his short hair was styled to stand inches above his head and sweep back at the top. Sybil couldn't believe this eccentric character was Mordecai or any king had allowed him to be an advisor for ten years. Seeing this Mephidilea led her to admire the king for his decision to let him go.

"Have you been to court before?" Sybil asked Keijin as they started the second course.

"A few times," he replied, somehow ignoring the intense stares of the ladies sitting next to him. "But not for many years. The last time I visited, King Elias was just a prince, and a young man at that. He had actually asked me to accompany him on an adventure. He wanted to get out of the palace, see the world, and possibly help some people along the way if he could, but his father would hear nothing of it." Keijin laughed. "Come to find out a year later, he escaped the palace and traveled around the kingdom for years. He's probably the only noble in the kingdom who has ever met the Enlightened."

"You're kidding," Sybil breathed, looking over at the king.

He was laughing with his wife about something, and she realized how unusual he was for a king. His methods of rule and peculiarity as a noble might have been the reason why someone was going to such great lengths to kill him. Honestly, though, if Sybil didn't know Mordecai was him underneath, she would have suspected Mephidilea.

"So, what brings you to the royal palace, wizard?" one of the ladies sitting next to Keijin asked Sybil, bringing her back to the table.

"The Enlightened sent me to connect with the king," she replied, being as vague as possible. Gibbous Tower wants to maintain a strong relationship with the throne."

"Don't you also work for the Enlightened, Sir Keijin?" one of the lords asked. "You two must know each other."

"Only in passing," Keijin said and then chuckled charmingly. "But it would be false of me to say I didn't notice her the few times I saw her."

How many women were going to become jealous of Sybil from what Mordecai and Keijin said while they were here?

"You flatter me," Sybil muttered, turning away.

"Do you plan to stay long at the palace, Sir Keijin?" the same lady as before asked, trying to keep the attention on her.

"At least long enough to recover from the feast tomorrow night," Keijin answered with a laugh. "Wouldn't want to miss all the revelry, after all."

"Then, perhaps, we could have a dance together?" she asked, her cheeks flushing as she did.

"It would be my absolute pleasure," Keijin said to the lady, though his eyes were still on Sybil.

The king turned in early that night, wanting to rest up for the events of the next day. Feeling drained from all the interactions, Sybil had Malic show her to her chambers. King Elias would be under guard all night, and he and the queen had been moving from room to room to keep anyone but Malic and his most trusted guards from knowing where they were on any given night. Just as she was heading into her room, Sybil noticed Mordecai's silly character heading into the one across from hers. It was good to know he would be so close, but she had no idea where Keijin or Giselle ended up.

Sybil's room in the palace was equal to the one in the Queen's Resort, but she was glad to not have any windows with Shuheyr's giant statue looming outside. Exhausted, she collapsed on the bed and heaved a sigh, not having a single clue who, if anyone in the palace, was responsible for killing the king's double. Perhaps, there was a way for them to get in and out undetected through some magical means. It would be hard to navigate the halls while invisible due to all the doors to go through and people to weave around, but it was doable.

Sybil kicked off her boots and rolled over in bed, not bothering to undo her robes. After all the time camping out on the road, she no longer minded sleeping in them. While she was sleeping, something happened to her she had never experienced before: a flash of a dagger, stabbing through the air, and the feeling of it piercing into her chest. It felt real, causing her to sit up in bed clutching where she had felt the knife.

Then, she realized there was someone with her in the room: an assassin, wielding a dagger.

Seeing Sybil sit up caused the assassin, a woman covered head to toe with tight-fitting black clothes, to stagger back and hesitate, but after a moment, the assassin lunged toward her. Without having time to think, Sybil sent her flying back with a wave of a hand, causing the assassin to smash against the door with a loud thud. She let out a groan, but immediately regained her footing and rushed toward Sybil. She rolled out of bed, and the dagger landed right where she had been sitting. With the bed between them, Sybil tried to think of what to do before the assassin jumped across the bed, dagger first. Sybil threw a lightning bolt at the assassin, sending her toppling back over the bed. The combination of the electric shock and the impact on the floor caused the assassin to fall unconscious.

As soon as things were still, Sybil moved to the assassin and jabbed her in the side with her foot to see if she would stir. Knowing the assassin was out cold, she rushed over to Mordecai's room and knocked repeatedly on his door. He pulled her into his room and shut the door in a flash. It surprised Sybil to see Mordecai back in his usual form and clothes, even though he needed magic to wear those as well.

Mordecai looked annoyed and asked, "Why are you here? I thought we agreed we were going to pretend we don't know each other."

"Oh, I'm sorry," Sybil said, and then pointed her thumb toward the door. "I guess I'll save the information about an assassin just trying to kill me in my room for my other friends."

"What? No, wait, I'm sorry. I just…" He groaned, pinching the bridge of his nose. "Sorry, I'm being an ass again. Are you okay?"

"Yeah, I'm okay," she said, appreciating that he was trying, even if he was doing a terrible job at it. "Come on, I'll show you."

They entered her room, and the assassin was still lying unconscious where Sybil left her. Mordecai bent down to inspect her for a moment before turning to Sybil and saying, "It's fortunate you were awake when she attacked."

"Actually, I wasn't, or not until she was in the middle of attacking, that is," Sybil replied, rubbing the back of her neck. "I had some sort of vision in my dream about it, which woke me up just in time. I would've been killed if not for that."

This seemed to bother Mordecai, and he glared down at the assassin before asking, "What should we do with her?"

"I could try to dig out where she came from, how she got into the palace in the first place," Sybil suggested, surprised he was asking her. "But then again, I've always wanted to experiment on altering someone's memory but never felt right doing it. With this person… it feels right."

Mordecai, clearly intrigued with the idea, agreed, and Sybil entered the assassin's most recent memories. With a pull and twist of magic, she altered the memories enough to make the assassin believe she had been successful in her mission. The spell made the assassin believe, before Sybil managed to get out the lightning bolt, she stabbed her right through the chest. In the memory, Sybil was still able to get her spell out just as she was stabbed to account for the assassin's lost time, and Mordecai helped sell this by creating an illusion of a stab wound in Sybil's chest. Once everything was in place and Mordecai was invisible in the corner, Sybil created an invisible scrying eye, awoke the assassin, and played dead.

Through the scrying eye, Sybil watched as the assassin got up from the floor and started to unpack her new memory. She moved across the room to Sybil and saw she was dead, falling for the ruse. The dagger on the floor next to Sybil had also been illusioned to look bloodied. Mordecai was so skilled at this spell the blood even dripped from the blade as the assassin picked it up and splashed onto the floor. All of this convinced the assassin and after a few more minutes of inspecting and thinking, she left the room, closing the door silently behind her.

Sybil immediately lunged to her feet, and Mordecai grabbed her hand before turning her invisible with him. They followed after the assassin as she moved hastily through the halls, turning left and then right around the corners. Eventually, she reached a place along the wall in the middle of the corridor and pressed in a piece of the molding. A door popped open, and within a moment, the assassin flitted around it and disappeared into an unknown tunnel.

When they approached the door, Mordecai gave a huff and said, "This shouldn't be here. As advisor, I knew all of the secret passages inside and out of the palace. I've never seen this one before."

"If you didn't know about it, possibly the king and his guards don't know about it either."

"If I didn't know about it, I can assure you they don't," he corrected.

"So, this is how the assassins were able to get in unnoticed. They must be scrambling, trying to figure out how to get to the king after messing up the first time. I wonder why they tried to kill me, though. Wouldn't that have just raised more of an alarm for them?"

"It's possible they had changed their plan to attacking in the day, while you've been watching over the king," Mordecai said. "We should get the others; we don't know what we'll find down there."

Back in Mordecai's room, Sybil pulled out the messenger stone Keijin had given her back in Taragpass and used it to call him over, grabbing Giselle on his way. Once the party was together again, they headed back to the secret door. Giselle's race were able to see in nearly absolute darkness, just like the dwarves, so the others let her lead them down the corridor. It struck Sybil how she had recently become uneasy in the darkness, as if there was always something reaching out to grab her.

A light ahead of the adventurers started filling the tunnel as they made their way down it, and slowly they could start making things out in the dim light. Giselle put her hand up for her companions to stop, and they moved slowly around the corner to see a group camping out in an underground storm drain. This place had been designed to prevent flooding in the City, but all it really was was a large stone room with tunnels leading to all sorts of places across the City, a perfect hideout for assassins.

There were six of them, a surprisingly large group for a job which required a great deal of stealth. They had a couple of tents, and it looked like they had been camping down there for a while. Sybil wondered if the assassination of the king was the only mission they were running or if they had several in motion from this position.

"They'll be able to dart in all different directions from this spot," Mordecai whispered to the others. "If they run, we just need to grab one to question. If they decide to fight us, leave at least one of them alive. We can seal the tunnel, but we still need to find out who's behind all this."

"I have a hunch," Giselle said, pulling her daggers from their sheaths along her thighs. "But, I suppose, getting solid evidence would be better."

Four people were standing around a makeshift table, and one of them was giving orders to the others, so the party decided he would be the best person for them to grab. Not wanting to attack first, Keijin decided to step out and speak with them while his companions were ready with their first moves. The sound of his footsteps moving toward the assassins got their attention first, and as all six turned to him, their hands on their weapons, he called out, "Hello! What an interesting hideout you all have here. I wonder if-"

Mordecai's prediction was correct. As soon as Keijin finished his first sentence, the leader shouted, "Move," and the other five sprinted in opposite directions toward the various tunnel entrances. All of them stopped dead in their tracks when Sybil lifted up the water from the drainage and blocked off each of the tunnel's entrances. None of them seemed familiar enough with magic to know it was safe to jump through, but as the other three were heading into combat, she froze the water for good measure.

The assassins, all of them now spread out across the area, turned to the party and readied themselves to fight. Mordecai started pulling together dark energy between his hands and sent a thick tendril of it straight toward the assassin who had tried to kill Sybil. The tendril stabbed into her chest, causing the assassin to let out a cry of pain, and it started draining the life out of her. Her skin turned pale to gray, and her eyes lost their brightness. One of the assassins ran up to Keijin, who tried hitting her with his sword, but she was too fast for him and sliced him in the side. Giselle, on the other hand, was even more dexterous than the assassin she was fighting and made quick work of him by weaving around and stabbing him in the neck at the base of his skull. The assassin dropped instantly.

A light blazed from the table, and Sybil looked over to see the leader burning papers they had been examining on the table when the party arrived. She turned to him and held him in place, reaching the full capacity of her spellcasting, holding him and the walls of ice at the same time. She had never exerted her power this strongly and could feel the strain running through her. Still tethered to one assassin, Mordecai sent a small, black sun flying toward two others, knocking one of them off their feet. The assassin fighting Keijin had managed to get a few slashes in around the vulnerable parts of his armor, so blood was starting to drip down the plate mail.

While Sybil was distracted with Keijin's predicament, an assassin had managed to sneak around her and stabbed her in the lower back, managing only a flesh wound, despite how painful it was. Before they could do any more damage, Giselle flashed over to the assassin and slit their neck. The pain and surprise from her wound caused Sybil to lose focus on the ice walls, and they instantly melted and all came splashing down. Two of the assassins instantly darted for the passageways, and the third, who was fighting Keijin, was slashed across her back with Keijin's sword as she moved toward the closest exit. The leader tried to move as well, but Sybil still had a magical hold on him, keeping him right where he had been standing at the table.

"Cal!" the wounded assassin shouted, turning back toward the leader.

"Go, now," he replied, and after a moment of hesitation, she did as he commanded. The adventurers let her go and approached the leader. He was glaring at Sybil and asked, "Who the fuck are you people?"

"Funny, we were going to ask you the same question," Giselle replied with a laugh. "How about you go first?"

"Bite me," he replied.

"Oh, there will be plenty of time for all that," Giselle breathed, moving her face closer to his with a mischievous gleam in her amethyst eyes. "But first, we're going to get the answer from you we want, whether you like it or not."

Keijin grabbed him and tied him up with some rope he found next to one of the tents. Once he was secure, Sybil was able to let go of him. The others then looked at her.

"Oh, wait, you want me to question him?" she asked, clutching the wound on her lower back.

"No, we want you to read his mind," Mordecai replied gruffly.

Sybil shook her head and said, "That could kill him."

"He's as good as dead, anyway."

"We don't have to resort to that just yet. And besides, Sybil's injured," Keijin said with a huff. As he started healing her, he continued, "Let's get him back to the palace, inform the guards of the entrance to this tunnel so they can seal it off, and question him once he's in a cell."

This irritated Mordecai, but he gave a wave of his hand and said, "Fine, whatever. Let's just drag this out then."

Chapter Fifteen

The party, dirty and bloodied yet again, stood in the middle of the king's study. Sybil had found Malic in the chambers across the room from hers. He was disappointed because he thought she was there for a middle of the night romp but directed them to the king's study to wait there while he woke the king. Sybil looked over at Mordecai and asked about his disguise, as he still looked like his regular self, but he shook his head and said, "I'm ready to retire Mephidilea. He served his purpose for this mission."

When the king arrived nearly a half hour later, he had a scowl on his face, and his hair was still a little unkempt from being woken in the middle of the night. When he made it to his desk, he leaned against the front of it and his eyes darted Mordecai.

"What's going on? Who's this?" the king asked.

"Your majesty, in addition to Sybil, the three of us," Keijin said, gesturing from himself to Giselle and Mordecai. "Were sent by the Enlightened to aid the crown's guard in protecting you from those who wish to see you killed. A couple of hours ago, Sybil was attacked in her room by an assassin, who entered the palace through an old, unknown passageway, which Malic has your guards working on closing as we speak. Following the assassin down the tunnel, we found a hideout in the sewer and found a whole group of them. We killed a few, others escaped, and we managed to capture their leader for questioning."

The king listened intently to Keijin, and once Keijin was done, the king sighed.

"What has he told you?"

"Nothing yet," Keijin replied. "One of the others called him Cal, but we thought it would be best to bring him to you for questioning, and your guards put him in a cell."

"If need be, though, we have other means of getting answers from him," Mordecai added, causing the king to eye him suspiciously.

"Very well..." the king said. "If it is true that you have means of getting answers from the prisoner, I would like the four of you to go with Malic to the dungeons. Find out what you can from him, particularly who funds his operations."

The adventurers bowed to the king and followed Malic to the dungeon. Sybil was surprised to find it so close to the throne room. Malic turned to her with a smile and said, "Keep your friends close."

Another guard led the party down the steps, and Malic returned to the king. There were lanterns on the wall lighting their path, but it was dark and dingy and so far unlike the rest of the palace. They passed several cells housing unknown prisoners, most of them sleeping, as the guard brought them to a cell in the middle of the dungeon where Cal, the most recent occupant, was standing in the center, his expression impossible to read.

Mordecai stepped forward and asked, "Who do you work for?"

"Someone who's going to flay the skin from each of you for messing with his plans," Cal said, his low voice echoing off the stone walls around him. He didn't say it as a threat but a fact. "The four of you have stepped in something you ought not to have stepped in."

"Why were you targeting the king?" Mordecai asked, unfazed by what he said.

"Because he's stepped in things, as well," the prisoner said with a smirk.

"What kind of things?" Keijin asked as he moved closer to the cell. "This king has cracked down on the criminal underworld of the City. Your boss some sort of gang leader?"

"Fuck off," Cal breathed, looking away. Sybil could tell they were onto something with his reaction.

Giselle laughed and said, "Quite the suggestive one you are. Tell me, are you prepared to die a horrible death to protect this boss of yours? I seriously doubt he'll ever think twice about you after you're gone."

"I know he doesn't care about me; it's not him I'm protecting."

"That woman, the one who called you Cal," Sybil recalled. "Your lover? Sister?"

The prisoner grabbed the bars of the cage tightly and growled, "Screw you."

"Enough of this," Mordecai said. "Use your powers, go into his mind, and get the answers we need."

"With his conviction, I'll probably kill him," Sybil breathed.

"If you're so concerned with that," Mordecai said with an eyeroll before offering her his hand. "I can help you."

Sybil took his hand and extended her free one toward the prisoner. Closing her eyes, she focused her spell, saying the incantation under her breath, and launched her consciousness into Cal's. It felt like the wind was knocked out of her as Sybil hit the wall around his mind. He must have practiced years building to defend against attacks like this. With Mordecai's help, though, she was able to find a gap and started seeing bits and pieces of his memories, despite how hard he was working to push her out.

Sybil saw flashes of the Outer Ring, dilapidated houses in the mud and the sick and feeble lining the streets. Then, a regal carriage drove by, and the time seemed to flash forward several years. There was what appeared to be a tavern, but every table had crowds of people playing different types of games with coins and other trinkets in the middle, and people were dressed in expensive and fashionable garbs. Suddenly, she was in the back room, and that's when Cal started to fight harder.

"No," he gasped. "Don't."

With how hard he was fighting, she was surprised this wasn't killing him.

The memories continued, and Sybil found herself in a dingy back office where a rather frightening looking man was sitting behind a desk. He had three claw marks over his left eye, which was milky white, and his large frame was looming over his desk, making it look small in comparison. She only saw him for an instance but knew she would be able to pick him out of a crowd. Then, there was a flash of a woman's face. Cal let out a yell.

"Sybil, stop," Keijin said, grabbing her arm and snapping her consciousness back. "You're going to kill him."

The man's ears and nose were bleeding. His will had become impenetrable when she found the woman in his memories. He would rather die a horrible death than give up her secrets.

"I-I think I have enough," Sybil said, her entire body shaking from the spell. "Let the guards ask their questions."

The party once again found themselves in the king's study. After giving him the description of the man Sybil saw in Cal's memories, the king, Mordecai, and Giselle seemed to know exactly who it was.

"That bastard," the king nearly yelled. "I can't believe I'm still having to put up with his bullshit. If my father had any idea how to run a kingdom, let alone a city, that monster wouldn't still be running amuck here."

"Brynmor of Easthaven,'" Mordecai went on to explain to Sybil and Keijin. "Has been the main instigator of the crown and the City for nearly twenty years, getting his start as the main boss back when most of us in this room were children."

"Forgive me, your majesty," Keijin said, stepping forward and looking a little uncomfortable. "But we were assigned to assist you with the issue of assassins making their way into your palace, which we did. I doubt very seriously the Enlightened would want us getting wrapped up in dealing with a mob and the politics of the Outer Ring."

"Yes, of course," the king said with a wave of his hand "You all have already done enough, and I thank you for it. Brynmor of Easthaven is the crown's issue to deal with now. Please, trouble yourselves no more with this matter and get some rest so you can enjoy the festivities tomorrow. You are dismissed."

Giselle was very clearly disappointed. But having been dismissed the party bowed before heading out of his office. Keijin headed to his room on the other side of the palace, and Giselle needed to return to her contact to keep him from getting suspicious. While she didn't need him any more for this mission, she wanted to maintain her deception for any future needs.

Once they were alone, Mordecai walked up to Sybil, offered her his hand again, and said, "Come on. You need to get some rest."

Mordecai lead her to her chambers, and Sybil stared into her darkened room and thought about the idea of someone creeping around in the night.

"Would you stay with me tonight?"

"What?" he inhaled with furrowed eyebrows.

"I just… never mind."

"No, go on."

Sybil sighed and said, "After what happened earlier, I'd just feel safer with you around."

"Can't imagine how," he said with a shrug. "But I don't see why not. Keeping you company would at least give me something to do."

"As amiable as always," she muttered as they headed inside.

Mordecai sat down on her bed and propped himself up with a couple of pillows as she readied herself for bed. Her robes had been dirtied and bloodied in the fight, so she needed to sleep in her undergarments. He was watching her for a moment or two as she undressed, so she frowned at him and moved behind the room divider next to her to finish changing.

Sybil heard him chuckle and say, "Oh, so it isn't that sort of spending the night together."

Hidden behind the divider, she allowed herself to smile as his teasing. "You knew it wasn't, you ass," she replied, causing him to chuckle again.

She realized that was the first time she heard him genuinely laugh. At least, she thought it sounded genuine, which was a hard thing to be sure of with him. As she was getting into bed, she asked, "So is that your real voice or part of your disguise?"

"Real voice," he replied, leaning back against the pillows. "It would be exhausting to use a fake voice all the time. The only part of my disguise that's magic is the visual, unless I play a ridiculous character like Mephidilea."

"Wow, then you're a fantastic actor."

"One of my many talents."

"Why did you really stop wearing the Mephidilea disguise?" she asked, turning on her side to face him.

"I told you already," he replied, but when she made a face, he sighed. "Perhaps, it could have partially been because I didn't like the way you looked at me when I was him. I wanted to go back to seeing the way you're looking at me now."

"And what way is that?" she asked, the sleepiness starting to take control over her eyes.

He reached over and ran his fingers through her hair, causing her to close her eyes, and said, "The way that tells me, despite all you know about me, there is a place for me in your heart."

Sybil smiled but was too tired to speak another word and soon found herself drifting off to sleep.

The next morning, Mordecai had to tie up some loose ends before saying goodbye to Mephidilea for good, and Giselle was off entertaining various nobles around the palace. That left Keijin and Sybil to wander around without much to do. Keijin asked if she would like to see the palace gardens, and wanting to get away from the busyness of the palace as it readied itself for the feast, she agreed.

Once they were outside, walking through a small orchard of apple trees, he said, "There seems to be something on your mind. You've been thoughtful since we arrived in the City, more so than usual."

Sybil nodded and said, "I've learned something of myself recently, and I knew bringing it up in the middle of our mission would only distract us."

"What is it?" he asked, concerned.

"Keijin, what do you know of Soul Children?"

He thought for a moment before shaking his head.

"Not much, unfortunately. They're said to be tied to a specific god or goddess at birth, and it takes a special ritual for them to come about. But before you, I had always thought them to be a myth, something clerics and cultists created as wishful thinking."

"My tie with Shuheyr, it's much stronger than I thought," she breathed as they moved to sit at a bench between a couple of trees. "The other night, he came to me in my dream and told me Soul Children were the actual children of gods or, at least, as much as they can be between the mortal world and the immortal realm. He told me I'm his daughter."

Keijin fell silent and his face went serious as he thought about this. While he did, Sybil stared up at the sun, what the ancient people used to believe was Shuheyr himself. So many stories had been made up and revised over the years about the gods that, for most people, it had become impossible to know what was true about them and what was false.

"Did he say that he wanted something from you? What would be the purpose for a god conceiving a mortal child?"

"He told me there were many reasons, but only shared one: he wants me to destroy the darkness threatening this world, he wants me to destroy Haborym," Sybil replied, feeling like this impossible task was no longer a choice but an obligation.

"Have you told Mordecai about this?"

"Not yet," she breathed, crossing her arms. "Honestly, I'm worried that it would change the way he thinks of me. He wants to kill Haborym more than anyone, and I fear he would only see me as a weapon if I told him about my true nature."

"At least you would know. And you're strong enough to keep him from using you, if the worst should happen. Despite the feelings you have for him, I've seen you push back against his will many times."

Sybil sighed and said, "You would never even think to use me for your own personal gain. I don't understand why I have these feelings."

Keijin's face turned pained for a moment before he was able to correct it.

"No, I value you as you are far too much," he replied, taking her hand in his. "But, as much as it pains me to say it, perhaps your heart is telling you there's something bonding you and Mordecai together. You're both very much alike, while in many ways being opposites of the other. It only makes sense that you feel connected to one another."

"What about all that talk in Taragpass about him being dangerous and how I shouldn't trust him?"

He thought for a moment and sighed before saying, "I think I spoke before truly understanding the nature of your characters. A lot has happened since then, and I've seen a lot of growth in both of you."

"Keijin," she said, heaving a sigh. "I think I love him."

"Yeah, I think so, too," he breathed, a sadness in his voice.

She turned to him, tears welling in her eyes, and said, "I'm sorry."

"Don't be. We can only do so much to direct our hearts, and at the end of the day, it chooses for us. You have nothing to be sorry for. I just hope he doesn't hurt you because I'd hate to have to kill him."

They laughed softly before falling silent for a few minutes, just enjoying the beauty of the garden and each other's company, still holding hands. Eventually, an elven lady's maid found them in the garden, gave a bow to each and said, "Pardon the interruption. I am Saria and have been instructed to ready Lady Sybil for the evening's events."

"Well, you didn't think the king was going to want you wearing your robes, did you?" Keijin asked with a laugh when Sybil looked over at him. "You are, after all, his personal guest at the palace."

Saria extended her hand, and Sybil took it. She pulled Sybil up from the bench and led her through the palace, gliding with the elegance of one who has been at court her whole life. They arrived at Sybil's room, and Saria opened the door. Inside the room was a rack of gowns in various colors and boxes of makeup and jewelry. She had Sybil stand in the middle of the room and eyed her for a moment before pulling three dresses off the rack.

"The king told me to be sure to dress you in the crown's colors to show everyone you are an honored guest," Saria explained as Sybil gawked over these fine gowns. "Which one strikes your fancy?"

"I suppose the silver one," she muttered, the red and blue embroidered flowers of the dress catching her eye. "What do you think?"

Saria smiled and said, "The silver one's my favorite."

Having never been dressed in an actual ball gown before, Sybil was taken off guard when Saria pulled out a corset and told her to raise her arms. As she laced it up, it felt impossibly tight, so Sybil told her it was too small. But Saria simply responded with "if you can hardly breathe, then it's the right size."

Sybil turned to her and said, "I admire your fortitude dressing like this every day."

Saria laughed and rolled her eyes before asking Sybil to take a seat at the vanity in the corner. She opened the box of jewelry first, fitting dangling, diamond earrings to Sybil' ears and placing a matching necklace around her neck. The makeup was the longest and most excruciating part. Sybil had never worn makeup before and could hardly stand Saria putting sparkling powder and inky black substances around her eyes and on her lashes. When Saria was done and allowed her to finally look in the mirror, though, Sybil was delightfully shocked at her appearance. Saria might as well have used magic to enhance her features.

"That's incredible," Sybil said, moving her head around to see her face at different angles.

"It's what I do best," Saria replied as she closed the boxes. "I'm sure Sir Keijin will be impressed."

With that, she left the room with the boxes under her arms and didn't see Sybil's face fall when she made that last comment. Staring at herself in the mirror, Sybil tried to understand why she didn't feel the same way he felt about her. Things would be so much simpler, but like Keijin said, that wasn't how the heart works.

Just as Sybil was about to head to the grand ballroom on her own, there was a knock on her door, and she opened it to find Mordecai standing there. He was in a black vest with a white cravat, and the silver buttons on his vest matched the embroidery on his black jacket in both style and color. Whether it was an illusion or not, he was extremely handsome, and a little flutter ran through Sybil when she saw him standing there. He had a red rose in his hand and handed it to her.

"You look exquisite," he said in his low, charming voice.

Sybil brought the rose up to her nose to hide her silly grin and asked, "Have you come to escort me?"

"Indeed, I have," he answered, offering her his arm.

Wrapping her arm around his, Sybil felt like a princess in the fairytales she read as a child. The way he was dressed and the warm, affectionate look in his eyes made Mordecai seem like a dark, but honorable prince, no longer the cloaked villain. They headed down the corridor, and the sounds of music and people laughing and talking grew as they approached the grand ballroom. A couple hundred people, at least, were all around the massive room with some at the tables lining the walls and everyone else dancing to their hearts' content in the center. As Sybil and Mordecai entered, some curious guests watched them and whispered to each other, making wild guesses and spreading rumors they had heard about who these strangers were.

A butler offered them glasses of a drink pale in color and bubbled like near-boiling water. It surprised Sybil to feel the glass was cold when Mordecai handed one over to her. The drink was sweet and tart, and the bubbles caused her tongue and nose to tingle, but she quite liked it. Mordecai led her over to a far corner of the room, so they were out of the way of the dancers and people coming and going into the ballroom. For a while, Sybil watched the dancers in wonder while sipping on her drink, never having seen dancing like it. In her village, there had been dances around the bonfires during important holidays, but nothing so specific and refined like what she was seeing now.

Mordecai finished his drink and set down the glass on a nearby table before offering Sybil his hand. She didn't know what that meant, but she set down her glass as well and took it. Catching her off guard, Mordecai pulled her onto the dancefloor, and she quietly shrieked that she didn't know how to dance.

"Just follow my lead," he muttered, pulling her close to him.

With their chests pressed together and his arm wrapped around her waist, Sybil felt her face start to burn. Looking down at her, Mordecai grinned, causing her heart to pound. Something about him had changed, as if all at once, and even though she liked it, Sybil wondered what changed him. The way he looked at her and held her in his arms, made all the walls he had put up and all the disagreements they had suddenly melted away, and all that was left was how much he cared for her. Did he feel the same way for her that she did for him? Sybil wished for that as he twirled her around, nearly causing her to lose her footing, and she let out a laugh when he spun her back toward him.

The music ended, and everyone turned to applaud the band, but Mordecai kept his eyes fixed on Sybil, still holding her close. Then, to her surprise and in front of all those people, he kissed her, pressing his cool lips passionately against hers and pulling her even tighter to him. When he pulled away, Sybil stared up at him, her heart swelling, wondering if this was all just some dream her mind was playing out.

As the next song started, Mordecai led Sybil off the dance floor, acting as if he hadn't just shown more affection in an instant than he had in the entire time she knew him. She was feeling a little dizzy and asked if they could sit down, and when they found a table, servants brought them plates of food. A few people joined them at the table, including Giselle, who was wearing a slim black dress and a silver necklace filled with amethysts that matched the purple hue of her skin. She flashed her perfect, white teeth at her companions, but continued telling her story of the time she faced a group of bandits alone to the three gentlemen with her.

"The worst part about them, really, was their smell," she said with a laugh, throwing her head back.

Sybil glanced around the room for a moment and watched the king and queen dance with bright smiles on their faces. Then, she found Keijin standing in a corner with six ladies, of all various ages, wearing an assortment of pastel-colored dresses. He was looking as handsome as ever wearing a vibrant, green tunic with golden trim, and his face had been clean shaven and his hair trimmed. With all of these women vying for his attention, his face showed a mixture of flattery and anxiety, but Sybil didn't watch him long enough to see if anything happened between him and the ladies. She was still acutely aware of Mordecai's presence next to her.

After they finished their meal, they started dancing to another song. Halfway through the dance, though, a nobleman with golden blonde hair and blue eyes, not much older than Sybil, asked to cut in. Keeping with the manners of the nobles, Mordecai obliged but had a scowl on his face as he did so. Before she knew it, Sybil was in the arms of another man, and Mordecai stood on the side of the dancefloor watching, seething.

"I know every woman here except you," the nobleman said, his voice smooth and charming. "That got me curious. Tell me, what brings you to the king's palace?"

"Perhaps you could provide me with your name, at the very least, before I give you details of my business here," Sybil replied, annoyed at his arrogance.

"Surely, you know who I am," he said with a laugh. When she didn't reply, he frowned. "How could you not recognize the king's nephew? I am Archduke Finlay, at least until my aunt produces an heir."

"And what will you be then?"

"The third most important person in the kingdom," he said, flashing a smile. "Just because I might not be king, doesn't mean I won't have a legacy." He twirled her around. "Now it's your turn. Who are you and what's your business here?"

"Sybil Dawn, the apprentice to the Enlightened," she replied, wishing the song would hurry up and end. "My official business is between the king and me."

"Oh, quite the mysterious woman you are," he said with a grin. "And who's that strapping young man who looks like he wants to impale my head on a stake. Seems like he's just a commoner, wealthy, but a commoner all the same. Not the same class of people as the two of us, destined for greatness."

"You really like the sound of your own voice, don't you?" she asked, and her heart filled with gratitude as the music stopped.

Sybil tried to walk away from him, but he grabbed her arm and snarled, "You rude, little bitch. How dare you talk to me like that."

Mordecai was between them so fast that Sybil almost thought he had used magic to move. He didn't strike the man, knowing well who he was, but he did place his hand on his chest to push him away from her.

"That's enough, your highness," Mordecai hissed, the spite oozing from every word. "Go bother a lady who would feel fortunate to listen to your nonsense."

The look on Mordecai's face and the terrible sound in his voice caused the archduke to back away. Finlay's eyes stayed fixed on Mordecai for a moment, as if he were about to strike, and Mordecai led Sybil outside the ballroom. They found a quiet alcove with windows facing out into the gardens, and Mordecai heaved a sigh before saying, "I hope that didn't spoil your evening."

"No, I can handle an ignorant man's words," she said with a soft huff. "But thank you for standing up for me. For a moment, I thought you were going to kill him."

"When I heard what he called you, I thought I was, too," he said and then chuckled. "What a mess that would've caused."

"It would certainly have been a story, something to add to the tapestries," she replied, giggling a little. "And I'm sure the king wouldn't have been too pleased. Do you think we would've made it out of there?"

"Between the two of us, and the chaos it would've caused, I have no doubt," he said, smiling down at her.

Then, a silence fell between them. Not an awkward one where neither of them knew what to say, but one that showed nothing needed to be said.

"Sybil, I haven't felt this light in my entire life. Even with the danger looming over us, I feel like I can breathe easily for the first time."

Mordecai brought his fingertips up to her cheek and ran them down to her jaw. The way his eyes stared deep into hers, it felt like the entire palace just melted away around them. Without being able to hold in the words any longer, she said, "I love you."

At first, Mordecai seemed to jerk back from her proclamation, causing her entire body to grow hot. But then, he smiled.

"I never thought I could love anyone before I met you," he said with a quiver of pain in his voice. The next words were hard for him, she could tell by how he seemed to chew on them, trying to get them out just as quickly as she was able to. Just when she was about to interject, to tell him that it was okay if he wasn't ready to say it, he breathed. "I love you, too."

He leaned down to kiss her again, and Sybil could feel her heart and soul swell with joy. She could not think of a time when she felt happier than she did at that moment.

Mordecai walked her back to her quarters after the feast, and they both headed inside. She turned to him, the skirt of her ball gown taking up most of the floor space, and said, "I, uh, don't know how to get out of this thing."

"I could help you if you like," he replied in his gravelly voice, stepping closer to her. "But I might have to see you undress to do so."

"As if you weren't looking all those times before," she said, rolling her eyes a little.

He placed the back of his fingers against her bare arm and ran them down, causing a shiver to run through her.

"How could I not?" he asked and then smiled. "I want to see all of you."

Stepping around her, he started working on the strings of the gown that kept it affixed to her body, and as his fingers worked, she felt his lips press against her neck. She let in a quick breath of surprise and pleasure as his lips glided down her neck. The gown dropped to the floor, and he spun her around. She was now in nothing but her undergarments and corset, but she didn't feel exposed, she wanted him to see the rest of her. Filled with excitement, she stepped closer to him and kissed him greedily. His hands ran up her back and started pulling at the strings of her corset, and once he got it loose enough, he pulled it off and tossed it across the room, causing her to laugh.

Picking Sybil up in his arms, he wrapped her legs around him and started walking to the bed. He threw her down, and she let out a soft shriek of exhilaration, causing him to grin mischievously at her. He pulled off his jacket and cravat before moving on top of her, pressing himself between her legs, making her feel like she was going to faint from all this excitement. As he pressed into her and kissed her lips, neck, and shoulders, she undid the buttons of his vest and ripped it off him. He pushed up the skirt of her undergarments, and she sat up for a moment so he could pull it the rest of the way off, showing all of her.

Taking a step back for a moment, he undid his pants and kicked off his boots as he scanned her body. When he was back against her, he whispered in her ear, "You're the most beautiful woman I've ever seen."

They made love well into the early hours of the morning, thoroughly exploring each others' bodies and becoming one in a passionate melding, body and soul. When they had reached a point of exhaustion, they both lay there together, staring at the other and enjoying how it all felt. Mordecai was running his fingers over her bare skin from her thigh up to her collarbone and back down again.

Eventually, Sybil fell asleep, blissfully unaware of the horrible incident happening elsewhere in the palace.

Chapter Sixteen

Sybil was no longer in bed next to Mordecai. She was sprawled on a cold, marble floor in nothing but a nightgown, feeling as though she had fallen from the sky. The chill of the floor and the air surrounding her had pierced deep into her core, so much so that her body didn't even bother to shiver. Lifting her head, she found that she was in the empty throne room, only moonlight illuminating the space through the stained-glass windows. She rose and turned toward the throne, which was filled by a shadowy figure, the one she had seen in the tower.

"You cannot defeat him," the shadow said, its voice reverberating off the walls. "The insatiable hunger will not be stopped."

Up until it spoke, Sybil had believed this shadow to be Haborym, or an extension of him, but she wasn't so sure anymore. The darkness from this creature, this form, was weak as if the smoke of a dying campfire was given form. It didn't thicken the air or threaten to envelop her. Almost like a memory, it was barely there.

"What are you?" Sybil asked, her words filling the room.

The shadow leaned forward, watching her without eyes. Then, in a slow, weak hiss, it said, "The Eaten."

Sybil tried to take a step forward and ask it another question, but all at once, the throne room around her vanished, and she was back in bed being shaken awake by Mordecai.

"Wake up, we have to leave," he told her in a hushed tone. "The king's dead."

Ice shot through Sybil, and she jolted up in bed, completely awake. "Dead?" she choked. "But how?"

"We don't have time to find out," Mordecai said, tossing her robes onto the bed. "I went out to grab us breakfast, and the entire palace was in a panic. We need to leave before someone pins it on us."

Using the messenger stone, Sybil once again asked Keijin to grab Giselle and meet in her room. They arrived as soon as Sybil had dressed. Mordecai led his companions down several corridors, turning quickly right and then left, avoiding any guards who were heading down the opposite way. The party stopped at what appeared to be a dead end. Grabbing one of the sconces on the wall, Mordecai revealed a hidden passageway as the door clicked open. He hurried them inside and closed it before anyone saw. There was still no time to waste, though. They had to grab their horses and make it out of the Inner Ring before the guards managed to shut it all down.

Being cautious, Mordecai led them to the Outer Ring and brought them to a safehouse he used in the City when he needed to hide out for a while. Like many of the residences in the Outer Ring, it was a dilapidated and dingy little place, barely big enough to call a room, let alone a house, but it gave the party a place to safely talk while remaining in the City.

"How could this have happened?" Keijin asked, placing his hands to his face. "We stopped the assassins, and the king was heavily guarded all day and night."

Sybil felt sick knowing the king, who she had just watched dancing happily with his wife less than twelve hours ago, was dead. Unable to sit still, she paced back and forth between Giselle and Keijin.

"A number of things could have happened that were outside of our control," Mordecai told him, leaning against a table with his arms crossed. "But he's dead, and whoever's responsible for it must benefit from his death in some way."

"The archduke seemed like he would be the type," Sybil remarked, stopping for an instant before continuing her pacing.

"Him? He might have orchestrated it, but I doubt he fell the knife… or poison, or whatever it was," Giselle said and, growing irritated by her movement, grabbed and pulled Sybil onto the grimy couch with her. "Brynmor would very much enjoy the archduke becoming king. When his assassins failed, he might have moved to some other method."

Taking the others by surprise, Keijin kicked over the chair closest to him and shouted, "How could we have let this happen?"

"We dealt with the assassins and had them seal up the tunnel," Mordecai grumbled. "It wasn't our job to protect the king from every possible threat. That would have been impossible. If anything, it's on him for knowing someone was trying to assassinate him and letting so many people into his palace anyway. There could have been a dozen different people looking to find their opening to kill the king last night, and one of them was successful."

"Archduke Finlay will become king, then?" Sybil asked, thinking back to his brutish behavior the night before. "What does that mean for the kingdom?"

"It means the City will return to the hands of Brynmor of Easthaven to start," Giselle said with a huff. "From there, who knows how deep his corruption will affect the kingdom."

Keijin, who was starting to calm down, asked, "What if we took Brynmor out of the equation? If we can get rid of the mob, we can minimize the damage."

"Weren't you the one who told the king that Leon wouldn't want us getting mixed up in the mob?" Mordecai asked with a frown. "And how do you suggest we go about toppling a man who has been running the City's underground for twenty years?"

"I believe we can think of something," Sybil said, her guilt over the king's death turning to vengeance. "We always do after all."

There was a moment of silence before Giselle breathed, "Fuck yeah," with a gleeful grin.

Before the party continued on with their mission, Sybil had to take care of something back in the Inner Ring, which could only stay closed for so long. While Mordecai escorted her to the Inner Ring, both of them wearing new disguises he designed, Giselle decided to do some digging into the casino Sybil saw in Cal's memories. Keijin, on the other hand, wanted to research more about the line of succession for the royal family, so he went off on his own to do that. They would all meet back at the hideout by nightfall.

"Why do you want to go to the temple of Shuheyr?" Mordecai asked as they made their way down the uneven road of the Outer Ring on their horses. "I thought you were trying to avoid him?"

Sybil chewed on the inside of her cheek for a moment before saying, "I'm his child."

There was a long moment of silence before Mordecai finally asked, "You're his *what?*"

"Did you know that gods can conceive mortal children?" she asked him, staring up at the sky. "If the conditions are right and the vessel is willing, then gods are able to pass on part of themselves into a child, creating an unbreakable connection with them and bestowing that child with some of the god's power."

"When did you learn all this?"

"Our first night in the City," she replied. "When Shuheyr came to me in my dream, he explained everything to me… well, he explained enough to me."

"So, you're not tied to him like I am to Haborym. You're not his servant, but there's a part of him in you that connects you to him," Mordecai said, solidifying all these wild ideas in his mind. "A Soul Child. That name makes more sense now. You're the embodiment of Shuheyr's soul in mortal form, which means we could have only just scratched the surface of your powers."

"Possibly," Sybil breathed as they entered the busy market street in the Middle Ring. "But I'm not sure I want to test the limits of Shuheyr's powers. I've already grown so much in developing my magic, outside of his influence, and I don't like the idea of relying on his power when I have my own magic to wield."

People were in a frenzy all around them about the king's death, which had either not yet made word to the Outer Ring or, Sybil figured, the people there just simply didn't care with all the other woes they had to deal with.

"You're a powerful wizard in your own right," Mordecai responded. "But we'll need every ounce of power we can get to defeat Haborym. Perhaps, you could make a deal with Shuheyr, just utilize his power for the time we need it and return to your own magic after."

"I don't know," she said, shaking her head. "This is all still so new to me, and I have a lot of questions. After I speak with Shuheyr, I'll be able to make a more informed decision about this."

When they reached the gates to the Inner Ring, it took quite a bit of convincing from Mordecai for the guards to let them in. It wasn't until they were sure he was part of the upper class that they let them in. Coming from a small village, it surprised Sybil how many more doors being rich opened than keys.

Once they were through the gate, Mordecai and Sybil rode up to the temple and got off their horses. She couldn't help but gaze up at the towering statue of Shuheyr. It looked far more ominous than it had through her window at the inn.

"You go in without me," Mordecai said, taking Dusk's reins from her. "A place under the God of Light is not a pleasant one for me, being tied to darkness and all."

Wanting to remind him of their intimacy from the night before all this madness inflicted the City, Sybil moved closer and kissed him on the cheek. He turned to her and gave what he would consider to be a smile, and Sybil headed inside the temple.

The temple of Shuheyr was just as grand as the palace, though significantly smaller. After the entryway, the temple opened up to a room about the size of the throne room with a smaller version of Shuheyr's gilded statue that stood outside in the middle. The room had a domed ceiling, plated with gold stamped with intricate designs, and with all the torches and lanterns, it glimmered like the sun. Along the walls, there were several doors leading to other areas of the temple and benches and pews for patrons to worship. Only a few people were there at this hour, praying in panicked whispers, surely over the death of the king. As Sybil approached the statue of Shuheyr, one of the nuns walked over to her with a sad smile.

"May the light of Shuheyr shine upon you," she said in a brittle voice. "Is there anything I can help you with today?"

The question Sybil had made her feel a bit silly, but she asked it anyway: "How would one go about directly speaking to Shuheyr?"

This surprised the nun, and she asked, "Whatever do you mean, my dear? We can always speak to Shuheyr through prayer."

"I…" she started but then looked up at Shuhery's statue. "Never mind, thank you. May I sit in one of the pews here?"

The woman nodded and let her be, heading over to a row of candles and lighting a few while chanting prayers. Sybil wondered what Shuheyr thought of this. Was it strange to watch mortals dedicate so much time and energy to you or did it build up too much of an ego for you to care?

"Okay, I'm here," Sybil said in a quiet voice so none of the nearby patrons could hear her, leaning her arms against the railing in front of the pew. "Now what? How do I talk to you?"

Nothing followed her questions, so she just sat there, waiting and staring up at his statue. What a gaudy, ugly thing it was. How many people in the Outer Ring could his two statues have fed and housed for a year? It was no wonder so many people no longer worshiped the gods.

"What my followers choose to do with their gold is not up to me," Shuheyr said to Sybil in her head, causing her to jump.

"So, you can read my mind."

"Only when you let me in," he replied, and suddenly his form appeared beside her, looking just as he did in her dream with the same golden hair and bright blue eyes. "And even that has its limits."

Sybil leaned back in the pew and sighed.

"Why am I here?" she asked, after a nun walked past, not seeing Shuheyr next to her.

"It was a bit of a test, I suppose," he said with a smile. "I wanted to see if you were willing to go out of your way to come to my temple and speak with me. You've never been to one of my temples before."

"It doesn't appear I've missed much. Besides, I've learned all I need to know about you from Morningbreak."

"Is that so?" he asked before crossing his legs. Why did he bother with the mannerisms of mortals? "I guess it is true that villages like the one you grew up in have a far deeper understanding of me and my powers. They have been following me long before the temples were ever built, nearly as long as I have existed."

"And how long is that?"

"Back when this kingdom was only but a dream, when the elves ruled over this land," he replied. "The number of years have since escaped me."

"What do you know of Haborym?"

He eyed her for a moment and heaved a regretful sigh.

"There is only so much to know. He was once a mortal creature, but he sought an unthinkable amount of power, relying on the darkness of the universe to fuel it, and it ended up twisting him into a monstrosity that later became the very embodiment of darkness."

"You're the god here, not me. Why not destroy Haborym yourself? Why must this fate rest on my shoulders?"

Another smile spread across his face before he said, "Sybil, it's not that I need you to do this. You are not some chosen savior or someone destined to rid the world of darkness. No, this is simply a mission I am giving you, similar to ones you have accomplished for Leon, but if you cannot do it, then I will let this world be overtaken by the darkness."

"Why?" she asked in a gasp. "Your light is supposed to protect the world."

"And what is light without darkness?" he asked. Sybil never thought she would see a god shrug his shoulders, but Shuheyr was full of surprises. "You are my child, and I love you dearly. But if your choices lead to your death and the death of thousands more, I will not intervene."

"You saved my life once before, though," she told him, staring down at the pew railing.

"Did I?" he asked, raising a golden eyebrow. "Or did you use your connection to me to harness the powers you were gifted with at birth? In that moment, down in the dungeon with the hag, you trusted me enough to feel my power and allow the connection between us to become unwavering, just as you did against Haborym's disease in the woods."

"It's that simple, then? I just have to trust you."

"Yes. But then again, has trust ever been simple for you? Even the man you love is someone you are suspicious of."

"There are reasons for that."

"Well, whatever the reasons, if you are going to successfully defeat Haborym, you are going to have to trust both of us completely."

Anger bubbled up inside her.

"At least Mordecai has done things to earn my trust. What have you done, *father*?" Sybil asked, her voice full of spite. "You men think you can just say 'trust me' and I'll go 'oh, well there's an idea.'"

Shuheyr laughed and shook his head before saying, "I will see you again soon, my child." And as the last word was uttered, he disappeared.

Sparks started to crackle from Sybil's hands as she clenched them together, frustration filling her. How could she possibly trust him? She wasn't one of his mindless followers who were worshiping around her. For an instant, her vision lost sight of the temple around her and instead turned to Morningbreak, the village she grew up in. She didn't know if it was a memory or a vision of it in the present, but what she did know was that Shuheyr was making her see this and telling her to go back. But what could she possibly find there that would benefit her in any way? Was that place more important than she realized?

When her vision returned to normal, Sybil rose from the pew and headed outside. She had almost forgotten Mordecai was wearing another face and didn't recognize him at first when he stood up from a bench next to Shuheyr's statue. He joined her by the horses and studied her face for a moment before asking, "I'm guessing it didn't go the way you had hoped for."

"Not exactly," she muttered before mounting Dusk.

As they rode back through the Middle Ring, Sybil told Mordecai everything said between her and Shuheyr, leaving out the part when he acknowledged she was struggling to completely trust Mordecai.

"He's not going to help us, not directly at least. Fortunately, he seems to believe that, if I utilize his powers, we'll be able to defeat Haborym."

"So, what's the next step then? We only have two weeks before the Winter Solstice," Mordecai reminded her. "We are still wildly unprepared for whatever Haborym and his servant plan to throw at us."

"He didn't say it outright, but I think he wants me to visit my old village, Morningbreak. Perhaps there's something for me to learn there, or he wants me to make peace with my people, which I admit is the main reason why I don't trust him," she explained. "But I want us to finish our business here first, if we can. What's the point of saving this kingdom from darkness if it's just going to fall apart from corruption afterward?"

When they arrived at the safe house, it was late afternoon, but Giselle and Keijin were still not back yet. Back in their usual appearances, Mordecai seized the opportunity of them being alone to pull her into his arms and kiss her.

"I had hoped we would've been able to spend the entire morning today laying around in bed together," Mordecai breathed, staring deeply into her eyes. "This place is disappointing compared to the lavish accommodations we had last night. I wouldn't even dare to undress you here. It's not good enough for you."

Sybil kissed him again, running her fingers through his hair, and when they pulled apart, she asked, "Can I see your true form again?"

"He might find us," Mordecai replied, pulling away slightly.

She reached up her hand and recited an incantation. A seal full of symbols representing the words she spoke flashed for a second on the ceiling.

"There, that should last for a little while."

Mordecai laughed, looking up as the seal began to blend into the ceiling and said, "Did you learn wards just so you could see my face?"

"I might have," she answered, blushing a little.

With a small smile, Mordecai revealed his true face again, his eyes and hair returning to their brown hues and the scars reforming in his tanned skin. Though his face usually looked closely shaved, there was a bit of stubble, nearly long enough to count as a beard, along the lower half of his face, matching the auburn of his hair. She ran her fingers over his face, and he closed his eyes, enjoying the pleasure of her touch. Once again, she found herself lingering over his scars, and this time she felt bold enough to ask him where they came from.

"I had a run in with Brynmor and his men once before, nearly ten years ago now, when I was sixteen, barely a man yet," he explained, bringing her hand up to his jawline. "That's how I got this scar. They caught me in the act of pretending to be one of his left-hand men, trying to get information about someone, and he gave me this scar in the midst of escaping."

"And the one across your eye?"

He brought her hand up to that one, as if her touch was soothing those old wounds, and said, "I was only a child when I received this one. It was one of many scars the man who bought me from the orphanage left me with. Even though he was violent and cruel, he never touched the face unless one of his slaves tried to escape. This was the mark of a disobedient slave, one that was not to be trusted." Pain wavered through Sybil as he said this. "It was through trying to hide this scar that I learned how to create disguises for myself."

"I hate him, whoever that man was, for doing such horrible things to you," she said in barely a whisper.

"Ivellios," Mordecai said, his voice filled with a malice of which she had never heard before, even from him. "My biggest regret in life is letting him live."

"Perhaps, we'll be able to correct that one day," she told him, feeling his anger as her own.

Mordecai squeezed her hand and said, "I love you, you know."

"And I love you."

The door opened, causing them both to jump, and in a flash, Mordecai returned to his known persona. Both Giselle and Keijin walked through the door, looking like their day had turned around.

"Great news," Giselle said, sitting down at the table in the corner. "I've been able to request four seats at the casino tonight for me, my sister, and our two escorts."

227

"Sister?" Sybil asked.

"Yes, dear one," Giselle said, extending her arm out to Sybil. "Because while we are not related by blood, I do consider you to be a kind of sister to me." Then, she shrugged. "Plus, I wanted to see if Mordecai could make you look like me. Not an exact replica of course, but enough to where we would easily pass as kin."

Annoyed, Sybil turned to Keijin who had a pleasant look on his face, which was a stark contrast from the devastation he was feeling earlier, and asked him what he learned at the library.

"Nothing much," he replied, but something had changed about him. The weight of the king's death seemed to no longer be pressing down upon him. "I investigated the royal lineage to see who might have rights to the throne other than Archduke Finlay. But unless the queen is with-child, and it is rumored she is not able to conceive, then the only clear heir is Finlay."

"What about Finlay's father, the king's brother?" Sybil asked, remembering the king was the younger of two sons.

"He's been dead since Finlay was a small child," Mordecai said with a shake of the head. "Mysterious circumstances."

"Does Finlay have any known tie with the mob?"

"No, but before King Elias, most nobles did," Mordecai grumbled. "Mephidilea was practically a middleman between the two. Finlay has spent many a night in the casino and other mob-run businesses, though. I would be shocked if he didn't have dealings with Brynmor."

"Fortunately," Keijin told his companions, staring at the floor. "I also learned that the laws of the kingdom state that when a king is killed whether through assassination or in battle, there's a month interim before the next king is crowned out of respect for the king's untimely death. The queen will rule the kingdom in the meantime, which gives us some time to prove whether Finlay had any involvement. Even though he's next in line, he would be executed for treason if we can prove it before he is made king."

"And who would take up the throne instead?"

Keijin's face turned serious.

"That's a great question. From the research I did today, it could be a few different people. Two cousins of the king, stemming from his great-grandfather's line, or his illegitimate sister, though she has made it clear on multiple occasions that she wants nothing to do with her royal blood. I believe she's a privateer, captain of her own ship, in fact."

"Either way, it would leave the throne disjointed," Mordecai said. "The throne has passed from parent to child of the same, legitimate bloodline since the kingdom was established."

"That's better than having it in the hands of the mob," Sybil retorted with a shrug. "But it's ultimately up for the nobles to determine. If Finlay is responsible, then he shouldn't get the throne no matter who else is next in line."

There was a lull in the conversation, and after a few minutes, Giselle clapped her hands together and stood.

"Well, what are we waiting for?" she asked. "We have a casino to get to. Mordecai, change my lovely sister here to look like me, perhaps with a bit redder skin tone and wavy hair instead of straight. Yes, that should be good."

Mordecai did as she asked, and Sybil realized that he had never made a snide remark to Giselle before. He must have respected her for her abilities or, at least, knew it was better not to cross her. After a moment of thought, he waved his hand over Sybil, and from head to toe she changed into a completely different person, no similarities between her regular self and this new form other than her height, which already matched Giselle's. There were no mirrors in this safe house, but she could see her arms were now the color of boysenberry juice, and her hair was now red-black and wavy, falling over her chest.

"Beautiful," Giselle said as if she were looking at a piece of artwork. "Your skills in magic are truly wonderful, Mordecai."

Giselle and Sybil had their arms linked with Keijin and Mordecai, both of them in their own disguises in the fashion of the noble class, as Giselle led them to an establishment in the Outer Ring. On the outside, it looked just as dingy as the other buildings in this region of the City, but people in elaborate garbs, some fitting the same style of Mephidilea, were coming and going from this place in particular. Two large figures, one a human with bulging biceps and the other a half-orc with sharp tusks jutting upwards from his lower jaw, stood outside the front door, stopping the party when they tried to enter the casino.

"The Zaxibis sisters plus escorts," Giselle said, flashing a gorgeous smile at them.

One of the men pulled out a scroll and read through a list of names. Then, he looked to the other and gave a nod. Just like that, they were in the casino.

It was just as Sybil had seen in Cal's memories. A half dozen tables, large enough to easily fit eight people, were scattered about the room. Elegantly designed chandeliers dangled from the ceiling, cascading shimmering light across the room, and a small wooden stage with velvet rope jutted out into the room in the left corner. There was a bar in the right corner, across from the stage, with three full shelves of liquor bottles that lined the wall and a nicely dressed man behind the counter serving people. Around sixty patrons were here, plus another dozen guards or so.

The adventurers headed to the bar, and Giselle ordered cocktails for the girls and two pints of ale for their gentlemen escorts. Keijin downed half of his while scanning the room, but Mordecai just held his, like he was holding it for someone else. The drinks Giselle ordered for herself and Sybil were far sweeter than anything Sybil had experienced before, tasting of an assortment of berries with only the slight hint of alcohol as she swallowed. It was so good that Sybil didn't even realize how quickly she was drinking it until it was gone, and she could feel a warmth radiating from her belly. As Giselle and Keijin headed over to one of the tables where people were starting to gather for a card game, Sybil turned to Mordecai and asked him why he never drank.

"Same reason I try not to sleep," he replied. "It compromises my mind to outside forces. I've only been drunk once, but Haborym nearly took control of my mind. It's not that it's sure to happen, but it isn't worth it."

"Surely one drink can't compromise you that much," she offered, gesturing to the pint he was holding.

"No, but as soon as I drink this, I'll get cocky and believe I'm strong enough to keep him out no matter what," he replied before setting the drink down on the bar. "It's a slippery slope."

Mordecai suggested they find a table to play a game, and they found one hosting a game he taught Sybil that night in Blackridge as they were waiting for the rain to stop. It was one of Redbeard's favorites, though possibly not after Sybil beat him twice that night. Three other patrons and the card dealer were at the table already, and they didn't seem to pay any mind to the newcomers as they sat down, but the lady next to Sybil did stare down at her reddish-purple skin for a moment. People of Giselle's race, along with the other races who do not blend in with the dominant human population, were rare in cities and villages, often keeping to themselves or making a living at establishments off the beaten path, like at the Crossroads. However, it appeared that people were used to the sight of an infernally born persons here, probably due to Giselle's career within the City, particularly in places like this.

The party played various games well into the night, but there was no sign of Brynmor. Finally, as Giselle and Sybil were hanging out near the stage where a woman in a sparkly blue dress was singing with a band behind her, a man with strawberry blonde hair and a bulky frame walked in.

"It's Douglas, Brynmor's right hand," Giselle whispered as they watched him roaming through the room. "We have a history, of sorts. I think I can find out where Brynmor is from him. Just give me a minute."

Giselle glided over to him, and Sybil watched for a while as they spoke to one another. At first, he didn't seem pleased to see her, but the more they talked, and the more she flirted, the more he relaxed around her. Mordecai found Sybil after the table he was playing at ended their game and put a hand on her shoulder. She gestured over to Giselle and this Douglas guy, so he joined her in waiting. Keijin, meanwhile, was still playing a game at another table, and seemed to be winning because there was a huge grin on his face and the other patrons looked irritated with him.

Eventually, Giselle returned to Sybil as Douglas went inside the back office. She had a smile on her face that immediately faded as soon as Douglas was out of sight.

"He's not here," she told her companions. "In fact, he's not even in the City. Apparently, he's been in Easthaven all week."

"Sounds like he's trying to create an alibi for himself," Mordecai said, and Giselle nodded along with his idea. "He never leaves the City unless he really has to. Doesn't like leaving everything for his men to take care of."

"So, what now?" Sybil asked.

"You know, this might actually prove beneficial for us," Giselle said. "Here, he's protected by the very systems he helped put in place. But in Easthaven, he's vulnerable and exposed. We could go to Easthaven and capture him, get his confession, and then bring him to someone we know would uphold the law."

Mordecai didn't look pleased with the idea but said, "That does appear to be our best option at the moment. But let's not speak anymore of this here."

Just as his companions were starting to wind down for bed, Mordecai told them he needed to see to a few things and left without any further explanation. It bothered Sybil, but it wasn't like it was any different from his usual methods, so she tried her best to ignore it. She and Giselle shared the small bed that night as Keijin slept on the couch, and around an hour after they laid down, Giselle asked Sybil if she was still awake.

"It's hard to sleep in a place like this," Sybil replied and then lifted her head to look over at Keijin who was snoring softly. "Well, for me at least."

"I agree, especially with how nice our stays at the Queen's Resort and the palace were," Giselle said and then groaned softly. "My pillow smells like old shoes."

Sybil gave a laugh, trying to stay quiet for Keijin.

"Hey, can I ask you something?"

"You can ask me anything," Giselle breathed with a smile. "We're sisters now, after all."

"Oh yeah," Sybil said, returning the smile. "I was just wondering about you and Tanele. Do you... love her?"

"I think so," she said, frowning as she thought about it. "It's sometimes difficult to tell. But I know she loves me."

"You two seem happy together."

"Yes, well, I'm sure she would be less than pleased to learn about the real me, to know all my secrets," she said with pain in her voice. "That's why it's difficult to tell if I love her. Can you love someone who doesn't know who you actually are? Or is it the other way around? Can she ever love me without knowing these things?"

"What's something you want to tell her but don't feel you can?"

Giselle thought for a moment before answering, "Even though I could live without this lifestyle, I enjoy the things I do. The methods I employ to get what I want, learn what I need to learn, and take out my targets, I love those things. I think she believes they are just a means to an end, but I never would've tried them if I didn't want to do them. She feels like she needs to save me from this lifestyle." She gave a sigh, warming Sybil's face with her breath. "But I'm afraid she would see me as tainted if I told her. So many people already think my race is disgusting and vile... it would kill me for her to see me that way."

"Well, I don't see you that way," Sybil replied. "And I've had a far more sheltered life than Tanele."

"Yes, but you also fell for someone like Mordecai, who has more flaws than all of us put together," she said with a smirk. "You aren't a good baseline for other people's judgment."

Sybil laughed quietly and said, "I suppose that's true. But wouldn't it be better to know if Tanele is someone who will judge you and end it than to live a lie with her?"

"Sure, it's easy to say it, but my heart feels such fear to think of her loving eyes turning to disgust," Giselle whispered. "I see my future with her… I know I won't be doing these things for the rest of my life. It's just hard to think that who I am could make all of it go away."

Tears started rolling down her cheeks, and Sybil put her hand up to Giselle's face and said, "Trust her. Trust her love for you. And then let yourself love her back fully." As she said it, Sybil realized this was something she wanted to do, too.

Giselle nodded, wiping her tears, and there was a moment of silence before she said, "And what about you? It seems like you and Mordecai are a pendulum swinging from lovers to acquaintances, and quite frankly, it's giving me a bit of whiplash."

"Our situation is complicated to say the least," Sybil replied. "But we seem to love each other, and our goals are intertwined, and I suppose the rest is just going to have to be figured out as we go along. It feels like we have no time while also having all the time in the world, so it's a little hard for me to understand."

"Well, he's definitely changed for the better since he arrived at the tower. Every time I saw him that first week, I thought he was going to spontaneously combust into a rage. There was so much hate and anger in him. Don't get me wrong, there still is, but there's something more in there, something brighter. And the way he looks at you…" She gave a small laugh, tiredness starting to get to her. "It's a beautiful thing to see."

Chapter Seventeen

The door flung open, the early morning sunshine stirring the sleeping adventures awake, and Mordecai entered. He had been out all night and appeared displeased about something. It wasn't anything he wanted to talk about, Sybil could tell by the look on his face, but it was clear what it was about. His silver eyes were always darker for a while after nights he spent speaking with Haborym.

Without any further delay, the party packed up their stuff and headed out of the City on their horses. For their own reasons, they were all determined to find Brynmor and bring the king's murderer to justice as quickly as possible. Not wanting to camp on the road, they pushed through a good portion of the night and made it to Easthaven around midnight. Even though it was the oldest town in the kingdom, established when humans first settled in this part of the continent, the buildings looked as though they were newly and intricately built, having no signs of wear and tear as structures from other towns. This town was far more affluent than the others: old families with hundreds of years of wealth built up and industries spread across the kingdom.

The focal point of the town square was the tavern, a three-story building with a gilded wooden sign that read "The Duck and Dog." As the party entered the tavern, they found it still alive with music and the voices and laughter of its patrons, despite the hour. Hungry, they found a table and ordered a late dinner. There were a couple dozen people, both patrons and workers, in this place, and Sybil even recognized the singer of the band to be the same elegant dwarf Redbeard had sung along to in Taragpass. She wondered if anyone here knew where they could find this Brynmor character, but she didn't know how to ask without drawing attention to herself.

All four of them were exhausted from the ride, and Keijin suggested they get at least a few hours of rest before trying to track down Brynmor. Sybil didn't like it, but even Mordecai agreed it would be better to wait until morning. They just had to hope he didn't leave before they could find him the next day.

On the top floor of the Duck and Dog, there were rooms for rent, and Giselle asked for two rooms from the young man sitting behind a counter. She gave one to Sybil with a wink before announcing that she and Keijin would share a room. Keijin looked a little startled but didn't say anything as he followed Giselle up to their room, leaving Sybil and Mordecai standing awkwardly at the bottom of the stairs. They hadn't had a chance to talk about what happened the other night with everything else going on.

With a huff, Mordecai took the key from Sybil and headed upstairs. She followed him, after a moment of hesitation, and they entered their room at the far end of the hallway. He closed the door, and suddenly, she found herself feeling extremely nervous, more so than she had ever felt around him. Things had changed between them, and she didn't know how to act. It felt like she was doing everything all wrong.

"Why are you shaking?" he asked, moving closer to her. "Are you scared of me?"

"No, no," she said, shaking her head. "Nothing like that. I mean, I'm scared but not because I'm worried you're going to hurt me or anything. I just… don't know how to do this. I don't know if we even should do this."

"Yeah, I know what you mean," he said and sighed, looking away. "A part of me wishes I didn't feel this way for you, and I've been trying to fight it since I met you." His eyes returned to hers, and she could see something deeper in them than she had ever seen before. "But I don't want to fight it anymore. I want to be with you, in whatever capacity that might be for now. And if all goes wrong and Haborym defeats us, I want to make sure I spend what little time we have left together."

Sybil stepped toward him and put her arms around him, taking in a deep breath of his scent. He smelled of old books, fresh ink, and eucalyptus. It didn't make sense to her why they felt so strongly for each other, but she wanted nothing more than to be with him. Something was still nagging at her, though, and caused her to pull away.

"If we're to be together, we need to be completely honest with each other," she told him in a soft tone. "Is there anything that you're keeping from me?"

"Yes," he breathed without a moment of hesitation. "There's so much that I'm keeping from you. But I can't tell you everything. There are things you shouldn't know, and things I don't want to disturb you with."

"What *can* you tell me?"

Mordecai thought for a moment, moving to the bed to sit. It was clear he wanted her to know as much as he could share.

"Felix knows something about Haborym, something useful in destroying him, but I couldn't get him to tell me what it was," he said with a frown. "I did his dirty work for two days, and all he told me was that I wasn't ready yet. He said to come back when I was actually ready to betray Haborym, which is bullshit. I've been ready to betray him since I was a boy."

"Did he explain what he meant by that?"

"No," Mordecai growled, clutching the bedsheets underneath him. "After he said that, he opened up a portal and pushed me through it. The next time I see him, I might beat the answers out of him."

"Or," she said slowly as she sat next to him. "I could get them from him."

The realization sparked across Mordecai's eyes, and he ran a strand of her hair through his fingers as he thought.

"If we could catch him while he was sleeping and I were to amplify your powers, we might just be able to pull that off," he said, still thinking. "Perhaps, we should have you practicing that ability more. You've definitely improved on it in the past few weeks, but Felix's mind is as impenetrable as Leon's, so we'll need to have every advantage we can."

"I suppose we might need to use it against Brynmor to get some answers from him, if he isn't willing to talk."

"True, but you could also practice it on me," Mordecai suggested with a shrug.

Sybil stared at him for a moment, waiting to see if he was joking.

"Don't give me that look. Just do it."

"I don't know," she breathed. "The last time I was in your head, it nearly killed me."

"Yes, well, that was under much different circumstances," he replied as anger and guilt flashed across his face. "I won't let something like that happen to you again." His eyes turned hard. "Please, trust me."

Sybil nodded before holding her hand out toward him. With a hard swallow, she sent her consciousness into his mind, immediately hitting a wall. He was challenging her, seeing how much she could push his will, which neared the point of rivaling Leon and Felix. Pushing harder, he let her through and suddenly she found herself in a small, dingy room with no windows and only a bedroll on the floor. She was sitting with her legs crossed and could feel the cold floor and dirt on her bare skin. There were voices coming from the other side of the door, and she strained to listen.

"And you're sure he's healthy?" a male voice was asking. "I don't pay for sickly workers. He'll need to be able to do manual labor throughout the day."

"Yes, of course, sir," a small woman replied. "He's a bit skinny, but he's far stronger than the other kids his age. The boy will make a fine servant."

After a moment, the door was unlocked from the other side and a man walked through. He was finely dressed in a red tunic with matching red leather boots and a black overcoat with red tassels. Staring down at her with cruelty and malice in his eyes, he said, "You'll do. Come with me."

Then, he exited out the door, leaving it open.

Time flashed forward, and suddenly Sybil was in a room with wooden walls and floors, staring out a barred window at the moon. Below was a sprawling town with the warm glow of candles and lanterns shining out windows like stars in the sky. The door opened, and she swerved around to see the same man standing there, more or less in the same outfit, holding a young boy up by his upper arm. A cry escaped her as she noticed that the young boy's face was beaten and bloody, making him hardly recognizable. The man threw the boy down on the ground and yelled, "You rats are nothing. How dare you defy me."

The man slammed the door and locked it behind him. Sybil moved to the injured boy's side and hesitated before she put her hands on him to check to see if he was still breathing. The boy looked at her with his one open, bloodshot eye and tried to say something but didn't have enough strength to make the words. With her hands on his chest, she could feel his heartbeat grow weaker and less frequent until it stopped, and the boy let out his final breath. At first, she didn't move, didn't make a sound, until finally she stared down at her hands and saw the boy's blood on them. A horrible cry followed, and she quickly escaped Mordecai's consciousness before she felt any more of his pain.

A sob bubbled out of Sybil, and she felt like she still had the blood on her hands. When she looked over at Mordecai, hot tears streaming down her face, he was motionless, staring down at the floor. While his face was unchanged, his cheeks were wet with tears. She sat down on the bed next to him as she gained her composure but couldn't think of what to say to him.

"His name was Myles," Mordecai breathed, wiping the tears that were pooling under his chin. "He was the first person I had ever loved… the only person I had ever loved, until I met you. And Ivellios beat him to death to send me a message, to keep me in line. Myles didn't have many skills, had an average intelligence, and was the weakest of the other boys, but he had the kindest heart and the gentlest soul. Ivellios' only use for him was to cause me pain, and that day he went too far and took Myles' life."

Something inside Sybil, perhaps because of his scream in the memory, told her this was only the beginning of the story, so she asked, "What did you do after he died?"

Mordecai's face contorted before he was able to push back the pain again, and said, "That night, as I cried on the floor with Myles' body in my arms, was the first night Haborym came to me. He could sense my pain. It was so great it became a bright beacon for him to follow in the night.

"He told me he would be able to give me powers to defeat my enemies, earn my freedom, and protect those I loved. But I only felt hate, hate for Ivellios and hate for the world. I accepted his offer, but he told me I had to prove my loyalty to him first by making a sacrifice. My plan was to kill Ivellios, but by the time I was able to find the key to my room, he had left for the City and wouldn't be back for weeks. Instead, I figured out a way how I could hurt Ivellios just as he hurt me."

Mordecai paused, and Sybil could feel the shame and guilt radiating off him.

"What did you do?" she asked, placing her hand on his.

"Ivellios had a son, born from one of his servant girls, who he treasured as his heir," Mordecai said, and the air left Sybil's body. "I killed him in his sleep and snuck out of the estate, never intending to return to this town. He was innocent, only five or six, but I killed him, and my prize was moving from one form of imprisonment to another."

There was silence for a long time, and Mordecai kept his face turned away from Sybil. Finally, he breathed, "Please, say something."

"You were just a child," she told him, squeezing his hand. "You were in so much pain, and there were these two forces twisting your mind to be someone that, deep down, I know you're not. Ivellios drove you to the point of desperation, and Haborym took advantage of your pain. Anyone would have taken that path. It doesn't make you worse than anyone else."

"How can you be so forgiving?" he asked, his voice breaking a little.

It scared Sybil a little to see him so vulnerable, to see him being so completely human. She had always taken such comfort in his strength and willpower, even if it did make him hard to get along with.

"You forgave me for what happened near Blackridge, you forgave me for getting you tied up with Haborym in the first place, and you forgive me for this. Why? I've done nothing to deserve it."

She lifted his arm up and put it around her shoulders so she could hug him from the side, placing her head on his chest.

"Did you want to do any of those things? Did you seek them out?" she asked in a whisper, closing her eyes. "No, you didn't. And I didn't forgive you for those things because it wasn't your fault they happened. If it wasn't for Haborym, that boy would still be alive and my life wouldn't be in danger. It's heartbreaking he made you a tool for all those things, but you're working to make the world a better place and save it from darkness."

Mordecai fell back on the bed, pulling Sybil with him, and held her there, his face pressed into the top of her head. His arms were wrapped around her tightly, and she held a part of his tunic in her balled-up fist. After several minutes had passed, Mordecai breathed, "I love you," and with a small smile on her face, Sybil drifted off to sleep.

Something was different about her dream that night. It felt too real. She could only see snippets of things, like when she forced her way into people's memories, but eventually, she found herself bound to a chair, struggling to break free. A couple more flashes showed Ivellios with a horrible grin on his face as he stared down at Sybil and a room full of terrible, bloody instruments. This wasn't a memory; it was Sybil in that chair, in that room. She woke with a start, gasping for air, causing Mordecai to rush to her side to see what was wrong.

"I think I just saw the future," she breathed, wiping tears from her eyes, and told him what she saw. "I've been studying divination for years, but I've never had a vision of the future come to me like that."

"We're not going to let that happen," Mordecai assured her, placing his hand on her face. "I won't let that bastard get anywhere near you."

Sybil nodded, not entirely convinced because she didn't understand the nature of her visions. Many forms of divination could give its wielder possibilities of the future, but some also showed what was unchangeable, fate. Still, she couldn't let her fear get in the way of accomplishing their mission. For King Elias and for the sake of the kingdom, they needed to bring those responsible for his assassination to justice.

That morning, Mordecai and Giselle set out to use their skills and contacts to get a lead on Brynmor's last known location. He had a place of business in Easthaven, but it was heavily guarded and fortified. It would be best to know for sure if he was there or catch him unawares when he was somewhere else in town. Keijin and Sybil didn't serve much purpose in this, so they wandered around the town, hoping to happen across something useful.

"Things seem to be developing between you and Mordecai," Keijin noted as they entered the market district. "I got so used to the two of you bickering that it's a little strange to see you so at ease with each other. But if it's working, I'm happy for you."

"Thanks," Sybil breathed, glancing around a booth they were passing. "It's not too weird for you traveling with us?"

Keijin laughed and said, "It was at first, but I think I've come to accept it. In fact, I've done a lot of thinking about it the past couple of days, and I fear I may have been pursuing you for the wrong reasons."

"Such as?' she asked, moving aside for a man rolling a barrel down the street.

"Don't get me wrong, you're a wonderful person and someone I truly admire. But with your abilities as a wizard, and surely your tie with Shuheyr as well, you'll probably live ten times longer than any normal human, and you're to be the leader of Gibbous Tower one day," Keijin explained, looking embarrassed. "I think those things made me feel like you were the best match for me. I could be with someone I cared deeply for while not having to give up my oath. But with the assassination of the king, I started seeing things differently, and I think that someday very soon I'll be giving up my oath to settle down."

"Keijin, if this is because you feel responsible for his death," Sybil started, but he held up his hand.

"It's not that, not really," he replied. "At first, I was devastated by it. But then I started thinking of all the people I *have* saved. There have been a lot, spanning over centuries now, and I feel like with all I've done, I've fulfilled my oath." He stopped in the middle of the road and took her hands in his. "And that's why we can't be together. My journey is coming to a close, and yours is only at its beginning. Our relationship would require one of us sacrificing part of who we are for the other, and that would only be doomed to fail. But with you and Mordecai? It's going to be a rocky road for the two of you, but at least you will be walking that road together."

Sybil was surprised at herself to find that Keijin's words had made her a little teary-eyed, but she tried to shake it off and said, "Then, we need to find you someone to settle down with, huh?"

"Yes," he said with a laugh as they continued to walk. "I suppose that's true."

Giselle found them before Mordecai did. Keijin and Sybil had gone into a bookstore to browse and were just walking out when she came strolling down the road. Other than the confirmation that Brynmor was indeed still in Easthaven, Giselle wasn't able to dig up any specifics. As they were heading back to the tavern for luncheon, though, Mordecai found them. He was fuming, and after they had found a table in the corner of the tavern, away from the other patrons, Sybil asked him what he learned. Through gritted teeth, Mordecai said that Brynmor was staying as a guest at Ivellios' estate.

"Apparently, they're long-time business partners," Mordecai growled, hunching over the table. "Figures."

"This might be a good opportunity to take Ivellios out as well, especially if he's still up to his old tricks," Sybil suggested.

"As long as we don't let it distract us from our main mission here," Keijin reminded them. "We're here to capture Brynmor and bring him to justice. If we're able to deal with this other man, fine, but not at the sake of the mission."

"Don't worry your pretty little head about it," Mordecai grumbled, causing Keijin's eye to twitch. "We'll make Brynmor our first priority. I can always come back for Ivellios later."

"Who is this Ivellios character, besides an obvious ghost from Mordecai's past?" Giselle asked, looking over at Sybil.

"A trafficker of slave children and a murderer," she answered, not wanting to go into too much detail. "He's just as bad as, if not worse than, this mob boss we're after."

"Well, good. Killing him will stay my hand toward Brynmor long enough to get him back to the palace," Giselle said and ignored the warning glance Keijin was giving her. "So, Mordecai, you wouldn't happen to know an easy way to sneak in and out of this Ivellios' place, would you?"

"Ivellios has a lot of enemies, and ever since his son was killed in the estate, he's been extra careful with his defenses," Mordecai explained, folding his hands across the table. "The last time I was there, he had a seal across every door leading into the house which immediately canceled out any spells currently in use when crossed, such as invisibility or a disguise, so those are out." He thought for a moment. "Honestly, I think our best bet would be to break in the old-fashioned way, so we'll have to rely on Giselle's expertise for that. His estate is three stories tall, and the further up we go, the less likely we'll fall into any traps going through a window. The only ones that are barred are for the slave rooms."

Thinking back to his memory, Sybil winced.

"Okay," Giselle said with a nod. "Get me a shit ton of rope and something to use as a grappling hook, and I'll get you up there."

Back in their room, Mordecai made a map of the estate from his memory, trying to piece it all together the best he could remember after fifteen years. While he did this, Sybil worked on a spell she hadn't touched in a while, one she never fully learned how to use. It was a spell that would allow her to fly, but if she messed it up from three-stories high it could break her legs and ruin their whole mission. The incantation was easy enough to remember, but navigating it once she had it active… that was the real trick.

Sybil hovered in the air a few feet off the ground, moving forward and backward and left and right to get the movements down. Thirty feet up, it would be more or less the same, but if she bumped into something it could cause her to lose her concentration, and if she did that, even for a second, she would fall. At one point, Sybil tried to go left but darted right instead, knocking Mordecai in the head with her foot and then causing herself to tumble onto the bed and the map next to him.

"Sorry," she breathed, staring up at him.

He rubbed his head and growled, "Go practice in the other room."

Keijin was procuring the rope Giselle needed from town, so it was just Giselle in the room when Sybil came in and asked if she could practice. Giselle was just stretching on the floor, so she didn't mind Sybil hovering around the ceiling.

Trying to increase the spell's independence from her concentration, Sybil asked, "Break into many houses by scaling the wall?"

"A fair few," Giselle replied, bending completely over her left leg, pressing her forehead to her shin. "It's a thrill to do. I've just always found the tricky part to be getting out. If we're fortunate, our target will be on the floor we go in. But if we're not... well, that's why we're bringing Keijin along, isn't it?"

"Not just for his charming good looks?" Sybil asked, causing both of them to giggle and her spell to fail.

When Sybil was back on her feet, Giselle said, "It always feels better to have him around, don't you think? All my other missions away from the tower, I always felt on edge all the time. But he's a sturdy rock to lean on, and I know he'll have our backs no matter what. Plus, the healing's a nice perk."

"Yeah, I've always been thankful to have him next to me," Sybil said, sitting on the edge of the bed near her. "There are many times he's had to save the day. He's a true hero."

"I wonder what that feels like..." Giselle said as her face turned thoughtful, and Sybil couldn't tell whether it was a twinge of sadness or regret in her voice.

Sybil sighed and said, "Yeah, me too."

After nightfall, the party headed toward Ivellios' estate with the rope and makeshift grappling hook Giselle had requested and Sybil's spell good enough to keep her from fearing a painful fall. Ivellios' estate was a fortress on a hill just outside of Easthaven. From the west side, he could see all of Easthaven, watching over it like his very own kingdom. The adventurers snuck through the trees and came around the east side of the fortress, away from the eyes of the guards who were patrolling around the front and the sides of the estate. Without the plan they had in place, it would have been nearly impossible to break in, but the way Giselle looked over at Sybil, a gleam of delight in her eyes, she knew they were going to make it in.

What happened from there was anyone's guess.

Giselle tied some knots in the rope before handing it over to Keijin by the grappling hook. To gain momentum, he swung it around several times before tossing it high into the air. They all held their breath as they watched it fly and land onto the roof with a distant clang. Giving it a tug, Keijin was able to secure it to the edge of the building. As Giselle started scaling up the side, being mindful to avoid the windows, Sybil recited the incantation she had been practicing most of the day and floated next to Giselle as she climbed.

"That looks way easier," Giselle huffed. "You wizards are so pampered."

"Yeah, well, you look way more stylish than I do."

Giselle and Sybil reached a window on the third floor, and Sybil did her best to muffle the noise Giselle made trying to shimmy open the lock by putting a magical barrier around it. Eventually, the lock popped open, and they both froze for a moment after a part of it clinked onto the floor. When no sounds or movements followed it from inside, Giselle pushed the window open wide enough for them to get through. Keijin then started using the rope to climb up, and Sybil did her best to guide Mordecai up with the same spell she used on herself, but it was much tricker to keep him moving straight. He didn't seem bothered by the jerky motions, though, and kept his eyes to the ground, making sure a guard didn't happen across them.

Once all four of them were inside, Sybil closed the window as gently as she could, and they began their search for Brynmor. Mordecai was able to turn everyone invisible, but they still had to be mindful of the noise they made with their feet pressing against the wood panel floor. The entire third floor was dark, even though it was only early in the evening, and after searching and listening for a while, they were sure no one was up there.

Using as much of her magic as she could muster, Sybil cast a spell allowing her to see through walls and directed it toward the floor, seeing into the rooms and corridors below. After passing through a few rooms, some clearly meant for servants and slaves, she happened across a far nicer room at the end of the hall on the west side of the building. Brynmor was snoozing on the bed, completely unaware someone was watching him. With a grin, Sybil told them she found him.

Mordecai pulled out the roughly sketched map he had made of Ivellios' estate and explained that the stairwell was on the east side of the building, so they would have to travel all the way across the floor without being noticed. After that, they would have to grab Brynmor before he could scream for help, which Sybil could help with, making him fall into a deep sleep, and figure out how to get him out of the building without anyone noticing.

Sybil had a bad feeling about all this. They were in a tricky spot, and none of them had any idea what kinds of safeguards Ivellios had around his estate, not even Mordecai. The memory of her dream came back to her, and a wave of unease and nervousness shot through her. If she was captured by either of these men, they would not be merciful to her. Still, it could have been a nightmare or a flash of a future possible but not one she was destined to face. She took in a slow, deep breath to steady herself and pushed the dream from her mind.

Doing their best to stay together, the party made their way down to the second floor, and Sybil rammed into Mordecai's invisible arm because he stopped before heading out into the hall. A guard passed right by them, equipped with a shortsword and a mace, and once he was a safe enough distance away, they continued into and down the corridor, reaching the last door on the right. They were halfway there, but Sybil's heart sank when her foot stepped on something sticking up from the floor, and it pressed down with a click.

Two iron walls shot up from floor to ceiling, and Giselle and Sybil became visible, trapped between them. Mordecai and Keijin must have been on the other side of one of the walls because if the spell failed for Giselle and Sybil, it would have for them, too. Then, there was fighting, and a blast of something slammed against the wall behind them, causing them to jump. Sybil heard a muffled cry of pain, thankfully not from a voice she recognized, and then everything fell silent. Giselle and Sybil started to test around the seam of the walls to see if they could find a way to wedge them back down, but the walls were made of a thick sheet of metal and no amount of magic Sybil threw at them would make them budge.

A small hole appeared in the wall to their left and steam started billowing out of it. Giselle took Sybil's hand and gave it a squeeze. Before she even smelled the bittersweet gas, Sybil knew what it was, and as soon as it reached her nostrils, she collapsed to the ground.

Chapter Eighteen

However much Sybil didn't want to believe it, the vision she saw in her dream about her future predicament was true. When she came to, she found herself bound in a chair and fought back against the panic rising in her chest. She was in a stone room that was cold, damp, and eerily quiet, underground, probably a basement. Her head felt like it weighed a hundred pounds, and she struggled to keep her eyes completely open. Across from her, Giselle was in the same position, but her head was still slumped over, her red-black hair covering her face. To Sybil's left, metal instruments, some with dried blood still caked to them, were hanging on the wall, and above her were thick, jagged hooks affixed to the ceiling. Without even using her magical senses, she could feel the tremendous and horrible amount of pain that had been experienced here.

The only door in the room opened to Sybil's right, causing her to jump. A late-middle-aged man with short cut hair and a red tunic with dark trousers walked in. Though he looked far older and more tired than he did in Mordecai's memories, Sybil knew this was Ivellios. When he approached her, all she could see in his eyes was spite and rage.

"We have your friends in the other room," he said, his voice low and menacing. "Tell me why you're here and who sent you, and I won't make them suffer a slow and agonizing death."

Sybil's powers had grown strong, and she had spent enough time around liars, both good and bad ones, that she could pick up something she hadn't been able to notice in people before. There was no power behind his words, no surety. He was lying. They had no idea where Mordecai and Keijin were, which caused her heart to fill with hope. Still, she needed to play along or he might try to use Giselle to get answers out of her instead.

"Please, don't hurt them," she cried —her acting had been improving, too. "I'll tell you whatever you want to know. Just let my friends go."

"It doesn't work that way," Ivellios growled. "Your friends are as good as dead, but it's up to you how much they suffer in the process."

This man was cruel and unwavering with any idea of mercy. And even though she knew Keijin and Mordecai were safe, she hated him. For what he did to Mordecai and the other children, for what he was doing now, and for what she knew he was planning to do with her and Giselle.

"We came to capture Brynmor," she said, glaring up at him. There didn't seem much point lying to him. What was he going to do with the truth anyway? "We know he had the king killed."

"So then, you're the apprentice to Gibbous Tower my informants told me about," he said, his rage turning to amusement. "It's your lucky day then. You're sure to fetch a fine price, so unlike your friends, I'll be letting you live, but just barely."

Just then, the door opened again, causing Giselle to stir this time, and Brynmor walked in. Giselle looked up, still not sure of her surroundings, and recognizing her, Brynmor struck her across the face with the back of his hand. Her head jerked back, and she let out a yelp. Sybil fought against the ropes, nearly knocking over her chair.

"You bastard," Sybil screamed. "Leave her alone!"

"And who the fuck is this one?" Brynmor asked Ivellios, looking at him with his one good eye.

Ivellios, unfazed by Brynmor's entrance, just said, "A wizard."

"Well, whoever she is, you can kill her as long as I get to gut that one over there," he replied, shoving his thumb back toward Giselle, who was now glaring at him. "She's done a lot of odd jobs for me here and there, thought she was someone I could trust. I don't like people double crossing me."

"Yes, old friend, I'm aware," Ivellios said with a huff, as Brynmor moved over to the instruments on the wall and started to pick one out.

"I know who you are," Sybil said to Ivellios, her heart burning with hate. "I know all the terrible things you've done."

"Oh, do you now?" he asked, moving closer to her.

She heard the rattling of metal on metal as Brynmor pulled an instrument from the wall, a jagged blade with a stained wooden handle.

"And who told you that? The Enlightened?"

"No," she said, tilting her head. "The man who killed your son."

Ivellios' face turned white, and Sybil saw his adam's apple quiver as he swallowed.

"You know him?"

"I do," she breathed, enjoying the fear she saw in his eyes. "He won't leave me here for long, so I'd think carefully about how you treat me, if I were you."

The estate shook for the briefest of moments, but it grabbed everyone's attention. Ivellios shot straight up, his eyes wide and his mouth slightly opened, listening for any more noises or movement. Just when Ivellios was about to say something to Brynmor, two guards came running in, only terror in their eyes. They closed the door firmly behind them and turned to Ivellios and Brynmor.

"A terrible, dark creature has broken through the front door, my lord," one of the guard's squeaked. "He killed three of our men in one fell swoop."

"Quiet," Ivellios hissed, and his chest started to rise and fall rapidly.

A silence fell over the room, each of the men before Sybil standing portrait-still.

"So… this is it, then?" he asked no one in particular, his voice filling the air.

"What's happening?" Brynmor asked in a whisper, but just after he did, the door flew open.

Black smoke billowed into the room, snuffing out the lights of the lanterns along the walls around them. Stepping through the middle of the smoke was Mordecai, his eyes pitch black. Through all the smoke in the doorway, Keijin was barely visible, but Sybil could see how unusually pale he was and the hardness in his eyes. Mordecai's cloak was splattered in blood, and the dark magic he was wielding caused his hands to look as though they had been covered in soot.

Ivellios trembled as he stared at this horrifying version of Mordecai.

"You… you're the one who killed him," Ivellios breathed, staggering back. "The dark creature who murdered my son."

"Yes," Mordecai said, his voice echoed by another as he spoke. "If it was not for the pain you inflicted, I never would have entered your home. You drew me to your own ill-begotten fate."

Sybil's entire body went cold. The other voice speaking was Haborym, she was sure of it. To have enough power to save her and Giselle, Mordecai must have had to let him in.

Mordecai lifted his hand, and Sybil heard this faint, high-pitched sound, but the way Ivellios fell to his knees, clutching his ears, she knew he heard the noise at great intensity. His eyes, nose, and ears started bleeding, and he started screaming this horrible scream of agony. Then, to Sybil's horror, his head erupted from his neck, sending blood splattering across the room. The spell was so powerful it didn't stop with Ivellios, and the guards who were standing next to him started crying out in pain and collapsed to the ground as tears of blood streamed down from their eyes. They lay there, unmoving, with their red eyes staring up blankly at the ceiling. Then, Mordecai turned to Sybil and started to extend his hand, as if to grab her, but then he went stalk-still. He was fighting Haborym's hold on him with every ounce of willpower he had.

"No, that's enough," she heard Mordecai's real voice say. For a minute or so, everything went deathly silent, and then he stumbled back a bit. The smoke swirling through the room dissipated and the ash marks around his hands faded. His eyes and hair turned brown as he pushed Haborym's magic and influence out of his mind. He was no longer in his disguise, looking like his natural self for the first time in front of Giselle and Keijin. Keijin moved into the room, keeping a safe distance from Mordecai, to untie Giselle, and then, they both surrounded Brynmor who was balled up in a corner, crying.

"Please, please, don't kill me," he sobbed, tears and snot streaming down his face.

"Don't worry," Keijin said in a tired voice, standing him up and starting to tie a rope around his wrists. "You're not going to die today. I think the queen would much prefer your head fresh when she puts it on a stake outside the palace walls."

The three of them left the room as Mordecai approached Sybil and slowly started untying her ropes, looking absolutely exhausted from the exertion of Haborym's powers. He didn't look at her as he said, "I'm sorry you had to see that."

"Thank you for saving me," she breathed as a tear slipped from her eye and down her cheek. "Are you okay?"

"I will be," he said, pulling the ropes from around her.

He stood up, helping Sybil from the chair, and she fell into him, wrapping her arms around his torso. At first, he flinched, and his back went rigid, but the longer she held him there, the more relaxed he became, and eventually, he wrapped his arms around her and squeezed her tightly. He pressed his face to the top of her head and whispered, "I was afraid he was going to take you, too. It drove me mad just thinking about it. I'm so sorry, but I had to let Haborym in."

Sybil pulled away from him and looked him in the eyes, seeing his natural face and the genuine pain he was feeling. How many years of pulling away from Haborym did he reverse in order to save her? Her stomach grew heavy, but she said nothing about it. Instead, she told him she loved him and that they should go find the others.

Ivellios and the guards in the basement were by no means the only casualties of Mordecai's powers as he made his way through the estate. There was a guard dead on the stairs, the life sucked out of him by darkness, and in the corridor, there was a splattering of blood high on the wall, and a trail that led to the guard who lay on the ground below. Two more lay dead further down the hall, near the front, their chests hollow from the spikes Mordecai had shot through them. Only one of the guards he passed still survived, but he looked crazed and was muttering the same, incoherent words to himself over and over again. Even though she knew this was due to Haborym's influence, it made Sybil sick to think about how much suffering and violence Mordecai was able to inflict with his powers.

Sybil and Mordecai found Keijin and Giselle just as they were locking Brynmor in one of the slave rooms on the first floor. Mordecai headed up to the second floor to free any slaves up there, and Giselle went in search of Ivellios' office. When they were alone, Keijin took Sybil's arm and pulled her aside, his face still pale and eyes hardened.

"I didn't lift a finger in the death of those men," he whispered to her, as if he was worried Mordecai would hear him from the floor above. "Mordecai tore through them without an ounce of remorse, without a single flinch at their screams."

"It wasn't him," she said, keeping her voice low as well. "It's unfortunate those men had to die in such a way and you had to see it happen, but Mordecai allowed Haborym to work through him so he could save us. Brynmor was going to kill Giselle; he had the blade in hand he was going to use to do it."

Keijin let go of her arm and sighed.

"I suppose you're right. It's just... I have never seen evil like that before, especially not in someone I was beginning to think of as a friend. Truth be told, it frightened me."

"I think it frightened all of us," she told him. "Mordecai included."

"Are you sure he's safe for us to be around?"

Sybil thought for a moment before firmly saying, "Yes, I am."

Keijin gave a nod, his lips tightly pressed together, before heading to help Mordecai tend to the slaves, and Sybil went to find Giselle. She was by Ivellios' office door and had just jimmied the lock open when Sybil found her. The entire left side of Giselle's face had turned such a dark purple it was almost black from the hit she took from Brynmor. They moved inside the office, and Giselle headed straight for the desk, pulling out drawers and dumping their contents onto the ground. Sybil didn't bother asking her what she was doing; she would explain soon enough.

Once all the drawers were emptied and on the ground, Giselle sat in the desk chair and thought for a moment before a spark of insight flashed across her face. She reached under the desk and ripped a package out from under it. Waving it at Sybil, she said, "I knew he wouldn't keep it far from him."

Giselle tore open the package and pulled out a thick document, slapping it on the table in front of her. It was the deed to Ivellios' estate and the surrounding land, and when Sybil realized this, she couldn't help but grin. With the connections Giselle and Mordecai had, they would be able to put the deed in whoever's name they picked. This place could be put to good use, or they could just burn it to the ground. It was theirs to do with what they wanted.

In order to help them make a new life somewhere else, Keijin and Mordecai let the freed slaves ransack the house for any coin or valuables they could sell. They would spend the night there and be on their way to freedom after sunrise. A few of the children, though, seemed lost about where they should go, so Giselle walked them over to a nearby temple to have the clerics care for them. Once all the former slaves and servants were seen to, Mordecai could no longer stand being there, so Sybil followed him outside.

Just as they passed the estate, Mordecai turned on his heel and growled, "Don't follow me. I don't want you around me right now."

"Why?" she asked, a little pang of pain in her chest.

"Why do you think?" he replied, his voice growing louder with every word. "You saw what happened in there. I'm a monster. Haborym still has his claws in me; you're not safe around me."

"Mordecai, I wouldn't be alive without you," Sybil breathed as she took a step closer to him. "But is that really the issue? Or do you resent me for having to call on his power?"

His voice went quiet as he said, "I don't resent you. It's just..." He trailed off, and then anger bubbled up in him again. "You just don't get it. Everything you have, your magic, your powers from Shuheyr, the legacy you are set to inherit from Leon, all of it has just been handed to you. I've had to scrape and bleed and suffer to get to where I am, and yet, I'm still just a slave, a servant of darkness. I am nothing, a street rat whose only power has been gained through lies and manipulation. But you... you're the daughter of a god and the heir to Gibbous Tower. I am nothing compared to you. I am nothing to you but a threat, nothing but pain."

His words had made Sybil's chest feel hollow, and all she could manage to whisper was "That's not true."

"See?" he said, staring down at her face, as all of the anger and frustration left him. "I'm hurting you right now, aren't I?"

"Yes," she breathed, her hands clasped together against her chest. "Because of these lies you're saying about yourself you seem to believe. You're not nothing, especially not to me. You're the most important thing in the world to me. I would give up my powers and the tower and my connection to Shuheyr if it meant getting to spend the rest of my days with you because you mean that much to me."

Mordecai was looking away from her, and Sybil couldn't tell what he was thinking. This fear rose up in her chest as she wondered if he had fallen out of love with her or if he realized he had never truly loved her in the first place. She felt him slipping away, and there was something deep inside of her screaming to grab hold of him, to keep him from leaving. Without being able to stand it any longer, she stepped forward and pulled him close to her.

"I love you, damn it," she cried, squeezing him tightly. "I don't care what happens to me. Just please, stay by my side. You're not a threat, you're not pain. You're the smartest, most cunning man I know, and after we defeat Haborym, you will be able to become whoever it is you want to be."

Mordecai seemed to crumple around her, his forehead resting against her shoulder and his arms draped over her. She felt his body shudder as he let out a cry, but he didn't make any noise. Then, he said, "Thank you."

Sybil closed her eyes, feeling the tears which had been welling start to slide down her cheeks, as she held him there. After a few moments, he jerked back and let out a groan as black ichor started dripping off his skin. He took a few steps back so the liquid wouldn't touch Sybil before collapsing to his knees. She stood there frozen, unsure what to do, and watched in distress as he suffered from whatever symptom of Haborym's magic this was.

Eventually, he stilled and took a deep breath as the last bit of ichor dripped onto the ground. His brown eyes looked up at Sybil, all the suffering gone from his face.

"I-I don't know what that was," he breathed, standing upright. "It feels like I was able to fully push him out, but I've never been able to expel him that quickly. Something about what you said, how you made me feel, must have fought against his hold on me. That's... incredible."

Mordecai pulled Sybil into his arms and kissed her passionately, running his fingers through her hair and across the back of her head, causing the top of her head to tingle. The hollowness in her chest filled with joy and hope, and she wanted nothing more than to make this moment last forever.

When Sybil awoke, having dreamed of only the real nightmares she witnessed the day before, she found that Mordecai had also fallen asleep sometime in the night. His arm was limply draped over her hip and the other was tucked under his head and pillow. For the first time since she met him, his face was calm and unthinking, the weight of the world and his powers a distant concern. A short lock of his brown hair had fallen, the tips of the strands resting against his eyelid, and she moved it back into place while grazing her fingertips over his forehead. His face twitched for a moment, but he stayed asleep. Until the sun came up, she lay there watching him, soaking in the sight of him. Eventually, he did stir, and when his deep brown eyes met hers, he smiled a small, sweet smile.

"If I could wake up to your beautiful face every morning, I would ask for nothing more from the world." he breathed in a groggy, gravelly voice.

He brought his hand up to her cheek and ran his fingers down her jaw. Holding her chin, he leaned forward to kiss her, making her heart soar.

"It made me happy to see you resting," she said. "Did what happened last night make you safe from Haborym getting into your head?"

"Not exactly," Mordecai replied, his face turning serious. "He was able to get into my head last night when I called upon his powers. I let him see just enough that he thinks he knows what's going on, what I'm planning.

But I've been practicing compartmentalizing my thoughts for as long as I can remember, and if I was successful, he has no idea we're planning to destroy him. He has too much confidence in his powers to think I was able to get away with hiding something like that from him."

"Perhaps, we'll be able to continue using his underestimation of us to our advantage," Sybil suggested. "We just have to make sure that he doesn't figure out how capable we really are."

"Yeah, and that's a hard thing to keep from showing," he said, a small grin appearing on his face.

Later that morning, they returned to Ivellios' estate, and Sybil felt ready to question Brynmor and figure out the truth behind the king's assassination. Keijin brought Brynmor into Ivellios' study where Giselle and the former slaves had ransacked the day before and tied him to a chair in the middle of the room. Sybil leaned against the front of the desk with her staff resting on its surface behind her, while Giselle sat in the desk chair, Keijin stood off to the side, and Mordecai, who was back in his silver-eyed disguise, hovered by the door. Sybil's arms were crossed as she stared at Brynmor for a few minutes, and he stared right back at her with his one good eye. The other had gone white from damage, probably in the same moment he received the scars running over it. Even in the state he was in, Brynmor was an intimidating presence. She had to be smart about her interrogation; he was clever enough to use information to misdirect her.

"Those assassins you sent through the tunnels," she began. "We were able to apprehend one of them, and we received all the information we need to pin the king's murder on you."

"The king's dead?" he asked, his voice sounding shocked. "I had no idea. When did this happen?"

Sybil smiled, being familiar enough with manipulative tricks not to fall for his act, and continued, "You see, I have unique abilities, ones that I have developed during my tutelage under the Enlightened. Whether the person wants me to or not, I can peer into their mind and learn all their secrets. I did this with one of your men. Despite his best efforts, I was able to see him receive his orders from you to lead his team to kill the king in his sleep."

Brynmor sat there, listening to her intently, but did not seem fazed by the information she was presenting to him. Eventually, he breathed, "If you know I'm the one responsible, then why are you wasting your time here, questioning me? If you're able to prove that it was me, then why not just present me to the queen and be done with it?"

"Because you don't just do things on a whim, unless they're drugs or women," Mordecai growled behind him. "There's a reason you sent your assassins after the king; there's someone behind your actions. We want to know why you're involved and who hired you."

"There are plenty of reasons why I would want the king dead," Brynmor said, laughing. "That little prick has always stood in the way of my business, and when he became king, he practically had my organization in a stranglehold. Getting rid of him benefitted me in so many ways."

"You're protecting someone," Sybil noted, picking up on the fact he was awfully quick to confess to his crimes. "Who are you protecting?"

"Why would *I* protect anyone?" he asked with another laugh, though this one sounded different, more unsure. "I'm the head of my organization. There isn't anyone I find more important than myself."

"We'll see about that," she said, reaching over to grab her staff.

Pointing her staff toward him, the wolf totem glimmering in the candlelight of the chandelier above her, she said the incantation to send her consciousness into his mind. She felt sick as she shoved her way through his willpower and suddenly found herself in one of his memories. He knew he couldn't keep her out, so he forced himself to remember something different than what she was searching for.

Sybil was in the casino, sitting at a table surrounded by people. The cards she held in front of her looked good, and after a moment to keep the crowd in suspense, she slapped them down on the table. The crowd let out a cheer, and the dealer pushed all the coins over to her.

She pushed back against the memory, trying to dig deeper into his mind. For the first time since she had learned this spell, she actually heard the inner voice of the person she was trying to read.

"You'll get nothing from me," he boomed inside her head.

Sybil felt a hand touch her actual shoulder, and she knew right away it was Mordecai because she could feel his magic flow into her. With his help, she was able to break free from Brynmor's memory trap and push into one he was trying to keep closed. Unexpectedly, she was in the middle of the throne room, looking up at a different king sitting on the throne. He looked older and far more pampered than the late King Elias. She realized King Elias – Prince Elias in this memory– was standing right next to her, looking no older than sixteen, tall but scrawny with only the hint of a beard starting to grow in. The king dismissed the court, and Prince Elias turned to her.

"I don't understand why father keeps letting people walk all over him," he said with a sigh. "It's embarrassing really."

"He isn't letting people walk all over him," Brynmor's voice, younger but still of a man, said. "The crown needs funds. These people are providing it to him."

"Well, then, that's just corruption," the prince said.

Brynmor struck him and growled, "Never speak of father that way."

The memory vanished instantly, and Sybil was in a bedchamber, staring down at a woman who was holding a newborn baby. She didn't recognize this woman, but with the number of attendants around her, she knew she was someone of importance. The woman lifted the baby up to Sybil and said, "Elijah, meet your son."

Sybil took the baby boy in her arms, and he looked up at her with dark blue eyes.

"Finlay," Brynmor breathed.

The sound of yelling coming from Brynmor's mouth brought Sybil back into reality, her consciousness snapping back into her body. He was glaring at her with a fiery rage in his eye while he fought against the rope. She stared at him confused, not understanding how this mob boss could have once been the heir to the throne, the father of Archduke Finlay. It didn't make sense.

"Keijin, what happened to King Elias' brother? The crowned prince?"

After thinking for a moment, Keijin answered, "No one really knows. His wife was found dead in her chambers, strangled to death, and he was never heard from again. People suspected he was the one responsible for her death and fled to another kingdom, and after several years had passed, everyone suspected he was dead."

"Dead, and reborn into something different," Sybil added, staring down at Brynmor, his rage not bothering her in the least.

The realization hit Mordecai, and he caught on right away.

"So, you killed your wife and knew you would be charged for matricide and treason, lose your crown, and possibly spend most of your life in a cell, so you fled the palace, probably through the very tunnels the assassins used. Then, you took on a new identity, one which would give you just as much, if not more power, as the crown," Mordecai said, breaking it all down, and then laughed as he shook his head. "Impressive."

"Why kill your wife?" Sybil asked, ignoring Mordecai.

"Who can remember?" Brynmor replied with ice in his tone. "But, you're right, since she was a princess from another kingdom, I knew I wasn't going to get away with it. I would never be king after that. And who else would I pin it on? So I left. Traveled the kingdom for a bit before taking over the underground gangs and bringing them all under one banner, my banner."

"So, you killed the king to put your son on the throne, is that it?" Brynmor glared at Sybil.

"Yeah, that about covers it. The boy didn't know I was his dad, but he respects me and would've let me run things the way I've done for twenty years before my brother took the throne. Plus, the throne has been passed down from first born to first born since the kingdom was founded, and I guess you could say I'm a bit sentimental."

"Was Finlay in any way involved? Did he scheme with you?"

"Him? No, he ain't much of a schemer. Definitely takes after his mom in personality, the dote, but he would make a perfect king for my needs within the kingdom."

"Well," Giselle said, sitting up in her chair. "Sounds like we have all we need to bring this asshole to the queen and get him sentenced for regicide, matricide, and all the other terrible crimes he's committed around the City."

After sticking Brynmor back in his room, the party discussed the information they had gathered so far. Clearly, with his ties to Ivellios and his slave trade, they had at least enough to get him imprisoned for a few years. But without any proof to his scheme against the king and his past ties to the throne, it was still going to be tricky to pin this on him, especially if he denied it when they brought him to court.

"What if," Giselle started, looking at her companions with a gleam in her eyes that made Sybil a little nervous. "We broke into his office? He's sure to have documentation in there. Things he wouldn't even bother trying to get rid of because his office is nearly impossible to break into."

"And risk getting killed in a mob den?" Sybil asked with a humorless laugh. "Let's leave that as a last resort."

"Oh, please, it's not like we haven't been through worse," Giselle said with a wave of her hand. "But fine. Perhaps we could bring him to the queen and revisit that idea if she asks for proof beyond what we have to tell her."

"Yes, let's do that," Sybil said and then sighed. "Okay, well, we have some workings of a plan… should we start heading back to the City?"

Keijin found a horse on Ivellios' property and saddled it up so Brynmor could ride, tied up, alongside them, and once again, the adventurers headed to the City of the King to deliver the prisoner to the queen. Since they had a late start in the day, they had to make camp for the night a few hours from the City. To make sure he didn't try to run away, they tied Brynmor to a tree near the campfire. Sybil didn't like the idea of sleeping near him, so she decided to knock him unconscious with her magic, which would keep him out for most of the night.

The party sat around the campfire with the unconscious Brynmor next to them, and it was the first time they were all together without a plan to discuss, so an awkward silence fell between them. Giselle was poking the fire with a stick and, every now and then, would lift the stick up and wave it around to make shapes with the ember at the end. Sybil couldn't take the silence anymore, so she asked the first question which came to mind.

"So, Giselle, why did you join Gibbous Tower?"

Giselle's face was lit by the fire, making her look more red than purple, and she looked at Sybil with flames dancing in her eyes. She threw the stick into the fire and said, "At first, it was all about the money. Leon offered me a good deal of coin for the jobs he hired me for, so I started taking more and more jobs from him, leaving my old life behind in the City. Eventually, I found myself completely under his employ, and he only explained later that I would never have joined the tower if he just asked me outright, so he had to lure me in, in a way. He felt bad for the trickery, but he was right. I wouldn't have left my old life for the tower if I was just asked to do so, but I'm certainly glad I did."

"How did you come to live in the City?" Keijin asked, leaning back and supporting himself with his hands on the ground behind him.

Giselle pulled her legs into her chest, wrapping her arms around them.

"My mom brought me from the Homeland. I was about six, and the civil war was going on at the time, so a lot of people were fleeing," she explained, staring into the campfire. "Not many were traveling here because of how humans typically view our race as dirty or evil, so my mother thought there would be more space for us here and we could start anew. She was a very optimistic woman, my mother, always believing the best in people." She gave a sad laugh. "Obviously, I didn't take after her in that respect.

"Eventually, we made our way to the City after not being able to make a living anywhere else. Either places weren't hiring her or they would only pay her a fraction of what they would pay the other worker because 'she should be grateful for what she can get,' as they would always say. By the time we made it to the City, though, my mother's health was failing, and even though she was able to get a decent paying job, she couldn't work the number of hours needed to pay our bills."

Her voice grew quiet.

"After about a year of us living in the City, she became bedridden, and I had to do whatever I could to pay the bills, which is when I started working for Brynmor and working my way up in the City's underbelly. When she died, I just kept doing what I was doing, putting everything I had into my work, until Leon found me."

"We worked together once," Mordecai said with a soft laugh. "You were just a child back then, and I was wearing a disguise, so you wouldn't have remembered me. Honestly, it kind of pissed me off how skilled you were."

"Why didn't you tell me before?" Giselle asked with her eyebrows raised.

"Well, when we had finished our mission, that was the day Brynmor discovered that I was pretending to be someone else," Mordecai explained. "You definitely tried to kill me as I was escaping, and you managed to hit me with a throwing knife. When we met again at Leon's tower, I was still a little bitter about it, and I didn't know how to bring it up to begin with."

"You were that kid who fooled Brynmor," she said, the memory coming back to her. "That makes so much sense." She laughed, tilting her head back. "Well, if it makes you feel better, I was only trying to slow you down. I was too impressed by you to kill you."

The conversation started to die, but then Sybil looked over at Brynmor and asked, "What do you think's going to happen to the City when he's no longer in power? Is someone else just going to take his place?"

"Possibly," Keijin answered. "There's always been someone who has acted as a sort of leader to the Outer Ring of the City. Brynmor just manipulated the people's desperation toward crime and evil deeds, but if there was someone to take over his position who wanted the best for the people." His eyes flitted over to Giselle. "Then, perhaps, some dignity and good could be restored to the Outer Ring."

Giselle noticed the way Keijin was looking at her and asked, "What, me? I think you've taken too many blows to the head, sir knight."

"No, I agree with him," Sybil said with excitement. "You'd be the best person for the job. Who knows the City better than you? And you have a rapport with all of his people, his right-hand man looked like he would give his kidney to you, despite his best judgment, and you could maintain what draws people to that lifestyle while doing some good for the City."

"I don't know," she breathed, putting her fingertips to her lips as she thought about it.

"If you don't," Mordecai began. "Then, I'm going to have to. And nobody wants that."

"True," both Keijin and Sybil said at once.

Giselle laughed and said, "I... well, I guess I have something to think about, then."

Chapter Nineteen

When the City came into view the next day, Sybil suddenly grew nervous about returning to the palace. Honestly, it didn't look good for them. Shortly after the king was killed, they fled the palace and went into hiding. What if the queen thought they were bringing Brynmor to court to pin their crimes on him? There was no true evidence to prove their innocence or Brynmor's guilt. Still, if the queen was anything like her husband, she would handle this matter sensibly, listening to reason and not making any decisions based on snap judgment. And they had to trust she was, in fact, like her husband.

It was around midday when the party reached the Inner Ring. The guards at the gates did not seem pleased to see four travelers approaching them, especially with Brynmor tied and gagged on the horse behind them. One of the guards asked what their business was, and Keijin stepped up to explain to them they were bringing a highly important prisoner to the queen. At first, they were not convinced, but then Mordecai warned them that interfering in the crown's business would be punished severely. With that threat, they let the party through, but two of them mounted horses and escorted them to the palace.

As if he sensed their arrival, Malic was at the palace doors, glaring at the adventures as they rode up. They dismounted their horses, and Keijin helped Brynmor down.

Malic approached them and said, "Funny, I thought for sure I would never see the four of you again. But yet, here you are." His eyes landed on Brynmor. "And who's this?"

"The one responsible for the king's assassination," Sybil told him. "Brynmor of Easthaven."

"Very well," Malic said slowly, his brows furrowed. "I shall take you to the queen, then. She's holding court in the throne room."

Compared to how it was the first time Sybil walked through the palace only days ago, it felt like an entirely new place. The palace was bleak and practically deserted. They only saw a handful of people, mostly servants, who kept their heads and eyes down, not wanting to draw any attention to themselves. As though it had been made a requirement, everyone they passed was dressed head to toe in black.

Malic led the party to the massive double doors to the throne room, and they followed him inside. The dozen or so people in the room fell silent as the adventurers approached the queen, who was sitting on her late husband's throne. Her once vibrant blue eyes looked dull, and her face was pale. Even though it was clear she was trying to maintain her former appearance by the elegant gown she wore and the intricate styling of her hair, a silver crown resting on top of it, the grief and anger she felt over the past few days was apparent.

The queen stared down at the party from her raised, gilded throne as they stood in the middle of the room, surrounding Brynmor. The adventurers bowed, and the queen said, "The ones who were charged with protecting my husband have returned, despite their failure." Her voice was hoarse but powerful. "I was beginning to suspect the next time the four of you set foot in the palace would be in chains, but it appears you have brought another prisoner to me instead."

"Your majesty," Keijin said, giving another bow. "We bring you Brynmor of Easthaven, the one responsible for King Elias' death."

Scanning around the room, Sybil caught sight of Finlay who was standing near one of the statues next to two noblewomen. He was looking at them curiously but did not seem to be all that concerned with what was going on. Sybil stepped forward.

"The prisoner we bring before you, your majesty, has done more than just kill the king," she said, trying to push the nerves away as she spoke to the most powerful woman, the most powerful person, in the kingdom. "This man is, in fact, Prince Elijah, the eldest son of King Reginald."

Gasps came from several people in the room, and the queen looked annoyed at Sybil and said, "Prince Elijah has been dead for more than twenty years."

"Just shy of the time Brynmor of Easthaven has been in control of the mob, is it not?" she responded, raising her eyebrow. "Through my powers of divination, seeing into his memories, I have been able to learn that Prince Elijah murdered his wife and fled. His escape was through the very same tunnel he used to send his first wave of assassins, killing the king's double and nearly killing me, as well. He did this in order for his son to become king."

Finlay, who had turned several shades of red over the course of Sybil's explanation, took a step back toward the wall when she said this last part. The queen eyed her cowering nephew for a moment before returning her attention to Brynmor and asking, "How do I know what you are telling me is true? Can you show me these memories?"

Unsure, Sybil looked to Mordecai, who could only shrug, and said, "I've never done something like that, but it might be possible. I would need some time to prepare."

"Very well," she said and looked at Malic. "Take Brynmor to the dungeon and have your men escort these four to the study." Her eyes met Sybil's again. "You have an hour."

Malic waved over his guards and grabbed Brynmor by the arm, dragging him out of the throne room in the opposite direction the guards were leading them. The guards waited right outside the door while they entered the king's study. Once the door was shut, she turned to Mordecai.

"I don't think I can do this."

"Not that I don't trust your abilities, Sybil," Keijin said, moving across the room toward the desk. "But I've seen what happens to people when you use this specific spell on them, and to yourself from the exertion. Are we sure we want to put the queen of all people in that situation?"

"We could see if one of her men, someone she trusts, like Malic, would do it," Giselle suggested with a shrug.

"The queen sounded pretty damned sure she wanted it to be her," Mordecai said. "But we should definitely practice before trying anything with the queen. If you kill her, even if it's by accident, they'll sentence you to death for treason, so no pressure."

In order to practice this spell, Keijin would be the one whose memory Sybil would explore and Giselle would be the one she showed the memories to. Mordecai held her hand to amplify her magic, something she still didn't quite understand how he did, and she temporarily tied her consciousness to Giselle's. With much effort, she sent both of their subconsciouses into Keijin's mind, which nearly caused his knees to buckle out from under him. He tried to put up a fight for the sake of their practice, but he had no experience in combating another person's will, so she was able to slip in quite easily.

Sybil witnessed many events of the past couple of days from his perspective, seeing herself in most of them, a strange phenomenon. Then, Sybil saw a woman wearing fashionable leather armor with a bright green tunic underneath. She was wielding a short sword and round, wooden shield, painted green with an intricate design of knots in black. Keijin and this woman were fighting a swarm of giant spiders, hacking away at their abdomens, and the distinct gleam and glee in the woman's eye while facing such a terrifying foe reminded Sybil of Alina. This must have been one of their adventures together, and she now understood why Keijin was so enamored with her. Not only was she gorgeous, her blond hair dazzling as it swung around her shoulders, but she was fierce and courageous and a fantastic fighter. But all of those things were only able to last so long.

Pulling away from Keijin's memory and letting go of Giselle's consciousness, Sybil turned to them, still holding Mordecai's hand.

"She's cute," Giselle said with a grin, confirming the spell worked as Sybil had intended it to. "What's her name?"

"Can we please stay on task, Giselle?" Keijin asked with a frown.

Mordecai smirked and said, "What's wrong? Don't want to talk about your feelings for once?"

Keijin bristled and, ignoring Mordecai, asked Sybil, "Do you think you'll be able to perform the spell without hurting the queen?"

"I think so," Sybil said and looked over at Giselle. "Do you feel alright?"

"As well as I usually feel," she said with a shrug. "It was an unpleasant experience, but that's all."

"Your skills are certainly improving," Mordecai said with a nod, though she wasn't sure she would have been successful if it wasn't for his help.

Trusting in Mordecai's assessment, Sybil told them she was as ready as she was going to be, and they headed back into the throne room. This time, it was only the queen and the royal guards until Malic returned with Brynmor from the dungeon. Sybil's heart was racing as she stepped up to where the queen was waiting for her. Her nerves were firing rapidly, and it took her a few minutes to clear her mind, which grew more difficult as she could feel the queen growing more impatient by the second.

Taking a deep, steadying breath with her eyes closed and feeling Mordecai's hand firmly on her shoulder, Sybil connected her consciousness with the queen's. Brynmor let out a groan as she pushed into his mind, his will feeling even stronger than it had before as the desperation to survive fueled it. But after the encounter in the mansion and the uncomfortable nature of his traveling back to the City, he was exhausted and only able to put up an initial fight. After one final push, causing both Brynmor and the queen to quiver, Sybil dug around for the memories she had seen in Easthaven. Curious and feeling a little bold, she even searched for the last memories he had of his wife, seeing her face cringing in pain as his large hands squeezed firmly around her neck, confirming Mordecai's theory of what happened to Finlay's mother.

Once Sybil had shown the queen everything, she dropped the spell, and their minds were all their own again. Only Brynmor was showing any adverse effects from the spell. With his palms pressed into the floor, he was hunched over and breathing heavily.

"He is indeed the long-lost prince," the queen breathed, staring down at her brother-in-law. Then, her back went rigid and her eyes hardened. "Prince Elijah, or Brynmor of Easthaven as you are known to the City, I sentence you to death for the assassination of the king, the murder of your wife, and for all the crimes you have committed against the City and our kingdom. Your execution will take place tomorrow at dawn."

Brynmor's face turned pale, but he said nothing and made no gesture to show he had heard the queen's words. Malic stepped forward and took him by the arm, and just as he was being led away, he asked the queen, "May I see my son before I die?"

"If Finlay wishes to visit you in the dungeon, then I shall allow it," the queen replied. "Now, get this man out of my sight."

When Malic and Brynmor were gone, the queen returned to the throne. She looked like a broken woman, tired and grief-stricken. Sybil wondered what she would do once Finlay was crowned king, where she would go.

"Thank you all for ensuring the king's murderer was brought to justice. I will be sure to send a handsome donation to Gibbous Tower to repay your services and send you with a servant who will make sure you get the best accommodations at the Queen's Resort for as long as you wish to stay. If you will excuse me, though, I have an execution to prepare for and wish to do so in peace."

Everyone bowed as the grieving queen rose from the throne and exited through one of the side doors, her servants following after her. Malic was quick to start leading the party back through the palace, so he didn't have to deal with them any longer.

In her room at the Queen's Resort, Sybil stood by the window staring at Shuheyr's statue, thinking about the conversation she had with him in the temple. At the base of the statue, workers were starting to construct a stage where Brynmor was to be executed the next day, and noticing this, she closed the curtains. Mordecai, back in his natural appearance thanks to the wards she placed around the room, was sitting at a small table in the corner, reading from one of his tomes written in an ancient, dark language. Turning to him, Sybil watched Mordecai read for a few minutes. It hit her in that moment that she did, in fact, trust him, despite all the things she had seen him do and heard him say which told her she shouldn't. However, she was still finding it hard to trust Shuheyr, to give into the powers of her birthright. She still didn't understand why he created her, which led her to believe there was something he was planning, some way he was going to trick her. If he didn't create her to stop the darkness, what was his purpose for her?

Sybil had time to get that answer from him, and she didn't want to think about it right then. Instead, she crossed the room to Mordecai, and standing behind him, she wrapped her arms around his chest, staring down at the text she could not comprehend. He put his hand on her forearm, rubbing her skin with his thumb as he continued to read. But when she kissed him on the neck, she pulled his attention away from the tome. He turned around in his seat and kissed her on the lips, his index finger and thumb lightly pinching her chin.

Mordecai rose from the chair and pulled Sybil into his arms, his hands running up her back as he continued to kiss her. Before she knew it, he had her on the bed and their bare bodies were pressed together. As she felt the strength of his shoulders and back with her roaming hands, she wrapped her legs around his, wishing their love could always be this intimate and simple. They both let out groans of satisfaction before Mordecai moved to lay next to her, both of them panting and smiling. Sybil looked over at him, admiring his natural features.

Unlike his silver-eyed disguise, everything about the true Mordecai looked warm: his brown hair and eyes, his lightly tan skin, and the smoothness of his features. Sybil ran her fingers down his broad chest, causing goosebumps to rise on his skin. He closed his eyes and let out a satisfied sigh. She wished they could just run away and go somewhere where Haborym and Shuheyr couldn't find them. But they would have had to cross planes of existence to do something like that, which even with their powers combined, they would never be skilled enough to do. Instead, Sybil could only enjoy the time they had together. Laying her head on his shoulder, entangled in each other's limbs, she fell asleep.

In her dream, a man with fiery red hair and a pale complexion stood near a table with instruments of torture similar to the ones Ivellios had on his basement wall. His frame was tall but slender, and even though he wore rough spun commoner's clothes, he looked strikingly unique. The more time Sybil spent in this room with the man, seeing it as one would a story in their minds rather than a memory, the more she could see of it. They were inside a flour mill, the noise of the giant stone grinder filled the air as it spun, crushing the bits of wheat beneath it. On the other side of the room, mostly hidden from where she stood by the grinder, was a young woman with tangled blonde hair tied up against the wall, her thin arms strung up by the rafter above her.

The man picked up a saw, its thick blade gleaming in the moonlight and candlelight illuminating the room, and moved over to the woman. As he approached her, her chest began to rise and fall rapidly and her eyes widened, staring at the saw. When he was only a couple feet from her, Sybil heard her soft cries as she begged, "Please, Tomas, don't do this. You're a good man; I know you are. Please, please, don't hurt me."

"You know, it's funny," Tomas said, his voice calm as if he were commenting on the weather. "Whenever I am about to hurt someone, they always tell me I'm a good man." He brought the saw to the woman's chest, pressing the serrated blade gently against her skin. "The thing is, I'm not a good man. I'm a very, very bad man. I want to see you hurt, so that's just what I'm going to do."

Despite the horrible things Sybil saw, she couldn't make herself wake up from this dream. She had to unwillingly watched this man tear into the woman's flesh, her screams filling the room as blood trickled down her body, Sybil felt the memory of the hag tearing into her own flesh and the warmth of her blood as it drenched her clothes. She knew what this woman was feeling, both the pain and the fear, except there were no powers to save her.

The woman's head finally fell forward, and her entire body went limp. She was dead, and the man breathed in a deep, satisfied breath. Sybil didn't know who he was, save for his name, but she wanted to kill him, to do what he just did to that innocent woman right back to him. Just as she thought this dream had nothing else to show her, a voice filled up the room, making the wheat grinder fall silent. It was the same voice she had heard before when Haborym was haunting her. Though the voice seemed to have startled him at first, the man seemed to understand what it was saying and smiled a wicked smile.

"The Shadowed One, I have waited a long time to speak with you," Tomas said, giving a bow.

The voice spoke again, hissing in his ear.

"Yes, of course," he replied, staring at the wall in front of him. The voice whispered back, and the man responded, "If you lend me your power, I shall serve you to the end of my days."

The moonlight faded from the windows, and the flames of the candles dimmed to only tiny specks. A black shadow appeared in front of him, just like the one Sybil had seen in the tower and throne room, and it dissipated into smoke. The thick, black smoke surrounded the man, and he held out his arms to his sides as he felt the power of Haborym seeping into him. His eyes turned black as the last of the smoke seeped into his tear ducts. The man turned, looking directly at Sybil with his horrible eyes, and just as their eyes met, she woke up from the dream.

Mordecai looked up at Sybil from where he was reading at the table as she sat up suddenly in bed. Her entire body had a thin layer of sweat from the dream, and her teeth and jaw hurt from clenching through the woman's pain. Pulling her legs to her chest and wrapping her arms around them, she took a deep, steadying breath and decided she needed to tell Mordecai about these dreams.

"I've been seeing things," she told him, in a tired voice. "I don't know if it's Haborym haunting me, my divination magic growing stronger, or a combination of both. But the more things I see, the more this horrible feeling in my gut grows."

After explaining to Mordecai what she had seen so far, both in her waking and sleeping states, he said, "I think this man you saw is the one we're going to face. One of Haborym's followers, though I don't know him by name or appearance, has fully given into his powers, and from what it sounds like, it's this Tomas you saw in your dream."

"So, if he has fully committed to Haborym, that means facing him would practically be like facing Haborym," Sybil said, thinking back to how much power Mordecai was able to wield by only a temporary connection.

"There would be a few limitations for his mortal form, but yes," Mordecai replied, his face turning grave. "It will almost be like we were fighting Haborym."

The weight of this set in, and she heaved a sigh. They weren't ready for something like this, but they were running out of time to get ready. Soon, the Winter Solstice would be upon them, and they still had no idea where this servant of Haborym would appear.

The morning of the execution, a small crowd gathered outside the palace, facing a large stage which had been constructed next to Shuheyr's statue. Sybil and Mordecai met Giselle and Keijin outside the Queen's Resort to watch Brynmor's fate unfold. Malic led Brynmor up onto the stage and had him kneel, his arms and legs free of restraints, and the queen stepped up after them.

"Prince Elijah, son of King Reginald and brother of King Elias, has been found guilty of the crimes of regicide, matricide, treason, and further violations against the crown and the City," the queen announced to the people below her. The crowd was deathly silent. "The punishment for these crimes is death and the stripping of legacy across the kingdom. No one shall breathe the name of the man who kneels before me again and all mention of him in historical archives will be removed."

Brynmor looked up at the queen in horror. For a man like him to have his legacy removed was far worse than death. The queen met his gaze, not even a twinge of pity in her eyes.

"By the power of the crown and with the blessing of Shuheyr, I sentence you to death."

Malic lifted up his greatsword, the morning sun gleaming off the metal for an instant, and dropped it over Brynmor's neck. After a long moment, his head fell into a basket below and his body slunk limply to the stage.

Sybil turned away, looking to the others who stood with her. Mordecai was unfazed, while Giselle had a satisfied smirk on her face. Keijin, however, seemed troubled, as if he had been hoping for Brynmor's execution to bring him peace about the king's death. But while Brynmor was dead and Finlay was due to inherit the throne in less than a month, the kingdom's fate was still uncertain.

Just as the crowd was beginning to disperse, a mail carrier approached Keijin and handed him an envelope from Leon. This mail carrier kept his face hidden and vanished as soon as he stepped into the crowd of people, as if he were an apparition. Keijin opened the letter and held it out so he could read it with his companions.

Dear adventurers,

Despite your best efforts, the loss of the king's life seems to have been fated. You did well apprehending those responsible and providing a more promising future to the City than if you had otherwise not been involved. It is time three of you return to Gibbous Tower as there is still much to prepare for. Giselle, however, must stay in the City as she has a great deal of business to attend to within the Outer Ring.

—Leon

Sybil looked over at Giselle, whose face was contorted with the conflicting feelings of excitement and disappointment. When she noticed Sybil looking at her, Giselle smiled and shrugged before saying, "Tanele will just have to visit me here."

"I know she'll understand," Sybil said, taking Giselle's hand and giving it a squeeze.

"Yes, I'm sure she will," Giselle replied but the sound of her voice said otherwise. Clearing her throat and raising her chin, Giselle turned to Keijin and Mordecai. "Well, it seems like you all have one more errand to do, so you should be on your way. I should probably head to the Outer Ring. I'm sure as soon as Brynmor's head took a tumble, his organization did the same, the underbosses will probably all be at each other's throats, so I should make sure they don't all kill each other. I might need a couple of them."

Just as she was about to turn to leave, Sybil pulled her into a hug. They held each other for a moment, before Sybil pulled away and said, "Be careful."

"Always am," Giselle said with a wink. "If ever you need any help in the City, you know where to find me."

After a quick clasp on the shoulder by Keijin and an awkward nod from Mordecai, Giselle made her way out of the Inner Ring. The others watched her leave, and Sybil could feel a pulsing pang of sadness in her chest, knowing that it may be some time before she saw her friend again.

"Well, I suppose there's nothing left for us to do here," Keijin said once Giselle was out of sight. "We best be on our way back to the tower."

The adventurers left the library without a word, mounted up their horses, and set off toward Gibbous Tower. Nearly an hour of riding went by in silence, and Sybil and Mordecai were following Keijin, who kept pace several horses ahead of them. Eventually, Sybil turned to Mordecai and said, "we only have a little over a week before the Winter Solstice, and we still don't know where Haborym plans to strike."

"I'm aware," Mordecai grumbled. "He's wanting to catch us off guard, but he'll have to attack somewhere other than the tower. Leon and his forces are way too powerful for one of his servants, even one who's fully committed. Somehow, he'll find a way to get us away from the tower."

"And if we try to stay away, if we try to ride out the Winter Solstice, he'll find something we care enough about to draw us out," she said, understanding more and more about how Haborym's mind works.

"All we can do now is prepare as best we can," Mordecai responded, not sounding particularly optimistic about it. "This person Haborym will be controlling is still mortal, despite whatever ancient magic he might wield, so between the two of us, we have a chance."

Chapter Twenty

The sun had already set behind the trees with only a little lingering daylight, and just as the adventurers were nearing Gibbous Tower, a spear flew through the air between their heads, and stabbed into a tree near Keijin. This sudden attack caused the Captain to rear as Keijin drew his sword, and Sybil and Mordecai turned in the direction of where the spear came from. A gang of hobgoblins came out from the woods, and they groaned to see it was the same ones from before. Even though he was still wearing his black cloak, the hobgoblins must not have recognized Mordecai as the one who terrified them so badly last time.

"Oi," the leader of the hobgoblins yelled. "How about ya give us them horses and we won't gut ya?"

Including the boss, there were five of them. The party could have easily slaughtered them if they engaged, but while they were brutish creatures, they weren't evil or hateful. And even to common travelers, they didn't pose much danger because they got what they wanted through threats and other intimidation tactics. Annoyed, and not feeling in the mood to kill a bunch of idiots, Sybil slid off her saddle and started walking toward the leader. All the hobgoblins were confused by this, and their eyes went wide with shock as she reached up her hand and caused their boss to fall asleep, crumpling to the ground with a snore.

"Gather him up and be on your way," she told them, igniting her fingers with flames. "Or I shall burn your fur down to the point it doesn't grow back."

Once again, the hobgoblins fled in terror, this time carrying their boss, each of them holding a limb. Sybil hoped this would be the last time they attempted to ambush people on the road, but they were clearly not the smartest bunch. When she returned to her horse, Keijin sheathed his sword, pleased not to have used it.

They continued on their way and soon Gibbous Tower came into view. It had been four years since Sybil had seen the tower from this angle, back when she first rode up with Keijin at sixteen. Built with a combination of expert architecting and powerful magic, the tower stood thirteen stories tall, rows of windows and edges of stone showing each level. It was made, inside and out, with the same dark gray stone, and the wood of the rafters jutted out before each new story. The only building Sybil had seen that could compare to the tower was the palace, but even it was not as much of a marvel with how tall the tower stood.

The stable hands ran out to greet the party as they reached the front steps of the tower. After handing off the reins and removing their bags from the saddle, the weary adventurers headed inside. Mordecai's disguise seemed to melt away as he stepped through the main doors to the tower; it was safe to be himself here. They headed up the many flights of stairs to reach Leon's office on the seventh level. With everyone in the tower finishing up their work before dinner, they didn't see anyone else until they found Tanele speaking to Leon, who was sitting leisurely at his desk. Tanele turned to the others entering her peripheral, and Sybil could see her eyes were red, on the verge of tears, and her pale face was hard. She didn't look around the room at any of them. Leon must have just told her Giselle stayed in the City instead of returning to the tower with the rest of the party.

Tanele gave a nod to Leon before turning on her heel and leaving the office. Leon magically shut the door and asked the party to share what happened since they last left the tower. They just stuck to the facts, sharing details about events at the palace and what happened at Ivellios' estate, but none of them mentioned Sybil's conversations with Shuheyr or the relationship developments between her and Mordecai, or even Keijin for that matter. It wasn't that they were trying to keep things from him, or at least Sybil wasn't, but all of the other stuff just felt strange to say out loud. She knew she would sit down with Leon at some point and would explain everything to him then, anyway.

After their debrief, he dismissed the party just as the dinner bell chimed throughout the tower and happily informed them that they were having smoked chicken that night. Neither Mordecai nor Sybil was feeling all that hungry, so they decided to head to the library to figure out their next steps. Sitting in their usual spot with a notebook between them, they wrote out what they knew, such as Haborym planning to attack on the Winter Solstice, his servant, Tomas, who Sybil had dreamed about, and the understanding that Haborym would find a way to draw them out.

"Our greatest weapon is your light," Mordecai said, looking up at Sybil from the list. "You need to practice using it as much as you can while we're here. Strengthening some of your other spells would help, as well, in case he decides to throw something else at us, like the necromancers did with the Blackridge victims."

"And what do you plan to do?" she asked when she recognized the scheming look on his face.

He thought for a moment, his illusory-silver eyes scanning her face, before he said, "There's something I've been keeping from you. Those texts I've been studying over, the ones you've asked me about before, hold the secrets to Haborym's powers."

Sybil frowned and asked, "What does that even mean?"

"It means," he said with a sigh. "That Haborym learned the power he wields. A few years ago, I was able to catch a glimpse of Haborym's past life, his mortal life, and learned about the books which taught him to wield his power. They are texts outdating even the elves, held together for so long through magical means. I found them in the Northern Lands, across the sea."

"If you're studying them the same way he did, aren't you worried you'll end up like Haborym?"

"Haborym was an idiot," Mordecai said with a frown. "He thought he could take in all the power of darkness this universe had to offer without there being any consequences. Furious with his hubris, eldritch horrors sought him out and changed him into one of them, but I won't let my powers grow that strong."

Sybil stared at him, watching his face for a moment, and asked, "What are you not telling me about this? And, please, don't use the excuse of you trying to protect me again."

Looking away, Mordecai let out another sigh.

"You'll think my motives for wanting to destroy Haborym are purely selfish when I tell you this, but I can assure you that my desires have changed in this matter, specifically because of you." His eyes met Sybil's again before he continued, and she could see the sincerity in them. "Despite all I've studied and all I've done to wield the dark magic on my own, I cannot fully control it until Haborym is dead. He has hoarded too much of it, so much so that he practically rules it. Once he's dead, though, I'll be able to wield it to my fullest potential without being overcome by it due to greed."

"I don't know if this is the best idea," she told him, feeling weighed down by his plan.

"There's more to consider, though," he said, sounding frustrated. "If I don't take the bulk of Haborym's power, then it'd be free to be taken by another. It's likely it would go to one of his servants, someone who, in time, would grow to be the same monstrosity Haborym is now. We might not see the day, but it could still result in this world being destroyed by the darkness."

"Okay," Sybil breathed. "If you believe this is the best option, that you'll be able to keep yourself from falling down the same path as Haborym, I'll support you in this."

He gave a nod but said nothing, and all at once, the exhaustion of the day hit Sybil. Excusing herself, she headed up to her room, knowing from the determination in his eyes she would not see him until sometime the following day. Being alone again for the first time in what felt like a year, she lay down on her bed and stared at the ceiling. She didn't get much sleep that night, but, not in the mood for any more nightmares, she was fine with not risking it.

Shortly after breakfast the next day, Sybil headed to Rani's workshop. When she arrived, though, Rani was standing in the center of the room arguing with Luvodert, the enchanter and weaponsmith who crafted Sybil's wand and staff. Neither of them noticed her, so she just sat in her usual spot on the stool in the corner to watch.

"That's your solution to everything," Luv yelled, throwing his hands up into the air. "Just use a potion. I've lost a limb: potion. I want to be taller: potion. I want super speed: potion. Where's the craft? Where's the skill?"

"The skill comes from me ya daft git," Rani shouted back. "When I give someone a potion, I don't have to also provide them with a manual for how it works or require them to spend years of training before they can actually use it. They can just take the potion and carry on with their business."

"Easy solutions for easy problems," Luv responded with a wave. "Sure, you're talented, but you're just giving these people a reason to not try harder. Your potions are excuses."

"Excuses? Why ya little-"

Coughing, Sybil made her presence known before the argument could get any further out of hand. When Luv turned and saw her, his cheeks flushed red for a moment, and Rani huffed.

"Whatever," Luv said, his chin lowering. "I see it's useless to argue, and I have better things to do."

Luv then marched out of the room, slamming the door behind him. For a moment, Rani stared at the ceiling before looking over at Sybil, giving a laugh, and saying, "I think the fool might be in love with me."

"Not sure who to pity more, you or him," Sybil said with a chuckle.

"Oh, him for sure," Rani replied with a smirk. "It's good to see ya back."

Even though Rani had heard some of the stories Keijin told during dinner the night before, Sybil shared with her all the events that had transpired since she and her companions had left for the City of the King. When Sybil reached the part about what happened with Mordecai in Ivellios' estate, though, Rani's face turned grave, and when she finished her tale, Rani asked, "And ya weren't scared of him? Mordecai, I mean. The powers he wields and the things he can do to a person... it sounds terrifying."

"No, I'm not scared of him, though I certainly have been in the past," Sybil answered, looking down at the floor, her gaze soft as she thought about him. "I don't know why or how, but I love him. And I am ready to face all the dangers of the world by his side."

"Never thought I'd see the day," Rani muttered with a shake of her head. "But I suppose, if ya like him, he can't be all bad."

"There's certainly worse people out there," Sybil replied before sighing and standing to leave. "Mordecai and I are going to be fighting someone who might just as well be the epitome of evil, so I'm going to either be practicing my spells on the training floor or studying in the library, if you want to find me."

"Ya think ya'll need some potions?" Rani asked with a gleam in her eyes.

Sybil shrugged, a small smile tugging at her lips, and said, "It couldn't hurt."

After several hours of practicing spells, Sybil was back in her usual spot with Mordecai, who had been there all night and most of the morning. There were several books sprawled out in front of them, and the librarian found them and asked if they needed help with anything. Sybil told her they had everything they needed for now and thanked her. As the librarian carried on with her work in the library, Sybil watched her for a little, trying to get a sense of what sort of person she was.

Sybil must have been staring at her for a while, watching as she organized books and carried herself with confidence through the library, because Mordecai nudged her and gestured to the book in front of them. They were running out of time, she needed to keep studying. Blinking a few times, she turned her attention back to the book on evocation magic she had been reading. It struck her then why she had been staring at the librarian for so long. Sybil was jealous of her. Her life seemed so pleasant and easy. With all the terrible things Sybil and her companions had been through and the darkness looming over her and Mordecai, she wanted to have the librarian's life.

To take a break from all the practicing and studying, Mordecai and Sybil went for a walk around the tower. Soon after they were alone, Sybil asked him, "What do you think your life will be like after we defeat Haborym once and for all?"

Mordecai's eyebrows furrowed at this question, and he looked like she had asked him something silly, like if he had to choose, what animal would he be? After thinking for a moment, he said, "I have no idea. Unfortunately, looking to the future is a luxury I don't feel like I can afford right now." When their eyes met, he asked, "Why do you look like I've disappointed you?"

"You haven't disappointed me," she replied. "I just, I don't know. Something got into my head about living a normal life, and I can't stop thinking about it."

Mordecai stopped walking and turned to her.

"You know a normal life is not in the cards for people like us," he said. "We're not normal, and even when all of our threats have been eliminated, we'll never be normal. What, you want to go live on a farm somewhere when you can literally harness the powers of the sun? And what about me? If I am able to harness all of Haborym's powers… well, quite frankly, I have no idea what life will look like for me after that. We are both dealing with powers on the same level of the gods. Our future is something we can't even comprehend yet."

Sybil turned away as tears started filling her eyes, still not comfortable with letting him see her cry. With a sigh, he pulled her into his arms, giving her a start, and held her there for a minute as a few tears rolled down her cheek. She put her face to his chest and said, "I'm sorry. I just… hate not having a choice in all this."

"You do have choices, though," he said, pushing her away to look her in the eyes. "You chose to fight alongside me, to be with me." His cool hand wiped away another fallen tear. "You chose to grow your powers as both a wizard and a Soul Child and to work with Shuheyr. Even though you didn't choose your powers or your connection with a god or even your love for me, you've been able to decide your fate along the way and will continue to do so."

Sybil was quiet for a moment as his words sunk in and said, "I've never thought about it that way."

"Well, you typically only think about things one way," he said with a teasing grin. "That's why I'm better than you at most things."

"You're an ass," she replied with a laugh.

"Yes, but somehow you love me anyway," he said and his grin turned into a genuine, loving smile.

As Sybil was heading to dinner one night, Tanele was walking down the corridor with a packed bag slung around her shoulders. She ran to catch up with Tanele and asked where she was going. She turned to Sybil, looked down, and said, "To the City. I need to find Giselle."

"Don't be mad at her that she stayed there," Sybil said. "She's trying to do what's best for the people."

"Mad? I'm not mad," Tanele said, shaking her head which caused her black hair to fall like ink on a page around her white face. "I'm worried about her. I want to make sure she's okay. Even though I hate the idea of living in the City, I'll live there to be with her."

Sybil smiled and placed a hand on Tanele's forearm.

"You should ask her about her past," she suggested. "She's afraid, so she needs you to tell her it's okay and listen to everything she has to say."

Tanele frowned at Sybil's words and thought for a moment before saying, "Does she think I'll judge her for her past, that I would leave her?"

"Something like that," she replied with a nod. "She loves you, though, and she wants to share those things with you, but something just keeps getting in her way. Some sort of fear she has."

"Thank you for telling me this," Tanele breathed. "I love her, too, so much that being apart from her has been unbearable. I don't want her thinking that I would ever judge or leave her because of some part of herself. She's crazy and dangerous and loves things that don't make sense to me, but I love every part of her, altogether."

Tanele pulled Sybil in for a hug, squeezing her so tightly she couldn't breathe for a moment, and thanked her. Then, she hoisted her bag back up on her shoulder and headed out of the tower. As Sybil watched her leave, she hoped for the best between Tanele and Giselle. Everyone deserves love, and sometimes you have to work at it harder than others.

After she was out of sight, Sybil headed to the dining hall, sitting between Mordecai and Keijin. Nearly halfway into dinner, Rani came up to the table carrying a bag nearly the same size as her and set it up in front of Sybil. The three of them watched Rani, either chewing or with food still on their forks, as she unpacked vial after vial of various potions, drawing the attention of the entire room.

"Of course, ya have yer standard healing potion," she announced, waving a hand over a stack of vials all colored the same shimmering red. "Then, ya have yer potions that make ya resistant to various elements. Fire, ice, acid, ya name it really. And this guy." She held up a vial of what looked like liquified silver. "This will cure any ailments, be it venom, a curse, or poison. And speaking of poison, I can get ya plenty of poison if ya want. I just didn't think it would be best to bring in here."

"I think we'll be able to make do without poison, Rani, thanks," Sybil said, setting her fork down on her plate.

Rani nodded and said, "Well, if ya have any other specific needs, I can make potions that can do an assortment of fun things. Just let me know. I'll leave this in yer room."

After gathering up all her potions again, the glass clinking together, she slid the bag over her shoulder and headed out of the dining hall, grabbing a couple of rolls and a slice of ham as she did.

"She's very passionate about her craft," Sybil said with a shrug to Mordecai and Keijin who were both looking at her.

After dinner, Mordecai came up to Sybil's room with her, knowing that she hadn't been sleeping well on her own lately. With each passing day bringing them closer to the Winter Solstice, it wasn't surprising. And now, there were only two days left. Laying together in bed, he held her in his arms, running his fingers through her hair, and as if he were the cure to all her ailments, she found herself easily drifting off to sleep.

Sybil was back in Morningbreak. It was midday and everyone was making themselves busy, readying the village for the Winter Festival by putting up decorations and painting the wooden statue of Shuheyr that stood in the center of the village. The day of the Winter Solstice was used to celebrate all the light Shuheyr had provided the people of Irminshu through the other seasons and to prepare for the months after, during which they would stay inside for most of the day in silent prayers. The sun shone brightly over the village, and Sybil found herself standing in the very center of it. All the cottages, lined in a circle, faced into the center of the village, which was where they held all their festivities and rituals, and the Main House stood right in front of her. The Main House was a large building, several times the size of an average cottage, where the elders of the village lived and some of the more private ceremonies and rituals took place. Sybil's birth, for instance.

The people she was able to recognize looked several years older than she remembered them, which told her she was seeing it in the present day, on the day of the Winter Festival. She didn't understand why she was seeing her old village, usually something happened in her visions of the future that was significant. But then the sky started turning dark, causing her stomach to drop.

Everyone in the village stopped what they were doing to stare up at the sky as it turned to night, the sun just a faint glimmer through the darkness. Then, the Main House exploded, sending shards of wood and pieces of rock up into the air, falling fatally on some of the villagers below. A man stepped into the center of the village, only a few yards away from Sybil. He was wearing black from head to toe and had fiery red hair. It was the man from previous dreams: Tomas. There were dozens of black veins running up his neck to his face, and his eyes were pitch black, filled with evil and hate. His hands, raised up to wield his magic, looked like the skin had been burnt to soot. Three villagers near Sybil tried to run away, but he grabbed them with the same black tendrils she had seen Mordecai wield and sucked the life out of them, dropping their desiccated corpses to the ground. Then, his black eyes landed on her and dark magic started drifting toward her.

Sybil was screaming, and Mordecai was holding her in his arms, trying to console her. As soon as the room was back in her vision, she quieted and calmed, shaking and feeling embarrassed for her sudden outburst. Once she could manage the words, she said, "Haborym's going to destroy my village. That's where the servant's going to be on the Winter Solstice." Then, she turned to Mordecai with determination in her eyes. "We have to stop him."

His eyes stared back at her, hard and sure, and he said, "We will."

Chapter Twenty-One

The sun had barely started to peek over the trees when Mordecai and Sybil made their way to Leon's office. As if he had been expecting them, Leon was sitting upright at his desk, his frail hands folded on top of it, and his golden eyes shimmered in the early morning light

"And what is it that you need my help with?" he asked them before they could say anything.

As if he didn't know, as if he hadn't known these things for a while now. Sybil stepped forward, trying her best to hide her irritation, and said, "We need your help getting back to my old village. There's not enough time for us to get there on horseback."

"I can get you across the Cormyr River," he said. "But I have never been to your village and, due to the nature of my magic, it is waning as the solstice approaches."

"The nature of your magic?" Sybil asked, unable to help herself. "I thought the thinning of the vail on the solstice caused magic wielders to grow stronger."

"For most it does," Leon replied with a single nod. "But for those in my order, it grows weaker. There is much you both have to learn about the magic of this world and its history, but there is no time for that now."

Leon had them gather their things and meet him outside the tower with their horses. Sybil had thought about finding Keijin to see if he would help him, but she decided this wasn't his fight and didn't want him getting caught in the middle of it. Standing near the front steps of the tower, he raised up a thin, wrinkled hand and a blue portal appeared at the start of the road.

"Trust in your power, both of you, and you will make it back here in one piece. After which I will tell you all you wish to know."

Sybil nodded, hating the vagueness of his prophecies, and turned to look at Mordecai who was staring hard at the portal. She thanked Leon for his assistance and offered her hand to Mordecai. Together, they stepped through the portal with their horses following behind them, and their feet moved from gravel and onto grass as they found themselves in the middle of an empty field, the Cormyr River flowing just a few yards behind them.

"No turning back now," Mordecai mumbled. "How far is Morningbreak from here?"

"If memory serves," Sybil said, glancing in the direction they would be riding. "A little less than a day's ride. We'll need to make camp or…" She realized there was somewhere on the way to spend the night: Roland's old cottage. "Or, if it's still standing, there's a place I know we could stay."

"Okay," he said, his mind barely there with her and surely fixated on the fight ahead. "We should start making our way there, then."

Sybil nodded, his behavior making her feel uneasy, but she didn't say anything about it. Instead, they mounted their horses and headed onto the road toward Morningbreak. While they were riding, she asked Mordecai if he had ever met the man she had seen in her dreams, but he hadn't. In fact, there had only been one of Haborym's other servants he had been in contact with, but it was long ago, when he was still a child.

"He sought me out to help me learn how to control my powers. But he never told me his name as there is power in a name," Mordecai went on to explain. "He trained me for nearly a month before disappearing in the middle of the night. I doubt Haborym wants any of us getting close to one another because together we might be able to defeat him."

"Do you think we would be able to recruit some of them?" she asked as the idea came to her. "Maybe some of them are like you."

"Depends on how saturated they are in his magic," he replied. "From how you described the one in your dream, for instance, it sounds like he has fully submitted to the whims of Haborym, letting go of his humanity completely."

"And there's no turning back from that?"

"No, there isn't," he said, saying so much in so few words. "Haborym is a cancer. Once there's enough of him in you, the part of you that's left fades to nothing."

Roland's cottage was smaller than Sybil remembered it being, and it was surprising to see light shining out through the cracks in the window curtains as they rode up. What was even more strange was the raven that sat on the very middle of the roof, seeming to be staring right at her. It cawed and flapped its wings, its feathers gleaming in the moonlight, before taking flight and disappearing into the trees.

At first, she thought about just moving down the road and making camp for the night, but something drew her to the cottage. She slid off Dusk and dropped her reins over the branches of a nearby tree before heading straight to the door. Mordecai watched Sybil from his horse, his eyebrow raised as she approached this clearly occupied home.

Reaching up with a shaky fist, she knocked on the door. There was motion in the cottage, and the curtains shifted, but Sybil didn't look over soon enough to see the person peering out. Then, the door flung open, and a woman stood there, her icy blue eyes wide as she stared at her.

"Sybil?" she gasped, bringing her hands to her mouth.

It was like staring in a mirror twenty years into the future as this woman had all her same feature, the black hair, freckles, and fair skin all with the hint of aging. Sybil was looking upon the face of the woman who gave birth to her, the person she acknowledged as her mother but who she had never loved like one. Sybil didn't know what to say, and it took her a moment before she realized her jaw had dropped and closed it quickly.

Finally, Sybil said, "What are you doing here?"

"Please, won't you come in?" her mother asked and then peered around the doorframe. "You and your friend?"

Glancing over at Mordecai, Sybil gave him a nod. He shrugged before getting off his horse and meeting her at the door. Her mother moved into the cottage, sitting in a chair by the fireplace where a small fire was blazing. There was a small couch across from her where Sybil and Mordecai sat together. She was staring at Sybil, her eyes scanning her face, taking in every detail.

"Why are you living in Roland's cabin?" Sybil asked again, shifting uncomfortably in her seat.

"Roland," her mother breathed, staring up at the ceiling. "Yes, that was his name. I couldn't for the life of me remember." Her eyes met Sybil's again. "I came to live here shortly after you left. The elders told me not to go searching for you, that I would be banished if I went against their wishes, but I just couldn't sit around while you might have been hurt or lost. After nearly a year of searching to no avail, I tried to return to the village, but the elders were true to their word. Hoping that you would one day return, I came to live here, so I wouldn't be too far away."

"Why did you come after me?" Sybil asked, frowning.

"Because you're my daughter," she replied as if the question surprised her. "Even though the elders tried to keep you away from me, to raise you as theirs and not mine, I still loved you."

This knowledge hit Sybil like a bag of bricks. There was a time Sybil yearned for the love of her mother, but as the years passed, they became nothing but acquaintances connected by blood.

"Even though it was a great honor to serve Shuheyr and give birth to his child, it broke my heart everyday to have to watch you grow up from afar. When you ran away, I knew that not showing my love to you had been part of the problem, so I set out to find you and bring you home. I had this idea in my head that I would be able to convince the elders that you needed to be with me, with your mother, to live happily in this village. I just hate that it took you running away for me to realize this."

Mordecai, who always seemed to have a comment for every situation, was dead silent, and all Sybil could do was just stare down at the floor. The fire next to them popped and crackled, and her mother just stared at her, waiting for her to say something. Eventually, she stood up and moved across the room to grab an old journal off a table.

When she returned to her chair, she handed it to Sybil and said, "I started this journal shortly after you were born. It was my way of being close to you, even though I was forbidden to interact with you. You can have it if you want."

Sybil took the journal from her and held it in her lap before asking, "Why did they keep us apart?"

"They believed you would grow stronger without a mother, that you would rely on Shuheyr's light to guide and comfort you," she replied, anger clear in her voice. "But none of them understood the power of a mother's love. Even if I had to watch you from a distance, my love for you only grew stronger with every passing day. When you ran away, I just couldn't stand it anymore and realized just how wrong the elders were for keeping us apart.

But after months of searching, and nearly getting myself killed in the process, I returned here to wait for you."

"I'm sorry I didn't understand all of this," Sybil told her and decided that she was due an explanation. "When I left here, I was heading to Gibbous Tower, a place where I've lived for the past four years. The Enlightened rules the tower, and I left to become his student. After understanding the scope of my powers and dedication to the study of magic, he made me his apprentice. I never intended on returning to Morningbreak."

"How did you learn of this wizard? How did you come to study magic?" she asked, her face contorted in confusion as she tried to piece it all together in her head.

"I learned it from Roland," Sybil said, glancing around the cottage, seeing all the interesting books and trinkets she used to always gaze at when she was here. "I had attempted to run away once before, when I was far younger, about seven or eight, and he found me crying in the woods. To soothe me, he created colorful lights which danced around his fingers, and instantly I became drawn to magic." She showed her mother the spell, just as she had done for Gingy, the little girl in Spindlewood. "Every week, while the elders were in their daylong meeting, I would come here, knowing people would assume I was with the elders, and he would train me in all sorts of magic. Eventually, I surpassed his ability to teach me, so I had him tell me of another wizard who would allow me to be even more powerful."

Sybil stopped her story there. Mordecai had heard the rest, about how her mentor didn't want to give her the information she sought about Leon and his tower and how she took it from his mind, unknowingly killing him in the process. It would be exactly four years ago on the solstice. Even though they didn't have much of a relationship, Sybil feared the look of shame appearing on her mother's face.

"If you found what you were looking for at this tower, why return here?" her mother asked.

Sybil stared down at her hands which were folded in her lap and sighed.

"My connection to Shuheyr has put a bit of a target on my back, and I've recently made a powerful enemy, a being who's the embodiment of darkness," she explained, causing her mother's face to turn grave. "One of his servants seeks to destroy Morningbreak to get to me, and we're here to stop him."

"Destroy it?" she asked with a gasp. "One person to destroy an entire village? Surely, there can't be a servant of darkness so powerful."

"I assure you, there can," Mordecai spoke up, his gritty voice filling the air.

Sybil's mother, who's gaze up to this point had been locked onto her daughter, stared at Mordecai for a moment before saying, "And you would know because you're one of those servants... I can see the darkness in your eyes." Then, she turned to Sybil. "How did the Daughter of Light come to side with a servant of darkness?"

"Fate?" Sybil said, looking over at Mordecai. "We were brought together at Gibbous Tower, and now our destinies are intertwined."

Her mother gave her a knowing look and said, "In more ways than just combating the forces of darkness it seems."

"Yes, well..." Sybil trailed off, not sure how her mother was so insightful about her relationship with Mordecai, and decided to change the subject. "Would we be able to spend the night here and set out for Morningbreak at first light? Tomorrow is the Winter Solstice. The servant of darkness is going to strike then."

"What do you plan to do?" her mother asked, nothing but concern in her voice.

"Hopefully, stop him before he kills anyone or destroys the village," Sybil replied with a frown, thinking back to her dream.

Just like with the dream she had about being captured by Ivellios, there was a chance that the vision she saw of the devastation of Morningbreak could just be a possible future. If they got there in time, they might be able to stop it.

Yet again, Sybil found it impossible to fall asleep. If they did get there in time, there was still a possibility of casualties and one or both of them falling in battle. She had no idea what this follower of Haborym was capable of, but if it was anything like what she saw in the aftermath of Mordecai's siege on Ivellios' estate, they were in trouble. Mordecai's connection to Haborym had been weakened from what she said to him the other night and the love they shared, but she had no idea to where his power had developed through studying the ancient texts on his own. All she could hope for was that Shuheyr's magic would come to her when she needed it and that Mordecai would be able to muster up enough of his power to keep himself out of harm's way.

At some point, she must have fallen asleep because she was awoken by Mordecai, who put a finger to his lips and gestured to her mother who was still sleeping. He didn't want Sybil to wake her, which she figured was a good idea. If her mother allowed herself to be banished from the only home she ever knew to follow after Sybil, she might try to follow them to Morningbreak. Despite their broken relationship, Sybil couldn't live with the guilt of her mother getting caught in the crossfire.

As carefully as she could manage, Sybil slid out of bed and put her robes and boots on before grabbing her staff and following Mordecai outside. Just as they were about to mount their horses, he turned to her and asked, "Are you ready?"

"As ready as I can be, I suppose."

It looked like he was about to just nod, but then something compelled him forward, and he kissed her as he held her tightly against him. When he let go, he said, "Alright, let's go stop this bastard."

From a distance, Morningbreak appeared to be just like any other village, but the closer someone came to it, the more unusual it seemed. All of the villagers wore the same outfit, white tunics and pants or white cotton dresses, and there were totems and ruins hung and painted along the walls of the buildings and carved into rocks and the earth. In the center of the village, there stood a wooden statue of Shuheyr, something Sybil used to think of as a bit overdone until she saw the statues of him in the City. Every year during the Winter Festival, the statue was repainted, so there were bowls and tins of paint around the base of it. As Sybil and Mordecai rode into the village, people stared up at them in fear as visitors were a rare occurrence, usually just traveling merchants who thought they could convince these simple people to buy their shoddy wares.

A young man ran up to them, his face a mixture of excitement, confusion, and worry. When Sybil saw him, she flinched because, though she didn't recognize him from her past, he was one of the people who the servant killed in her dream.

"Sybil, by the light, what are you doing here? Where have you been all this time?" the young man asked, and it was his voice that reminded her who he was: Caleb, one of her childhood friends. She was technically forbidden to have friends, but her and some of the other children had managed to form bonds behind the elders' backs. His appearance had completely changed in the past four years since she had seen him.

She dismounted her horse and put her hand on his shoulder.

"It's good to see you again, Caleb, but I must speak with the elders immediately."

"Yes, of course," he said, extending his hand to take Dusk's reins from her. "They're in the Main House, preparing for the day's events."

"Thank you," she replied as she handed him the reins. "Please, tell everyone to leave the village, or at the very least stay inside. There's danger coming to Morningbreak."

Fear flashed across his face, and he asked, "What's going on?"

"Please, just do as I ask," she said, and he nodded before turning to leave. The tie Sybil had to Shuheyr still gave her rank above everyone who wasn't an elder, and Caleb knew to follow her commands.

With haste, Sybil led Mordecai to the Main House, noticing that the sun was close to reaching the middle of the sky. Despite running out of time, she hesitated at the door. Not only had she been conditioned to wait outside while the elders were busy, but this had been a place of great pain for her. Trapped behind these walls for weeks at a time, she had been isolated not just from her village but from the entire world. There were spans of time she couldn't even remember, blocked from her mind because of how horrible they were. What she did know was it had something to do with the elders trying to harness her powers, powers that were now going to save all of their lives. Shaking all those thoughts and conditioning off, Sybil pushed open the doors and found the elders sitting in a circle, all of them looking the same as she had left them years ago. They turned to look at her, and in an instant, she could see the look of recognition light up their faces. One by one, they stood in surprise at her sudden return.

"Our prayers have been answered," Hywel, the elder closest to her, said and raised his hands up. "The Soul Child has returned to us."

"There's no time to delay," Sybil said to them, her voice booming in a space where once it was so weak. "We must evacuate the village."

"Or is it an enemy disguising itself as our Soul Child?" the oldest of the elders, Nerissa, asked in a frail voice.

"Listen," Sybil urged them. "A servant of darkness is coming to destroy you all. He'll be here soon."

"How do you know this?" another elder, Alexina, asked and then jabbed a crooked finger toward Mordecai. "And who is this stranger you bring into our sacred halls? I can feel his darkness."

289

"Shuheyr sent us to protect this village from a creature of darkness known as Haborym," Sybil said, and the mention of Haborym caused all of them to gasp. So... they knew who he was all along.

Just as another one of the elders was about to say something, the ground trembled under their feet, causing some of the artwork on the walls to tumble and crash to the floor. Sybil's heart sank; she thought they'd have more time. She opened the door and yelled at the elders to leave the building, and with horrified expressions they scurried out of the Main House. Just as Sybil and Mordecai stepped outside behind them, the sky turned dark. They headed into the center of the village, standing at the base of Shuheyr's statue, all the paint splattered around at their feet, and watched as the sky turned black. Terror filled the villagers as they ran around screaming and crying for Shuheyr to save them, and it broke her heart to know, after all their faith and dedication to him, he cared so little for them. Sybil's thoughts were snapped back to the danger at hand when, just like in her dream, the Main House exploded into millions of tiny pieces. Thankfully, though, her warning to Caleb and the elders had kept everyone out of harm's way from the falling shards and rocks.

As the dust of the Main House was settling, the man from her dream, Tomas, stepped forward, his red hair even more vibrant than in the vision. Smoke billowed out of his robes, and he stared at Mordecai and Sybil with his hauntingly black eyes. The black veins running up his neck pulsed as he moved forward, and Sybil knew there was nothing human left in this creature heading toward them. Mordecai moved his hands around, seizing what power he had within him, and created a dark orb that he shot in the creature's direction. It hit him, causing him to stagger back, but the cold, determined expression on his face didn't change.

"You weak fool," the man said, the voice of Haborym coming through as an echo. "The power you possess is only a remnant of the true power you could have wielded. Instead, you decided to let this wizard, this woman, make you feeble and useless."

Sybil could feel Mordecai tense beside her as Haborym's words hit his pride. But then, an energy started to radiate off him, and she felt darkness surging more powerfully from him with every passing second. When she turned to look directly at him, she saw that his arms were lost in a smoke forming around them.

"For years, I have been studying the ancient, forbidden magic, the one you studied so long ago," Mordecai explained, his eyes turning black. "I no longer need your darkness, for I control my own."

The man reached his arm out and giant, black tendrils shot out of the earth and engulfed Mordecai, causing him to let out a moan of pain as they crushed him.

"Your new magic is no match for one I have been perfecting for a millennium," the voice said in a hiss.

Mustering up all the light she could, Sybil shot the energy toward Mordecai, dissolving the tendrils around him and causing him to fall to his knees, which switched the servant's attention to her. Her hand was still glowing as she brought it to her chest and flashed a teasing grin toward the servant as Mordecai stood back up and started forming shards of dark magic in the air around him.

"This woman," Mordecai said, his voice calm and collected. "Is going to be the one who destroys you."

A sound mixed between a snarl and a shriek came from the servant's mouth along with inky black liquid splattering onto the ground, sizzling like acid. Jabbing her staff toward him, Sybil unleashed a giant ball of flames right where he was standing, but as it exploded, the servant seemed to form into smoke for an instant, only the hem of his cloak singed from the flames and returned to his physical shape. Mere magic, the kind learned through books and simple practice, did not seem hurt him.

The ground started rumbling again, causing the houses and statue near them to rattle and crack, and the darkness of the sky started closing in around them. Then, Sybil heard the most horrible noise, something she could never have imagined, as if every voice in the world was screaming at once. It caused every nerve in her body to fire wildly, causing her heart to race uncontrollably and her entire body to tremble. Even when she covered her ears, Sybil could still hear it as it pierced deep into her brain. All memories of comfort and contentment left her, as if she had only ever known this pain. She screamed with all the strength of her lungs but couldn't hear it through the noise.

Then, the light burst from Sybil's chest, freeing her and Mordecai from the servant's mental hold. There was blood trickling down both their ears, and the spell he used had left them exhausted, but they jumped back into action right away. She threw beams of light at the redhead as Mordecai unleashed spikes of dark magic. He was able to dodge out of the way and put up a magical barrier to deflect most of these, but one of her beams hit him in the shoulder, causing him to lurch back for a moment, long enough for one of Mordecai's spikes to hit him in the side. With a roar of pain, the servant drew up balls of dark magic in fast succession and threw them at his enemies. One landed square in Sybil's chest, sending her flying back and landing hard on the ground. He tried to throw another attack at her, but Mordecai stepped in front of her and deflected it back toward him.

There was a small group of terrified people watching all of this play out behind a nearby house, and when the servant noticed them, he used the opportunity as Mordecai helped Sybil back up to her feet. He reached out and sent black smoke wafting around them. Sybil watched in horror, struggling back onto her shaky legs, as their eyes went milky white and their faces turned deranged. Then, they all darted off into different directions.

"He's controlling their minds," Mordecai told her. "Go. Use your powers to remove the darkness from them before they kill the other villagers. I'll hold him off here."

Sybil was going to object, to stay by his side, but the cry of a villager being mangled by one of their own people pulled her away from him. Running toward the screams, she unleashed a beam of light, throwing it over both the one being controlled by the darkness and their victim. The light was so intense that both of them passed out, and after checking to make sure they were still breathing, she chased after the others. One had gone into a house and was chasing a woman around her couch. Her arm was bleeding from scratch marks, and she had a red mark on her face from being struck. She threw a beam of light at the attacker, who collapsed onto the floor, and the woman fell to her knees crying. There were more screams coming from the next house over, and when she reached it, a man was lying dead on the porch.

These people weren't fighters and rarely ever saw violence, so someone attacking them, trying to kill them, was something they just weren't prepared for. The man who was possessed in this house had another man on the floor in the kitchen, strangling him even though the man was clearly dead already. He was the last person the servant had possessed, and when she entered the house, he swerved and bolted straight at her. His speed was unexpected, catching Sybil off guard, and he managed to grab her by the forearm, digging his nails into her skin, and flung her across the room. Sybil hit the wall, and he rushed her again. This time, she managed to get her hands up and sent him flying back with a beam of light. Once he was down, she raced back to Mordecai.

The center of the village looked like it had been leveled, the only traces of Shuheyr statute remaining were little splinters at the base. Three other buildings had been completely obliterated, and there was a thick shroud of smoky darkness billowing out from where the servant and Mordecai were fighting. The servant looked more or less unharmed, but Mordecai was barely standing, and blood was streaming down from his nose and mouth. Reaching out his arm, the servant held Mordecai high in the air with a thick tendril, Mordecai's head falling back as his eyes closed, and flung him through the air.

Mordecai landed hard against the porch stairs of a nearby house, shattering the wood and causing a cloud of dust to shoot up into the air. Even though she wanted to rush to see if he was okay, this left the servant wide open. Angry and scared and knowing that if she didn't stop him he would destroy everything she cared about, Sybil called out to Shuheyr.

I trust you, father, she declared in her mind. *Now, let me fully wield your power.*

Shuheyr answered her call, a pillar of light beaming down from the sky. Light and love and radiance filled every inch of her, knowing the true power of the God of Light. Sybil unleashed all the power she felt surging in her, aiming it all directly at the servant, and engulfed the world around them in a bright, shimmering light, turning her vision and everything around her white. Once she started using this power, though, she couldn't seem to stop it. It was just flooding out of her like a burst dam. It all became too much, and she lost consciousness.

Chapter Twenty-Two

Sybil was standing in a field of long grass flowing in the wind. When she turned her head to the left, Shuheyr was standing beside her with a big smile on his face and his arms crossed behind his back. She glanced back around the field, not recognizing any of it.

"Am I dead? What is this place?" she asked, no longer able to feel any of the pain she had just experienced at the hand of Haborym's servant.

Shuheyr turned to her, his eyebrow raised, and said, "You really are quite dramatic, you know that?" When she frowned at him, he looked back toward the field. "This was what the land of your village looked like back in my time."

"Your time? Isn't your time still now?"

"Sorry," he breathed. "I meant back in my mortal time, when I walked this earth, the same as you do now."

"You were mortal?" she choked. "But you're a god... how can that be?"

Shuheyr started walking through the grass, and she had to move quickly to keep in step with him, as a small child struggles to keep up with the gait of their parents.

"The gods you know today, the ones belonging to my pantheon, were all once mortals. There are elven gods who came before us, known now as the Old Gods, and gods before them so mysterious even I do not know of their true origin," he explained to Sybil, his words hitting her so hard she had to stop walking. This information changed... everything. "I was once a mortal man, one of the first to live in these lands, a chieftain among my people. The village of Morningbreak was one I founded, though I did not live here for long. I was too much in pursuit of power to stay in any one place for a significant amount of time. Eventually, my power grew so great I could no longer keep myself tethered to the mortal world and was welcomed into my pantheon, the third of six. I had lived on this plane of existence for nearly five centuries by that point, and many had already begun to revere me as a god."

"Why are you telling me all of this? And why have a mortal child in the first place?"

"This is not the time for those answers, but it will be soon," he replied, his back facing her. "For now, you must focus on the goal you have set with Mordecai in defeating Haborym. After that, I will answer whatever questions you wish to ask me. Or, at least, the ones I can answer."

"Shuheyr," she breathed, causing him to turn to her. "Could I become a god?"

A gentle smile formed on his face, and he said, "I think there's someone waiting for you to wake up."

Sybil's mother, of all people, was by her side when she came to. Her dark brown hair was pulled back into a bun, and her blue eyes stared at her daughter with concern. Sybil was on a small bed in one of the cottages, but she had no idea whose. Across the room from her was another small bed where Mordecai lay unconscious, his face tilted toward her. A deep cut stretch across his right cheek to his ear that had been cleaned and was already starting to scab. It would be the third scar on his handsome face.

"Don't sit up," her mother whispered as Sybil started to stir, wanting to be by Mordecai's side. "You took a terrible blow to the head when you lost consciousness and fell and lost a lot of blood."

When her mother mentioned her head, Sybil could suddenly feel it throbbing.

"What are you doing here?"

"You were gone when I woke up, so I came to the village, knowing you would be here," her mother explained. "I arrived just in time to see you defeat that horrible man."

"So he's dead?"

"Disintegrated is the more appropriate word," she corrected, her voice calm but her face worried. "When your light faded, there was nothing left of him but a shadow burned into the ground and a pile of ash."

"He was so closely tied to the darkness, his mortal form must have reacted just the same to Shuheyr's light," Sybil suggested before her eyes returned to Mordecai. "Is he okay?"

Her mother looked over her shoulder at Mordecai and said, "He will be. When the clerics finally got to him, the Goddess of Death practically had her fingers around his throat, but they were able to stabilize him. Their magic is weak, though, compared to what was done to him, so I would give him a few more days until he's conscious."

"Could you bring me my bag, the one with my horse?" Sybil asked her, remembering the potions Rani made for them. "It has something I need in it."

"If you promise me you'll stay in bed, then, yes," her mother said, and Sybil gave a short, painful nod in reply. "Very well, then."

As soon as her mother was gone, Sybil called out to Mordecai, who didn't even stir at her voice. Then, she turned her head to look out the window near her and saw that the villagers, despite the near destruction of their town, were starting up the Winter Festival with what little they had left. A few people were even working on a new statue for Shuheyr in the middle of the village with a giant block of wood they stored for an occasion such as this. Many people were praying, singing, and chanting loudly as they worked, some crying while they did so, to thank Shuheyr and his Soul Child for saving them. Villagers brought out another block of wood, a little smaller, and set it next to the first one, and it gave Sybil an uneasy feeling when she realized they were adding a second statue next to Shuheyr's. Were they going to start worshiping his Soul Child now, too?

A few minutes later, her mother returned and set the bag of potions on the table next to her. She tried to keep Sybil from sitting up again, but she waved her mother away. Her legs dangling over the side of the bed, Sybil opened the bag and pulled out one of the vials with the sparkling red liquid and popped open the top. Her mother watched with wide eyes as she downed the potion and the cuts and bruises on her exposed skin immediately started to heal. Sybil's head still hurt, but there was no outward wound. With the three other potions in hand, she got out of bed and moved over to Mordecai's bedside. His body shifted slightly when she sat down next to him and after popping the top off another vial, she turned to her mother and asked her to leave them.

Her mother opened her mouth, probably to object, but then she thought better of it, nodded, and left. Moving his head straight and opening his mouth slightly, Sybil poured the potion into his mouth, hoping he wouldn't choke on it. After a moment, the cut on his cheek healed into the scar she foresaw earlier, and the bruises and busted lip he had faded away.

Several more moments passed until his face moved into a frown, and he opened his eyes.

"Well, I guess you're a fighter, after all," he breathed, his voice even more gravelly than usual.

Sybil laughed softly and kissed him, cupping his face with both hands.

"Told you so."

Since he was still in bad shape, she opened up another vial and gave it to him to drink. Soon after the liquid passed his lips, she heard bones popping, and Mordecai winced. Some of his ribs had been broken in the fight. He took in a deep breath and sat up.

"He's dead, yes?" Mordecai asked, swinging his feet over the edge of the bed.

"Nothing but a pile of ash," she replied, causing Mordecai to nod. Even though there was relief on his face, he also looked concerned, his eyebrows seeming to be permanently stuck together. "We defeated him, isn't that a good thing?"

"You defeated him," he said as his hands turned to fists. "I was nothing but his punching bag. My magic was nothing compared to his."

"It will be. You've just got to give it time."

"We're running out of time!" Mordecai yelled, his voice still too hoarse to make much noise, as he stood up. "Haborym will be upon this world soon, possibly as early as the next Winter Solstice, and that servant was nothing compared to Haborym in his full strength. He has the power to darken worlds, not just villages."

Mordecai was in the center of the room at this point, so Sybil stood and walked over to him. He looked at her with fire in his eyes when she placed her hand on his arm and calmly said, "A couple months ago, I would have said facing an opponent like what we just did would be impossible. We have an entire year, if not longer, let's just take a deep breath and trust that we will make ourselves ready for the next fight."

Taking in a slow steadying breath, Mordecai calmed himself.

"Sorry," he breathed as he pulled her into his arms. "You're right. I'm sorry."

"It's okay," she told him, squeezing her arms around him. "Everything's okay."

Now that they were both back on their feet, they decided to head back to Gibbous Tower immediately. As they were leaving the cottage, her mother embraced Sybil and asked her to return to her when she was able so they could build their stole relationship. Sybil wholeheartedly agreed, but hesitated before saying she would. Would it even be possible?

Once outside, many of the villagers came up to her, trying to give her gifts, which she declined, and praying over her, and chanted scripture from their holy text. They forced their way through the crowd to the stables where the horses were. She saw a few of the elders standing in a circle near the blocks of wood, staring at her from the corner of their eyes. Asking Mordecai to ready the horses, she approached them, causing all of them to back a few steps away from her, either in fear or reverence, it was hard to tell.

"I want you to allow my mother to return to the village."

"But she broke our laws," Hywel said, putting his hand up to his chest. "We must banish anyone who leaves our village because they risk us being in danger from the outside world, just as your return has done this day."

"My mother was compelled to search for me when I left, wanting to protect the Soul Child, her child. You cannot punish her for something like that."

"We have never reversed a punishment once the elders have decreed it," Alexina remarked, looking at the others.

"If you wish to show me your loyalty, show me your gratitude for saving you and your village from the darkness, you will do me this favor," Sybil told them, using her powers and title to her advantage in the village for the first time. "I could have let you all die, remember that."

The three elders bowed, agreeing to what she asked. Frowning at them, hating all they did to her as a child, she turned to walk away. Maybe someday she would get back at them or make them change their ways, but for now, she just wanted to return to the tower and rest.

Sybil and Mordecai rode to Roland's cottage, arriving just after nightfall, and as he explored some of the books around the room, she made a fire to warm them up. All of Roland's books were blank, and when Mordecai showed one to her, Sybil recited an old incantation she hadn't said in years, returning all the text to the page.

"He didn't want just anyone reading his books without his permission," she explained with a shrug.

After reading a few pages, Mordecai said, "This is a book that Roland wrote himself. The way he speaks of history, like he was there, makes me suspect that he lived it, possibly making him as old as Leon." He paused, thoughtful for a moment. "It reminds me of a story I heard once, about three brothers who were born without magic but learned to harness it anyway. It's just a story told to children, but as we've learned through our own experiences, there's truth in them."

"Do you think Roland was one of the three brothers? And Leon and Felix?"

"It's possible," he said, turning the page. "But the brothers' part could have just been added later. Perhaps they were just colleagues who learned magic through studying it together. It's interesting because many magic users who are born with their magic claim that wizards are unnatural, that they have cracked some sort of code but will never be able to harness it as nature intended."

"Is that why wizards can't enter the Mirrored like mages and other natural magic users can?"

"I'm not too familiar with the Mirrored, as my powers are unnatural to me as well, but there are definitely signs that show us it falls outside of the natural order, such as the long life we've seen with Leon and the mutation of Haborym." He heaved a sigh. "There's still so much I don't understand about magic."

"I'm starting to believe it's impossible to know it all," she told him, moving to sit at the table with him. "Perhaps that's why there would be three of them. Leon is knowledgeable, but there are things he still doesn't know, things he has hinted to Felix knowing instead. I wonder if there were things Roland knew the other two didn't, and together they held all the information between them."

"Leon and Felix are powerful, though," Mordecai said with a shake of his head. "You were able to kill Roland by accident while still learning your powers."

Sybil winced, thinking back to that day and how scared she felt when she saw Roland's lifeless body on the floor. Why had he fought so hard to keep her from learning about Leon? Her stomach rolled; it was a question she never thought to ask before. Was he protecting her or did he fear her powers growing? Staring down at the table, Sybil felt cold and wished that she could speak with him now.

"Mordecai, why do you think Leon took me on as his apprentice?" she asked, looking back up at him. "Do you think he really intends to pass down the tower to me, or do you think he has something else in mind?"

Frowning, Mordecai thought about this for a while before saying, "Even though wizards are thought to be well-known, there are only four of them I can think of who actually existed in this kingdom, you being one of them. You're a rare breed of magic user, and it could be possible Leon wants to train you to develop your magic toward his methods or is keeping you close so Felix does not try to manipulate you to his darker magic. Another possibility, though, is that he's training you to become a weapon against his enemies, of which he has many."

"What do you think it is?"

"I don't know," he said, shaking his head. "But I think, for now, it's important that you stay the course with Leon, staying aware of what he says and the decisions he makes. He might be exactly who you think he is, but a man like him is bound to have secrets."

"Yes, I suppose you're right," she replied before crossing her arms as if she was cold, despite the fire she built. "I'm afraid, after everything we've been through, I'm getting more suspicious of all these things I used to feel so sure about. I don't know what to believe anymore."

"The things that can be sorted will sort themselves out soon enough," he told her, and there was a flash of something in his eye, something she knew he wasn't going to tell her about. It almost seemed like guilt or regret. "And everything else, we'll just deal with as it comes."

"So, what now, then?"

"Now, you need to get some rest," he told her, sliding the book he placed on the table into his lap.

Even though he was holding himself calmly and his face was expressionless, she could feel something was off, could see it in his eyes. But she trusted him and knew that he would tell her what was going on as soon as it became something she needed to know.

Sybil kissed him, told him she loved him, and went to bed.

The cottage was empty when Sybil awoke the next morning, but she didn't think anything of it as she sat up and stretched out her arms and back. Mordecai often left in the middle of the night to return in the morning, so she waited for him to get back by flipping through her mother's old journal she had given her. After some time had passed, though, she started to grow a little worried. Heading outside to see if he was somewhere nearby, she noticed a small note stuck to the door in Mordecai's script, causing her stomach to twist. She pulled it off the door and read what he had written:

Sybil,

You will not understand this, at least not at first, but there are things I must do on my own. If we are to defeat Haborym and end his tyranny on this world once and for all, I will need to grow stronger, and I must do so alone. It's fine if you are angry with me, and I'm sorry if this hurts you, but please trust me when I say that I will return to you one day. You have my heart, and I hope that I still have yours.

-Mordecai

Crumpling his letter in her fist, Sybil sat down in the closest chair. Her chest was hollow and the blood in her veins had run cold. Uncrumpling it, she read the letter once more to make sure she hadn't missed something and let out a soft cry of pain when she reached the end. She couldn't believe it. After everything they had been through and all the trust she put in him, he just decided to leave without a slightest bit of warning.

Anger swelled up inside her, and she tossed the half-crumpled letter to the floor. *That bastard.* If he thought she was just going to accept this and carry on with her life, he was sorely mistaken. She was going to find him, and when she did, there would be hell for him to pay.

When Sybil exited the cottage, Dusk was standing alone where she left her. Casting an assortment of spells and trying her best to use what little tracking skills she picked up from Redbeard, Sybil tried to figure out which direction he went. But he knew she would do these things and was sure to cover up his trail. Standing on the porch of the cottage, a lump formed in her throat as she tried to figure out what she could have possibly done wrong to make him leave.

No, it isn't my fault, she thought with clenched teeth. It was his decision to leave, and whether or not it had something to do with her, it was on him. Taking a deep, steadying breath, she decided to head back to Gibbous Tower. If anyone could help her find Mordecai, it was Leon. With a hard shell forming around her heart and a stomach that felt like lead, Sybil packed up her stuff and headed back to the tower. She was sure, beyond a shadow of a doubt, that she would find him.

The first winter snow was starting to fall when Sybil made her way out of the cabin. Just as she was about to mount Dusk for her journey back to the tower, her eyes caught sight of the small gravestone she had made for Roland. After she discovered her magic had killed him, Sybil spent the entire night digging his grave with only a small spade, sobbing through most of it. Once he was buried, she found the biggest rock near the cottage, about the size of a cantaloupe, and carved his name on it the best she could. It was mostly covered by leaves and had been shifted to its side, so when she bent down, she cleaned it off and straightened it.

"How was I able to kill you?" Sybil asked, staring down at Roland's grave. "You were ancient and powerful, so how did this happen?" No answer came, of course, and she sighed "I'm sorry for what I did, for all the wrong things I've done. I promise, I'll make things right."

A raven landed on a branch only a couple feet away from her and made a low, gurgling croak. Ravens were rare in these parts, so it must have been the same one she had seen the night before. Standing, Sybil turned to it and saw its bright blue eyes staring back at her, a trait she had never seen in a raven before. She and this creature just stared at each other for a moment before it flapped its wings, giving her a start. It stayed on the branch, seeming to have only made that motion to scare her, and she frowned at it.

"Yes, then? What do you want?" she asked, having a suspicion it was able to understand her.

It cawed loudly as if she could understand it, too, but she just shook her head and said, "That's not an answer at all."

It made a sound like a growl, as if it was frustrated with her, reminding her of Mordecai. With a huff, Sybil started walking back toward her horse, and the raven flapped its wings again, this time taking flight, and glided over to her saddle. It stood on the saddle horn and cawed again, causing Dusk to turn her head toward it in confusion.

"I don't understand what you want from me, but you can join me on my travels if you wish," Sybil told it, only feeling a little strange she was talking to a bird. Stranger things have happened, after all. "You'll need to move, though, so I don't crush you."

The bird hopped from the saddle horn to Sybil's shoulder, its silky feathers grazing her left cheek as it did. Once the bird was firmly on her shoulder, her vision changed from the forest around Roland's cottage to a large room designed strikingly similar to the throne room in the palace. The throne was made of wood and level to the floor and the walls were free of all the statues of the gods and banners of regions and kingdoms which normally covered them. The room was empty except for a young man who stood near the throne, his back facing her when Sybil first arrived. It did not surprise her to see Shuheyr turn around and sit on the throne, smiling at her.

"Funny, I thought your bird was a dove. Aren't ravens a little too dark for you?" she asked, tired of his games.

"Ravens have always been my bird, always my symbol, even if it was changed by my worshippers," he replied as he leaned back in his throne. "That's why you felt so compelled to make it your own sigil." He pointed to the design threaded in her robes across her chest. "Dove's are nothing but glorified pigeons, but ravens? They are the smartest of all birds, they are survivors and soothsayers, just as we both are."

"And you sent this one to keep an eye on me?"

"I sent this one to aid you," he replied, annoyed. "Save for when you're in the tower, I already keep an eye on you, just as any good father would."

His thinking of himself as a good father irritated Sybil.

"How will this bird aid me?"

"There are many ways, which I will let you discover for yourself."

Sybil sighed and looked around before asking, "Why are we in the throne room?"

"Because, after our last conversation, I decided I wanted to share with you a bit more about my mortal life," he responded, running his hand over the arm of the throne. "This has been long forgotten, as I went by a different name when I ruled, but I was the first king of this kingdom. My brother and I were among the first humans to step foot in these lands, and we slowly built our civilization over decades until the kingdom was officially founded.

"Though the people simply believe monarchs of Irminshu are ordained through my blessing, every king and queen who has sat on the throne has been one of my direct descendants, including this Finlay boy you dislike so much."

"If so much of you is tied in with this kingdom, why are you so willing to let it be swallowed up by darkness?" she asked, shaking her head. "Haborym would erase everything you've created, but you just stand by to let me handle it on my own."

"Are you really this dense, my dear girl? Have you not figured out what I am trying to accomplish with you by this point?" Shuheyr asked, tilting his head in genuine confusion.

Through gritted teeth, she replied, "Perhaps, if you just tell me so I stop having to guess at all your wild intentions."

"Very well," he said with a sigh and stood from his throne to walk over to her. "You have done much to grow in your skills as both my Soul Child and a wizard in your own right, but it wasn't until the moment of desperation you felt when you saw Mordecai about to be killed that you unleashed your true potential."

Shuheyr paused and shook his head.

"I do not wish to see this kingdom overrun by shadow, but I know it will be the only way for your true power to grow. You are so determined to focus on the lesser magic of your wizard spells that you do not even understand half of what your powers entail."

"Why is this so important to you? Why risk everything you've built so that I may become more powerful?"

Shuheyr frowned as he thought for a moment.

"Because my time is coming to an end," he said, a twinge of sadness and regret in his voice. "And you, Sybil, have a great destiny laid out before you. You are to be the next God of Light."

Acknowledgements

There are many people to thank for the creation and development of this book, but first and foremost, I must thank who this book is dedicated to: Forrest Hallstrom. Not only has he been a supportive husband and the love of my life, but the characters of Mordecai and Keijin would not exist without him. They are both pieces of him that I nurtured and developed and placed side-by-side with Sybil and Redbeard who are a reflection of myself. Thank you for all the many hours you helped me brainstorm ideas and listened to me read scene after scene until I got things just right.

I am truly blessed for such a great support system in my family, namely my parents, who have always encouraged my writing, even when it got in the way of other responsibilities. You both pushed me to stick through the rough years of college until I discovered my truest joy comes in all things writing. Oh, and thank you for all financial support, as well.

Though he will never read this, I also what to thank my grandfather for passing down his writer spirit to me. You wouldn't have enjoyed this book, but I know you would have been proud to see me accomplish this. I'm sorry I wasn't able to do so sooner.

Last but not least: Emily, Micaela, Marion, Hollay, Tricia, Susie, and Mike. Without all of you, I would not have had the strength and courage to put my words out into the world. I feel so lucky to have each of you in my life.

About the Author

A nerd of all things fantasy, C. Sloan Lewis has begun her author career with her debut novel, *The Soul Child*. She has lived in and around Dallas, Texas all her life and has a BA and MEd in English. Since 2019, she has helped to broaden the minds of young readers and stoke the fires of their imagination as an English teacher and the Department Head of English on her campus. When she isn't teaching or writing, she is spending time with her daughter and husband, playing RPG tabletop and video games, and exploring nature.

Find C. Sloan Lewis on social media:

@c.sloanlewis

C. Sloan Lewis

@csloanlewis

authorcsloanlewis.wordpress.com

www.ingramcontent.com/pod-product-compliance
Lightning Source LLC
LaVergne TN
LVHW090609260325
806752LV00001B/27